PRAISE FOR
ZOO CITY

"Beukes's energetic noir phantasmagoria, the winner of this year's Arthur C. Clarke Award, crackles with original ideas."
— Jeff VanderMeer, *New York Times Book Review*

"Beukes (*Moxyland*) delivers a thrill ride that gleefully merges narrative styles and tropes, almost single-handedly pulling the 'urban fantasy' subgenre back towards its groundbreaking roots."
— *Publishers Weekly,* starred review

"*Zoo City* is a fabulous outing from an extremely promising writer . . . it has so much fabulous wordplay, imaginative settings and scenarios, and such a dark and cynical heart that I was totally riveted by it."
— Cory Doctorow, *BoingBoing*

"In *Zoo City* we have an unfamiliar land full of familiars, a broken Johannesburg of the near future peopled with damaged wonders. Proving her debut novel was no fluke, she writes better than I wish I could on my best day. If our words are bullets, Lauren Beukes is a marksman in a world of drunken machine-gunners, firing her ideas and images into us with a sly and deadly accuracy, wasting nothing, never missing. I'll follow her career as long as she's willing to write and I'm able to read."
— Bill Willingham, creator of *Fables*

"*Zoo City* is a story of mysteries unfolding, and it is a story well told. But it's the world around the story, and the words that guide us through, that make it something more than simply marvelous. With her subtle, intimate descriptions of the roads we walk in this crazy city; with characters so deeply twisty you could lose a giant squid in their nebulous hidey holes, and with turns of phrase that are as likely to conjure up Rudyard Kipling, Brenda Fassie, or Credo Mutwa as they are to invoke Japanese anime, Doctor Who, or the crack in Johnny Cash's voice as he sings of his greatest loss, this canny authoress has brought real magic to everyday life in Jozi, in what I'm afraid I really am going to end off by describing as an act of unadulterated literature."

—Matthew du Plessis, *Times Live*

"This book is a must read for lovers of South African fiction and urban fantasy alike. It is edgy and pacey and like a rollercoaster ride, it sweeps you up, spins you around, turns you upside down and dumps you out on the other end, heady and breathless and yearning for more." —*Exclus1ves*

"Lauren Beukes is an awfully smart writer. In *Zoo City* her characters ooze attitude, their dialogue is snappy, and her vivid imagery is both original and arresting. What's more, with an inspired blend of pop-culture savvy and fantasy (just enough, not too much), her depiction of Johannesburg, magical charms and all, feels eerily real. . . . In fact, it feels as incomplete as real life. It's gritty, it's tangled, and it's flawed;

nothing is polished, nothing perfect. That's what makes *Zoo City* so disturbingly, hauntingly, uncompromisingly brilliant."

— Jonno Cohen, *MiniMonologues*

"At times the witty and lyrical prose is sheer magic, the story captivating and the characters exotic, cruel, and beautiful while the backdrop of Johannesburg seethes with hidden, lurking dangers around every corner, *Zoo City* is quite simply captivating."

— *SciFi & Fantasy Books*

"With her second release, Lauren Beukes stuns with a richly textured venture into a pseudo-fantastical Johannesburg of the future where criminals are magically partnered with animals, and unscrupulous record producers run amok."

— *SciFiNow*

"We all know there is a fine line between genius and madness. So it is with *Zoo City* . . . a story that is remarkable for both its inventiveness and the sharpness of its writing."

— Jason Baki, *Kamvision*

"A contrast of fragility and extreme imaginative strength, Beukes's books are going places. She'd better ready herself for one helluva wild ride."

— Mandy De Waal, *The Daily Maverick*

"*Zoo City* is pure originality . . . a book that had me reading it reveling in Beukes's magical way with words." — SF Signal

ZOO CITY

Also by Lauren Beukes

Moxyland

The Shining Girls

Broken Monsters

ZOO CITY

LAUREN BEUKES

MULHOLLAND BOOKS

Little, Brown and Company

New York Boston London

Mulholland Books / Little, Brown and Company
Hachette Book Group
1290 Avenue of the Americas, New York, NY 10104
littlebrown.com

Originally published in hardcover by Angry Robot, January 2010
First Mulholland Books paperback edition, August 2016

Mulholland Books is an imprint of Little, Brown and Company, a division of Hachette Book Group, Inc. The Mulholland Books name and logo are trademarks of Hachette Book Group, Inc.

The publisher is not responsible for websites (or their content) that are not owned by the publisher.

The Hachette Speakers Bureau provides a wide range of authors for speaking events. To find out more, go to hachettespeakersbureau.com or call (866) 376-6591.

ISBN 978-0-316-26792-2
Library of Congress Control Number: 2016939900

10 9 8 7 6 5 4 3 2 1

RRD-C

Printed in the United States of America

SPECIAL THANKS

I'm very grateful to the three people who contributed original chapters to this book: Music journalist Evan Milton "interviewed" Odysseus Huron, Charlie Human wrote the psychology paper abstract on Masks of Existence, and Sam Wilson wrote the prison diaries.

PART ONE.

1.

IN ZOO CITY, *it's impolite to ask.*

Morning light the sulfur color of the mine dumps seeps across Johannesburg's skyline and sears through my window. My own personal bat signal. Or a reminder that I really need to get curtains.

Shielding my eyes—morning has broken and there's no picking up the pieces—I yank back the sheet and peel out of bed. Benoît doesn't so much as stir, with only his calloused feet sticking out from under the duvet like knots of driftwood. Feet like that, they tell a story. They say he walked all the way from Kinshasa with his Mongoose strapped to his chest.

The Mongoose in question is curled up like a furry comma on my laptop, the glow of the LED throbbing under his nose. Like he doesn't know that my computer is out of bounds. Let's just say I'm precious about my work. Let's just say it's not entirely legal.

I take hold of the laptop on either side and gently tilt it over the edge of my desk. At thirty degrees, the Mongoose starts sliding down the front of the laptop. He wakes with a start, tiki tavi claws scrabbling for purchase. As he starts to fall, he contorts in the air and manages to land feet first. Hunching his stripy shoulders, he hisses at me, teeth bared. I hiss back. The Mongoose realizes he has urgent flea bites to attend to.

Leaving the Mongoose to scrolf at its flank, I duck under one of the loops of rope hanging from the ceiling, the closest I can get to providing authentic Amazon jungle vines, and pad over the rotten linoleum to the cupboard. Calling it a cupboard is a tad optimistic, like calling this dank room with its precariously canted floor and intermittent plumbing an apartment is optimistic. The cupboard is not much more than an open box with a piece of fabric pinned across it to keep the dust off my clothes—and Sloth, of course. As I pull back the gaudy sunflower print, Sloth blinks up at me sleepily from his roost, like a misshapen fur coat between the wire hangers. He's not good at mornings.

There's a mossy reek that clings to his fur and his claws, but it's earthy and clean compared to the choke of stewing garbage and black mold floating up the stairwell. Elysium Heights was condemned years ago.

I reach past him to pull out a vintage navy dress with a white collar, match it up with jeans and slops, and finish off with a lime green scarf over the little dreadlock twists that conveniently hide the mangled wreckage of my left ear— let's call it Grace Kelly does Sailor Moon. This is not so much a comment on my style as a comment on my budget. I was always more of an outrageously expensive indie boutique kinda girl. But that was FL. Former Life.

"Come on, buddy," I say to Sloth. "Don't want to keep the clients waiting." Sloth gives a sharp sneeze of disapproval and extends his long downy arms. He clambers onto my back, fussing and shifting before he finally settles. I used to get impatient. But this has become an old routine for the pair of us.

It's because I haven't had my caffeine fix yet that it takes a little while for the repetitive skritching sound to penetrate — the Mongoose is pawing at the front door with a single-minded devotion.

I oblige, shunting back the double deadbolt and clicking open the padlock which is engraved with magic, supposedly designed to keep out those with a *shavi* for slipping through locked doors. At the first crack, the Mongoose nudges out between my ankles and trots down the passage towards the communal litter tray. It's easy to find. It's the smelliest place in the building.

"You should really get a cat-flap." Benoît is awake at last, propped up on one elbow, squinting at me from under the shade of his fingers, because the glare bouncing off Ponte Tower has shifted across to his side of the bed.

"Why?" I say, propping the door open with my foot for the Mongoose's imminent return. "You moving in?"

"Is that an invitation?"

"Don't get comfortable is all I'm saying."

"Ah, but *is* that all you're saying?"

"And don't get smart either."

"Don't worry, *cherie na ngayi*. Your bed is far too lumpy to get comfortable." Benoît stretches lazily, revealing the

5

mapwork of scars over his shoulders, the plasticky burnt skin that runs down his throat and his chest. He only ever calls me "my love" in Lingala, which makes it easier to disregard. "You making breakfast?"

"Deliveries," I shrug.

"Anything interesting today?" He loves hearing about the things people lose.

"Set of keys. The widow ring."

"Ah, yes. The crazy lady."

"Mrs. Luditsky."

"That's right," Benoît says, and repeats himself: "Crazy lady."

"Hustle, my friend. I have to get going."

Benoît pulls a face. "It's so early."

"I'm not kidding."

"All right, all right." He uncocoons himself from the bed, plucks his jeans from the floor, and yanks on an old protest t-shirt inherited from Central Methodist's clothing drive.

I fish Mrs. Luditsky's ring out of the plastic cup of Jik it's been soaking in overnight to get rid of the clinging *eau de drain,* and rinse it under a sputtering tap. Platinum with a constellation of sapphires and a narrow gray band running through the center, only slightly scratched. Even with Sloth's help, it took three hours to find the damn thing.

As soon as I touch it, I feel the tug—the connection running away from me like a thread, stronger when I focus on it. Sloth tightens his grip on my shoulder, his claws digging into my collarbone.

"Easy, tiger," I wince. Maybe it would have been easier to have a tiger. As if any of us gets a choice.

Benoît is already dressed, the Mongoose looping impatient figure eights around his ankles.

"See you later, then?" he says, as I shoo him out the door.

"Maybe." I smile in spite of myself. But when he moves to kiss me, Sloth bats him away with a proprietary arm.

"I don't know who is worse," Benoît complains, ducking. "You, or that monkey."

"Definitely me," I say, locking the door behind him.

The blackened walls of Elysium Heights' stairwell still carry a whiff of the Undertow, like polyester burning in a microwave. The stairway is mummified in yellow police tape and a charm against evidence tampering, as if the cops are ever going to come back and investigate. A dead zoo in Zoo City is low priority even on a good day. Most of the residents have been forced to use the fire escape to bypass this floor. But there are faster ways to the ground. I have a talent not just for finding lost things, but shortcuts too.

I duck into number 615, abandoned ever since the fire tore through here, and scramble down through the hole in the floor that drops into 526, which has been gutted by scrap rats who ripped out the floorboards, the pipes, the fittings—anything that could be sold for a hit.

Speaking of which, there is a junkie passed out in the doorway, some dirty furry thing nested against his chest, breathing fast and shallow. My slops crunch on the brittle glitter of a broken lightbulb as I step over him. In my day we smoked crack, or mandrax if you were really trashy. I cross over the walkway that connects to Aurum Place and a functional staircase. Or not so functional. The moment I swing open the double doors to the stairwell and utter darkness, it becomes obvious where the junkie got the bulb.

"Well, isn't this romantic?"

Sloth grunts in response.

"Yeah, you say that now, but remember, I'm taking you with me if I fall," I say, stepping into the darkness.

Sloth drives me like a Zinzi motorbike, his claws clenching, left, right, down, down, down for two stories to where the bulbs are still intact. It won't be long until they too find a new life as *tik* pipes, but isn't that the way of the slums? Even the stuff that's nailed down gets repurposed.

After the claustrophobia of the stairwell, it's a relief to hit the street. It's still relatively quiet this early in the morning. A municipal street-cleaning truck chugs up ahead, blasting the tarmac with a sheet of water to wash away the transgressions of the night. One of the transgressions in question dances back to avoid being sprayed, nearly stepping on the scruffy Sparrow hopping around between her high heels.

Seeing me, she pulls her denim jacket closed over her naked breasts, too quickly for me to figure out if they're hormone-induced or magic. As we pass, I can feel the filmy cling of a dozen strands of lost things from the woman, like brushing against the tendrils of an anemone. I try not to look. But I pick up blurred impressions anyway, like an out-of-focus photograph. I get snatches of a gold cigarette case, or maybe it's a business-card holder, a mostly empty plastic *bankie* of brown powder and a pair of sequined red stilettos—real showgirl shoes, like Dorothy got back from Oz all grown up and turned burlesque stripper. Sloth tenses up automatically. I pat his arm.

"None of our business, buddy."

He's too sensitive. The problem with my particular gift, curse, call it what you like, is that everybody's lost *something*. Stepping out in public is like walking into a tangle of cat's cradles, like someone dished out balls of string at the lunatic asylum and instructed the inmates to tie everything to everything else. On some people, the lost strings are cobwebs, inconsequential wisps that might blow away at any moment. On others, it's like they're dragging steel cables. Finding something is all about figuring out which string to tug on.

Some lost things can't be found. Like youth, say. Or innocence. Or, sorry Mrs. Luditsky, property values once the slums start encroaching. Rings, on the other hand, that's easy stuff. Also: lost keys, love letters, beloved toys, misplaced photographs, and missing wills. I even found a lost room once. But I like to stick to the easy stuff, the little things. After all, the last thing of any consequence I found was a nasty drug habit. And look how that turned out.

I pause to buy a nutritious breakfast, aka a *skyf* from a Zimbabwean vendor rigging up the scaffolding of a pavement stall. While he lays out his crate of suckers and snacks and single smokes, his wife unpacks a trove of cheap clothing and disposable electronics from two large *amaShangaan,* the red-and-blue-checked bags that are ubiquitous round here. It's like they hand them out with the application for refugee status. Here's your temporary ID, here's your asylum papers, and here, don't forget your complimentary crappy woven plastic suitcase.

Sloth clicks in my ear as I light up my Remington Gold, half the price of a Stuyvesant. This city's all about the cheap knockoff.

"Oh come on. One. One cigarette. It's not like I'm going to live long enough to get emphysema." Or that emphysema isn't an attractive alternative to being sucked down by the Undertow.

Sloth doesn't respond, but I can feel his irritation in the way he shifts his weight, thumping against my back. In retaliation, I blow the smoke out the side of my mouth into his disapproving furry face. He sneezes violently.

The traffic is starting to pick up, taxis hurtling through the streets with the first consignments of commuters. I take the opportunity to do a little advertising, sticking flyers under the wipers of the parked cars already lining the street outside *The Daily Truth*'s offices. You have to get up pretty early in the morning to invent the news.

I've got ads up in a couple of places. The local library. The supermarket, jammed between advertisements for chars with excellent references and second-hand lawnmowers. Pasted up in Hillbrow among the wallpaper of flyers advertising miracle AIDS cures, cheap abortions, and prophets.

LOST A SMALL ITEM OF PERSONAL VALUE?
I CAN HELP YOU FIND IT
FOR A REASONABLE FEE.
NO DRUGS. NO WEAPONS.
NO MISSING PERSONS.

I've resisted going mass market and posting it online. This way it's kismet, like the ads find the people they're supposed to. Like Mrs. Luditsky, who summoned me to her Killarney apartment Saturday morning.

To the old lady's credit, she didn't flinch when she saw Sloth draped across my shoulders.

"You can only be the girl from the ad. Well, come in. Have a cup of tea." She pressed a cup of greasy-looking Earl Grey into my hands without waiting for a response and bustled away through her dingy hallway to an equally dingy lounge.

The apartment had been Art Deco in a former lifetime, but it had been subjected to one ill-conceived refurbishment too many. But then, so had Mrs. Luditsky. Her skin had the transparent shine of glycerine soap, and her eyes bulged ever so slightly, possibly from the effort of trying to emote when every associated muscle had been pumped full of botulinum or lasered into submission. Her thinning orange hair was gelled into a hard pompadour, like the crust on *crème brûlée*.

The tea tasted like stale horse piss drained through a homeless guy's sock, but I drank it anyway, if only because Sloth hissed at me when I tried to turf it surreptitiously into the exotic plastic orchid next to the couch.

Mrs. Luditsky launched straight in. "It's my ring. There was an armed robbery at the mall yesterday and—"

I cut in: "If your ring was stolen, that's out of my jurisdiction. It's a whole different genre of magic."

"If you would be so kind as to let me finish?" the old lady snapped. "I hid in the bathroom and took all my jewelry off because I know how *you people* are—criminals, that is," she added hurriedly, "No offence to the animalled."

"Of course not," I replied. The truth is we're all criminals. Murderers, rapists, junkies. Scum of the earth. In China they execute zoos on principle. Because nothing says guilty like a spirit critter at your side.

"And what happened after you took it off?"

"Well, that's the problem. I couldn't get it off. I've worn it for eight years. Ever since the Bastard died."

"Your husband?"

"The ring is made with his ashes, you know. They compress and fuse them into the platinum in this micro-thin band. It's absolutely irreplaceable. Anyway, I know what happens when they can't get your rings off. When my neighbor's cousin was mugged, they chopped off her finger with a bloody great *panga*."

I could see exactly where this was going. "So you used soap?"

"And it slipped right off, into the sink and down the drain."

"Down the drain," I repeated.

"Didn't I just say that?"

"May I?" I said, and reached for Mrs. Luditsky's hand. It

was a pretty hand, maybe a little chubby, but the wrinkles and the powdery texture betrayed all the work on her face. Clearly Botox doesn't work on hands, or maybe it's too expensive. "This finger?"

"Yes, dear. The ring finger. That's where people normally wear their rings."

I closed my eyes and squeezed the pad of the woman's finger, maybe a little too hard. And caught a flash of the ring, a blurred silver-colored halo, somewhere dark and wet and industrial. I didn't look too hard to figure out the exact location. That level of focus tends to bring on a migraine, the same way heavy traffic does. I snagged the thread that unspooled away from the woman and ran deep into the city, deep under the city.

I opened my eyes to find Mrs. Luditsky studying me intently, as if she was trying to peer into my skull to see the gears at work. Behind her bouffant hair, a display case of china figurines stared down. Cute shepherdesses and angels and playful kittens and a chorus line of flamenco dancers.

"It's in the drains," I said, flatly.

"I thought we'd already established that."

"I hate the drains." Call it the contempt of familiarity. You'd be surprised how many lost things migrate to the drains.

"Well pardon me, Little Miss Hygiene," Mrs. Luditsky snapped, although the impact was diminished by her inability to twitch a facial muscle. "Do you want the job or not?"

Of course I did. Which is how I got a look-in to Mrs.

Luditsky's purse for a R500 deposit. Another R500 to be paid on delivery. And how I found myself shin-deep in shit in the stormwater drains beneath Killarney Mall. Not actual shit, at least, because the sewage runs through a different system, but years of musty rainwater and trash and rot and dead rats and used condoms make up their own signature fragrance.

I swear I can still detect a hint of it underneath the bleach. Was it worth it for R1000? Not even close. But the problem with being *mashavi* is that it's not so much a job as a vocation. You don't get to choose the ghosts that attach themselves to you. Or the things they bring with them.

I drop off a set of keys at the Talk-Talk phone shop, or rather the small flat above the shuttered store. The owner is Cameroonian and so grateful to be able to open up shop this morning that he promises me a discount on airtime as a bonus. A toddler dressed in a pink fluffy bear suit peeks out between his legs and reaches for them with pudgy grasping fingers. The same one, I'm guessing, who was chewing on the keys in her pram before gleefully tossing them into the rush-hour traffic. That's worth fifty bucks. And it's more in line with my usual hustle. In my experience, the Mrs. Luditskys of the world are few and far between.

I walk up on Empire through Parktown past the old Johannesburg College of Education, attracting a few aggressive hoots from passing cars. I give them the finger. Not my fault if they're so cloistered in suburbia that they don't get to see zoos. At least Killarney isn't a gated community. Yet.

I'm still a couple of kays from Mrs. Luditsky's block, just

turning off Oxford and away from the heavy traffic, which is giving me a headache, the kind that burrows in behind your temples like a brain termite, when my connection suddenly, horribly, goes slack.

Sloth squeaks in dismay and grips my arms so hard his long claws draw little beads of blood. "I know, buddy, I know," I say and start running. I clamp my fist around the cold circle of metal in my pocket as if I could jump-start the connection. There is the faintest of pulses, but the thread is unraveling.

We've never lost a thread. Even when a lost thing is out of reach forever, like when that wannabe-novelist guy's manuscript blew out across Emmarentia Dam, I could still feel the taut lines of connection between him and the disintegrating pages. This feels more like a dead umbilical cord withering away.

There's an ambulance and a police van outside Mrs. Luditsky's block, strobing the dusty beige of the wall with flicks of red and blue. Sloth whimpers.

"It's okay," I say, out of breath, even though I'm pretty damn sure it's anything but, falling in alongside the small cluster of rubbernecking pedestrians. I guess I'm shaking, because someone takes my elbow.

"You okay, honey?"

I'm obviously not remotely okay, because somehow I missed these two in the crowd—a gangly angel with huge dark wings and a dapper man with a Maltese Poodle dyed a ludicrous orange to match the scarf at his neck. It's the man who has attached himself to me. He's wearing expensive-looking glasses and a suit as sharp as the razored edge of his *chiskop* quiff. The Dog gives me a dull look from the end of its leash and thumps its tail half-heartedly. Say what you like about Sloths, but at least I didn't end up with a motorized toilet brush. Or a Vulture, judging by the hideous bald head that bobbles up and down behind the woman's shoulder, digging under its wing.

The woman falls into the vaguely ageless and androgynous category, somewhere between 32 and 58, with a chemotherapy haircut, wisps of dark hair clinging to her scalp, and thin overplucked eyebrows. Or maybe she just tries to make herself look ugly. She's wearing riding boots over slim gray pants and a white shirt with the sleeves rolled up. It's accented by leather straps crossing over her chest from the harness that supports the weight of the hulking Bird on her back.

"You know what's going on?" I say to the Dog guy.

"There's been a *mur-der*," the man stage-whispers the word behind his hand. "Old lady on the second floor. Terrible business. Although I hear she's *terribly* well preserved."

"Have they said anything?"

"Not yet," the woman says, her voice, unexpectedly, the malted alto of jazz singers. Her accent is Eastern European, Russian maybe, or Serbian. At the sound of her voice, the Bird stops grooming and a long neck with a wattle like a deflated testicle twists over the woman's shoulder. It drapes its wrinkled head over her chest, the long, sharp spear of its beak angled down towards her hip. Not a Vulture then. She lays one hand tenderly on the Marabou Stork's mottled head, the way you might soothe a child or a lover.

"Then how do you know it's murder?"

The Maltese smirks. "You know how most people's *mashavi* and their animals don't line up?" he says. "Well, in Amira's case, they do. She's attracted to carrion. Mainly murder scenes, although she does like a good traffic pileup. Isn't that right, sweetie?"

The Marabou smiles in acknowledgement, if you can call the faint twitch of her mouth a smile.

The paramedics emerge from the building with a stretcher carrying a sealed gray plastic body bag. They hoist it into the ambulance. "Excuse me," I say and push through the crowd. The paramedic shuts the double doors behind the stretcher, signaling the driver to kill the lights with a wave of his hand. The dead don't need to beat the traffic. But I have to ask anyway.

"That Mrs. Luditsky in there?"

"You a relative?" The paramedic looks disgruntled. "'Cos unless you are, it's none of your business, zoo girl."

"I'm an employee."

"Tough breaks, then. You should probably stick around. The cops are gonna want to ask you some questions."

"Can you tell me what happened?"

"Let's just say she didn't pass in her sleep, sweetheart."

The ambulance gives one strangled whoop and pulls out onto the road, taking Mrs. Luditsky with it. I grip the ring in my pocket, hard enough to embed the imprint of the sapphires into my palm. Sloth nuzzles into my neck, hiding his face. I wish I could reassure him.

"Ugly business," the Maltese tuts, sympathetically. "Like it's any of yours."

I'm suddenly furious. "You with the cops?"

"God, no!" He laughs. "Unfortunately for this one," he says, nodding at the Marabou, "there's no real money in ambulance chasing."

"We're sorry for your loss," the Marabou says.

"Don't be," I say. "I only met her the one time."

"What was it that you were doing for the old lady anyway? If I may ask? Secretarial? Grocery runs? Nursing?"

"I was finding something for her."

"Did you get it?"

"Always do."

"But sweetie, what a *marvelous* coincidence! Oh, I don't mean marvelous, like oh, how marvelous your employer just died. That's ghastly, don't get me wrong. But the thing is, you see—"

"We're also looking for something," the Marabou cuts in.

"Precisely. Thank you," the Maltese says. "And, if that's, you know, your *talent*? I'm guessing that's your talent? Then maybe you could help."

"What sort of something?"

"Well, I say some*thing,* but really, I mean some*one.*"

"Sorry. Not interested."

"But you haven't even heard the details."

"I don't need to. I don't do missing persons."

"It's worth a lot to us." The bird on Marabou's back flexes its wings, showing off the white fléchettes marking the dark feathers. I note that they're clipped, and that its legs are mangled, twisted stubs. No wonder she has to carry it. "More than any of your other jobs would have paid."

"Come on, sweetie. Your client just turfed it. Forgive me being so frank. What else are you going to do?"

"I don't know who you are—"

"An oversight. I'm sorry. Here." The Marabou removes a starched business card from her breast pocket and proffers it between scissored fingers. Her fingernails are immaculately manicured. The card is blind embossed, white on white in a stark sans-serif font:

Marabou & Maltese Procurements

"And 'procurements' means what exactly?"

"Whatever you want it to, Ms. December," the Marabou says.

Sloth grumbles in the back of his throat, as if I need to be told how dodgy this just turned. I reach out for their lost things, hoping to get anything on them, because they obviously have something on me.

The Maltese is blank. Some rare people are. They're either pathologically meticulous or they don't care about anything. But it still creeps me out. The last person I encountered with no lost things at all was the cleaning lady at Elysium. She threw herself down an open elevator shaft.

My impressions of the Marabou's lost things are weirdly vivid. It must be the adrenaline sharpening my focus— all that hormone soup in your brain messes with *mashavi* big time. I've never been able to see things this clearly. It's strange, like someone switched my Vaseline-slathered soft-focus perspective for a high-definition paparazzi zoom lens.

I can make out the things tethered to her in crisp detail: a pair of tan leather driving gloves, soft and weathered by time. One of them is missing a button that would fasten it at the wrist. A tatty book, pages missing, the remainder swollen with damp, the cover half ripped off. I can make out sepia branches, a scrap of title, *The Tree That—*. And a gun. Dark and stubby, with retro curves, like a bad prop from a '70s sci-fi show. The image is so precise I can make out the lettering on the side: V*ektor*.

Oblivious to me discreetly riffling through their lost things, the Maltese presses me, grinning. His painted Dog grins too, pink tongue lolling happily between its sharp little teeth. "We really need your help on this one. I'd even say we can't do it without you. And it pays very, very well."

"How can I say this? I don't like people knowing my business."

"You advertise," the Marabou says, amused.

"And I don't like your attitude."

"Oh don't mind Amira, she comes off mean, but she's just shy, really," the Maltese says.

"And I don't like small dogs. So thanks, but you know,

as far as I'm concerned, you should go fuck the carcass of a goat."

The Maltese squinches up his face. "Oh, that's disgusting. I'll have to remember that one," he says.

"Hang onto that," the Marabou indicates the card. "You might change your mind."

"I won't."

But I do.

2.

From: Livingstone Mission House [mailto: eloria@livingstone
.drc]
Sent: 21 March 2011 08:11 A.M.
To: Undisclosed Recipients
Subject: A message in a bottle.

To whom it may concern,

My name is Eloria Bangana. I live in the DRC or Democratic Republic of Congo. I am 13 years old. When they killed my family I had a choice. I could be a prostitute or pretend to be a boy and work in the coltan mines.

Lucky, I am very small for my age. Most people think I am 9 or 10. So, I choose the mines, because I can crawl into tight spaces with my little bucket for sifting and my spade, although mostly I use my fingers. Sometimes my fingers get cracked and bleed from scratching in the dirt.

They say coltan makes cell phones. I do not know how you make cell phones from mud. Also computers and video games. All your technology runs on mud. Isn't that funny?

My cousin Felipe says he has played a video game in Kinshasa, he said you just press buttons to fight, buttons to walk or kick or punch. He said it was boring.

Felipe likes soccer more. I used to play soccer with him, but it wasn't really soccer. It's a game called 3 tin, because we only have tins to kick. The rules are similar. Maybe one day I can teach you. We don't play 3 tin anymore, because the rebels say there isn't time. We are here to work, not play. They shot my cousin Felipe in the back when he tried to run away. He died. It was very sad. We were very scared.

I get seven cents American for every kilogram of coltan. The rebels weigh it on the scales but they cheat. The lady at the mission station, Sister Mercia, says coltan is worth 100 times what they pay. She says they use us like slaves.

Sometimes it is hard to understand her because she is from America. She is helping me translate this because I speak French and my English is not so good. She is very helpful and very nice. She shows me how to use the computer. And she fixes my clothes and sometimes she gives me oranges.

Maybe you are wondering why I am emailing to you? Sister Mercia says we need to wake up the world about what is happening here. She says to tell you, don't worry, we are not asking for money. We are asking for help.

The orphanage where Sister Mercia works and I live now that the Vainglory Ministries rescued me, we have a problem. The rebels have cut off our phones and all our communication. We have one cell phone that we hide from them and it has WAP so we can send email, if you go stand at the top of the hill when the rebels aren't watching.

It is like a message in a bottle. We send it floating into the ocean and hope that someone finds it.

But this is not our real problem. The man who runs the orphanage, Father Quixote, has been kidnapped by the rebels and they want us to pay $200,000 for him to come back safe to us.

Father Quixote is very brave, but he is also very clever. He has locked all the orphanage's money away in his bank account in America. The rebels cannot get to it, but we can't either using just a cell phone with WAP.

We have the password and the authorization (Sister Mercia says you will know what this means) which means a Good Samaritan could help us.

We need money to feed the other children here (there are many babies as well as little children, some of us wounded and sick) and to pay Father Quixote's ransom.

Please, can you help us? If you can access Father Quixote's bank account, you can wire transfer some of the money to us. Sister Mercia says we do not expect you to do this for nothing. She says we can pay you a fee of $80,000 for taking the risk to help us. She asks you to email her directly at dogood@livingstone.drc.

Sister Mercia says we must pray for this message to find its way to someone who is good and kind and strong. I pray this is you.

Yours truly,
Eloria Bangana

3.

THERE ARE TWO things in the interrogation room with me and Inspector Tshabalala. The one is Mrs. Luditsky's ring. The other is twelve and a half minutes of silence. I've been counting the seconds. One alligator. Two alligator. 751 alligator.

She's forgetting I've done jail time. 766 alligator. That if you're smart, prison is just a waiting game. I can wait when I have to. I can wait like nobody's business. 774 alligator. Sloth is the one who gets fidgety. He huffs in my ear and shifts his butt around. 800 alligator.

It's supposed to make me nervous. Nervousness hates a vacuum. 826 alligator. Nervousness will blurt right out with something, anything, to kill the silence. 839 alligator. Unless nervousness is kept busy doing something more useful. Like counting. 842 alligator.

The inspector's face is perfectly, studiedly neutral, like a 3-D rendering of a face waiting for an animator to pull the strings. 860 alligator. Watching her watch me gives me the opportunity to study her. She has a round face with cheeks like apples and baggy pouches under her eyes that look like they're settling in for the long haul. She wears her hair in braids tied back with a clip. Not exactly practical for *ipoyisa*, but then she's an inspector, not a patrol grunt. There is a tiny scar where she once had a nose piercing. 884 alligator. Maybe she still wears a *diamanté* stud off-duty. Maybe she has a whole secret life, a sideline in punk rock or a night-class PhD in Philosophy. 902 alligator.

Her navy suit has a food smear on the lapel. I'd venture tomato sauce. 911 alligator. Maybe blood. Maybe she beat up another suspect in another gray room just before she came in here. 922 alligator. I'd feel her out for her lost things, but cops and police stations are all equipped with magic blockers. It's regulation infrasound. Low-frequency sound waves below the range of human hearing, but which still resonate in your body, the kind that scientists use to explain experiences of haunted houses or the divine, usually brought on by something as mundane as an extraction fan or the low notes of a church organ. 932 alligator. That was before the world changed. It's a fragile state—the world as we know it. All it takes is one Afghan warlord to show up with a Penguin in a bulletproof vest, and everything science and religion *thought* they knew goes right out the window. 948 alligator.

Inspector Tshabalala leans across the table to pick up the ring, idly rolls it between her fingers. 953 alligator. She takes a breath. 961 alligator. Caves.

"Hardly seems worth it," she says. Sloth startles with a hiccup, as if he'd just been dropping off to sleep, which is not unlikely. He sleeps around sixteen hours a day.

"You think?" I'm annoyed that I have to clear my throat.

"You could probably get a good price for it. R5000 if

27

you had the certification. But let's assume you don't, which means you're looking at what, R800 max, at a pawnshop. You that hard up for cash, Zinzi?"

She flicks the ring over her knuckles and back, the kind of cheap magic trick you might use to impress girls in high school.

"I don't know how *Mr.* Luditsky would feel about that."

"Feel about what?"

"Being pawned. Bad karma. He might haunt me." I incline my head at Sloth. "And I'm haunted enough already."

"What are you talking about?"

"The ring? It's made with dead guy. Do your homework, Inspector."

She blinks, but just the once. "All right, so what were you planning to do with the ring?"

"Return it. It was a job. Like I told your guys outside her building. Repeatedly."

"Your fingerprints were all over the scene."

"I was in her apartment two days ago. She made me tea. It was undrinkable. You going to tell me how she died?"

"You tell me, Zinzi."

Sloth grazes my shoulder with his teeth, which is his way of kicking me under the table. I sort of specialize in social *faux pas.*

"All right," I say, causing Sloth to bite down on my shoulder *hard.* I shrug him away. "Let's see. She died on the scene. In her apartment. Gunshot?" I'm imagining a retro number with the word *Vektor* printed down the side, even though that's ridiculous. "Stabbing? Blunt object? Choked on a piece of stale biscotti?"

Inspector Tshabalala flicks the ring, backwards, forwards, palms it. Then she reaches into her bag and places a brown cardboard police docket on the desk. After a moment, she flicks it open to reveal the photographs. She fans them out, hoping to get a reaction. "You tell me," she says again.

There is a woolly sheepskin slipper lying in the passage by the front door. There is stripe of blood over the toe of the slipper that continues in an arc across the wall and a framed print of waterlilies.

There is a bloody smear against the wall, as if someone had fallen against it and scraped along, using the wall for support.

There is a black raincoat in the bathtub, a puddle of plastic and blood under the full blast of the shower. There are pink streaks down the bathroom sink.

The display cabinet is overturned. There are drag marks in blood across the floor. Someone trying to crawl away.

There is the shrapnel of china figurines everywhere. And I mean everywhere. A cherub's rosy buttock in the TV room. Little Bo Peep smiling blandly up from the kitchen tiles, decapitated, among the splintered remains of her little lamb.

Mrs. Luditsky is sitting on the floor, slumped against the couch, her legs splayed out in an A. Her head lolls backwards and to one side at an uncomfortable angle. If it weren't for the wrinkles and the wounds, she could be a sloppy drunk, a teenage girl at a house party after one alcopop too many. She is wearing a voluminous silk blouse soaked in blood. It gapes in the places where it has been sliced through, revealing a beige bra and bloody gashes. She is wearing one slipper. The toenails on her other foot are painted a dark plum. Her eyes are open, as cold and glossy as Little Bo Peep's. Her *crème brûlée* hairdo is half crushed against the arm of the couch.

"I'm going to venture it wasn't stale biscotti," I say. Nor gunshot. Tshabalala exhales through her teeth and glances at the door.

"That," she says, tapping the photograph, "is not your everyday burglary. Seventy-six stab wounds? That's personal."

"Was anything taken?"

"We're checking with her housekeeper. She's still in shock. Why? You got something *else* you want to hand over?"

"The TV? The DVD player? Other jewelry?"

"You're the one with the ring in your pocket," Inspector Tshabalala smirks.

"I didn't do it," I say.

She strings out the silence. 97 alligator. 99, 128. "It's not like we don't know what you're capable of, Zinzi," she says, finally. I lean back in my shitty gray plastic chair. I've heard this tune before and it's nothing but cheap Muzak. She's reaching, which means she's got absolutely nothing.

"That's unconstitutional, Inspector."

"Save it for the animal rights people."

"That's the SPCA."

"What?"

"The animal rights people. Dogs, cart-horses, cats, lab rats, neutering programs. I *know* you didn't mean to say anything that could be construed as racist, inspector. Something that could go on your permanent record."

"All I'm saying is that you've murdered before."

"The court said accessory to."

"That's not what the thing on your back says."

"He's a Sloth."

"He's *guilt*. You know how many people I've shot in eleven years on the force?"

"Do I get a gold star if I guess right?"

"Three. Non-fatal, all of them."

"Maybe you should spend more time at target practice."

"A good cop doesn't need to shoot to kill."

"Is that what you are? A good cop?"

She spreads her hands. "You see a furry companion at my side?"

"Maybe your conscience is on the fritz. There have been studies: sociopaths, psychopaths—"

"The difference between you and me?" she interrupts, the ring re-materializing in the crack of her fingers like a jack-in-the-box. "The Undertow isn't coming for *me*."

She flicks the ring into her palm and replaces it neatly, exactly in the center of the table. I let her have her moment. One alligator. Getting the last word is all about the timing. Two alligator.

"Don't worry, Inspector," I say. "You've still got plenty of time to fuck up."

By the time I get out of Rosebank police station, the bright and shiny coating on my day has started to peel off. The cops kept the ring, confiscated the R500 in my wallet as "evidence" and made me sign a hundred billion forms.

The security cameras on Mrs. Luditsky's building provided a clear record of my comings and goings. Arrived Saturday 11h03, signed in, departed 11h41. Arrived again this morning, 07h36. Departed in the back of a police van in plastic cuffs after a heated argument on the street: 08h19.

But, really, it's thanks to my criminal record that they eventually had to let me go. Because they have my details on file.

Ref: Zinzi Lelethu December #26841AJHB
ID 7812290112070
Animalled 14 October 2006
(see Case SAPS900/14/10/2006 Rosebank cf:
Murder of Thando December) Ability to trace
lost objects.

Which means that my story checks out. Although the charming Inspector Tshabalala still insists that Benoît comes down to sign an affidavit about my whereabouts at 06h32. That's when the security cameras mysteriously fritzed out and Mrs. Luditsky's neighbors reported hearing screams, right before they rolled over to go back to sleep, figuring it was probably just a violent show on TV with the volume pumped up, because maybe the old lady was finally going deaf. Tshabalala told me that much before she chucked me back out on the street.

People are such assholes.

4.

The Daily Truth 22 March 2011

POLICE FILE
Crime Watch with Mandlakazi Mabuso
Mall Rats

YOH, MENSE. Another nightmare day in dream city. Killarney Mall gets hit by armed robbers on Friday, and yesterday the same gang hits Eastgate! No one got killed but believe you me, the shoppers are plenty shook-up by having okes with AKs storming around. The *tsotsis* hit a jewelry store and emptied the tills at Checkers before clearing out while mall security twiddled their thumbs. Okay, maybe understandable when witnesses report that the gangsters had a lion with them. Makes me wonder if we don't need a pass system for zoos after all!

Jump over to Linden for a happy ending (for once). A young mom was hijacked on her way back from crèche yesterday, but the baddies took pity and dropped the baby off, still in his carseat, by the traffic lights a couple of kays away. *Ag voeitog.* Even gangsters have a heart sometimes.

But maybe not a nose. Over in Cyrildene, the cops found several million rands worth of *perlemoen* rotting in a garage. The *okie* who owned the place was bust when the neighbors complained about the reek of *vrot* sea snot that's supposed to be a potent aphrodisiac—and a protected species! Tell that to the Triads shipping them off by the rotting bucket-load to China, my china.

And over in *larney*-ville Sandton-side, it turns out Bafana boy Kabelo Nongoloza is a good striker off the field as well as on. His long-time girlfriend and debutante, Queenie Mugudamani, laid charges of assault against the young soccer star on Tuesday and is sporting a nasty bruised and swollen face as Exhibit A. Sounds like time for another nose job for Queenie. Pity you can't get a makeover for your bad taste in men!

5.

PEOPLE WANT TO believe: you just have to feed them plausible constructs. The help-poor-widow-of-defunct-government-minister-get-$25-million-out-of-the-corrupt-country is so stale and overused that even my mother wouldn't fall for it. And I know from personal experience that my mother would fall for a lot. I brush the dusting of Mongoose fur and flea eggs off my laptop, and flick open the screen to see if the phish have been biting.

I've become a master builder in the current affairs sympathy scam. A broken levee and an old lady with a flooded mansion, desperate to sell her priceless antiques cheap-cheap. A Chechnyan refugee fleeing the latest Russian pogroms with her family's diamonds in tow. A Somali pirate who has found Jesus and wants to trade in his rocket launcher and ransom millions for absolution.

It's all topical. All rooted in the hard realities of the world. Ironic that Former Life I never watched the news. But then, lifestyle journalists don't have to. And normal people don't have to pay off their drug debts by writing scam letters for syndicates. Or hide their sideline from their lover, who would definitely not approve.

There are 2,581 replies waiting. Not a bad hit rate out of the 49,812 that I sent out on Monday, not including the tens of thousands that bounced off spam filters. There are 1,906 "out of office" replies, which at least marks the email addresses as active, 14 irritated missives that range from "fuck you, scamfucks" to "pull the other one." Add 292 kanji variations, 137 in French, 102 in German, 64 in Arabic, 48 in Spanish and 12 in Urdu, all of which I'll plug into my translation software later. This leaves six potentials, two responding with cautious interest and the rest with abject confusion. I forward them all on to Vuyo, who is my catcherman. If people would just read the damn email properly, they would have responded to him directly.

And then there's an anomaly that chokes my auto-filter. Two stark sentences that read as either nonsense or poetry, or both.

When you eat, you are eating things from planes.
The plastic forks, they leave a mark on you.

There is no link. No return address. No point to the message at all. It makes me nervous.

There is also an email from the dentist, a friendly reminder that it's time for my six-month check-up, please contact Ms. Pillay to make an appointment. I haven't been to a dentist since I went to jail three and a half years ago. This is code for "contact me immediately," which is worrying because I'm not due to report in until next week. I log in to Skype chat where Vuyo is already online. Probably talking to "clients" in other windows.

>>Vuyo: Yes?

He answers right away, curt as always. Vuyo is not his real name, of course. It's probably one of several not-his-real-names that he uses in the course of business.

I like to think of him hanging out in a huge sprawling Internet café adjoining a raucous street market in Accra or Lagos, kinda like a 419 sweatshop, but the truth is he's probably in a dingy apartment like this one, maybe even right next door. Flying solo, because it's all carefully decentralized.

>>Kahlo999: Hey, hello. How are you? Got a very strange msg. No return address. About forks. I'll fwd it.

>>Vuyo: No! U dont know what it is girl. Might b a virus. Might b bad muti.

>>Kahlo999: Or a msg about cutlery.

>>Vuyo: U dont know. Could b rival syndicate. Police. Click here.

>>Kahlo999: What am I downloading? It's just, you know, I have very particular tastes in porn.

>>Vuyo: Proprietary firewall 4 viruses spyware malware muti. And delete that thing.

>>Kahlo999: So what's with the dental appointment, boss guy? I haven't been flossing enough?

>>Vuyo: I need u 4 an interview. 2pm. Rand Club. Frances format. Clients want to meet her.

I turn cold. Frances is a refugee in a camp in Côte d'Ivoire. Twenty-three years old. Suitably flirtatious if the *moegoe* on the other end of the line is a man, a good chaste Christian girl if it's a woman. More or less. Most characters are designed to be slightly flexible depending on the operator, although Frances is fairly one-dimensional. After the rebels attacked, she fled to safety, got stuck in the refugee camp, and now she can't access her father's fortune. Bog standard format. That is to say, not one of mine.

>>Kahlo999: Sorry. Not in my contract.

>>Vuyo: Not neg.

>>Kahlo999: Let's talk remuneration.

>>Vuyo: Will deduct it from ur total. Dont worry, Im keeping track.

>>Kahlo999: It would be nice if I could keep track too. Not that I don't trust you.

>>Vuyo: U forget who u dealing with girl.

>>Kahlo999: My own personal knacker. The guys who bought the lame horse of my drug debt for cheap-cheap to turn it into glue.

>>Vuyo: Lame horse? Ur horse is expensive.

>>Kahlo999: Do you know how much racehorses go for? R150,000 is cheap at the price. So, here's the thing. Where do we stand you and I? What's my lame horse ass worth?

>>Vuyo: R55,764.18.

>>Kahlo999: Profit?

>>Vuyo: Ha. No. U still owe us R94,235.82.

>>Kahlo999: That's impossible. How many moegoes have I hooked for you?

>>Vuyo: Is v. possible. U forget interest. Normally 45%, but u get employee discount. Only 34%. And it is not fish on the hook, it is the fish in the bucket that counts.

>>Kahlo999: Fuck you, Vuyo.

>>Vuyo: This deal will bring in 50 Titos. If u do well, it is worth 10% to u.

>>Kahlo999: And if I don't?

>>Vuyo: Of course u will do well. U R practically a pro. Ur dealer told us about all the stories u came with, crying about ur mama with cancer + ur dead granny + being mugged just when u were coming to pay for ur coke. This will b easy for u.

>>Kahlo999: I mean, if I don't do it at all.

>>Vuyo: I will have to add a penalty to ur total. 20% + usual interest. So that is . . . let me work it out.

>>Kahlo999: I got it, thanks.

>>Vuyo: 2pm at the Rand Club. Dress nice. But not 2nice.

>>Kahlo999: Refugee chic.

>>Vuyo: Good girl. BTW ur new format—the coltan—its doing well. Head office likes it.

>>Kahlo999: What can I say? I'm all about the job satisfaction.

>>Vuyo: Cheer up girl. Greed is a bad thing. They deserve it.

Part of me thinks I do too.

I sign off and delete the forks message, but not before I've copied and pasted it into a Word doc. And I leave the install icon on the firewall waiting patiently in its folder, uninstalled. I know how the Company works. Who knows what else their firewall will do?

The Rand Club is a relic of Johannesburg's Wild West days, when it was frequented by Cecil John Rhodes and other colonial slumlords who would sit around divvying up diamond fields and deciding on the fate of empires. A hangout for power people rather than two-bit crooks like Vuyo, who is waiting for me . . . at the curved stretch of bar that folds itself around the room. I assume it's Vuyo because he's the best-dressed guy in here, in a suit and pointy shoes like shiny leather sharks.

The patrons pushing the boundaries of their liquid lunch hour have the same aura of clingy colonial nostalgia as the venue, with its chandeliers and gilded railings, caricatures of famous members, mounted buck-heads and faded oil paintings of fox hunts. Vuyo, by comparison, has the air of the fox that's escaped the painting and doublebacked to raid the kitchen. I'd always pictured him as a skinny weasel of a guy with bad posture from hunching over his computer all day, but he's well-built, with swimmer's shoulders, broad cheekbones, a neat goatee, and an easy smile. Generically handsome with a ruby stud in his ear that hints oh-so-tastefully at danger. All the better to scam the pants off you.

I extend my hand and he clasps it in both of his, as if we are old friends instead of only online acquaintances. "Mr. Bacci, I can only imagine?" I say.

"Frances. It is so good to see you," he replies. I shouldn't be surprised that he speaks better than he types. Or that he's South African. Why should the West Africans and the Russians have all the fun of fleecing rich foreigners?

"Mr. and Mrs. Barber are waiting for us upstairs. They're excited to meet you at last," he says smoothly, as if the podgy bankers round the other side of the undulating bar might be listening in. But as he escorts me up the grand staircase, he hisses under his breath, "Less attitude, girl. You are a refugee, not a prostitute."

"Mr. Bacci! Does that mean you don't like my dress?" The white shift is the plainest thing in my wardrobe, but I've touched it up with clunky beads and a *shweshwe* head-wrap, with the perfect refugee touch, a red-, blue-, and white-checked rattan carrier bulging with the weight of an exceptionally grumpy Sloth.

"It means, be soft," warns Vuyo, aka Mr. Ezekiel Bacci, financial director of the Bank of Accra.

"Can you qualify that? Are we talking demure African

princess soft, proud but humble and desperate to reclaim her throne? Or broken Janjaweed-gang-rape survivor soft?"

"It means none of your jokes. Keep that tongue tamed."

"You realize you employed me based on my writing skills, not my acting ability?"

"Just do what I tell you. Don't open your mouth unless I ask you something specifically. You read the emails?"

"Yes." Poor bastards.

We step into the grand library with shelves and shelves of books that look like they've never been cracked open. A couple the wrong side of middle age are waiting anxiously. Mrs. Barber is sitting with a magazine on her lap, but I'm guessing she hasn't read a word. It's open to a double-page spread advertising a three-year-old conference on the economics of environmental reform. Mr. Barber is standing facing away from us, fiddling with the standing chessboard.

"You know, honey, I think these are ivory," he says, holding out a white bishop to Mrs. Barber, his consonants a flat Mid-West drawl.

"You never know where you might find hidden treasure in Africa," I say, in my best Queen of Sheba voice.

"Oh," Mrs. Barber says, looking at me. "Oh!" And then she gets up, envelops me in a crushing hug, and bursts into tears. I stand there awkwardly, but with great grace, as befits a girl who has weathered the ravages of losing her throne, her family, and, temporarily, a great fortune that Mr. and Mrs. Barber have had the great fortune to help her recover.

"My friends," I murmur softly. "My friends."

Mr. Barber sits down heavily, still holding the bishop, looking shocked. I gently extricate myself from Mrs. Barber's fervent embrace, only for her to grab me by the hand. I manage to maneuver the pair of us onto the couch.

"So, you see, here she is, after all," Vuyo says. "Safe and sound, as I told you."

"We weren't sure. We didn't know. After everything . . ." Mrs. Barber's sentence declines into another bout of juddering sobs.

"You look different from the photographs," Mr. Barber says, an obstinate flicker of suspicion flaring up. Considering they have already given Vuyo over R87,000 for various clearance certificates, passport application fees, bribes for corrupt government officials, and exchange-rate commissions, and he's demanding a further R141,000, I'd say he was justified.

"Yes," I say with dignity, "I've been through a great deal." Mrs. Barber pats my hand, and I lean my head against her shoulder and close my eyes as if the ordeal has been unspeakable. A contemptuous bark comes from my bag. I ignore it.

"You have brought the money?" Vuyo says.

"Well, yes, but——" Mr. Barber squirms.

"Why are there buts? Buts are for goats! Are you a goat? Jerry, in three days' time, you will have 2.5 million dollars in your account."

"It's only that it's my pension."

"Our savings."

"Look at this girl, Jerry. Look at her! You have done this. You have got her away from that hell. You and Cheryl have done a good thing. A life-changing thing." Vuyo takes Jerry's face between his hands and gives him a little shake for emphasis, a cross between an evangelist and a corporate teambuilder. "And here. Your certificates from the Reserve Bank, as you requested. Everything is in order. It's almost over, Jerry."

"It's almost over, Jerry," Cheryl repeats. She glances over at me and her chin starts to wobble all over again. I imagine staples fixing my smile in place and dip my head, as if equally overcome with emotion. The whole thing is grotesque, yet some perverse part of me is getting off on it. The same way I ticked off points on a scoreboard when my parents actually believed the bullshit I spun them about my car breaking down, about needing help paying the fees for a master's degree in Journalism that I never even registered for.

Jerry is looking over the certificates, immaculately forged, complete with the holographic seal of the Reserve Bank. "Of course, I'll need to get these verified by my lawyer," he says, but it's obvious that he's bluffing. The smell of money is too strong now. It bellows like a vuvuzela, drowning out the whisper of doubt.

"Of course, yes," Vuyo says, but he allows a hint of concern to smudge those generic good looks.

"What is it, Mr. Bacci?"

"Please, we are all friends here. Call me Ezekiel."

"What is it, Ezekiel?"

"It is only that it might cause a delay."

Cheryl moans.

"What kind of delay?"

"No longer than a couple of weeks. Two months maximum."

"Now you just wait a minute, we have been through *enough*. This is everything we have in the world. Our pensions, our savings. I borrowed money from my son! Do you realize how much it costs for us to fly out here? This is the third time!"

"You have been very understanding, Mr. Barber. It's only that there is a window period. It is the end of the tax year in Ghana, and the government locks down all banking transactions for the reconciliation period."

"That's the stupidest fucking thing I ever heard!"

"Jerrr-ry . . ." Cheryl says.

"It is Ghana," Vuyo shrugs.

"So what can we do?"

Vuyo considers it and then allows illumination to spread across his face. "I have it. The bank has bearer bonds. I will give you bearer bonds to the value of your cash deposit. These will take a month to clear, but they are not subject to the restrictions of the government's reconciliation period. So you will be safe. And we can go ahead with the final transaction."

"I don't know, that sounds awfully complicated. Maybe we should wait."

"The waiting was the worst," I say, absently.

"What was that, dear?" Cheryl squeezes my hand.

"Not knowing if they were going to kill us. They would

play games with us. Sometimes taking girls at random. Other times they made us choose, made us decide who it was going to be. And then they would take someone else instead. But you had to live with it, live with the betrayal of what you'd done."

"Oh, sweetheart. Oh, sweetheart," Cheryl chokes, her palm clamped over her mouth. "Oh, baby, if that was our Mandy. Can you imagine? Oh."

"I just want to say thank you," I say, looking down at my hands clasped together in my lap.

"Oh," says Cheryl. "Oh, baby."

"Okay," Jerry says, defeated. "Bearer bonds, huh?"

"Only for 72 hours. And then the 2.5 will be cleared," Vuyo says.

While the menfolk sort out the matter of exchanging a tog-bag full of cash for phony bearer bonds from a nonexistent bank, I order tea for both of us.

"May I ask what you are going to do with the money?" I say to Cheryl.

"Buy a house. For us and the kids. Amanda and Simon and their families. I mean, two-and-a-half million bucks, you could buy a place in Malibu. But we're going to stay in Aurora, get Mandy to move back from Chicago, so we can spend more time with the grandkids. Wait a minute, here's a photo." Cheryl pulls out her phone to show me a snapshot of an unfortunate-looking baby covered in slobber and a smiley girl with pigtails and a strawberry birthmark over her cheek. "That's Archie, and this is Becky—Mandy's little ones. And Simon, well, Simon and his partner are planning to adopt."

"So cute." I hand the phone back.

"What about you, dear?"

"I will try to make a new life as best I can. It is better here in this country."

"And the orphanage?"

"Oh yes, the orphanage. Um. We have been looking at buildings. There is an old retirement home that we could convert. It's lovely. Big garden with a mulberry tree, swimming pool. Near the botanical gardens. It will be lovely." I am thinking of a version of the house I grew up in.

"It's nice to feel like suddenly you have possibilities, isn't it?"

"Yes."

We lapse into silence.

"Did you have much trouble getting out of the camp?"

"Please, Cheryl, it is too painful to talk about." I bury my face in my hands for emphasis. Through the gaps between my fingers, I can see my bag start to squirm again. I prod Sloth with my shoe to make him cut it out.

"Oh. Of course." She puts her arm around my shoulders and pulls me into an awkward embrace, stroking my back. "There, there," she says. "There, there."

"All taken care of." Jerry is grinning broadly, like a man who has had an incredible burden lifted from his back. Doubt weighs a lot. "Can I give you a hand with this, Frances?" He hefts the rattan bag before I can stop him. "Whoof, what do you got in here, all your earthly goods?"

"Jerry!" Cheryl says, scandalized.

"Oh, sorry, I didn't mean..." and then Sloth pokes his head out and bleats grumpily.

Jerry drops the bag. Luckily, it's only five inches to the floor, but Sloth yelps like he's gone over the Victoria Falls.

"Mary, Mother of God! What is that thing?"

"Jerry Barber! You know perfectly well what that is! Oh Frances, honey, you should have told us." Over her shoulder, Vuyo is giving me a stare that says "You better fix this."

"I was—ashamed," I mutter.

"Now, baby, there's nothing to be ashamed of. It doesn't mean you're a bad person. It just means you've done bad things once upon a time." She shoots Jerry a fierce look. "You're a good girl, honey, a good girl." Her eyes brim with tears all over again.

We watch Cheryl and Jerry pull out of the parking lot packed with X5s and A4s in their white VW Polo rental, and wave cheerily until they pull around the corner.

"You *are* a good girl," Vuyo says, imitating Cheryl.

"Shut up, Vuyo."

"We should do this again."

"I want twenty percent."

"Next time, maybe."

"This was a one-time-only event. I'm not doing a repeat performance."

"I have R94,235.82 that says different."

"I'll write more formats."

"I'll double your interest rate."

"I don't care."

"What was your brother's name again?" he says slyly. "The dead one?"

"Fuck you."

"And your lover? That handsome *mkwerekwere?* Benoît, is it? Be careful, Zinzi. You know what happened last time you fucked with gangsters."

Vuyo gets into one of the X5s. I memorize the license plate. It's undoubtedly fake, but I'm a packrat for information. I rap on the window. He slides it down. "What is it?"

"Give me a ride."

"Get a car," he says and pulls away, wheels spinning.

6.

MAKHAZA'S PLACE IS already vibey at three in the afternoon. This is a reflection of the lack of recreational facilities in the area. Although Mak's popularity in a neighborhood packed with bars and churches can be ascribed to two things: the Lagos-style chicken, and the view. The bar is situated on the second floor of what used to be a shopping arcade back when this part of town was cosmopolitan central, with its glitzy hotels and restaurants and outdoor cafés and malls packed to the skylights with premium luxury goods. Even Zoo City had a Former Life.

There was big talk about comebacks and gentrification a few years ago, which led to months of eviction raids by the Red Ants, with their red helmets and sledgehammers and bullhorns, and bright-eyed landlords buoyed up on the property boom bricking up the lower stories of buildings. But the squatters always found a way back in. We're an enterprising bunch. And it helps to have a certain reputation.

Mak's is situated in what used to be an oversized display window looking out over the street. It was modeled on Macy's, rotating exhibits of aspirational fashion and lifestyle products, roomy enough that they once put a convertible

Chevrolet in here as part of their Christmas display, Santa in shades and a Hawaiian shirt at the wheel.

Mak kept some of the mannequins for the ambience; a double-amputee guy in sharp-pressed corduroy pants, a lime sweater vest and a fedora, and a woman with a pockmarked melamine face to match her moth-eaten white mini-dress and go-go boots, both arrested in some forlorn pose of retro cool. The patrons don't dress half as nice.

I shrug Sloth off at the holding pen by the door. He sways himself onto the branch of a dead tree hung with fairylights and already well populated. A doughy Squirrel quickly stuffs the remains of a chocolate bar into her mouth and chitters reproachfully at Sloth, then bounds higher, past a preening Indian Mynah and a Boomslang looped casually from a fork in the branch, as motionless as the mannequins.

"Don't get too close, buddy," I warn Sloth. Unofficially, there's a code of conduct, but animals are still animals. And animals can be assholes, too. The Mongoose is curled up in the corner in the sawdust. He slits his eyes open, then pretends to go back to sleep.

Benoît and two of his boys, his roommate Emmanuel and that *sgebenga* D'Nice, are in the usual spot by the foosball table. I pick up a tonic water at the bar (the closest I get these days to the full equation of gin &), and drop down next to them in the corner booth. The aircon is on the fritz as per usual and their beers are sweating. D'Nice's Vervet Monkey is sitting on the table surrounded by at least two rounds of 750 ml empties, toying with a coaster nicked from the Carlton Hotel circa 1987.

The TV is blasting some godawful crunk rap thing, jiggling sweaty bodies intercut with gritty images of a city burning. Giant fireballs light up the Las Vegas skyline. The singer, wearing a leopard-print vest and chains, skulks between the girls with a Hyena padding beside him. The animal snarls in close-up, baring yellowed teeth. It's an act so dramatic, it causes the girls to burst into flames too. Luckily, it doesn't seem to bother them too much. Flames lick over their taut gyrating bellies, fiery arcs tracing the curve of buttocks peeking out from sprayed-on hot pants.

"That for real?" I say, indicating the TV by way of greeting.

"You're kidding." Emmanuel is deeply shocked. He's a sweet Rwandan kid, only twenty, working piecemeal jobs. Doesn't have an animal, but there's no rule saying it's obligatory. We're all about tolerance in Zoo City. Or mutually assured desperation.

"Give me a break, Emmanuel. I'm thirty-two. I don't know this shit anymore."

"*Cha!* Zinzi! How do you *not* know Slinger?"

"What kind of a name is Slinger? That's so metal."

"You hurt me. Your words. They physically hurt me."

"You haven't seen me try to hurt you, Emmanuel."

"Yes, it's *real!*" he says, defensively. "Nigga took a bullet to the face and lived to tell. Bounced off the side of his skull, shattered his jaw, they had to wire him up, reconstruct the whole thing."

D'Nice chips in, waving his beer, slopping it around. "You know a hyena's jaws are stronger than a lion's. Got to get through skulls, to the marrow." The Vervet Monkey perks up at the sight of the spillage. She drops the coaster and leans forward with great deliberation.

"Skulls don't have marrow," Benoît says. I realize they're all already slightly drunk.

"You know what I mean," D'Nice mutters. The Vervet Monkey wipes her paw through the puddle of beer. She raises her hand to her face and examines it before licking her palm. She shivers at the aftertaste. Then licks her hand again, pink tongue searching out the cracks. Did I say slightly drunk?

"Listen!" Emmanuel says. "So Slinger's not standing for that, right? Gets out of hospital, half robot with all the metal bits they've had to graft into his head, and goes looking for the niggas who did this to him. Finds them in some strip joint in South Central. Walks right through the front doors. And *bam! bam! bam!*" Emmanuel mimes blowing the motherfuckers away with an imaginary gun so gigantic he has to hold it with both hands.

"Takes them out, like eight of them. Half don't even get a chance to react, the other half get as far as reaching for their guns, maybe standing up before he blows them away. Strippers running out of the building naked and screaming and stuff, all covered in blood!"

"You know, I think I saw that movie."

Emmanuel's grin drops from his face like a kicked puppy, bounces on the pavement, and tumbles into the gutter with a little pitiful yelp. On the TV, Slinger and his Hyena have given way to a Mouseketeered kwaito duo, a boy and a girl, all sweet teen provocado.

"Zinzi, stop being a mean old cynic." Benoît's breath smells like three, maybe four rounds of *lengolongola*. "I'm sorry, Emmanuel. I can't take her anywhere."

"Ha. Like you *do* take me anywhere. Sorry, Emmanuel. Didn't mean to disrespect your boy." I punch his arm to show no hard feelings. Emmanuel looks less downcast—in fact, looks like all is entirely forgiven, and to show just how forgiven I am, he's going to regale me with more riveting details of Slinger's totally-not-fabricated biography. I cut him off as he takes the breath that will power the next paragraph of Slinger trivia, throwing a proprietary arm over Benoît. "So, you boys talking business or can I take this one away?"

"What's the rush, Zee-zee?" D'Nice is one of those guys who assign nicknames unasked for. He's also one of those guys with his fingers gravy-deep in all kinds of dodgy pies. He's wearing a woolen beanie, his mouth hanging slightly open, like always, which makes him look stupid. But you'd be stupid to underestimate him.

"Stay and have a drink with us," he says.

I raise my tonic water. "Sorted, thanks, *nicey-nice*. And cut it out," I add, as I feel something like insect feet brushing against my temples. His Vervet is leaning forward, tense, suddenly focused through the glaze of alcohol. An animal at work.

"Cut what out?" he says innocently, as if he weren't extending little magic suckers towards me, but the skittery sensation fades away and the Monkey leans back in disappointment. She gives D'Nice a dirty look and goes back to fumbling with the beer.

"You've been hitting them heavy, Zee-zee," D'Nice says, but he's trying to deflect attention because Emmanuel isn't in on his party trick.

D'Nice is the opposite of nice. His *shavi* is soaking up little moments of happiness, absorbing them haphazardly like a sponge. He lies about it, of course. A lot of zoos have a cover story for talents more deviant than normal. If you ask him, D'Nice will tell you his talent is scavenging information and, admittedly, he does a lot of that too. He lifts it off the street and flips it for cash to whoever is paying—but his snitching isn't magically enabled.

You'd think if you were a serotonin vampire, you might internalize some of that happiness. Not D'Nice. As far as I can tell, Benoît is his only friend, or at least the only person who can tolerate him for longer than twenty minutes sober.

"You know me, D'Nice. Party animal. Speaking of which, I think yours has had one too many." The Vervet topples the bottle.

"Fuck's sake," D'Nice says, grabbing for it, but not before the Vervet has managed to pull it over, dominoing three other glasses and the remains of my tonic water in the process. Emmanuel leaps up with a shout, knocking over his chair in the scramble to avoid spillage. There is the crash of glass. D'Nice is yelling, alternately at the Vervet for being an idiot, and for Mak to bring a rag to clean up the mess—and a new round, while he's at it, on the house 'cos it wouldn't have happened if the table wasn't wonky like all the shitty reject furniture in here. Mak disagrees with the diagnosis, loudly, which gets

Carlos, the very large, very bald Portuguese bouncer involved. Emmanuel wisely uses the opportunity to take a slash or get another drink and melts away.

The chaos gives Benoît and me a moment to converse like grown-ups.

"You okay?" he says, being the kind of smart, sensitive guy who picks up on not-so-subtle hints. Not so smart and sensitive that he's discerning about his friends and roommates, but hey.

"As shitty days go, this one's been raw sewage so far."

"What happened with Mrs. Luditsky?"

"She died. Murdered, if you want to be technical. I was practically there and the connection just...withered up." Saying it, I feel the kick in my gut again. Like a lost heart attack that's wandered into my intestines by mistake.

"Is that where you've—"

"Cops. Three hours. Total bullshit. Oh, and they need you to go down to the station in the next couple of days and give a statement about my whereabouts this morning."

Benoît doesn't say anything. His hand goes absently to the burn scars on his throat where the skin is Barbie-plasticky and shiny under the collar of his t-shirt.

"Sorry, Benoît. I know it's a pain in the testicles." His thumb traces tight little spirals up his neck to his jawline, and I lose my patience. "Is it your papers? Because I thought your extension came through last week. If it's a hassle, I can ask one of my other lovers to cover for me."

Benoît smiles wanly. FL, the idea of other lovers would

have been more than credible. But since Sloth I've been so monogamous I make the demonstration banana that AIDS educators use to show how to put on a condom look slutty.

"I got a phone call," he says.

"From?" But I know. I know exactly who it is.

"Come on, Zinzi. My wife. My family."

And there's that feeling again. Twice in one day. Heart attack in the guts. A wrenching squeeze and twist. From the other side of the room, Sloth looks up with an enquiring squeak. I give the tiniest shake of my head.

"That's great, Benoît. You must be . . ." There are a lot of words I could fill in here. None of them quite match the cocktail of emotion burning a hole in my stomach right now: a mix of Stroh rum and sulfuric acid. And who knew? Who knew that she'd be alive after all this time? Not me. Because I don't do missing persons.

"*Ai*. Who died?" D'Nice says, directing Emmanuel to set down the fresh round of beers he's brought over from the bar. D'Nice pushes one in my direction.

"You shouldn't pick up *stompies*. You might burn your fingers," I snap.

"Benoît tell you his wife called?" D'Nice says, slyly. So much for discretion. "Great news, hey?"

"Unbelievable," I say. The heart attack has moved up to its proper place, like a poison flower in my chest. "Amazing. I have some stuff to do. I'll catch you later, Benoît."

I lean over to kiss him. His mouth tastes sweet and yeasty. I wonder if it's one more thing I'm going to have to swear off.

7.

ON MY WAY home, the dull crackle of automatic gunfire, like microwave popcorn, inspires me and a bunch of other sensible pedestrians to duck into the nearby Palisades shopping arcade for cover.

The cops don't usually use automatic weapons, which means it's either gang war or an armored car heist. The cash-in-transit vans usually get taken on the highways, where there's more room for quick getaways, but the gangs have been getting more brazen in the inner city. Gunfire has always been part of the nocturnal soundscape of Zoo City, like cicadas in the countryside. But it's only recently that it's become part of the daytime routine.

We wait it out, tense, between Mr. Pie, the Milady budget shoe store, and the Go-Go-Go travel agency, which obviously took the imperative of its name too seriously, because it's upped and gone. The window is wallpapered with a mix of TO LET signs, faded posters of exotic locales and *Unbeatable Travel Deals!*

The elevator to the atrium opens to disgorge an old lady carrying a pharmacy bag, who has to be held back from blundering outside into the gunfire. It takes some convincing, and finally she retreats, grumbling and muttering, back into the elevator, as if next time the doors open, it will be onto another place.

Benoît and I met in Elysium's elevator. Back when the elevator still worked. Back when I still used to try to disguise Sloth under a baggy hoodie. Back when I was raw out of Sun City — the prison that is, not the casino playground. There aren't any water slides or showgirls at Sun City, aka Diepkloof, where I spent three years as a guest of the government. It's an oversight of the prison system. Reform might be more effective if they taught you useful life skills — like the high kick and the titty jiggle.

They call prisoners clients these days. It's all in the semantics. "Clients" still get served slop and *pap,* still have to sleep fifty-seven to a room designed for twenty, still have to exercise in a grim concrete yard with the outside world taunting, only a mesh fence and a gun turret away. Clients still get kicked out onto the street when their compulsory state-funded vacation is up. With zero support except for an overloaded parole system that can't keep track of who you are, let alone what you're supposed to be doing.

I didn't phone my parents. We hadn't had a meaningful conversation since that spring night in 2006 when they'd come out to find me in the ambulance parking lot of Charlotte Maxeke, the shadows retreating, Sloth curled up in my lap like my own personal scarlet letter.

It was inevitable I'd end up in Zoo City. Although I didn't realize that until after the fifth rental agency had sneered over their clipboards at Sloth and told me they didn't have anything available in the suburbs—had I tried Hillbrow?

Elysium Heights wasn't the obvious choice of location for Starting Over. There were other, nicer blocks I looked at. But when Elysium's security guard agreed to show me the vacant apartment on the sixth floor when I asked him, there was something comforting about the barbed wire and the broken windows, the way all the buildings connected via officially constructed walkways or improvised bridges to form one sprawling ghetto warren. It reminded me reassuringly of prison. Only here, the doors open when you want them to.

I moved in that afternoon, with only the stale cash in my wallet and the Sloth on my back. I spent most of that first day hiding inside the apartment, trying to figure out what my next move was. In prison, you can drift between the Klaxons that regiment the day, just doing what you're told, like a ball in a slow-mo pinball machine. I missed those Klaxons.

It was late afternoon by the time I got up the guts to go outside, and then only because Sloth was mewling for food. The Sun City canteen served up slightly wilted leaves or dead insects or hay or raw offal, depending on your animal's dietary requirements. They're good that way in prison. Outside prison, well, baby, you're on your own. Got to find your own wilted leaves and slop.

Armed with the battered and scratched plastic keycard that grants access through Elysium's unwieldy turnstile gate (also reassuringly like prison), I locked up the apartment and pulled my hoodie up over Sloth's head. He snuffled in dismay.

"Tough luck, buddy," I said. I wasn't used to being seen in public with him yet. I still cared about what other people thought, even when the other people in question had animals of their own.

The lift took a long time. You could see that it had been recently refurbished. The metalwork was shiny and new against the peeling duo-tone paint job on the wall that framed it. I was just considering taking the stairs when the doors slid open revealing a pack of men, all with animals.

In Sun City, I would sometimes go along to the Neo Adventists' services. If you sat through the whole spiel, including the one-on-one counseling sessions afterwards, they would give you a proper meal, five food groups and everything. They said that the animals were the physical manifestation of our sin. Only marginally less awful than the theory that the animals are *zvidhoma* or witches' familiars, which would qualify us for torture and burning in some rural backwaters. The Adventists' sermons were torture enough, going on and on about the animals being punishment that we were going to have to carry around, like the guy in *Pilgrim's Progress* lugging around his sack of guilt. Apparently we attracted vermin because we were vermin, the lowest of the low. They said everyone could be saved, but I've yet to meet anyone who has had their animal magically dematerialized, like Pilgrim's sack of sin. Not without the Undertow coming for them.

But the men in the lift didn't carry their animals like burdens, certainly not the giant in front with the burn scars creeping down his neck underneath his t-shirt, and a Mongoose slung across his chest in a customized baby sling. They carried them the way other men carry weapons.

The Mongoose snarled at me, and I may have hesitated for an instant before I stepped into the lift. It didn't go unnoticed. I turned to face the doors as they slid closed, turning my back on the men and their menagerie, although I could see their warped reflections in the shiny aluminium, like a cheap funhouse mirror by way of Hieronymus Bosch.

"Aren't you afraid," asked the giant in a voice like silt, "to be in here with all us *animals?*"

"You should be afraid to be in here with *me,*" I snapped, not bothering to turn around.

In the reflection, I could see the giant's face distending as he grinned, a grin that broadened until it swallowed his whole face, before he burst into laughter. The other men cracked smiles. Not big smiles, but big enough that no one hassled me after that, especially after I stopped trying to hide Sloth.

The next time I saw him was a few weeks later. The brand-new lift was already out of order, and I was dragging a portable generator up the fire escape, kerlunking the unwieldy yellow bastard up the stairs one at a time, Sloth wincing at every metallic clang.

"What's that for?" said the giant companionably as he walked up behind me. He was wearing a dark khaki security-company uniform, slightly too small for him, with a name badge featuring the silhouette of a Spartan helmet that read

SENTINEL SECURITY and *ELIAS*. He didn't offer to help, which I appreciated. In theory.

"Work."

"Stealing electricity too good for you?"

"Too potentially electrocutey for me." Most of the tenants shared illegal hook-ups, jerry-rigged wiring running between flats, sometimes between buildings—flaccid tightropes for a decrepit circus.

"I could organize a sideline for you charging cellphones. Lots of people don't want the hassle of going all the way downstairs to the phone shops."

"And I don't want the hassle of dealing with lots of people. Thanks."

"All right," he said and squeezed past me up the stairs, whistling and swinging his security baton. It took me twenty minutes to heft the generator up on my own.

The third time, he knocked on my door, brazen as that. When I opened it, he was standing there with a hotplate tucked under his arm and the Mongoose slung across his chest, looking sulky.

"I know you don't like lots of people," he said. "How about one?"

"Depends," I said. "What does one want?"

"I have this hotplate."

"I see that."

"And ingredients for dinner." He indicated the grocery bag at his feet. "And nowhere to plug it in." He grinned.

"Stealing electricity too good for you?"

"I'm a terrible thief. But a great cook."

It turned out he wasn't a great cook. But neither was I.

He was surprisingly easy to be around. My *shavi* is a bitch. Most *mashavi* are. But I was cynical about people *before* I could feel the threads of lost things radiating from them, like cracks splaying out from a hole in a windscreen. He didn't have any threads. Lost things, yes, incredibly faint and blurred around him, but no connections. Obviously, he had something horrible in his past, viz the Mongoose, but he wore it well, like a soft old shirt that's been washed many times. It turned out this wasn't a coincidence.

It also turned out that his name wasn't Elias. Elias was just the guy he filled in for when Elias was sick. The rest of the time, Benoît hustled. Odd jobs, man-on-the-side-of-the-road stuff, bouncer, laborer, fixer, entrepreneur, as long as it was legal, or mostly legal. Seducer of women was not part of his résumé, he claimed, until he met me.

In fact, I was the one who kissed him.

"I didn't expect you to be so forward," he said, surprised.

"Better than being backward," I said. The texture of his burns under my palm was like cellophane.

"Must be nice to wear your scars on the outside," I said.

"I'm not the only one," he said, touching the ruin of my left ear where the bullet had caught me. But he only told me about his wife and kids in January, four and a half months after we'd first started sleeping together.

We were perusing the wares on a food stand downstairs,

when he dropped the bomb that his wife's mother used to have a fruit stand in Walakase.

"Wife present tense?"

"Possibly. I don't know."

"You failed to mention a wife." I thought I was speaking at an appropriate volume, but I was loud enough to perk up all the hawkers on the corner. Even the upstanding young drug dealer on the corner with the unnaturally wide-eyed Bushbaby craned his neck to see what was happening. Sloth ducked his head. He hates it when I make a scene. "Maybe you should have told me about *your wife,* Benoît."

"You didn't ask," Benoît said calmly, picking up a mango from the fruit stand, turning it over in his hands. He squeezed it gently. Ripeness check, aisle three.

"I thought those were the rules we were going with. Former Life out of bounds. No questions."

"Why?"

"Because it's none of my business. I didn't want to know."

"And now you do. And this is my fault?" He swapped the mango for another candidate and handed it over to me, while the fruitseller pretended not to gawp. "What do you think of this one?"

"I think it's soft in the head."

"Would it have mattered to you, if you knew, *cherie na ngayi?*" I knew the textbook answer. The manual of morality dictates that I should have said "of course" or "how can you even ask that?" but I've never been a dependable liar. Or a good person.

"That's what I thought," he said. "It doesn't change any-thing, Zinzi." He moved to kiss me, but as I tilted my head up, he pressed the mango against my lips instead.

"Idiot," I said, wiping my mouth, mainly to hide my smile.

"Adulterer," he grinned.

"Unwitting accomplice!"

"You weren't so unwitting last night. And besides, *polygamie* is legal in Congo."

"Did I call you an idiot already?"

"Only as much as I deserve." This time he did kiss me.

I handed over twelve bucks for the mango and tucked my-self under his arm, forcing Sloth to shuffle over begrudgingly.

"Are we a terrible cliché?"

"Isn't everybody?" he said.

The full story only came out later, and then only in snap-shots, images caught in a strobe. The last time he saw his family, they were running into the forest, like ghosts between the trees. Then the FDLR beat him to the ground with their rifle butts, poured paraffin over him, and set him alight.

That was over five years ago. He'd sent messages to his extended family, friends, aid organizations, refugee camps, scoured the community websites, the cryptic refugee Face-book groups that use nicknames and birth orders and job descriptions as clues—never any photographs of faces—to help families find each other without clueing in their perse-cutors. No dice. His wife and his three little children had vanished. Presumed dead. Lost forever.

The reason I didn't sense any of this? The reason I thought

he was safe and sane and well-adjusted? His *shavi* is dampening other people's. He's the static to our ambient noise, the fuzzy snow that cancels out other frequencies, but only in how it affects him. A natural resistance to magic. Don't let that get out. If there was a way to synthesize his *mashavi*, gangsters and governments would both be after him. He lied to the Home Affairs officers on his refugee application, listing his talent as "charm"—and he was charming enough to get away with it.

I thought it didn't matter. But now that his wife is no longer a theoretical construct of a tragic past, it suddenly does. That's the thing about ghosts from Former Lives—they come back to claim you.

In the shopping arcade, the brittle ack-ack of gunfire has cut off, replaced by the wail of multiple sirens. People start venturing out, some newly supplied with pungent-smelling meat pasties from Mr. Pie. Who says violent crime is bad for business? I'm tempted to get one myself, but I'm held up by the signage in Go-Go-Go Travel, or more specifically the list of specials.

The place names are a list of well-worn exotica: Zanzibar. Paris. Bali. Amazing deals! Airport taxes not included.

These are places that do not feature: Harare. Yamoussoukro. Kinshasa. These are places that require alternative travel arrangements.

Border official bribes not included.

I'm woken by a scritching at the door. I don't know what time it is, barely remember falling asleep reading a three-month-old *You* magazine, with its gleefully scandalized headlines about minor league South African celebrities and moral degeneration in general. It's been doing the rounds on this floor for a particularly torrid piece on "Forbidden Love! My Zoo Story Romance," about some corporate banker and her reformed gangster lover—complete with Silver-backed Jackal. Sample quote: "The biggest challenge, after my parents, was getting over my allergies!" Tabloid journalism at its finest.

The lights are still blazing, which is no good for my generator. I make a note on my mental shopping list to get more petrol (along with food, any description), and stumble, cursing, to open the door.

The Mongoose is sitting to attention on the spot where my doormat used to be. Add another item to the shopping list. That's the third one in six months. Maybe this time I'll get one with an anti-theft charm woven in. There's a tailor in the flat opposite who has a real talent for it, as opposed to the placebos they sell at Park Station.

The Mongoose gets to his paws and pads off down the corridor towards the fire escape. He pauses and looks back expectantly over his shoulder.

"Really?" I say. I'm wearing a t-shirt, panties, and a pair of socks, and it's freaking cold out there.

The Mongoose sits down again and waits.

"Okay, hang on. For fuck's sake." I close the door and yank

69

on my yellow leather coat with the ripped lining. Sloth mumbles sleepily.

"S'okay, buddy. I think I can handle Operation Retrieve Drunken Idiot Boyfriend on my own." Sloth makes approving chewing noises and goes back to sleep.

I button up the coat, deciding on impulse to forgo jeans. The coat only comes down to my thighs, but it covers the objectionable bits. I will come to regret this. Also not putting on shoes. Because Benoît is not just down the hall, he's all the way at the bottom of the stairs, lolling against them like a drunken cowboy, his pageboy cap tilted rakishly over his eyes, and necking a *zamalek*. The burst vessels in his eyes when he looks up to see me suggest he hasn't let up since this afternoon.

"Lost y'r shoes?" he slurs mournfully.

"It happens," I say. It's not worth explaining.

"I think they're st'len. Everythin' gets st'len h're."

"I think you're drunk. Want me to get you to bed?"

"Y'r bed."

"You really up to facing the sunrise bouncing off Ponte tomorrow morning at 6 a.m.?"

"Sh'ld knock it down."

"Or get curtains. Come on, big guy." I wrestle him to his feet, using the railing for leverage. And then we start making our way, very carefully, up six flights of stairs, the Mongoose scampering ahead.

As soon as I open the door, the Mongoose scoots inside and heads for the warmth of my laptop. I let him get away with it, this time, mainly because I'm preoccupied with shuffling Benoît inside one lurching step at a time.

I try to get him onto the bed, and realize it's going to be easier to drag the mattress onto the floor and just tip him onto it.

"Want'd t' talk," he says, sprawling onto his back, narrowly avoiding concussing himself on the wall as he goes down.

"Plenty of time," I say, pouring some bottled water into a tin cup, because the landlord has shut off the water again. I tilt it into his mouth and he gulps it down. I tuck him in and position a wastebin next to his side of the bed for ease of puking, then peel off my filthy socks and climb in next to him.

"Y'r feet are fr'zin," he complains.

"At least they're not stolen."

It's at that moment that the generator splutters and gasps and runs out of gas, plunging us into darkness, and saving me from getting back up to turn off the light.

8.

Get Real: The Online Documentary Database

THE WARLORD & THE PENGUIN
The Untold Story of Dehqan Baiyat (2003)

User Rating: 7/10 (17,264 votes)
Directors: Jan Stephen Samara Khaja
Writers: Jan Stephen (narrator) Nikolai Wood
Interviews: Dehqan Baiyat Gul Agha Baiyat General Rashid "The Wrestler" Dostum Lt. Corp. Al Stuart Matthias Weems Brigadier Jon Chafe

[MORE]

Runtime: 180 minutes
Language: English / Dari / Pashto with subtitles
Company: League Pictures, London
Country: United Kingdom
Certification: Mature / Unrated

Genre: Politics / Culture / History
Aspect Ratio: 1.85:1
Sound Mix: Dolby SR
Filming locations: Afghanistan, Pakistan, New York, London, Guantánamo
Release date: 9 October 2002 (UK) on BBC1
14 March 2003 (US/Worldwide)
Awards: Academy Award Best Documentary 2004 Sundance Film Festival 2003 International Documentary Association 2003 BAFTA 2004 Genie 2004 Golden Gate Award 2004

[MORE]

Synopsis: Warlord. Icon. Patient Zero? The life and death of Dehqan Baiyat.

Full Summary: (SPOILERS) Dehqan Baiyat was a New York film student turned machine gun–toting, motorcycle-riding Afghan warlord who became notorious in the late '90s, not for his opium trafficking or his brutal tactics in fighting both the Taliban and NATO troops—but for the penguin always at his side.

After rumors began circulating among British troops of a warlord accompanied incongruously by an Antarctic bird in a flak jacket, investigative journalist Jan Stephen tracked Baiyat down to the opium fields of the Helmand province and spent two years with him in desert and mountain hideouts, trying to uncover the mystery of the man and the bird.

This documentary tracks the life and death of Dehqan Baiyat. Descended from an Iranian clan that once fought against Genghis Khan, he became known, incorrectly, as Patient Zero for what was then called the Zoo Plague and, later, AAF or Acquired Aposymbiotic Familiarism.

Baiyat was filmed on several occasions at public gatherings feeding his penguin strips of meat he claimed was the flesh of his enemies. It was said that he could torture a man without touching him. The rumors intensified: it was claimed to be black magic, genetic modification, Hollywood special effects. Or all of the above.

After the assassination of his penguin in a Taliban ambush, his very public death by the "black cloud" (or *Siah Chal* in Persian) was televised internationally. It was the first time the event had been captured on camera, and it caused widespread panic, leading to the establishment of quarantine camps in many countries and executions in others.

Unfairly compared to Gaëtan Dugas, the Canadian flight attendant alleged to have been at the center of the spread of HIV in the US, Baiyat was, in reality, simply the most high-profile case in an epidemic that had nothing to do with disease.

Initially suspected to be the eccentric quirk of a charismatic and self-indulgent sociopath, other theories postulated that the outbreak of the animal phenomenon in Afghanistan was a result of the fallout of Pakistan's nuclear tests in the neighboring Chagai Hills in 1998.

Now, it's believed that cases of the animalled may date back to as early as the mid-'80s, based on anthropological reports coming out of New Guinea, Mali, and the Philippines. The earliest recorded case, uncovered in retrospect, was that of notorious Australian thug Kevin Warren, who was gunned down by police during an aborted bank heist in Brisbane with his "pet" wallaby in 1986. Coming out of the animalled closet twelve years later, Baiyat was not so much the start of it all, as the poster boy.

But who was Baiyat really?

The film interrogates not only the mythos that sprang up around Baiyat in the turmoil and chaos of Taliban-led Afghanistan, but also everything we understand about the animalled and the ontological Shift that happened around him.

Featuring interviews with embedded journalists, mujahedin leaders, British troops, Taliban fighters, and the Baiyat family, the film is an unflinching portrait of a man at the public center of the Shift.

QUOTES:

"Why did I come back from film school in America? [Laughs] Because my father asked me to. Because this is my country. Because here I am a rock star. I have 18,000 men under my command. People respect me. Whole villages come to pay tribute. Because here I can fuck or kill whoever I like."   —*Dehqan Baiyat*

"Think of it as my mascot. Let's say you have your lucky rabbit's foot. I have my Penguin. You keep your rabbit's foot safe in your pocket. I keep my Penguin safe in customized body armor."   —*Dehqan Baiyat*

"This romantic idea you have of some, I don't know, playboy magician warlord is all wrong. He's a drug dealer, a rapist, a killer, and a spoiled little shit with his own private army and a bunch of tribal hocus-pocus pulled out of his arse."   —*Lt. Corp. Al Stuart*

VIEWER REVIEWS: (1218 total)
[Flagged for moderation]
20 March 2010
Username: JodieStar1991 **10/10**
AWESPOmE!
gr8 movie!!! IT made me hot for zoo s3x!!!! Found gr8 site for free zoo p0rn!!!! Check it out!!!! See for yuporself!!!!!!!!!!!!! http://zoo.Ur78KG
[3 Comments]

[12 out of 16 people found the following review helpful]

14 February 2010
Username: Rebecca Wilson **7/10**
An unflinching perspective on a troubled (& troubling) icon

The third in Jan Stephen's Conflict Quartet (Israel / Liberia / Afghanistan / Burma) is perhaps the most harrowing for its no-holds-barred close-up of a man reviled, adored, and mostly misunderstood.

Baiyat's role in determining public reaction to what the media called the Shift cannot be over-emphasized. Where some saw a romantic figure, a film school dropout turned freedom fighter, others saw a symbol of the unknowable. For a time, before the animalled hit the tipping point, Baiyat became the embodiment of the question of human morality.

But was the Penguin his Jiminy Cricket or the devil on his shoulder?

It's an issue the film skirts, or rather Baiyat skirts in the film, turning cagey whenever the topic turns to the bird, leaving *this* viewer wishing the filmmakers had... **[MORE]**
[9 Comments]

[126 out of 527 people found the following review helpful]
28 December 2009
Username: Patriot777 **0/10**
Give me a break

Get it together, people, apos aren't human. It's right there in the name. Zoos. Animalled. Aposymbiots. Whatever PC term is flavor of the week. As in not human. As in short for "apocalypse." This is part of the stealth war on good citizens disguised as apo rights.

It's in Deuteronomy: Do not bring a detestable thing into your house or you, like it, will be set apart for destruction. Utterly abhor and detest it, for it is set apart for destruction. Also Exodus: Thou shalt not suffer a witch to live.

Do I need to spell it out for you? Familiars. Hell's Undertow. Destruction of the detestable. God is merciful, but only to actual, genuine, REAL LIFE human beings. Apos are criminals. They're scum. They're not even animals. They're just things and will get what is... [MORE]

[1031 Comments]

[720 out of 936 people found the following review helpful]

23 December 2009

Username: TuxBoy **10/10**

Cannibal penguin FTW! That is all.

[118 Comments]

[MORE REVIEWS]

Recommendations

If you enjoyed this, Get Real thinks you might also like:

- The Shift (2001)
- *Des Anges au Bestiaire* (1998)
- Zoologika: Perspectives from Chinese prisons to Chicago's ganglands (2007)
- Great White Totem (2003)
- Traffic (2006)
- Warlord of Kayan (1989)
- Steering by the Golden Compass: Pullman's fantasy in the context of the ontological shift (2005)
- Claws Out: The Rise of the Animalled Rights Movement (2008)

9.

"CAN I JUST say, wow! I am *so* surprised you called!"

Maltese is driving up Empire at a fair clip, about 50 kays over the speed limit in an old Mercedes in '70s gold, with the Dog on his lap, head out the window, tongue flapping. They insisted on picking me up, even though it would have taken half the time if I'd caught a taxi.

"Mm. We thought we were going to have to hunt you down," Marabou says from the back seat. Her bird flexes its wings and refolds them, feathers scraping the roof. The car isn't really built for carrion-eating storks needing to stretch to their full wingspan. There is a horrible smell in the car, a sweet and rotten undertone to the scent of leather and the Maltese's citrusy cologne. He notices me wince and mouths the words "Bird breath" with a wrinkle of his nose.

Sloth makes a grumbly sound in the back of his throat, his claws padding my arms like a cat. This is why I can't play poker. Nothing like having a giant furry tell to ruin your bluff. I try to keep my grip on the door handle casual as the car races up Empire and barrels through another orange light. Sloth buries his face into my neck. I focus on the newspaper headline posters to fight back carsickness. CORRUPTION

CASE POSTPONED. HOMELESS MAN BURNED TO DEATH. AIRPORT DRUG BUST.

"I still don't like little dogs," I say.

"That's okay," says Maltese says, remarkably chipper. "You won't be working for us anyway."

"I might not be working for anyone at all. This is just a look-see."

"You're such a tough guy. I *love* it."

We pull up to a boom marking the entrance to a gated community. The uniformed guard has a Rat in his pocket, its pink snuffling nose poking out just above the Sentinel Armed Response logo. Zoos do okay in the security sector, especially with Sentinel, which is the largest and therefore, as a matter of practicality, the most open-minded armed-response company in the city.

The Dog bristles, and as the guard leans down to look in the car window, it springs up, in a frenzy of yapping and snarling. The Rat blinks at the Dog, whiskers twitching, but it doesn't budge.

"Down, biscuit! I'm sorry, Pierre. You know how excited he gets."

"It's João, Mr. Mazibuko. But it's no problem."

"Gosh, I'm *sorry*. You'd think I'd remember such a handsome boy. I promise I won't forget again." He looks at the guard calculatingly. "I don't suppose you can sing, by any chance?"

"Mark." The Marabou's voice is sharp and low.

"No, of course not, how silly of me. Never mind, Felipe.

João. Whatever your name is. Can you let Mr. Huron know we're here? If you don't mind doing your job, sweetie?"

"Yes, sir." Unfazed, the guard takes a smart step back from the car, speaks into his radio, and then raises the boom to allow the Mercedes through. There's something about the way he does it, a staccato snap to his movement that says ex-military. That's the thing about Africa. There are a lot of wars. A lot of unemployed ex-soldiers.

The car pulls away, a little more vigorously than required, under the boom, over a speed bump, and into the rotten heart of leafy suburbia. The suburbs are overshadowed with oaks and jacarandas and elms. Biggest man-made forest in the world, or so we're told.

The grassy verges on the pavement are more manicured than a porn star's topiary, running up to ten-meter-high walls topped with electric fencing. Anything could happen behind those walls and you wouldn't know a thing. Maybe that's the point.

"Huron. Odi Huron? As in the big-shot music guy?"

"The producer, yes," Marabou corrects me.

"As in Lily Nobomvu."

"A tragic loss."

"Bit of a Howard Hughes thing going on there."

"He has a condition," Marabou says, with an elegant half-shoulder shrug that her Stork imitates, like an avian Siamese twin on a one-second time delay.

We turn down a cul-de-sac, past an open plot, wildly overgrown and worth five million at least, and pull up outside a comparatively low brownstone wall overgrown with ivy, real ivy. The ironwork gate reveals rolling lawns leading up to a Sir Herbert Baker stone house, which must date back to the early 1900s, with a small rugged hill or *koppie* rising behind it. It sticks out in this neighborhood like a hairy wart on the face of cool modernity.

"And a lost thing," I press.

"Person," Maltese corrects.

"And this person is . . . ?"

"Oh, sweetie. Patience is a virtue. Virtue is a grace—"

Marabou chimes in, the old rhyme sounding weird in her East European lilt: "Grace is a little girl who never ate her face."

"Washed her face," Maltese corrects automatically. They have the well-grooved antagonism of siblings or a long-time couple. Marabou ignores him, and he continues, "He's a wonderful man, sweetie. You'll like him."

"No little dogs then?" I say.

"*Definitely* no little dogs." Maltese presses a remote and the ironwork gate creaks open to allow us entry to the sprawling property.

We drive round the side of the house to a newly built four-car garage squatting in ugly counterpoint to Sir Herbert Baker. One of the doors is open, revealing a well-maintained Daimler in dark blue with wood paneling. Clearly Huron travels in style, which is funny, because the impression I had was that he didn't travel at all. A heavy in a chauffeur's hat is washing down the rims of the wheels. He stands up when he sees us approach and indicates to Maltese to park on the left. Then he takes the bucket and stalks away into the garage, slopping soapy water in his wake.

"Friendly guy."

"Friendly isn't in his job description," Marabou says. She opens the back door and slides out of the car, cradling the Stork's naked head against her chest to prevent it hitting the doorframe.

Maltese stays behind, drumming the edge of the steering wheel with his thumbs. "You guys go ahead. I'm going to see if John can't give the Merc a bit of a spit and polish while he's got the bucket out."

"His name is James," Marabou says.

"Whatever. I'll catch up."

"The entrance is this way." Marabou leads me round the side of the garage and up the sweep of driveway to the house. Close up, the property is practically derelict. There are weeds with thorny leaves and dandelion heads nudging up between the paving stones, setting them off kilter. The rolling lawns flanking the driveway are dry and yellowing, patrolled by a lone ibis, poking around for bugs in the grass. The tennis court far down near the bottom of the garden has holes in its fence and cracks in the concrete. The net sags over the center line like a beer *boep* on an aging athlete. The scent of yesterday-today-and-tomorrow hangs heavy in the air, the purple and white flowers in late bloom. Sloth mutters in the back of his throat. I know what he means. It feels abandoned.

I needle Marabou for the hell of it. Plus, I'm curious. "So

what does 'procurements' mean exactly? Corporate head-hunting? Rare antiquities? Hostage negotiation?"

"It can mean anything you want—a lot like your line of work, Ms. December." The Stork makes a guttural croaking, throat sac jiggling.

"Oh, come on. What were your last three jobs?"

"Discretion is one of our guarantees. As it is yours, I hope?"

"Money makes all things possible," I agree. "So, you're not even going to give me a hint?"

"We are like an exclusive concierge service. We do what the job requires. For Mr. Huron we have escorted musicians on tours and facilitated deals, most recently with a German distributor, where we accompanied the artist to Berlin."

"Sounds more like A&R than 'procurements.'"

"Before this, we smuggled a shipment of seventeenth-century crucifixes out of Spain in a container packed with ceramic tiles."

"Really?"

"Maybe. Maybe I am lying to get you excited. How would you check?"

She presses her finger to the doorbell. The door is a dark heavy wood with a stained glass rosary window. Inside the house, a chime trills and echoes. A moment later, the door swings open, revealing a woman in a cardinal red pantsuit and a blond bob. She seems delighted to see us, smiling like she's had a sunbeam shoved down her throat. "Oh, wow, hey. You're super early. Odi's just finishing up something."

"Carmen is one of Mr. Huron's protégées," Marabou says in answer to my raised eyebrow.

"Oh yaa, sorry," Carmen says, giving me a flash of white teeth. "Are you, like, media?"

"Not anymore."

She loses interest instantly, although her sunbeam wavers only briefly. "Well, come on in. If you want to head out to the patio, I'll bring you guys some tea."

She turns and clatters away on a pair of shiny red platform heels, leading us through a house that seems too fusty for such a bright and cool young thing to be breezing through. Faded Persian carpets laid over wooden floors mute the clop of Carmen's shoes. The furniture is overbearing, heavy teaks and yellowwood railway sleepers. Sloth hugs me tighter, and I catch a snatch of a rank mineral smell, like week-old vase water.

We pass a dining room where the yellowwood table has places set for twelve under a huge chandelier that resembles a wedding cake turned upside-down. Lethargic dust motes swirl in sunlight that has managed to penetrate the choke of ivy and leaded glass. Someone has left a scattering of choco-late raisins to fossilize under the table.

"Did Mr. Huron just move in?"

"Oh no, he's been here for ages and ages," Carmen says. "I know what you're thinking, though. Like, it's not very rock'n'roll."

"You know, that is exactly what I was thinking."

"I know, right? It weirded me out at first, when I came to

audition? But it's part of Odi's philosophy? 'Cos it's actually about the music."

"As opposed to?"

"The image. The glitz. The glamour. All that *interference*."

The passage is lined with framed plaques and awards, gold records, platinum records, SAMA and MTV and Kora certificates, with names familiar even to a music heathen like me. JumpFish. Detective Wolf. Assegai. Keleketla. Moro. Zakes Tsukudu. Lily Nobomvu. iJusi. Noxx. The dates read 1981, 1986, 1988, 1989, 1990, 1992, 1995, 1998. And then a jump to 2003, 2004, 2005. 2008. "What's with the hiatus?" "Mr. Huron has other business interests," Marabou says.

"And he was sick," Carmen chips in. "But don't worry, he's almost, like, totally over it now."

We pass a study, set up with a video edit suite, surrounded by bookshelves lined with files and weird bric-à-brac. And then the passage ends abruptly in an authentically retro lounge with glass doors opening onto a bright patio overlooking the swimming pool. There is a hanging egg chair and a heavy silver coffee table, only slightly scratched, hemmed in by low-rise chocolate brown leather couches. Two tall, slim speakers, designed to be fuck-off low-key, pump out syrupy R&B.

"Here we are," Carmen says, pushing open the glass doors onto the poolside patio. She stoops to brush leaves off the cushions on the fussy ironwork chairs arranged around a matching table under a vine trellis. The very pretty view looks over and up at the *koppie,* which is covered in scrub brush and succulent aloes. There is a low bunker-style building with glass sliding doors across the way at the foot of the hill. Definitely not original Herbert Baker.

"That's where the magic happens," she says, wafting a hand sales-model-style at the bunker. "The Moja studios. If you ask nicely, maybe Odi will give you the tour." She winks, adorably. "Be right back!" and clip-clops away into the cool dark of the house.

The pool is an enormous old-fashioned square, with mosaic tiles and a classical water feature of two maidens pouring out a jug of water. But the tiles are chipped, the lapis-lazuli blue faded to a dull glaucoma. The brackish water is a vile green, a skin of rotting leaves cloying the surface. Lichen has crept over the two maidens. Moss clogs the folds of their robes and the crooks of their elbows, blanking out their features like a beauty mask gone wild. Like someone ate their faces.

I shrug Sloth off onto the table. He sprawls on his belly and curls his long claws through the ironwork curlicues. The Marabou folds herself into one of the dainty chairs, leaning forward so as not to put any weight on the Stork strapped to her back.

"You ever take him off?"

"It's a she. And only when I sleep."

"What happened to her legs?"

"She had a run-in with another animal. She came off worse. It wasn't a dogfight, if that's what you're thinking."

"I wasn't. I'm surprised it doesn't happen more often.

Herbivores and carnivores all mixed up together. We should probably segregate."

"Mmm," she says, her attention drifting.

"What was the book?" I say, just making conversation. But the Stork raises its head sharply, looking down its beak at me.

"The book?" Marabou is offhand, in stark contrast to the Bird's reaction.

"One of your lost things." I concentrate on the strands, but this time the image is frustratingly blurry. I can't read the writing on the gun anymore or make out the detail on the gloves, and the book could just as well be a piece of old brick. I fudge from memory. "The cover is torn. The pages are moldy and swollen with damp. Something about a tree?"

"Is that how your talent works, you can see things?" She looks amused. "How practical. I don't know what the book was called. But one of the other girls used to read it to us in the container."

"Container?"

"They shipped us over. Packed like tuna fish." She strokes the Stork's throat and it rucks its head in appreciation. "Some of the tuna fish died. I started a different life."

"I could try to figure out what the book is. If you wanted. You could get another copy."

"What if it is not as good as I remember? Some things are better left lost."

"I hope you're not talking about my girl!" Mr. Huron, I presume, emerges onto the balcony with a flourish. He's not so much a barrel of a man as a bagpipe, all his weight loaded in front, straining a t-shirt that bears the legend *Depeche Mode Rose Bowl Pasadena 1987*. He's balding on top, but he's grown the rest of his hair and pulled it into a thin scraggly ponytail. The genuinely powerful, unlike the Vuyos of this world, don't give a fuck about making an impression.

"Sorry to keep you waiting. Amira. You're looking lovely. Botox working for you? Maybe you should try some on the bird. And you, you must be the new help," he says, engulfing my hand in his giant paws, like Mickey Mouse gloves. "Only kidding," he winks. "Mostly."

With a little moan, Sloth clambers off the table and into my lap. He's seeing what I'm seeing: a black tumor of lost things hanging above the big-shot producer's head, thrashing with severed stumps, like an amputated octopus.

It's one of the worst hack jobs I've seen. There are ways to cut the threads. A good *sangoma* can do it. But they'll eventually grow back thicker and coarser than ever. In the shadow of his black halo, his skin looks sallow, his jowls sunken, his eyes bright and flat.

"What's wrong with your animal?" Huron says, collapsing into one of the chairs and fingering a hole in his t-shirt.

"He's just shy around strangers," I say, stroking Sloth's head to calm him down.

"Amira and Mark brief you already?"

I have to force myself to look at his face rather than the writhing black stubs around his head. I concentrate on his fleshy lips, the large nose, slightly askew, as if he once broke it in a rugby game or a bar fight. "Actually, Mr. Huron, I'm still waiting to hear what this is about. Before I make up my mind as to whether I even want to be briefed."

"Call me Odi, please. Short for Odysseus."

"Sure. Odi."

We're interrupted by Carmen holding a red plastic tray that looks like it was molded out of the same material as her shoes. She sets down a clipboard and a pot of evil-smelling tea.

"Don't worry, it's non-alcoholic." Huron pours a cup and hands it to me with a smirk.

"You've done your research."

"Yes, I've heard all about your nasty habit. But it's not just you. Moja Records has a policy. No drink. No drugs. No neural spells."

"No *interference*." I take a sip gingerly. It tastes as foul and pungent as it smells.

"Buchu and mustard seed. Good for detoxing."

"Lovely." I smile and heap in five spoons of sugar. It makes the brew only marginally more tolerable. What does it take to get a decent cup of tea? "I'm not sure I can even help you, Mr. Huron."

"Call me Odi. Really." He puts an envelope on the table. "Open it."

I do. Sloth cranes his head to see. It contains a cluster of crisp blue R100 notes. I put it back on the table.

"What's this?"

"Two large, just to hear me out. If you like what I have to say, you take the job and consider this an advance. If you don't, you take the money, you don't repeat any of what I told you, we're all friends."

"This all seems very serious. Are you sure you have the right girl here?"

"Mark and Amira think so."

"Just in case I'm getting the wrong end of the microphone here—you do know I can't sing?"

"Like that ever got in the way of a pretty girl getting a record deal. Autotune is a beautiful thing." He laughs, but his eyes are cold. "Let me assure you, you are here for your other skills." He watches me closely. I take the envelope and slip it into my bag, ignoring Sloth scratching at my arm, the halo of black stumps waving around Huron's head.

"All right, good. Now, you're no doubt familiar with iJusi." He waves his hand impatiently at my blank look. "The twins? Song and S'bu?"

The name sounds vaguely familiar, another life glimpsed on the TV at Mak's, maybe on the cover of an old *Heat* magazine at the *spaza* shop. A boy and a girl. Twins. Beautiful. Wholesome.

Huron sighs, exasperated. "Well, you can do some research."

"Has something happened to them?"

"Officially, no. Absolutely not. Everything's just fine. They're keeping a low profile because they're in studio, writing new songs. The new album drops in three weeks. We've got a big party planned."

"And off the record?"

"Songweza is missing."

"Run away? Kidnapped?"

"Either is possible. She hasn't been home for four days, according to her house mother."

"Is that unusual?"

"You see the thing about iJusi, although you wouldn't know this, is that they're a little ray of sunshine in an ugly, ugly world." He pinches the corner of his lower lip and rolls it between his thick fingers. "They're good kids. Role models."

"And you want to keep it that way. No nasty real-world taint for Papa Odi's little girl."

"Amira said you had an ugly mouth." The stumps lash and twist.

"I prefer to think of it as a fast mouth. So, there's no boyfriend? Girlfriend, maybe?" I push.

"Plenty of time for that later."

"Because she's a good girl."

"You see. We understand each other."

"I don't understand why you're talking to me, rather than the cops or a private investigator. Four days is a long time. She could be dead."

"Now, Zinzi, that's not very discreet. Police. PIs. If the tabloids get a sniff . . ."

"I get it. You're making a mistake, but I'll take your money. How much are we talking?"

"If you bring her back before the official launch and *intact?*" He smiles thinly. I know what that means. Sweet. Innocent.

Un-animalled. "R50,000." Sloth takes a sharp breath at the amount. All very serious indeed.

"Make it two hundred, I'm your girl."

"Eighty-five."

"One fifty. Plus expenses. Don't worry, Mr. Huron, I'll submit receipts."

The Marabou looks pained. Huron gives me a slow, evaluating look. The tentacles pause, like they're holding their breath.

"Odi, please." And we share a conspiratorial grin. Or maybe we're just baring our teeth at each other, like chimps competing for dominance.

"Odi? There's a phone call for you," Carmen pops her head out the door, plaintive, like she thinks we've taken up too much of his time already. She is cradling a black Rabbit, stroking its ears. It does explain the fossilized chocolate raisins in the dining room. Who knew that Odi Huron's eccentricities included cultivating a personal menagerie of zoos? I can't help wondering what she did to get her Bunny.

"Ah, thank you, Carmencita," Odi says. "I think we're done here. Amira and Mark will brief you and make all the necessary arrangements. Whatever you need."

He stands up, all business, downs his drink and throws out the ice towards the pool. The blocks go skittering over the cracked tiles and plop into the water, sending greasy ripples across the surface to stir the leaves. By the time I look up, Odi is disappearing into the house. And I didn't even get the studio tour.

Sloth is pissed with me. I can tell by the way he clambers onto my back, stiff and cross. "You have a better idea?" I hiss at him.

"What was that?" the Marabou asks mildly, staring at the pool, at the lichen-blinded maidens and the ripples breaking at their bare feet.

"I was wondering if this is the best idea," I say. "There must be more qualified people."

"More qualified, but maybe less discreet. And harder to vanish if everything goes wrong."

"You know, I'm pretty sure no one mentioned any vanishing."

"You do this thing, you disappear. No questions asked. Back to Zoo City and your own small world."

"I see." But I'm thinking about her lost gun.

"Shall we? You should probably be getting started."

The Maltese is waiting in the car upfront. It's been polished and waxed to within an inch of its warranty. The interior is awash with pine air-freshener and just a hint of ammonia. The combination makes Sloth sneeze. Which means I was wrong about the guy. I was convinced "spit and polish" was a euphemism for sex. But I have no doubt that dear Odi is nailing sweet little Carmen sideways and backwards. Maybe even now.

The Maltese—Mark—seems eager to get going. The car is idling, he's already strapped in and the Dog is standing on his lap, its paws on the steering wheel. It yaps once, impatiently, like this is a Formula 1 pit stop and we're holding up the race.

"How was that, sweetie? Was he everything we said?" Mark says, putting the car into gear as I close my door.

"And more!" I say, in chipper imitation of Carmencita. "I'm on the case *and* I've been put in my place."

"Don't take it personally, sweetie."

As the car pulls away down the drive, Huron appears in the doorway. I turn to look back over the headrest, past Amira and her creepy Bird. He's rocking back on his heels, his hands embedded in the pockets of his jeans, just the picture of laidback cool. It's a junkie look. That desperately pretending that everything is hunky-dory, you're not stressed at all about anything in the world, when inside your jeans pockets, your hands are clamped into sweaty fists, fingernails leaving grooves in your palms. If Huron's grooves were an LP, they would be playing the Johnny Cash cover of Nine Inch Nails' "Hurt." And the tentacles would be waving along in time.

10.

CALEB CARTER
HM Barwon Prison
Australia

"I didn't have the Tapir when I got here. She came on the second night, after I was jumped by a couple of the 4161s from Melbourne. Lucky my mate Len was already inside, and knew their game. He gave me a shank when I arrived, and it ended up in the neck of this one guy, a tattooed fuckwit called Deke.

"That night, at about the same time Deke was dying in a hospital in Geelong, the Tapir appeared outside my cell. I heard her scratching at the door of solitary confinement. Scared the hell out of me. The guards said she was still covered in jungle mud when they found her.

"I mean, there's cameras everywhere. And this thing's from a different continent. How come no one saw her arrive? How did she get here? If she can walk through walls or fly or something, why can't she carry me out of here?

"Anyway, I love her. They let me look after her good, take

her on walks around the yard. She's a stupid-looking creature and she's dopey as shit, but when the guys here see her at my side, they remember what happened to Deke. They remember not to fuck with Carter."

ZIA KHADIM
Karachi Central Jail
Pakistan

"They keep our animals in cages in another part of the prison. We don't see them. When they want to torture us, they put them in the back of a car and drive away to Keti Bandar. The pain is unbearable, you scream, you vomit, and you say anything.

"My Cobra was with me when I was arrested. I was nine. The police saw me walking on the street with my Cobra round my neck, and they grabbed me. They said I robbed a house. I didn't do it, but they beat me until I said I did.

"When they brought me here, they threw my Cobra into one room with all the other animals. The animals would bite each other and get infected and die. The Undertow would come every night for the prisoners. Too many people died. Now they keep the animals in cages, but they still don't let us see them, not unless we give a big bribe, a month's salary for a guard. I don't have that money.

"I haven't seen my Cobra since I was arrested. I'm now fourteen years old."

TYRONE JONES
Corcoran
USA

"It's crazy in here. I know you can't tear a man from his animal. Ain't right. But some of these niggas got real wild animals, man. One guy's got a Cougar. You can't tell me that's right, letting a prisoner walk around with a Cougar.

"There's an order to things, too. Don't matter what you did, you got a badass animal in here, you're a badass too. And it don't matter how many people you killed, you got a Chipmunk or a Squirrel, you're gonna be a bitch. Way it is.

"Then there's me. I got a Butterfly. Keep it in a matchbox. I oughta be pissed off, man. You can guess what it's like being in here with a Butterfly. Except for the stuff it lets me do.

"See, when I go to sleep every night, I wake up as someone else. For the time I'm asleep, I live the day of someone else on the other side of the world. Man, I've been kids in Africa and India, I was once this old Chinese woman. Mostly I'm poor, but sometimes I get lucky and I'm rich.

"What I'm saying is, I can't hate the Butterfly. Butterfly breaks me out of here every night."

Excerpt from *Caged: Animalled Behind Bars*
Photography and interviews by Steve Deacon
HarperCollins 2008

11.

TRAFFIC IN JOBURG is like the democratic process. Every time you think it's going to get moving and take you somewhere, you hit another jam. There used to be shortcuts you could take through the suburbs, but they've closed them off, illegally: gated communities fortified like privatized citadels. Not so much keeping the world out as keeping the festering middle-class paranoia in.

"I'm going to need my own ride."

"What's wrong, sweetie? You don't like my driving?" the Maltese says, but the jibe is half-hearted. He's been off-kilter since we left Huron's. Even the Mutt is subdued, although we're still hitting the green lights at speeds better left to rocket ships.

"Not particularly. But mainly it's that whole little dog thing."

"You just don't let up, do you?" Mark whines. For the first time, it seems like I've got under his flea collar.

"I need to do this alone. It's how my *shavi* works. I need to talk to people, to pick up a sense of her." This is all monkey crap, but it's not like they know any better. I'm hoping to stumble on a lost thing that will lead me right to the girl, but I can't count on it.

"I thought you could just see things?" Marabou says.

"Sure. If the person is in the room. But then you wouldn't need me. So this is how we're going to work. You can introduce me to people, but then you have to piss off. You can't expect someone to open up to a crowd. One's an interview, three's an interrogation."

"Ve hav our vays und means," Marabou says from the back-seat — evidence that she may have a sense of humor after all.

"I don't need anything fancy."

"No. We wouldn't want you to be hijacked," Marabou says.

"That would be bad," I agree, but the words come out on autopilot, because I'm ambushed by the memory of the bullet that tore away half my ear before it ripped through my brother's skull.

"A Kia, then," Maltese says, oblivious to my mental picture of Thando sprawled in the daisy bushes, my mom screaming, running down the driveway in her favorite dressing gown with the Japanese print. Afterwards, she had the daisy bush ripped out, the grass concreted over.

"What?" I say, dragging myself back.

"Or something secondhand. A *skedonk* on its last tires. A car that fits your lifestyle. The kind of thing you'd expect a disgraced zoo girl to drive."

"Gee, thanks. How about if it doesn't drive at all? We could get me a gutted shell on bricks. That would suit *my life-style.*"

It takes us an hour and a half to get to Midrand and the golf

estate where S'busiso and Songweza Radebe share a townhouse next door to their legal guardian, Mrs. Prim Luthuli,
all generously sponsored by their record label. Another ten
minutes to get past the gate guard, who grills us and insists
that we all step out of the car to be photographed by the web-
cam mounted on the window of his security booth.

"Animalists everywhere," Mark says through clenched
teeth, as the guard raises the boom and waves us through.
"They'd bring back the quarantine camps if they could."

"What do you call Zoo City?" I say.

"Just be glad we don't live in India," Amira says.

Mark revs the Merc unnecessarily. "Because who knew
there was a caste *below* untouchable?"

The townhouses are variations on a theme of relentlessly
modern, with trim front lawns and rear-facing views onto
the golf course.

"I always get lost here," the Maltese says. The numbering
system is completely insane and the estate is huge, so it takes
us a few minutes to find H4-301. From the outside, it looks
identical to all the other cookie-cutter townhouses with their
perfect green lawns and chorus line of hissing sprinklers.

"Aren't there water restrictions?" I ask.

"Borehole. There are underground water reservoirs all
over this area. Costs a fortune to tap, of course, but if you
run a golf course . . ." he shrugs.

It would appear no one is home at H4-301, domicile of
one Mrs. Primrose Luthuli.

"Maybe we should have phoned ahead."

"We can talk to the boys in the meantime."

"Do they know?"

"No. And Mr. Huron would prefer if we keep it that way." Marabou walks up to the door of H4-303, ignoring the intercom phone with embedded camera, and raps directly on the door. She waits. Then raps again. And then pounds. There's no way to tell if it's penetrated through the hip-hop bass emanating from inside.

Heavy footsteps shuffle towards the door, suggesting a senile hippopotamus in fuzzy slippers. A moment later, the door opens to reveal a very fat, very white kid wearing a very loud hoodie patterned with neon pink robot monkeys. He is scuffing at his nose with the back of his hand, his eyes are red and the reek of dope has soaked right through the hoodie into his pores. He's muttering as he opens the door, "Listen, you people need to chillax, man, the residents' association can get a restraining order — Christballs!" His bloodshot eyes open very wide as he registers the Marabou. He falls backwards into the house, barely recovering his balance before scrambling away in his dirty socks, yelping, "Dude, it's happening! They're fucking here, man! Break out the hardware! Shit!"

Marabou strides into the townhouse, right behind him. I'm about to follow, but Mark puts his arm across the doorframe, like a security boom and gives a little shake of his head. From inside, there is the noise of gunfire, strangely hollow, and then a lot of shouting.

"Get the guns! Get the freaking guns!" fat boy squeals.

Another voice, pissed off, bemused (pissmused?). "Hey! You guys aren't supposed to be here—"

And a third, weary, "Dude, there are no guns—"

Fat boy screams. "No, no, no, don't you even fucking, don't you come near—"

Then there is a dull crunch, followed by whimpering.

Mark lifts his arm, wafts his hand ostentatiously to usher me inside. I enter the house, cautiously. It's done up in a mash of just-moved-out-of-home boy décor. They've made a bit of an effort. The classic movie posters: *The Godfather, Swamp Thing, Kill Bill,* all framed. The katana above the giant flatscreen TV is wall-mounted, the trophy cans of beer stacked on top of the bookshelf are perfectly lined up so that the labels all face outward.

There are two boys sitting on the plush red couch. One is bare-chested in jeans, the fly unbuttoned. He has natty little dreads and a small gold loop in his ear, and he's pouting like he ordered strippers for his birthday and got clowns instead.

The other I recognize from glimpses of a music video. The boy-half of iJusi has big heartbreaker eyes, an upturned button nose, and dimples. He'll grow out of it, maybe even in the next six months, but S'bu still has something beautifully childlike about him, and even his poser attitude can't undermine the sweetness that rises off him like fumes. He's practically edible.

They're both holding PlayStation controllers, the source of the gunfire, I now realize, and they're both staring at Marabou and the fat kid, who is holding his bloody nose with both hands. The Stork cranes its neck forward to nudge her hand with its beak. She looks at the blood on her knuckles with forensic distaste, and wipes it off on the side of the couch. Dazed, the fat kid collapses into the La-Z-Boy.

Mark sets the Mutt down, picks up one of seven remotes on the coffee-table—by coincidence, it just so happens to be the right one—and kills the stereo.

Half-naked boy opens his mouth to complain, "Hey, that's—"

The Dog gives a shrieky little snarl and Mark says, "Shut up, Des. No one's talking to you." He perches on the edge of the low black teak coffee table, pushing aside a gimmicky odor-free silver ashtray shaped like a flying saucer, and folds his legs. "Well, boys, this is quite the scene."

S'bu stands up and walks over to the ashtray. "I know, I know," he says, in the patented world-weary way of teenagers. He pushes down on the top of the UFO, which whirrs open with a buzz and strobing lights, and stubs out his joint.

"She bwoke by dose—" the fat white boy starts.

"Shut up, Arno. It's your own stupid fault," snaps the half-naked kid with the dreads.

"You know you're not supposed to be smoking, S'bu," Mark chides.

"Didn't I already say, I know, I know?"

"Can these two take a hike?"

He shrugs. "Arno and Des are my boys."

"We need to talk about your sister."

"Whad's up wid your sisduh, dude? You didn'd say budding about your sisduh. Whad's up wid da Song?"

"Shut *up,* Arno," Des and S'bu say in unison.

"'Cos she hasn'd been awound. Shid. When lasd did we see her?"

"Dude. When last did you see your arse?"

Arno looks hurt, although it's hard to tell if his hangdog expression is par for the course, or just a result of his eyes starting to swell.

"Is that the only contraband?" Amira says.

"Des is holding," S'bu indicates his friend. Des cringes, pulls out a *bankie* of weed, and gingerly hands it over to Amira.

"What's wrong, sweetie?" Mark asks.

"Nah, it's just, we thought you were—" Des says. "The cops."

"Zombies," Arno says at the same time.

"Why would you be worried about the cops?"

"I dunno. Just. 'Cos." He waves a hand vaguely in the direction of the ashtray. There's a couple of video game boxes lying next to it, starring flesh-eating undead and aliens. One, *Grand Theft Auto VI: Zootopia,* features a badass in a hoodie, packing a shotgun with a snarling Panther by his side.

"You know this means we're going to have to search the house. Again."

"Whatever," S'bu says, and slumps back into the couch, picking up the controller and going right back to his game, a first-person slayer. He's playing a miniskirted girl with spiky

green hair and a machine gun for an arm facing down sham-
bling hordes of particularly monstrous aliens.

"Do you want to go back to rehab, S'bu?"

"Doesn't bother me." But I notice he flinches, enough to
throw off his shot. On screen, an alien manages to gore his
arm, knocking his health down to 89 percent.

"This is Zinzi December. She wants to talk to you. Help
her out," Mark says.

"It's for a story for a magazine. *Credo?*" I bluff.

"Oh yeah?" S'bu isn't even vaguely interested, but Des
perks up dramatically.

"*Credo* cooks, bro," he says, nudging S'bu's arm. "You're in
Credo, you're in. Hells yes, lady. My boy is down."

"Great," I say.

"Whatever, you clear it with these guys," S'bu says, still intent on his game.

"Oh, we're 'down,'" Mark says. He whistles for the Mutt.
The Dog jumps off the red pouf and immediately starts sniffing around the room with great seriousness, tail wagging.
S'bu lifts his feet for the Dog as it snuffles around the bottom
of the couch.

"Just seeds, man," says Des.

The Dog follows its nose out of the room, Mark and Amira
behind it. We can hear them climbing the stairs. A minute
later, there is the sound of objects being thrown around.

"Shid, dude, whad if she breags by shid?" Arno says.

"Then I'll buy you more shit. Will you shut up? You're
wrecking my concentration."

Everyone is quiet for a moment. Des and Arno watch me watching S'bu kill aliens. Upstairs, there is more thudding. Impulsively, I shrug Sloth off onto the recently vacated pouf, squeeze in next to S'bu, and pick up Des's discarded controller.

"This is two player, right?"

"Yeah, but—"

"Killing aliens with S'bu Radebe. That's profile gold. *Credo* will love it."

"They're Cthul'mites, actually."

"Whatever. They all bleed the same." From the player screen, I select the huge black guy character with Mike Tyson tattoos on his face and whipblades mounted in his forearms. Nice to see game designers keeping up the stereotypes.

"You any good?" S'bu gives me a sideways glance.

"Fucking terrible. It's all you."

"Oh great." But he cracks the slightest of smiles.

"Anybone wand a beer?" Arno says, heading for the kitchen.

"Get them now before they're all confiscated," S'bu calls out after him.

"I'll have one," I shout, gutting a particularly loathsome specimen with slobbery jaws and elongated fingers with my whipblades. I'm already down to 46 percent health. It's only when Arno comes back, cracking the bottles of Windhoek open with his teeth, and sets mine, foaming, on the table in front of me, that I realize what I've done.

"Oh thanks, but actually, I'm gonna skip." I barely manage

to duck as an arachnidy thing with a wobbly glutinous mass on top, like the bastard love child of a jellyfish and a spider, spews a cloud of mechanical insects at me. Luckily S'bu is there to liquidize it, and most of the insect cloud terminates in shrieking sparks.

"Our beer too good for ya?"

"No, it's just that I don't particularly want to go back to rehab either."

"No shit, man," Des says. "That place is ill. All full of whining junkies with the shivers."

"Abnd zombies," Arno adds, hopefully.

"Don't you guys have some place to be?" S'bu snaps.

"No, man. We're here for the duration."

"Seriously, I think I heard your moms calling."

"Dude. Uncool."

"*Madoda.* Take a hint and *hamba.*"

"Fine. Come on, Arno, let's go aim for *hadedas* on the fourteenth hole."

"Bud I like *hadedas.*"

"*Gijima,* fatty boomsticks. Can't you see I'm in the middle of an interview?"

Des grabs the set of clubs leaning against the wall by the fridge, and heads out, not bothering to pull on a shirt. He gives S'bu the finger as he goes. Arno follows, dragging his feet, but taking his beer with him.

"You guys don't strike me as the golfing type," I say, stomping frantically on the remaining clockwork insects. Unfortunately, not before one bites me. A red haze over my POV indicates that I've been infected. Antibiotics required. "Where's a medpack when you need one?"

"Yeah, it's all right. I prefer playing on console. Being Tiger Woods and shit? The medpacks are red plastic drop-boxes, white cross."

My health is dwindling, one point at a time. I'm down to 22 percent. "So which rehab did you go to?"

"Listen, just 'cos we're both in recovery doesn't make us best friends or nothing."

"I did mine in prison. Involuntary."

"That where you get the Sloth?"

"Well, just before. But yeah, close enough. He helped me get through it."

"There!"

"What?"

"Medpack."

"Got it." I steer awesomely muscular black guy over to the first-aid box handily wall-mounted next to a fire alarm. Nearly missed it, thanks to the red throb of my infection. "What about your sister?"

"What *about* my sister?"

"I mean, was she there for you?"

"There for me?" He gives me a skew look, but still manages to frag the tentacle-faced frog creature that pads down the wall. "No. Song's there for herself."

"So you were just smoking weed? Little hectic to go to re-hab for that."

"Ha. Tell that to Mr. Odi."

"Uh-huh." From his earlier reaction, I thought maybe he'd been to Donkerpoort, or one of the other fundamentalist hellholes that rely on the scare-'em-clean-with-beatings-and-a-Bible model of addiction therapy. It's straight cold turkey. Kids chained up outside, naked and shivering out the sweats. Methadone is for weaklings. And if you're really bad, they'll bring out the dogs.

"Wasn't so bad, I guess. It's the detox therapy the old man's into that kills me. Lentils and colonic cleansing and shit," S'bu says. "Boss!" A grotesque spindly torso lumbers towards us. I lash out with my whipblade, slashing right through its chest and into its ribcage. The split halves reel obscenely, trying to reconnect. Then the cracked ends of the ribcage start lengthening, until the split chest becomes a mouth full of gnashing teeth.

"Gross. How did Songweza find it?"

"How does the Song find anything?"

"You tell me."

"She was cool with it. You know what they say? I'm only here because of her. That she's the talented one."

"I don't buy that—crap! Sorry."

I've died, impaled on the spiny teeth, my corpse spewing great fountains of blood as the boss lurches around, trying to find S'bu's punky schoolgirl.

"Don't worry, I'll reload." S'bu pulls up the menu and instantly skips tracks on history back to a moment when we were both alive and well.

"Wish they had a 'restore saved game' for the real world."

"Tell me about it," he snorts.

"What point do you wish you could go back to?"

"You first."

"The moment before I got my brother killed."

"Heavy," says S'bu, but I can tell he's impressed. And this is what I've come to, breaking out my worst personal tragedy to pry open a teenager. If I hadn't already hit my ultimate low, this would be a close contender.

"And you?"

"Before we signed."

"That's the worst thing that's happened to you? *Seriaas?*"

"I dunno, maybe we should have signed with someone else."

"Odi's a pretty intense guy."

"Yeah."

"Rehab must have been *really* shitty."

"Yeah." He squirms. "It's more like his philosophy? It's worse than straight-edge. Like, there's no fun at all."

"You seem to be doing okay."

"Yeah, right," he rolls his eyes up at the thumping noises coming from above. "That guy needs to take a chill pill, you know? Maybe literally."

"You think you would have got where you are without Odi pushing you?"

"Nah, man, I appreciate that, it's the keep-it-clean crap. I'm fifteen, yo. We're not little kids anymore. And I'm not even that bad. Songweza's the one who lands us in the shit the whole time."

"Where do you think your sister is?"

"I dunno. *Jolling* with her friends?"

"Any friends in particular?"

"Hey, what's this interview about, anyway?"

"The band."

"'Cos it sounds like it's about her."

"Can I level with you?" I say, jumping into the abyss.

"Sure."

"I've been hired to try and find your sister. The interview is just a cover."

"Fuck!" He flings his controller across the room. It narrowly misses the TV and smashes into the wall beneath the katana. The back pops off, spraying batteries across the floor.

"I'm just being honest with you."

"Oh, *now* you're being honest with me? So all that other bullshit was just, just . . . *shit?*" He looks like he's about to cry.

"No, I've really been to rehab. I really killed my brother," I say calmly.

"Whatever. Hey, lady, ever occurred to you maybe Song doesn't *want* to be found?"

"Or you don't want her to be found?"

"You are one whacked crazybitch. What, like I . . . I killed her or something?"

"Did you? No. I don't think that. But if she ran away with her boyfriend or whatever, it sounds like you wouldn't mind so much if she didn't hurry back."

S'bu shakes his head. "Lady, we have an album about to drop." He grabs a jacket slung over the back of the chair and heads towards the door, wiping at his eyes. "Where are you going?"

"Same place as Song. *Out*."

Sloth swats my arm in reproach. Like I meant to make the kid cry.

He storms out of the house, past Mark and Amira, who are sitting on the stairs, clearly listening in.

"And screw you guys too."

He slams the door.

"Didn't go so well, then, sweetie?" Mark says. His Dog pants happily, mocking.

"I've had worse interviews." This is true. The time I rocked up high to interview Morgan Freeman, for example. "You still trashing the place, or can I take a look?"

"Knock yourself out."

"Interesting ploy, the journalist," Marabou says, stroking her Bird's shriveled head.

"You'd be amazed at how people open up when they think someone cares. Listen, don't wait up. After this, I'm thinking of taking in a round of golf. I'll expense a cab home."

Maltese sneers. "One day on the job, and she's too good for us."

I watch them out the door and then set to snooping. I skip the kitchen, which, surprisingly for a house full of teen boys, doesn't require Health Department intervention, and head upstairs, stepping over an amp at the top. There are more instruments lining the passage. A bass guitar, a tangle of microphone cable. Deck the halls. It's not clear whether they're normally out here, or part of Mark and Amira's redecorating scheme.

The first room is hotel-anonymous. A monotone motif with a black-and-white print of Namaqualand daisies above the bed. Guest room. I move on to the next: two single beds pushed to opposite corners. Clothes are strewn around the room, cushions have been thrown on the floor, the mattresses upturned, the camo-print beanbag leans on its side. There are posters of Megan Fox and Khanyi Mbau taped up, spreads from fashion magazines, all featuring menswear, and a business plan mapped out on a whiteboard underneath a sketch of an old-fashioned Nintendo video game controller and the words "War Room."

Fashion label launch Jozi fashion week, last week in August (realistic???)

> *Logo meet with Adam the Robot*
> *Put out brief on t-shirt designs on 10and5.*
> *Gorata Mugudamani to sort publicity?*
> *Distrib!!!! Cross-pollinate w music stores?*
> *Int?*
> *Choose ringtone tracks. Re-mix?*
> *SOLO?!?!? Heather Yalo*
> *Can we do a fragrance? Market research.*

I take notes. Move on.

Bathroom #1. A scramble of boy stuff. Five different flavors of deodorant, slick electric razors, electric toothbrushes, shaving cream, moisturizing balm, exfoliator, anti-wrinkle eye cream—all for fifteen-year-olds. A shower with a curtain featuring mildew and Hawaiian flowers. Sodden towels puddled on the Italian tiles. But otherwise remarkably clean. No skid marks in the toilet. Nothing living in the bath. Well stocked on toilet paper.

Bathroom #2. Dramatically smaller. The first hint of Song. A bottle of perfume on the counter. A punky black bottle with the name *Lithium* etched in white, like chalk scratchings. Blue nail polish. Eyeliner. More eyeliner. Four different kinds of mascara: coal, black, ultra-black, and green. Eyeshadow in jewel colors. Gothpunk Princess Barbie. I spritz the perfume into the air. It smells like petrol and dead flowers. Sloth sniffs the air appreciatively. Clearly there are tones in there that human noses just can't appreciate. There is a glass jar of dried green leaves. I crush some between my fingers. It's fragrant. Not dope. Possibly *muti*. But for what? If only traditional healers would label shit. I wrap some up in a tissue and fold it into my pocket.

More helpfully, there is also an unopened pill container marked "Songweza Radebe" and "Flurazepam," "dosage: 1 per day with food." I look it up on my phone. It's a generic, used for anxiety or insomnia, especially for those with manic depression. The date on the label is Friday 18 March. So one day before she runs away, she gets a prescription for heavy-duty anxiety pills. Makes it seem like the script wasn't her idea. Interesting.

Next door is a full-on bedroom studio with egg-boxes studding the walls, mixing decks, a computer facing the tiniest voice booth you ever saw, but at least semi-pro, if I'm any judge of expensive. And I am.

Adjoining the studio is the final bedroom. This has been creatively adapted. It's barely a meter across because a slap-dash drywall has been erected in the middle of the room, forming the back of the recording booth next door. A double bed takes up most of the remaining space, under a block-mounted poster of Barbarella gazing into the depths of space, managing to look yearning and bold all at once. The cupboard has been thrown open, and clothes dumped recklessly on the bed among a spread of comics. There are more comics crammed into every available space on a long, low bookshelf that runs the length of the window. I skim through a few. Swamp monsters and teleporting houses, a muscled guy wearing the Union Jack.

A collection of movie monsters are posed all along the top of the bookshelf. On instinct, I pick up the one that looks like an upside-down dustbin with rows of studs down the side. As I do, it says "Exterminate!" and I nearly drop it. The head comes right off. There's a *bankie* of dope inside. And it's quality, if I'm any judge of substances. And I am.

I put the little robot's head back on, leaving the dope where it is, and replace him carefully between Arnold Sch-warzenegger, metal chassis gleaming from under ripped plastic skin, and a manga girl with a mane of bright pink hair and boobs popping out of the leopard-print bikini that matches her tail and ears. But I do take one of the A5 soft-cover notebooks ferreted away between the comics. It says *lyrics* on the cover. And © *S'bu Radebe*. I roll it up and slip it into my bag.

As we're heading back towards the stairs, Sloth chirrups. "My thoughts exactly," I say, stepping back into the anonymous hotel room, which is not in fact a guest room. I open the cupboard and face an array of pretty preppy clothing. White sundresses and Afro-chic numbers by Sun Goddess and Darkie and Stoned Cherrie. Perfect for a hip teen *kwaito* queen. But not for a Gothpunk Princess Barbie. There are empty hangers, like a gaptoothed smile. Wherever Song went, whoever she went with, she had time to pack.

I ransack the room for lost things, digging under the mattress, in the back of the cupboard. There are only dust bunnies and some spare change, a hair band. Nothing lost. Nothing to lead me back to Song. Which means I'm stuck with the investigative journalist angle.

"Uh-oh. Fweag aled," Arno says nasally as I approach. He's looking considerably less stoned, likely courtesy of the pain in his nose, although his eyes are still bloodshot.

"Just ignore her. Maybe she'll get the hint." Des lines up the tee, once, twice, and then swings hard, neatly chipping out a clod of earth to join the other clods of earth gathered around his trainers, which are *not* regulation golf shoes. But then, neither are mine. I've left distinctive tracks across three holes: the common kitten-heeled hustler.

"You play golf now as well as *Blood Skies*?" Des says, mockingly.

"No. I hate golf. It's the genteel version of seal-clubbing, only not as much fun."

"What do you want?"

"Background stuff. Color."

"Is bad a whide joke?" Arno bristles.

"As in painting a picture of iJusi's life. The people they hang out with, what goes down."

"You're bod gonna wide about de guns ding, are you?" Arno looks worried.

I laugh. "What *was* that?"

"It was the dope. He gets *lank* paranoid. *Doos.*" Des smacks Arno upside his head.

"Don't worry, I'll make that incident 'off the record.'" I take out my notebook and pen, and look at them expectantly. "So tell me about you guys. How do you know S'bu?"

They look at each other uneasily.

"If this isn't a bad time for you. Wouldn't want to interrupt your..."—I look down at the pitted grass—"gardening." They have the grace to look sheepish. "C'mon, I'll buy you a drink at the clubhouse."

Turns out Des and Arno already have a well-established reputation at the clubhouse. "Oh no," the waiter says, wearing a bow tie and gloves, like this is Inanda instead of Mayfields. "No shirt, no service. And no animals."

"Hi there," I say, sticking out my hand. "Zinzi December, journalist for *The Economist*. You've heard of *The Economist*, I trust? I'm interviewing these young men for a piece on the South African music industry, and I'd really appreciate it if you could accommodate us. I'd hate to have to include something in my piece on the appalling service at Mayfields."

"Do you have a business card?"

"Not on me." I give him my best fake-tolerant smile. He considers this, then breaks out his best fake-obsequious smile in return. "Right this way, madam. But please inform the young gentlemen that we won't be serving them alcoholic beverages. We confiscated their fake IDs the last time they visited with us."

We sit outside overlooking the gentle rolling greenery of the course. A shrike eyes our table, checking out the scraps. Also known as the butcherbird, it has a habit of impaling its prey on barbed-wire fences. People tend to think animals are better than humans. But birds have their own serial killers. Chimpanzees commit murder. The only difference between us is that animals don't feel guilty about it.

"How many of these people actually play golf?" I say, waving my glass of Appletizer at the townhouses.

"Dwo?" Arno guesses.

"Three max. It's like gym," Des says. "Everyone signs up and goes for like a month and then never goes again."

"So, who are you guys? Tell me about you."

"Um. Anoo Wedelinghaze. Dad's Har-he-duh-he-," he spells out, leaning over my notebook. Listening to him speak makes my eyes water.

"Redelinghuys. Got it." I wink. "How old are you? Arno?"

"Fifdeen."

"And you, Des?"

"Twenty-two. And it's Desmond Luthuli."

"You go to school with S'bu?"

"I do!" Arno chirps. "Bud Des moved hewe wid him. He's da woombade. I jusd hang oud and sleeb over sombedibes."

"Moved out from where?"

"Valley of a Dousand Hills? In Kwa-Zulu Naddal? Dey, like, gwew up dogeduh, besd buds."

"I can speak for myself, Arno." There's something hungry about Des. I get the feeling reflected glory isn't enough for him.

"Sorreeee, dude. Shid."

"Yeah, so S'bu and Arno are only, like, friends from two years ago. They both go to Crawford," Des says. "But me and S'bu, we grew up together. Tiny little village called KwaXimba in the Valley of a Thousand Hills. So *ja,* when iJusi signed and S'bu and Song moved out here—"

"How'd they get signed?" I interrupt.

"You don't know?"

"I just want to get your take on it. In your own words." Actually, Maltese and Marabou filled me in on the way. There was a big hoo-ha after they aced the Coca-Cola Starmakerz auditions when they were still a tender fourteen; the youngest contestants ever to qualify, and from a desperately poor background that almost immediately made them the great bright nation-building hopes of the contest. But they had to drop out just before the semifinals, after their grandmother died of lupus, barely two years after they lost both parents to AIDS-related complications.

They were adorable. They were tragic. They were at least half-talented. And the song they chose to sing was a wrenching cover of Brenda Fassie's "Too Late for Mama." How could the General Public resist? There was a massive rallying around them. Radio 702 started a fundraising drive to pay for granny's funeral costs and establish a trust for the new orphans. Coca-Cola put them up in a hotel for the duration of the competition, arranged minders to look after them, and gave them as much free Coke as they could drink. And hopefully paid for their dental work afterwards.

Sponsors leaped to look after them. They got free clothes, free medical aid, and free tickets to rugby games, where they got to sing for the Springboks and the President. And they got signed before the semi-finals even went to air, and dropped out of the competition on the advice of their new label, Moja Records.

Des sums this up succinctly: "Like, they were in Starmakerz and then they got signed and Odi paid for them to move."

"Acdually, de creeby bird lady and be dog guy came do dalk to dem eben befowe."

"Before Starmakerz?"

"Dey said dey were dalend scouds."

"Yeah, but I told them they shouldn't just take the first offer they got, even if it was from Mr. Odi Big-shot Huron," Des interrupts. "I got them to audition for Starmakerz instead. Worked out. They got more exposure and we landed with Odi anyway."

"And they just did what you said?"

"Yeah, I'm kinda like S'bu's manager."

"You're twenty-two."

"So?"

"His mbom is deir legal guawdian," Arno pipes up.

"Yeah, that too. When they came to Joburg, we moved up with them."

"Mrs. Luthuli. Right. So, where is your mom? Is she okay with you guys smoking weed and drinking beer?"

"Yeah, she's really chill. We earned it, man."

"You mbean S'bu earned id," Arno interrupts.

"And where's Songweza in all this? I couldn't help noticing that the house felt very . . . *masculine*."

"Song's a sduck-up bidch," says Arno, with all the venom of someone who has tended a secret crush in the basement of his heart, only to be met with a sweetly patronizing pat on the cheek the moment he brought it out into the sunlight of her attention. The seedling might have been burned, but that doesn't mean it's dead.

"Shut *up*, Arno. Song has got her own thing going on. She's only there a couple of nights a week. Maybe."

"And the rest of the time?"

"Who knows? Who cares?"

"Shouldn't your mom care? Considering she's the official guardian?"

"She cares. She looks after those two better than their own family."

"Oh?"

"Buncha money-sucking vampires. But that's private. Off

the record, hey?" Des jabs his finger at me, just like a real manager, all grown-up.

"No problem," I soothe. "So tell me about this management gig, Des. What does that involve?"

"I got some stuff going with the clubs, some sponsorship deals, and me and S'bu are working on a clothing label for men. Controller."

"But not Song?"

He ignores me. "T-shirts and accessories, but quality stuff, hey. None of this cheap rip-off crap. Got some stores that are interested. The Space. YDE even. It's not just about the music anymore, it's about the brand. You gotta be smart. CDs don't count for squat. It's all about the cell phone downloads."

"Wow. You want to be my manager too?"

"Depends." He assesses me seriously, for the first time. "What you got?"

"Not a whole lot, let me tell you. How about you, Arno?"

"Be?"

"No, shit-for-brains, the other fat white boy." Des smirks at me as if we're in on this together.

"I jusd, you know, hang oud."

"What do you enjoy most about him?"

"Uh. He's weally funny? And cool. And he's weally good ad gambes."

"He seems pretty tense about his sister, though?"

"*Ag*. They fight a lot, but they love each other. They're just pulling in different directions and S'bu's kind of . . . sensitive,"

Des answers, getting antsy at no longer being in the spotlight. "Are we done here?"

"Yeah, okay. I might want to check in with you guys some other time though, if that's cool? Here's my card."

I hand over an old card to each of them, from FL. Cringingly, it reads:

ZINZI DECEMBER WORD PIMP

That's just the kind of cocky idiot I was. "Wordsmith" was too wanky. But why I couldn't have just gone with "writer" or "freelance journalist," only my cocky idiot FL self knows. At least I managed to keep my old number.

"What's a word pimp? Like you rent out words by the hour?"

"For dodgy assignations in tacky motel bedrooms. Yeah."

"That's so random."

"I'm planning to get new cards."

"As your manager, I'd say that's a very good idea."

"Yeah. Id's jusd . . . lambe," Arno says.

"I'll take it under advisement. Thanks."

When I get back to the townhouse, there is a red Toyota Conquest parked outside, with the boot open as if ready to swallow the woman who is leaning into it to retrieve the shopping bags inside.

"Give you a hand?"

"*Ngiyabonga, sisi,*" says Prim Luthuli, emerging from the

car. She manages to contain her double-take at seeing Sloth, and hands over three bags in each hand, loaded with two-liter soft drinks and frozen mini-pizzas and chips. She is in her late forties, a large mama in a floral skirt and an over-bleached white blouse.

"Just a guess. Teenage boys?"

She smiles wanly, but there's a tightness to her face. "I try to cook healthy for them, but, *hei,* teenagers are difficult."

She fumbles open the lock, while balancing four bags, and bumps the door open with her hip, revealing a mirror layout of H4-303. The walls are a warm yellow, leading into a bright red kitchen with a corkboard against the wall, plastered with family photos and news clippings featuring iJusi.

I set the bags down on the counter, nearly knocking over a vase of white roses which Mrs. Luthuli deftly saves without comment.

"Do you live in the complex, dear?" she asks, opening the fridge and shelving a pack of strawberries, the milk, carrots, chicken pieces, tomatoes. "I don't think we've spoken before?"

"My name is Zinzi December. Odysseus Huron sent me to talk to you about Songweza."

She closes the fridge door and sits down heavily on one of the bar stools attached to the breakfast nook. She knots her hands in her floral skirt. She is clearly upset.

"You? Why hasn't he called the police?"

"You tell me."

She sighs heavily. "He thinks she's playing games. But even if she is, she could still be in danger! Who knows where she is. She's been gone four days." She starts sniffling.

For the second time in an hour, I've managed to make someone cry. At Sloth's urging, I go over and put an arm around her, awkwardly.

"It's going to be okay," I murmur. "It's going to be fine. Look, this is going to sound a little strange. But do you have anything of Songweza's she might have lost? Something with sentimental value? I don't know, a favorite earring that fell behind the couch? A book or a letter? A sock, even?" I'm clutching at straws or, worse, laundry.

"No. I don't know what you mean. I don't have anything like that." She looks at me like I'm crazy.

"Okay. How about her phone number?"

"I've been trying it every day. It just goes to her voicemail."

"Can I try it?" Because wouldn't it be crazy if she answered? Easiest money in the bank ever. But as predicted, it kicks straight to voicemail.

"You know who this is. If I feel like it, I'll get back to you." The voice is sassy, sexy. Even with the faux-bored veneer, it comes through like a dare.

It's followed by the automated network pre-record, a decidedly less enticing voice: "This mailbox is full. Please try again later. This mailbox is full. Please try again later." Okay, so it's not going to be that easy. Of course, just because it's on voicemail doesn't mean that she's not using the phone to *make* calls.

"Do you have any idea where she might have gone? No other relatives? No close friends she might be bunking with?"

"I called her friends from school. Nonkuleko. Priya. They haven't seen her."

"What about her friends outside school?"

She looks at me blankly. "No, I . . ."

"Never mind. How long have you been the twins' guardian?"

"When their grandmother died, she wrote in her will that she wanted me to look after them. We were neighbors. But I would have anyway. It's traditional to look after orphans."

"Helluva inheritance."

"It's hard. I get stressed. All the Starmakerz nonsense. The city, all the parties, *warra-warra*. It's a bad influence, Joburg. But they're good kids."

"I get the idea that the boys don't know about Song. I told them I was a journalist, don't worry."

"Des knows. My son. Did he mention . . ." She looks to me for acknowledgment that I'm up on the family ties. "He said I shouldn't tell them. They're young. They're emotional. Especially S'busiso. He takes everything to heart."

"I noticed."

"I think he gets bullied at school. He doesn't tell me, but sometimes he comes home with bruises. And what if something has happened to her? How would they deal with it? It's better that they don't know. They shouldn't have to carry the worry. I told them she's visiting a friend."

"What is she like, Songweza?"

"She's smart, very smart. A's at school. But she's not like S'bu. She's popular with the girls. And the boys too," she says, with a little grimace of concern.

I'll bet, if that voice is any reflection of the rest of the package.

"Does she have a boyfriend?"

"Oh no." She looks shocked. "Song would tell me. We have an agreement. No boyfriends until she finishes high school."

"Would you say she's happy?"

"Sometimes it feels like Songweza is angry at the whole world. But she doesn't really mean it. She just has her ups and downs."

"Which is why she's on medication?" She seems confused. "No, I don't think so."

"Nothing? Not even homeopathic? *Muti?*"

"Oh yes. Yes, she sees a *sangoma* once a month. They both do. He gives them treatment to help with the stress. All this stress of being famous."

"I'm slightly—concerned—that you might not know as much about the kids as you think you do."

"We talk all the time. I cook dinner for them every night. Make their lunch for school. We go to church on Sundays."

"You know they're drinking beer? Smoking weed?"

She twitches and then looks at me with frank appeal. "They're just letting off steam. They're good kids. Don't tell Mr. Huron. Please. They're good kids."

12.

I GET THE taxi to drop me off in Rosebank and find the nearest pay phone. It's an anachronism that the mall even has a working pay phone, but I guess it caters to the traders at the African market and teens who have run out of airtime. Or the dubiously agenda'd, like me. I don't want to use my cell phone, don't want my number showing up on caller ID, in case I still decide to hang up. As if he'd still have it saved on his phone.

Because the truth is that I don't know if I can do it. Unless Prim Luthuli can dig up a useful lost thing, I am going to need a backup plan. And the backup plan involves summoning up the demons of my Former Life. Sloth does *not* approve of this plan.

"Ninth Floor Publishing and Print," the receptionist says, in a tone shot through with contempt. "Hel*lo?*"

I find my voice. "Can I speak to Gio—Giovanni Conti, please. Features editor on *Mach.*"

"Deputy editor. Putting you through."

There is a brief snatch of radio playing a housey number with a marimba riff, and then there's that signature drawl. "'Lo?" Giovanni has bed-voice the way other guys have bed-hair, apparently careless, but in reality, as meticulously styled as his irony t-shirts and cultishly obscure Russian designer jeans.

"Hey, Gio."

There is a long pause for processing time. Maybe even response-modifying time. And then he says, "Zinzi? Holy crapola. Where are you?"

"Downstairs. Can I come up?"

"No. Wait. I'll come down. Meet me at Reputation. It's the hotel bar across the road."

"I think they have a policy," I say, leaving it hanging.

"Oh. Oh right," he says.

Which is how we end up meeting under the fluorescent lights of the local Kauai, attracting the rapt attention of a cluster of well-pierced teens sitting around a plastic table loaded down with bile-green smoothies. While other passersby, the black-diamond hipsters and mall rats and suits, spare me only the sliding glances reserved for people in wheelchairs and burn victims, the Goth kids have no shame. They're practically staking me out. I raise one hand, busted-celebrity-mode, acknowledging, yes, it really is me, now please leave me alone, for fuck's sake. It doesn't put them off in the slightest. It must be something about dressing all in black that gives you a sense of social invulnerability. I'd be tempted to try it, but they're only *playing* at being outcasts.

Gio puts his hand on my shoulder. "Zinz?" He hastily removes it as Sloth snaps at his fingers.

"You were expecting someone else?"

He leans in awkwardly to give me a hug, thinks better of it, and slips into the chair opposite.

"I like the beard," I say. "And the new cut. You're looking good."

"Thanks." He scrubs absently at the fine stubble over his skull with his palm.

But what I mean is, he's looking different. He's filled out, his face especially, and there's a hint of paunch under his button-up shirt. I wonder if he's quit the irony tees or it's just a button-up shirt kinda day. His sleeves are rolled up, revealing the tattoo that loops up his right arm, a neat line of dashes tracing the trajectory of a paper jet set to fly away up his sleeve; a tribute to idealism, to the absurd frailty of flight. I used to walk my fingertips up that line of dashes. It used to suit him.

I'm aware that he's evaluating me in the same way, comparing this Zinzi with the images in his database. Like a spot-the-difference game. Circle the lines around the eyes. Circle the torn left ear, where the bullet caught me. Circle the Sloth with his weirdly disproportionate arms draped over my shoulders like a furry backpack.

"So. Jeez. It's good to see you. What, how — I mean, the newspapers said ten years . . ."

"I got parole. Good behavior. Didn't you hear?"

"No, I —"

"It's okay. I haven't been following your life either."

"Well, it's not like you've been posting status updates. Look, do you want something? A smoothie? A drink?

A . . . what does that thing drink anyway?"

"Water, Gio. We're both fine. Don't sweat it. It's good to see you."

"Yeah. Yeah, it is." He ducks his head boyishly, but the effect is diluted in the absence of tousled fringe. The tectonic plates of whatever we were have shifted out from under us— call it contextual drift. Mind the gap.

We're saved from risking being the first to breach the divide, by the approach of Goth girl and her posse.

"Excuse me," she says, with the kind of boldness that means she doesn't give a damn that her blond roots are showing under the black dye (although she's still tried to obliterate her freckles under a thick coat of base).

"Nothing to see here. Run along, kiddies." Gio makes a shooing gesture.

"I'm not talking to you. Asshat." The girl scrunches her face in adolescent scorn and then touches my sleeve as lightly as a butterfly sneeze, like I'm a saint, or possibly a blood relation of Dita Von Teese. "I just wanted you to know, it doesn't matter what you did."

"Well, it does, actually," I say. But my retort bounces off her like a Ping-Pong ball off an armored car.

"We still think you're cool."

"Okay. Thank you." One alligator. Two alligator. Three alligator. The others watch reverentially, and when it's clear I'm not going to say anything else, or give her a blessing or something, she nods, and leads her posse off in the general direction of the movies.

LAUREN BEUKES

"That was odd," I say, watching the black pack ascend the escalator.

"It's that Hyena rapper guy, Slinger. He's made zoos cool. You're counter-culture aspirational, baby."

"My life's ambition." But the encounter has cracked the awkwardness between us.

"You still eat sushi?" he says, and we relocate to a conveyor-belt place round the corner.

"So, what's up, Zinz?" he says, shoveling a salmon California roll into his mouth with plastic chopsticks, errant grains of rice plopping into the soya sauce. I once saw MRI scans of sushi in a magazine. In the stuff prepared by a master sushi chef, the rice runs laterally, so it's less likely to come apart. Not a bad life philosophy. Stick close, keep your head down, and you won't fall to pieces.

"What brings you to this part of town?" Gio persists, spearing a maki roll with one chopstick and cramming it into his mouth. He always had a rough edge.

"Research," I say, skirting the clamor of questions I don't particularly feel like dancing with right now. "I'm working on something, and I thought you might be able to give me some pointers."

"Autobiographical?" He's fishing.

"Ah, no. It's an article, a book actually," I ad-lib. "It's pretty early stages. It's on that *kwaito* band? IJusi?"

"Aren't they more Afropop?"

"Same thing."

"Not quite. And isn't it a little early to be immortalizing

the one-hit-wonder kids anyway? They won't last six months."

"Okay, look, it's for a feature I'm hoping to sell to *Credo*, so I can maybe spin it into a book on music and Jozi youth culture, part coffee-table book, part trend bible. Something that might actually make money." Even I'm beginning to buy this.

"So this is it," he says, clacking his chopsticks at me for emphasis.

"What?"

"Zinzi's Big Comeback." I learned to speak in capital letters from Giovanni. Learned to use a crack pipe, too.

"Hope so. Of course, I'm handicapped," I tilt my head at Sloth, who has gone to sleep on my shoulder. "I suspect this guy's going to make it a little harder to get interviews."

"You'd be surprised," Gio says, breaking out his lopsided smile. I find it's grown on me.

13.

PEOPLE WHO WOULD happily speed through Zoo City during the day won't detour here at night, not even to avoid police road-blocks. They're too scared, but that's precisely when Zoo City is at its most sociable. From 6 p.m., when the day-jobbers start getting back from whatever work they've been able to pick up, apartment doors are flung open. Kids chase each other down the corridors. People take their animals out for fresh air or a friendly sniff of each other's bums. The smell of cooking—mostly food, but also meth—temporarily drowns out the stench of rot, the urine in the stairwells. The crack whores emerge from their dingy apartments to chat and smoke cigarettes on the fire escape, and catcall the commuters heading to the taxi rank on the street below.

I arrive home with a copy of every music magazine on the planet, or at least those available at CNA. I haven't seen Benoît all day. He was planning to fill in for Elias again, although when I left this morning, he was still passed out, reeking of beer.

Elias has called in the favor four times already this week. He's been sick, coughing his lungs up in the squalid room he shares with six other Zimbabweans. It looks like TB. D'Nice has been bugging Elias for sputum to sell on the black market to people who can use it to claim temporary government grants. But the sickness in Elias's lungs could just as well be asbestos or a reaction to the black mold. Proper diagnoses are as rare as real doctors round here.

There are plenty of the other kind. *Nyangas* and *sangomas* and faith healers with varying degrees of skill or talent, broadcasting their services on posters stuck up on telephone poles and walls. Some of them are charlatans and shysters, advertising cures for anything from money woes to lovesickness and AIDS with *muti* made from crushed lizard balls and aspirin. Guess which ingredient does all the hard work?

Object *muti* is easy, particularly when it's based on a simple binary. Locked or unlocked. Lost or found. Objects want to have a purpose. They're happy to be told what to do. People less so. A hack spell to scramble SMSs on your business rival's phone—easy. An affection charm to make someone feel more tenderly towards you, whether it's a teen crush or an abusive husband—a little trickier. Lab studies have shown that some spells work through manipulating hormone levels, boosting serotonin or oxytocin or testosterone. Simple on/ off equations. Most magic is more abstract. Capricious. It has a tendency to backfire. And the big stuff they promise, the AIDS cures, bigger penises, or death spells, are all placebo and nocebo, blessings and curses conjured up in your head. Not unlike glossy magazines, which also promise a better sex life, a better job, a better you. Trust me, I used to write those articles. And just look at me now.

Some folk have a real *mashavi* for healing, some can make genuine *muti*. But these are rare, and they tend to be out of the price range of someone like Elias. Which means another day of standing in line at the clinic from 5 a.m. onwards, hoping to get to front of the queue before the cut-off time at noon, so as to procure seven and a half minutes of time with the burned-out nurses who have seen it all before. None of which is conducive to keeping up with your shifts.

Which is why it's even more of a surprise when I realize that one of the cooking smells mingling through the building is emanating from *my* apartment. I push open the door to find Benoît, still in Elias's too-small uniform, standing at the hotplate, cooking hot dogs and *pap* and beans. The whole apartment has been swept and wiped down, and even the bed has been made. The generator is purring happily, a canister of petrol standing beside it.

"You're looking very chipper for someone who should still be suffering the mother of all hangovers. And what's this?" It will turn out that I have good cause to be suspicious.

"I can't do something nice for you?"

"Oh, I can think of several things nice you could do for me, with me, to me."

"You see how it could be if you just gave me a key."

"This was a one-time deal, mister, and only because you were still sleeping it off when I left. Don't get used to it."

"You don't like it?" he asks.

I relent, sling my arms over his shoulders and lean against his back. "S'all right. I guess."

"Get off, woman, I'm cooking," he laughs, shrugging me off. But he tilts his head all the way back to kiss me.

"Cooking? Or burning?" I tease.

"Merde!"

He insists that we take our faintly charred hot dogs up to the roof, leaving the critters behind. He's even bought paper plates and napkins, and two bottles of beer. He also brings out his camera, a battered and hopelessly outdated Korean generic, barely a megapixel, and held together with duct tape. It's seen a lot, that camera. Whole documentaries' worth. But the only photos Benoît has shown me are the ones he takes of himself.

He's obsessive about it. He's recorded every step of his journey from Kinshasa to Joburg, photographed every major landmark, every significant crossroad or place he stayed for the night, every person who showed him kindness. But it's not enough to photograph the people or the places. He has to be included in the frame. Like it's not only evidence that he was really there, but that he exists at all.

By the time we reach the rooftop, I'm out of breath. People don't come up here a whole lot, especially since the elevators died, except to hang laundry out on a sunny day. Sometimes there'll be a party on the roof, to celebrate a wedding or a birth or when one of the local gangs feels like buying some community goodwill with a spit-*braai*ed sheep and grilled offal. It can get ugly if people are drunk, at New Year especially. It's practically tradition for people to send appliances crashing to the street, stories below. There are reasons the cops and ambulances are slow to respond to "incidents" in Zoo City—if they respond at all.

Benoît ducks under a laundry line, sheets and dresses and shirts flapping like tethered kites. Everything takes on a muted quality fifteen floors up. The traffic is reduced to a flow and stutter, the car horns like the calls of mechanical ducks. The skyline is in crisp focus, the city graded in rusts and coppers by the sinking sun that has streaked the wispy clouds the color of blood. It's the dust in the air that makes the Highveld sunsets so spectacular, the fine yellow mineral deposits kicked up from the mine dumps, the carbon-dioxide choke of the traffic. Who says bad things can't be beautiful?

"Why don't we come up here more often?" Benoît says, uncharacteristically wistful.

"Too many stairs."

He gives me a reproving look, and I feel bad for spoiling the mood.

"Here. Sit down." He plucks a quilt off the line, impervious to the sharp nettle-sting of the protection spell handwoven into the fabric by the specialty tailoring team downstairs, and spreads it on the cement under the water tower. I oblige. The quilt is still damp and covered in a patchwork of wannabe Disney characters, poor cousins to ripoffs and barely recognizable. But it's not like Benoît to be so unconscientious. "Aren't you worried it'll get dirty?" I say.

He shrugs. "Dirt isn't a permanent state. It'll recover." It occurs to me that he is not talking about the quilt. "C'mere." I scoot over to him and he tucks me under his arm and raises the camera high, pointing towards us. "Say Jozi," he says. And I understand that he is leaving.

When he turns the camera around to check out the photograph, it reveals him beaming broadly straight into the lens, but I am a blur of profile jerking towards him.

"No good," Benoît declares, but he doesn't delete the picture. He extends his arm to take another photo. "Hold still this time. Try looking *at* the camera." He touches my chin with his thumb, gently adjusting the angle of my jaw so that I am staring into our tiny and faraway reflection in the lens.

"Can't you wait?"

"I don't think so, Zinzi," he says quietly.

"Two weeks," I say. In desperation, "One."

"I can't say."

"But you still need to get your stuff together. Organize transport." There are people smugglers who will get you across borders, sneak you under barbed-wire fences, ferry you across crocodile-infested waters, pay off border guards with cases of beer or bullets. Although usually it's the other way round. Not much demand for sneaking *out* of South Africa. Of course, he could just fly, but then there will be stamps in his passport that will have to be explained to the people at Home Affairs, who believe being a refugee means you can never go home again.

He sighs and lowers the camera to look at me. "I'm working on it. D'Nice says he knows some people."

"D'Nice would. How are you going to pay for it?"

"I'm working on that too."

141

"How?"

"Always with the questions, *cherie*. Can you stop being such a journalist for one minute?" He kisses me, as if that's an answer and, raising the camera again, teases. "Now hold still, will you?"

And I think: No, you.

The call comes later. At 2 a.m.—that hour of sleepless brooding.

"She's dwying to sabodage him," the voice says urgently into the phone, without so much as a *hola* or *unjani*. The only reason I recognize it is because of the nasal honk.

"Arno?"

"She's going to fug evewyding up. Song and da boyfwienb. Dey're supposed to be in sdudio. And she's jusd gone. She's so selfidg. She jusd wants to ruin evewyding for him." He is choking back tears, and I realize I was wrong about his crush. It's not on Songweza. It's S'bu.

14.

I SPEND THE morning making phone calls to a list of Song-weza's friends culled from Mrs. Luthuli and, more usefully, Des. Most of them are a bust, even though her friends open up to me like an oyster come shucking time at that magic introduction "I'm a journalist." Even vague proximity to celebrity turns people into attention whores, especially teenagers. They spill their guts on her first crush, how she cheated on a Maths paper in grade seven and got bust so the whole class had to write the test again, how much she loves music, how talented she is, how much she talks in class, and on her phone, on MXit, how much she loves to party. How sometimes she gets really down on the world, "like seriously dark, hey, but not, like suicidal" the girl called Priya tells me.

My notes give me an outline only. The details are lacking, like a Polaroid that is still developing. I get the idea that there are names missing on Mrs. Luthuli's list, names she might not approve of, like this boyfriend she doesn't even know about.

I look up the people written up on Des's action white-board. The designer and the publicity chick are dead ends, straight business, slightly perplexed as to why I'd be calling. The only person of interest is Heather Yalo, who just so happens to be the manager for mega names like Leah and Noluthando Meje. When I introduce myself, she says, "It wouldn't be appropriate to talk to the media yet," and hangs up on me. I wonder if Huron knows that Des is planning a coup.

I set something up for tonight, with help from Gio, who "knows people." I also put in a message to Vuyo.

>>Kahlo999: I need a favor.

>>Vuyo: I heard about ur mkwerekwere. I can help. U write the letter. Ill get an official letterhead.

I'm too busy wrestling the spiteful flip of hope in my chest to care about where Vuyo got his intel from. The Company has more eyes than the inner-city CCTV surveillance system when it comes to protecting its interests. And I have my suspicions about who has been informing on me. I wouldn't be at all surprised if his name is D'Nice Languza.

>>Kahlo999: What are you talking about?

>>Vuyo: "Tragically, the International Red Cross DRC were misinformed. Benoit Bocangas wife and children are dead."

>>Kahlo999: You are a twisted SHIT of a human being.

>>Vuyo: Could even provide photos of the bodies. U need to get me references for Photoshopping tho.

>>Kahlo999: Shut the fuck up, Vuyo. It's not an option.

>>Vuyo: Touchy.

>>Kahlo999: You're not listening to me. I need three things: I need to find out if a cell phone number has been used in the last four days. I need to access a MXit account. And I need to find out if a life insurance policy has been registered on a particular party.

>>Vuyo: Itll cost u.

>>Kahlo999: R5000. Add it to my tab.

>>Vuyo: 12. With interest. Send me details.

>>Kahlo999: Out of curiosity. Does the Company do trafficking?

>>Vuyo: Are u sure u don't have police sitting next to u?

>>Kahlo999: Pretty sure.

>>Vuyo: U havent installed the firewall.

>>Kahlo999: I think you're up in my business enough already. C'mon, Vuyo. Trafficking? Sex slavery?

>>Vuyo: Company has wide interests.

>>Kahlo999: If I wanted to find out if someone had been kidnapped? By a dealer? Forced into prostitution?

>>Vuyo: Not kidnapping if they come of own accord.

>>Kahlo999: I think our definitions of "own accord" may differ. Can I give you a name?

>>Vuyo: This is an expensive favor girl. There is a price for what happens next.

>>Kahlo999: I think I know someone who can pay that price.

It turns out that slipping back into Former Life is as easy as pulling on a dress. Fashion is only different skins for different flavors of you. Tonight, I am peach schnapps. Nervous as a fourteen-year-old trying to sneak into a club for the first time. Did I say "a" dress? I meant nine. Which is the total extent of what I own.

Sloth huffs grumpily, sprawled out on the floor with a bunch of cassava leaves I got at the market downstairs to placate him (along with a tub of wood lice for the Mongoose). If

I could leave Sloth behind, I would. But the feedback loop of the separation anxiety is crippling. Crack cravings have nothing on being away from your animal.

After trying on all nine dresses, twice, with an intermission period spent trying to recapture the wood lice that escaped when Sloth grumpily up-ended the tub, I settle on skinny jeans and a surprisingly tasteful black strappy top I borrow from one of the prostitutes on the third floor, after giving up in disgust on my wardrobe. When I say borrow, I mean rent. She assures me it's clean. For thirty bucks, I'm dubious, but it passes the sniff test, so fuck it.

I catch a taxi into Auckland Park with the late-night cleaners, the nurses, and the restaurant dishwashers: the invisible tribe of behind-the-scenes. I get off after Media Park and walk up to 7th Street with its scramble of restaurants, bars, and Internet cafés. Outside the Mozambican deli-cum-Internet café, a hawker tries to sell me a star lantern made of wire and paper and, when I decline, offers me marijuana instead.

I used to stomp here. Got bust smoking dope in my readily identifiable school uniform on the *koppie* and was suspended for two weeks. Did my first line of coke in the bathrooms of Buzz 9. Had snatched sex in a driveway on 8th before the homeowner called armed response. This should not be so intimidating. But when I see Gio fiddling intently with his phone on the curb outside the Biko Bar, it's a relief.

"Hey, you."

He looks up guiltily and stashes his phone in his jacket pocket. "Hey, baby, you made it! C'mon, the guys are already inside." He ushers me towards the velvet ropes that have seen better days, and a short, wiry bouncer who is wearing a t-shirt that reads TRY IT MOTHERFUCKER.

"She's with me," Gio says and, although the bouncer is not happy to see Sloth, he gives us the tiniest of head tilts to indicate, yeah, sure, whatever.

The Biko Bar is to Steve Biko as crappy t-shirt design is to Che Guevara. His portrait stares down from various cheeky interpretations. A hand-painted barbershop sign with a lineup of Bikos in profile modeling different hairstyles and headgear; a *chiskop,* a mullet, a *makarapa* mining helmet. Steve stares out with that trademark mix of determination and wistful heroism from the center of a PAC-style Africa made of bold rays of sunlight. Steve, with a lion's mane, is the focal point of a crest of struggle symbols, power fists, soccer balls, and a cursive "The most potent weapon of the oppressor is the mind of the oppressed." My academic dad would have hated it. Reduced by irony and iconography to a brand.

"I see they sell t-shirts," I say. "Do the kids' sizes come pre-soaked with acid?"

"Very funny, Zinzi," Gio says, steering me through to the back. "Don't worry, they're nervous about meeting you too."

Apprehension clenches in my gut like the moment before you go over the lip of the roller coaster. I never liked roller coasters. Gio swings me towards a table occupied by a small cluster of painfully hip people with expensive haircuts. There is a very pierced and inked woman with violently red hair and Bettie Page eyes, and two men, one in a hideous paisley print shirt and gelled spikes, the other in his early forties, a war photographer's waistcoat, and a crafted coating of cynicism. They're all clustered around a big camera with a serious lens, examining the display on the back.

"Oh, ick," says the woman, pushing the camera away just as we reach the table. "Why would you show me that?" She hits the photographer on the shoulder, but it's a playful punch, the kind that says, I really like you, even though you show me gruesome photographs, maybe even *because* you show me gruesome photographs. "What's Dave got you looking at this time?" Gio says.

"Photos of the homeless guy who was killed," says Laconic Photographer Guy, the Dave in question.

"Ooooh, cool," Gio says. "I'd dig to check those out. You know, we have this new gross-out feature in *Mach*. Gangrenous feet. Puff adder bites. Ideally tied in to some kind of extreme adventure that's gone horribly wrong."

"Not much adventure in getting beaten up and set on fire. Cut him up pretty bad. Especially his face. Cut off his fingers too."

"Are you really going to publish these in *Mach*?" asks Ugly Paisley Shirt, clearly thrilled at the prospect.

"We're a men's magazine," Gio shrugs. "Men are brutal." And then adds hastily, "I'm not saying women aren't."

"They just hide it better," I say. Everyone looks at me, and then they all simultaneously switch their focus to Sloth. Paisley Shirt smirks. I put up my hand, like a kid at school volunteering the answer everyone's waiting for. "Hi, I'm Zinzi."

"Sorry, yeah, guys, this is my friend I told you about?" Gio's tone is loaded with things left unsaid. "Zinzi December. We used to work together." Sleep together. Take drugs together. Sleep together while taking drugs together at work together. It was a simple relationship, really.

Piercing Girl scootches round to make space for us to sit on the plush velvet bank while Gio does the introductions— the *crème de la crème* of musos in his immediate social circle, plus Paisley Shirt, better known as Henry. Dave is, as surmised, a news photographer for *The Daily Truth*, although he photographs gigs as well—mainly jazz, but he's done Oppikoppi four years in a row, plus the occasional feature for lifestyle magazines on the side. Henry does social media at a below-the-line agency, and a big part of his mandate is the music scene. Gio invited him specially. "He's the fag to Songweza's hag," he told me on the phone beforehand. "If anyone's going to have the dirt on your girl, it's Henry."

Piercing Girl is a hardcore music journalist when she's not being mom to a two-year-old she calls Toddlersaurus. "Juliette writes for *every*one," Gio says. "All the local mags, as well as *Billboard, Spin, Juke,* and *Clash.*"

Piercing Girl/Juliette rolls her eyes in pleased fake modesty, which I take to mean it's all true. "And what do you do now, Zinzi?" she asks sympathetically, leaning forward, giving me the benefit of her full attention. It's only three-quarters patronizing.

"I find lost things."

"Like stolen goods?" Henry pipes up. "Because my parents'

place was broken into last week and they got my grandfa-
ther's watch. It was a fob watch, you know, the one with the
chain, like 102 years old——"

"No, like lost things. As I said. Car keys. Missing wills."

"For money?" He raises his eyebrows, as if this is more ludicrous than toasters with built-in MP3 players.

"I charge a reasonable rate for my time."

He warms to the idea. "Hey, you know, you could totally
work at an old-age home where they have, like, senile de-
mentia or what's that forgetty disease?"

"Alzheimer's," Piercing Girl provides.

"Yeah, I bet they lose stuff all the time, and you could take
it back to them and charge them, and they'd forget they paid
you already and you could charge them again."

"I don't think it works like that," Piercing Girl says, clearly
having decided to adopt me as her pet cause. "Does it, Zinzi?"

"Who knows how it works?" I know I'm being antagonistic.

"But aren't there tests? I thought they did a full analysis?"

"Human lab rats!" says Henry enthusiastically. "Only I
guess sometimes there are actual rats, right? That must be
confusing."

"In the US, Australia, Iran, places like that, they do a
full head-to-toe, CAT scans, brain scans, endocrine system
analysis, the works. In South Africa, we're protected by the
Constitution." And the prohibitive costs of all that invasive
testing. There are better things to spend government funds
on, like nuclear submarines or official pocket-lining. They do
a few basic measurements to try and quantify your *shavi,* but

mainly they rely on reports from the social workers and cops, along with basic demonstrations of what you can do.

"How are your parents? Do you still, uh——" Gio falters, sensing he's blundered close to the edge.

"It's all right, Gio. I Google them occasionally. They seem to be doing fine. Still divorced. My mom's living in Zurich now. Dad's in Cape Town teaching theory of film to rich kids who are more interested in special effects than subtext."

"I didn't know they were . . . oh. Right."

"Couple of months before the trial."

An uncomfortable silence stretches out. Drops into freefall, hits terminal velocity, and keeps on going.

"But Giovanni said you're writing again?" Piercing Girl prompts. As a professional interviewer, she's probably used to picking up conversations that have crashed to the floor and setting them spinning again. "A music piece? That's why you're here tonight?"

"I'm doing a book. A trend bible slash pop history of Jozi youth culture. Music, fashion, technology." The more I say it, the more credible it sounds. Do-able even. Possibly profitable.

"You got a publisher yet?"

"I'm starting with a feature article for *Credo*. We'll see what happens from there."

"*Credo*? Oh, I've done some work for them. They're fantastic. Isn't Lindiwe awesome?"

"She's great," I say. I haven't got as far into my cover as actually contacting the commissioning editor. I chalk it up on my to-do list. But things go more smoothly after that. Apart from the moment when I catch Henry trying to sniff Sloth's fur.

Dave doesn't say much, other than to offer to show me the photographs when an argument starts about whether it's morally bankrupt to print such horrific images. I skim them, scrolling as quickly as possible. They're as bad as you'd expect, taken with a forensic distance, even in the pics he's framed with shocked bystanders, for mood.

"Do they know who he was?" I say, handing the camera back.

"Drifter. Been sleeping rough. They're still trying to get a name. Might have been a zoo, they're not sure. Do you mind?" he says, raising the camera. "Atmosphere stuff."

"Uh."

"Group photo!" Piercing Girl yelps, and Dave snaps a couple of awkwardly posed shots, before disappearing towards the stage as the band makes its appearance, only an hour and a half late: an all-girl Afrikaans/seSotho glam punk electro-rock number called "Nesting Mares."

Take me, take me, take me to your spider den
I'll be your conscience, your accomplice, your inner zen
Let me in, don't question why
Let me, let me be your alibi

"They're pretty good!" I shout over the thrum of guitars and the alto growl of the lead singer. In spite of the noise, Sloth has gone to sleep.

"Lightweights!" Piercing Girl shouts back. "Wait for the Tsotsis!"

"Oh yeah? They the ones who wear ski masks?"

"Yeah, they're brilliant! Of course, it's not like their identities are really, really a secret. Like Mzekezeke. Your iJusi kids aren't bad either! Real talent. But they need to get the fuck away from Moja."

"Why do you say that?"

"Bad influence!"

"Bad influence how?"

"Too commercial!"

"Is that a bad thing? Experienced producer like Odi Huron backing them?"

"What?!"

"I said, Odi's experience——" I shout louder, but it gets lost in translation over the screaming chorus.

Kill me——Thrill me
Kill me——Thrill me
Take me away from it all

"Yeah, he owns Counter Revolutionary!" Piercing Girl yells back. This is a surprise. Counter Rev is the hottest club in Jozi. "Chi-chi with a bleeding edge," according to *011 Magazine*, which rates iJusi's hit single "Spark" four stars on the Earworm Meter——"ferociously upbeat teenybop Afropop."

"King of Clubs, baby," Piercing Girl yells. Gio taps her on

the shoulder and tilts his head at the bathrooms. She gets up to follow him, already hoiking the twist of paper out of the front pocket of her jeans, leaving me with Paisley Henry.

"Gio said you're friends with Songweza?!" I yell at him.

"Yeah. We used to hang out a lot!"

"Why used to?"

Henry shouts back something like "She's a honey numb."

"Do you want to go outside? I can't hear a thing."

Outside is a fire escape already crammed with smokers.

"What were you saying?"

"I said Song is a funny one. On her own *plak*. She was up for this TV series, right? But it was all about the navy and they asked her if she could swim and she said, of course she could swim."

"But she can't?"

"She couldn't, past tense. She basically taught herself in a weekend. We went to the gym and she just *sommer* dived in to the deep end. Nearly drowned."

"She get the part?"

He shakes his head. "She lied about her age. They needed someone who was eighteen for the sex scenes, you know? I dunno how they didn't know she was fifteen. She's *mal,* that one."

"You seem a little old to be hanging out with fifteen-year-olds."

"*Ag* man, Song was hanging out with *me*. I met her on the scene, she's always at the venues. Carfax, &Serif. She makes friends with the bouncers."

"What's this I hear about her boyfriend?"

"Which one? They come and go. She's too much of a butterfly for anyone to hang on to her." But I can see I've hit a nerve.

"No one special?"

"Well, there was Jabu. But he turned out to be a total dick."

"Oh yeah?"

"Dumped her via SMS. Can you believe that? I mean, she should have seen it coming. They met in rehab, for Pete's sake. She was sobbing on my couch for, like, hours. But you know Song—she got it out of her system, wiped her eyes, and moved right on."

"She dated anyone since?"

"Hmmm. I know she kissed some drummer last week, with, um, Papercut. That screech metal band? You know that joke, right? What does a girl do with her asshole in the morning? Takes it to drum practice. Hey, can I hold it?" he blurts, reaching for Sloth. He's clearly been dying to ask.

"He bites."

"I'll be gentle, I promise. Please? Just for five minutes."

"He comes with a disclaimer."

"*Ja*, it's okay."

I gingerly hand Sloth over, giving him a little squeeze to remind him to play nice. To my surprise, he clambers happily into Henry's arms and nuzzles into his neck.

"Whoa! He's *lank* heavy!"

"I know."

"But really, really soft. Wow."

"I know that too." I do not point out that Sloth is chewing the collar of his hideous shirt. "Think she might have done a runner with the drummer? Or maybe Jabu came back?"

He shakes his head. "Nah, when Song moves on, she moves on. No way she would ever forgive Jabu or take his skanky rehab ass back. And the drummer was too lightweight for her."

"Anyone else?"

"*Ag,* that bouncer at Counter Rev has been hitting on her hard recently. They were always talking. And that dude must be at least thirty." He rolls his eyes at the thought of such decrepitude. "He didn't get anywhere, though. Song might be a slut, but she's not stupid."

"He got a name?"

"Uh. Major hot guy? Biceps the size of your head. I don't know if he just gyms a lot, or shoots up 'roids, or if he's just a freak of nature. You can't miss him."

"When was the last time you saw her?"

"About a week ago? She was at Informer. In Newtown?"

"I'm a little confused. If she's into metal and punk, hanging out at rock venues, why is she in an Afropop band?"

"Why are you writing a story for *Credo*? 'Cos it's a step up, right? Today it's *Credo*; tomorrow, like, *Dazed and Confused* or whatever your thing is."

"Any idea why she's not answering her phone? She flaky like that?"

"Not if she wants to talk to you. And she'd want to talk to *you,* believe me. She's hungry for coverage."

"Part of the step up."

"Yeah. Can you take this back, now?" he whines, shoving Sloth back at me. He's finally figured out that zoo doesn't mix with paisley.

Back at the booth, Gio and Juliette have returned, and the girls have been replaced by a quartet of ski-masked youths with microphones. These can only be the Tsotsis. "Having a good time?" Gio says, his mouth right up against my ear because the Tsotsis are raucously loud—high-wire *kasi* hip-hop acrobatically riffing off *maskandi* folk.

"It's been educational," I shout back.

"Wanna get out of here?" Gio breaks out his best mischief smile. "Seven and a half minutes to my place."

"I'll take a ride back to Zoo City." I grin at his expression. "Don't worry. Your chances of being shot are only one in three." And then I'm blinded by a camera flash as Dave reappears and snaps a close-up.

"Say paparazzi," he says.

It turns into a group outing. The chance of a guided tour is too much for Dave to resist.

"You been into Zoo City much?" I ask him.

"Well, our offices are nearby. And I picked up Lily Nobomvu once about seven years ago, hitching from her crack dealer's place on Kotze Street," Dave says. "Covered in bruises. Her manager was beating her up. She seemed happy enough, though. Asked me to lend her a hundred bucks when I dropped her off in Parktown."

"Odi Huron, by any chance?"

"That's the one. Dodgy motherfucker, by all accounts." Dave leans forward between the seats to take photographs through the windshield, of the trees hung with plastic bags like Christmas decorations, the prostitutes outside Joubert Park posing under the streetlights (the working ones, anyway) like their own personal spotlights.

"You know they never found her body? She could still be out there."

"Lily? You mean like Elvis? I can see them cruising truck-stop bars on Route 66, playing drinking games with gray aliens." Gio giggles. "Hey, didn't Odious have a bar? Remember, Zinz? Bass Station?"

"I remember being too drunk to remember anything about Bass Station. Like I don't remember anything about 206 or Alcatraz."

"Oh, Bass Station closed down years and years ago," Dave says. "There was a robbery that went bad. Couple of people died, if I remember correctly. Maybe that's why it took Huron so long to make a comeback."

"We should go to Counter Rev, sometime. You'd like it," Gio interrupts.

"Sounds like hipster hell."

"All right, you'd find it interesting, then. Anthropological."

"Turn left and pull over at the sign for His Believers," I say, indicating the billboard for the charismatic church.

"This is the stuff you should be doing," says Dave, suddenly very animated. "Why are you writing about pop bands when you could write about Zoo City from the inside?"

"But would people read it? Dogfight exposés and vice?"

"What's a dogfight?" Gio pipes up.

"Use your imagination."

"I'm seeing glitz and blood, money on the table, fur in the ring, mobsters with glamour models on their arms watching from the sidelines."

"Minus the glamour and glitz, add a heavy dose of illegal, and you've got it."

"To the death?"

"Not unless it gets really ugly. We do try to avoid the Undertow as much as possible."

"Sounds like a good night out. Maybe we should do Counter Rev and then an evening at the dogfighting."

"Or not."

But Dave won't let up. "More like insight pieces. Scenes from the street, what it's like to live here."

"It's *kak*, Dave. What more do you want to know?"

"Just think about it."

"So, can I walk you up?" Gio asks as we pull over.

"You probably shouldn't leave your car alone in this neighborhood."

"It's cool, I'll stay," Dave volunteers.

"You can walk me to security. Longer than that, and I can't speak for Dave's safety."

There is a small group of men, teens really, sitting on the steps leading up to Aurum Place opposite. Spare time and beer make them dangerous. Candlelight flickers in the windows of the squatter blocks where the electricity has long since been disconnected. A thudding bass line ramps up from the chop shop in the alley. Testing the sound system. In the distance, sirens, the occasional gunshot. Gio flinches, pretends he hasn't. We reach the security gate and I turn to say goodnight. Gio pouts.

"I don't get to come up?"

"Next time. Maybe."

"It was good seeing you."

"Like old times." This is not necessarily a good thing.

"So Counter Revolutionary? Saturday? Consider it research."

"How about tomorrow?"

"Done." He moves to kiss me. I pull my head back just enough to thwart the intention.

"What are you doing, Giovanni?"

"Uh-oh," he says. "Full Name Rebuke. That's serious stuff. You won't let me walk you up? You won't let me kiss you?"

"We broke up. In bad circumstances."

"Four years ago. Things change. People change. You have."

"And you haven't. In the slightest."

"One kiss," he says. "Quick, before I get raped and murdered by the evil zoos."

"You just don't give up." I grab his button-up shirt and press my mouth against his. His lips are warm. Surprised, it takes him a millisecond to respond, and then we are kissing like starving people intent on devouring each other, familiar and new at once. Which is right when Sloth leans forward and bites his ear. Gio yelps, and the boys on the steps pause in their banter to look.

"Jesus! Get it off! Fuck! Ow!"

"Sloth!"

Sloth lets go and hides his head behind my neck. Gio grabs at his bleeding ear and raises his fist, snarling. I angle my head so that any blow will hit me first. "You're lucky he's an herbivore," I say, calmly.

"Lucky, fuck. That fucking thing nearly fucking bit my fucking ear off. " He touches his ear, which is only nipped, and examines the smear of blood on his fingertips.

"I can tell you work with words."

"Not now, Zinzi. Ow. Fuck. Do you think I need a tetanus shot? I'm going to have to go to the fucking ER."

"You'll be fine. Thank you. I had a wonderful evening."

"Yeah, great. No, okay, I mean it. Apart from Dr. Hannibal Lecter on your back."

"I'll see you tomorrow."

As the car pulls away into the night, D'Nice separates from the group across the road and saunters over, swinging an empty *lengolongola*. His Vervet Monkey hugs his neck for balance.

"What's a sweet darkie girl like you doing with an *umlungu* like him?" D'Nice says.

"Maybe he's my long-lost husband," I snap.

"Uh-huh," D'Nice says and there is something sharp and mean behind the drunk in his eyes.

15.

CREDO August 2010

The Once and Future King?

Moja Records' hitmaker has been in hiding for almost a decade. Evan Milton pinned him down for his first one-on-one interview in forever to talk teen pop, new club culture, and the second coming of Odi Huron.

"I believe in second chances," Odysseus Huron says, sitting behind the mixing desk in his analog/digital studio, an airy bunker built into the koppie at the back of his house, which is the base of operations for Moja Records. Necessary, as the notoriously reclusive Huron hasn't set foot outside this rambling Westcliff property since 2001. He's not talking about himself, perhaps because he's already on his third or fourth go-round of chances. This is a man who has been dogged by controversy and tragedy through four decades of music-making, who has somehow managed to rise from the ashes again and again.

He makes light of his past — and his recent return to prominence. "I don't think anyone walks through this industry unscathed," he muses. "The only thing you can really do is become better equipped."

Every era has its reclusive musical genius; every genre has its behind-the-scenes starmaker trailed by hints of controversy. Brian Wilson disappeared for decades before returning with *Pet Sounds;* James Brown always surfed a little too close to the law; and let's just say the name of the Death Row Records rap empire wasn't entirely coincidental. Closer to home, Africa's world music stars have been accused of human trafficking, embezzlement, and involvement with blood diamonds, while the Nigerian government slapped Fela Kuti with a currency smuggling rap.

Mzansi has Odysseus Huron, the multi-platinum selling producer behind No. 1 sellers like Lily Nobomvu, Detective Wolf, and Moro, and the man who launched Yeoville's ill-fated Bass Station nightclub — as close to a South African Shrine or CBGB as we've ever had. It used to be that Odi Huron made hits and created stars effortlessly. He's been part of South Africa's ever-evolving cultural fabric since the dark days of apartheid, right through the Rainbow Revolution and into the post–"Born Free" era. He's also the man who disappeared almost entirely from public view amidst rumors of ill health and depression after the Bass Station tragedy and Lily Nobomvu's death.

He is not an easy man to meet with or speak to. In fact, there's almost nothing easy about Odi Huron. For starters, he had to consult with a *sangoma* for an auspicious date to do the interview. This was followed by a credentials check to rival a visa application. Three weeks later, Odi's bodyguard/dogsbody, James, ushers me into the house and hands me a bullet-pointed list of no-go zones. "He doesn't want to talk about it," James warns. "Come in, come in, what are you, a mugger lurking in the doorway?" Huron gestures me impatiently into the lounge. He has a jokey way of putting people down, keeping them in their place.

Odi lives alone in this vast house. He orders his groceries online. Prospective artists email him their demos. For everything else, there's James.

The house has seen better days. This is no Ahmet Ertegun palace of genteel music-mogul diplomacy, but then, the man who started America's mighty Atlantic Records didn't get drafted into smuggling guns across the borders of apartheid-era South Africa for struggle activists. Odi's past has been checkered to say the least.

In the '80s, he was one of a handful of white producers (think Gabi le Roux and Robert Trunz) who were willing to take a risk on black artists at a time when the apartheid government frowned sternly on such "crossover" projects. Odi saw the musical potential of black artists — and their commercial possibilities. It would turn out to be a savvy career move.

Inside, it's not all pop-rock'n'roll. Perched on the edge of a chair, holding her handbag and looking very out of place among the swinging '70s décor, is a middle-aged lady. She stands up to greet me and introduces herself as Primrose Luthuli, fumbling to explain that she's the twins' legal guardian.

The twins are the reason I'm here. S'busiso and Songweza Radebe, aka iJusi, aka Odi's latest flash of musical genius, aka the latest recipients of the platinum touch. They're also the "second chancers" he's talking about, the raw-talent pair who spurned his production and management offer to enter *Starmakerz*.

"It's total trash, demeaning to real artists," Odi says of the show. And based on the increasingly embarrassing performances by winner Sholaine Pieters, he may have a point.

Odi approached the twins again just before the semi-finals, and this time they inked a three-album deal. There's not a sentient soul in South Africa who hasn't heard "Spark" — the sound of a million ringtones, according to the download stats. Infectiously catchy music is one thing (earworm, anyone?), but star status requires more than that, and Odi's touch could be seen in marketing coups like licensing the track for the Chevy Spark ad campaign. If the buzz is anything to go by, the new single, "Drive-by Love," looks set to propel them even higher.

The teenyboppers in question are messing around in a swimming pool outside, painted a dark, depthless blue to retain the heat. S'bu is sitting on the side, his gray school pants rolled up, his black lace-up shoes next to him, bare feet dangling in the water. Songweza is thrashing around in neon green armbands. She's enthusiastic in the water rather than adept, dog-paddling over to her brother to splash the young heartthrob whose face smiles down from many teenage walls.

The proverbial new leaf is one thing, but to see a man remade is another. Gone is the Odi who pioneered the dark, danger-thump club-swagger of Assegai or the brooding sexual undertones that powered Zakes Tsukudu's biggest hits. Now, it's all bright sunshine and two kids splashing around in a pool.

"No, man, Sooo-ooong!" S'bu yelps at his effervescent twin.

"Well, get in!" she teases. He lobs his school shoe at the voice behind the addictive chorus of "Spark." She ducks. It plops into the water and sinks without a trace.

"*Tsha!*" Mrs. Luthuli says, springing into action. "Who is going to pay for that?"

"Who said you should never work with kids or animals?" Huron quips. "They obviously didn't have Prim on their side." He yells out the door, "You two, come say hello!"

The pair come into the house dripping, and Mrs. Luthuli goes scuttling off in search of towels.

"*Heita*," Songweza bubbles, "I'm Song and we're iJusi and we're going to be massive!"

S'bu punches her arm, embarrassed. "Song! Be more modest."

Song frowns. "Why? It's true."

It probably is.

But while the twins may be the stars, this is undoubtedly the Odi Huron show. He indicates that we'll take a stroll across the garden to the newly refurbished studio to get a "sneak peek for your ears" of the new iJusi single, "Drive-by Love."

"iJusi is more than a band for me," he says, "it's a sign of the future. Song and S'bu are exactly what the new Moja Records is about. It's not about using the new beats in our deal with Babyface; it's not about getting every sub-Saharan Android phone pre-loaded with iJusi FutureSong credits. It's about this. People say the twins shine when they sing. I say that we should all shine; that we can all shine if we just focus, if we just get past what's holding us down."

To emphasize the point, he sips from his bottle of vitamin water, part of his detox routine. It's a far cry from the triple shots of tequila that were the order of the day during the Detective Wolf era. The evidently healthy and clearly still razor-sharp Odi exudes the air of being a remade man, and iJusi represent a new sound that may well see his Moja stable eclipse the already impressive achievements of JumpFish, whose brilliant rekindling of bubblegum Afropop swept both urban and pop-rock charts, and Keleketla, the devilishly clever electro-pop-meets-*kwaito* street jam that seemed to pulse along every street corner in 2004, before the band split with Moja over "artistic differences."

And hey, maybe Odi deserves a break after everything he's been through. "Do I regret any of it? Of fucking course I do," he says, adding, "I also regret James not making it fucking clear enough that I didn't want to talk about it."

I press. People want to hear his side of the story. The Bass Station deaths. Lily. He relents, pinching his lip, unhappily.

"You have to understand. It was the fucking noughties, not the easy-swing 1990s. We were worried about people getting *in* — not someone trying to get *out*." His brassiness fails him. "Look, there isn't a day I don't think about that padlocked gate, don't wish it had never happened."

What did happen was that armed robbers broke into the Bass Station in November 2001, half an hour after closing. It was still doing good numbers back then, even if it was attracting a seedier, druggier clientele than when it first opened as town's hottest nightspot two years earlier. When the robbers couldn't get into the time-delay safe, they took it out on the manager, Odi's business partner, Jayan Kurian, and a bartender, Precious Ncobo, who was helping him lock up. They tried to escape through the emergency exit, but in violation of fire-safety regs, the gate was locked. They were shot in cold blood.

"It was a terrible shock. That these men could just break in and do this to me? To me! I didn't feel safe. I couldn't cope. I just quit. Walked away. Right out of the business. I was finished with it." He looks over the mixing-desk at the recording rooms beyond, his face reflected on the soundproofed glass. "The doctors diagnosed PTSD."

Practically overnight, Odi disappeared from the music scene and removed himself from society. He locked himself in the house, spiraling into depression and illness. There were rumors of cancer, even AIDS. Certainly, the photographs of him back then, in his studio with a fresh-faced Lily Nobomvu, show a man wasting away.

"Lily was my angel, my saving grace," Huron says. It's no secret that the music side of Odi's business had been faltering since the mid-'90s. "The club was too distracting. The Hillbrow scene was rough. Gangsters and drugs and gun-running — and the gay scene and the sex that was going on, everyone sleeping with everyone else. I lost focus. The music suffered."

Lily was the turning point for Odi. After two years of "rattling around in here, feeling sorry for myself," he reinvented himself and adopted a new "life mantra" — his life philosophy. "I decided no interference. No drugs. No alcohol. Clean living," Odi says. "Good music that would reach out to people, touch them here, in their souls," he puts a hand on the back of his head. "People want things that stick. They're looking for something spiritual. They're hungry for that."

He discovered someone who could sate that hunger through one of his talent scouts: a single-mother church chorister from Alexandra township. Lily Nobomvu made her debut in February 2003, with "Kingdom Heart," a solidly built, catchy single that didn't pick up much airplay, but sold lots of CDs out of car boots. Odi persisted, pushing the gospel angle at a time when *kwaito* was ruling the charts.

In the wake of Brenda Fassie's fatal overdose in 2004, he positioned Lily as the pure alternative to the fast life of sex and drugs and disco soul that had claimed the "Madonna of the Townships." She went platinum within the month.

But on 18 June 2006, two years and two albums later, Lily drove her car off a bridge. She was only thirty. The rumors of depression emerged only afterwards. "What can I tell you?" Huron says. "It was a shock. It's not that we didn't know, it's that we didn't know how bad it was. This industry eats boys and girls in different ways."

Lily's nineteen-year-old daughter, Asonele Nobomvu, recently hired as the fresh design talent for the hip-hop-inspired fashion label Lady-B, feels differently. "[Huron] pushed her too hard," she said in a recent interview with the *Sunday Times*. "He was desperate for her to be the next Brenda, but how could she live up to that?"

The bereaved daughter is not Odi's only detractor. Moro, who defected to Sony BMG in 2007, pulled no punches when asked about the man he once described as his mentor. "The man's got expectations a mile high. He doesn't let up, you're in that recording studio night and day, and he's just sucking it up. He's obsessive is what it is. All that time in that big old house on his own, the dying and shit? He needs to catch a wake-up, live a little, is what I'm saying."

Odi scoffs at the advice. "What do you think I'm doing?" And it's true that things are happening for the once and future hit-maker. Whatever illness was dragging him down seems to be in remission, and he's got big things planned for the twins. "They're going to be bigger than Michael Jackson!"

And as part of his comeback, he's just opened a new club, Counter Revolutionary. It's all been done sight unseen, but he's quick to point out that he approved the architectural drawings and signed off on every decision, down to "what kind of flusher to put on the shitters."

True to form, the new venue is already drawing a lot of press for the controversial decision to feature animalled dancers. Odi grins as he talks about three separate concerned citizens' groups that have protested outside the club, drummed up Facebook petitions, and inundated the newspapers with complaints. It's a provocative move, but then, as Odi says cheekily, "Everyone deserves a second chance."

He's also started getting counseling from a psychiatrist who comes by twice a week to help him deal with the crippling fear that has kept him a recluse these long years.

"Give us a few months to figure out the right medication, and maybe I'll even see you on the dance floor.

"You ready to hear this?" he says, turning towards the mixing desk. He cranks the volume and hits "play" on the file called "Driveby." It's an irresistibly catchy head-bopper of a song, sweet and fizzy with dips into a dirty, grungy hip-hop beat on the chorus. Songweza is right. It's going to be massive. And so is Odi, once again.

Like Noxx raps in the remix of Moro's classic "Cul-de sac": *Eye on the ball, ma'gents, eye on the ball . . .*

173

iJusi headline the Mzansi Unite stage on Saturday, featuring HHP, Joz'll (featuring Da Les, Ishmael, and Tasha Baxter), Lira, PondoLectro, and R&B/ pop sensation JonJon (guest slots by Mandoza and Danny K), with DJs Chillibite, Tzozo, Jullian Gomes, and MP6-60. The World in Union stage features Mix n' Blend, Krushed n' Sorted, Animal Chin, Spoek Mathambo, Dank, and HoneyB.

(Grand Parade Fan Park, gates @ 4 pm for big-screen game; concert 7 pm; tickets WebTickets .co.za)

16.

MY NEW RIDE is a '78 Ford Capri in burnt orange and good nick, apart from a few rust spots and a nasty scratch on the passenger door. It's not the only one that's a little rusty. I haven't driven in three years and the car handles like a shopping trolley on Rohypnol.

Huron's heavy, James, handed over the keys without a word. Didn't bother to reply when I asked for the spare key. Wasn't there to help when it took me five tries to get the engine to turn over with a strangled choke, followed by a bout of spluttering and finally a sickly roar.

*With 22 years' experience in treating addictive behaviors and other compulsive disorders, **Haven** provides a multidisciplinary approach, including counseling, the 12-step program and cognitive behavioral therapy.*

*A residential facility set on a tranquil and secluded country estate near the Cradle of Humankind, **Haven** provides a safe and supportive environment in which to reclaim your sense of self.*

I take a drive out to Hartbeespoort Dam, that favorite watery weekend getaway for landlocked city dwellers. The urban sprawl thins out as the road deteriorates; kitmodel cluster homes, malls, and the fake Italian maestro-work that is the casino give way to B&Bs, stables, ironwork furniture factories, and country restaurants. The hawkers selling giant plastic mallets and naïve Tanzanian banana-leaf paintings and the guys handing out flyers advertising new townhouse complexes get increasingly pushy as the spaces between traffic lights grow longer. A grizzled bush mechanic sits under a corrugated-iron lean-to, rolling a cigarette and looking out for customers attracted by the badly hand-painted sign propped up outside advertising exhaust fittings. A tea garden proclaims itself HOME OF THE ORIGINAL CHICKEN PIE! And then civilization falls away. The road narrows to one lane and opens out into dusty yellow grasslands and farms cordoned off with electric fences under a ferociously blue sky, with puffy white cumulus clouds already threatening a late-afternoon thunderstorm.

I nearly miss the turnoff to Haven, despite the very specific directions I was supplied with when I phoned to lie about setting up interviews for a nonexistent story on the rise of rehab safaris for *Mach* magazine.

"After the sign to the lion park, turn right onto a dirt road. You'll see the sign," the warmly professional male receptionist had said. It would help if the name Haven was not one of nine small, precisely lettered arrows on a discreet sign pole, including the Shongolo Hunting Lodge, Moyo Spa, Vulindlela Country Hotel, and the Grassy Park Country Living Estate.

After doubling back (twice), I finally spot the sign and pull up at an intimidating black gate framed by electric fencing. I buzz the intercom and give my name. The gate slides open— Sim Sala Bim. I drive up the dirt road, if "drive" is the right word for what I'm doing with the Capri, which is behaving like a rhinoceros on roller skates spoiling for a fight. I compensate by accelerating, kicking up billows of dust behind the car as it skids through the corners, past a copse of trees and a blue satiny wedge of dam with cormorants in the reeds.

I barrel round the bend and a sprawling farmhouse comes into view. It's repurposed rustic chic: stables and warehouses converted to dormitories, judging by the neat rows of windows hemmed by sunny yellow curtains. There is an aloe garden in front, being tended by a twentysomething in denim overalls, her hair in cocky little twists. She looks up, shielding her eyes from the morning sun, and waves me towards an acacia tree and a row of white lines in the gravel that mark out the visitors' parking. I pull in between a Bentley in racing green and a white minivan with tinted windows and HAVEN stenciled on the side.

As I crunch up the drive, the girl gravitates towards Sloth, holding out a piece of succulent.

"Hi, Munchkin," she says in a baby voice. "Oh, he's so cute." Sloth leans forward to sniff the aloe leaf. He takes a tentative bite, leaving a smear of milky sap on his chin fur, and scrunches his nose at the bitter taste. "Aloe's really good for the skin," the girl says. "We also grow indigenous herbs and organic veggies in the fields out back."

"No cheeseburger stand?"

The girl restrains a smirk. Her lost things are like a halo of dandelion fluff. "So are you inmate or rubbernecker?" she asks.

"Rubbernecker," I answer without hesitation. "You?"

"I'm a screw. Or on staff, anyway. Used to be an inmate. Repeat offender. Crimes against my body. Puking sickness followed by heroin, which led to more puking sickness." I'd be surprised at her forthrightness, but that's addicts for you. The twelve steps crack 'em open and then they can't shut up.

"You should grow hoodia," I suggest. "Isn't that a healthier way to suppress your appetite?"

"More natural definitely," Overshare Girl agrees, "although I've never really got that argument. I mean, puff adder venom is natural. Dying of gum disease at thirty is natural. You know why the Khoi used hoodia in the first place? So they could pretend they weren't starving to death. How's that for messed up?"

"Pretty messed up." I push her a little to see what comes out. "This a good place?"

"'S okay. High on the spoiled little rich kids and schleb factor, but you only really catch the brunt of it when you're on the other side. But the food is good. Organic. You got a cigarette on you?"

"Sorry, I tend to bum off other people. Anyone interesting?"

"Schleb-wise? That British Big Brother star—the Pakistani girl? Melanie whassisface? She's really sweet. Not what you'd expect at all. She says they just made her look like a major-league bitch in the edit. Um. Some big-shot politician's son.

Minister of Parking, or whatever. Some people just do their time, you know?"

"You just doing your time?"

"Sure. It's in the coding, right? It's funny, 'cos I used to be really big-time into astrology. Had a woman I used to see like once a month, sometimes twice. She was cool, even though I think she was making it up half the time. But I really wanted to believe that there were these magic celestial bodies that would direct my life, tell me what to do, and it turns out it's not stars, it's some bits of screwy DNA. I'm just meat with faulty programming."

"That's why you've chosen to stick around?"

"That gate you came through? It's like a revolving door. You go out, you come back in. Might take years, might take hours. It's inevitable. They tell you this stuff about cognitive behavior and about breaking the pattern and being mindful. All I'm hearing is that there's no such thing as free will."

"They give you a rough time?"

She shrugs. "Some rougher than others."

"I have a friend who was here, S'bu? He doesn't even like to talk about it."

"S'bu Radebe? He was a sweetie. But really shy. He had a really hard time. Kid from the sticks. I mean, he shouldn't have been in here in the first place, even Veronique said, and he was having to listen to all these hardcore addicts talk about the bad shit they'd done, prostituting themselves, abandoning their kids—"

Killing their brothers, I add to the list, but only in my

head. What comes out of my mouth is: "He shouldn't have been in here?"

"*Ag,* you know. Issues are like weeds. Everyone's got them. You can pull them up, you can poison them, eventually they'll just grow back. S'bu's too sensitive for the world. He just needs to toughen up a little and he'll be fine. His sister, though? She was nuts."

"Aren't we all?"

"Her and the boyfriends. *Hei wena.*"

"You mean like Jabu?"

"Excuse me? Hi there! Can I help you?" I recognize the warmly professional voice I spoke to on the phone.

"I'd like to carry on talking to you," I say to the girl, as the husky man in a checked shirt and an earnest smile starts walking over. "Chat later?"

"Doubt it. The inmates are going on a day trip and I'm driving." She blows Sloth a kiss. "Bye, cutie!"

The receptionist leads me into the cool interior of the farm-house. Whoever decorated has decent taste in art or, quite possibly, psychedelics. The reception area has wooden floors half-covered by a cheerful orange, red, and blue woven rug. There is a print of Technicolor lunatic smiley flowers hanging above the hotel-style reception desk.

In front of the desk two cream-and-gold suitcases mono-grammed all over with distinctive LVs are parked beside an oversized couch half-occupied by a boy who sighs dramatically and reposes himself, jiggling his foot impatiently.

"I'll be right with you," says my guide, over his shoulder to the boy, ushering me down the corridor and through to an office marked DR. VERONIQUE AUERBACH— EXECUTIVE DIRECTOR on the door, together with the admonition PLEASE KNOCK.

He ignores this, flinging the door open to reveal the lady in question sitting tucked into the bay window that overlooks the garden, reading a magazine.

"Oh good," she says, slipping into her shoes and standing to greet me. I catch a glimpse of the cover of the magazine. *Mental Health & Substance Abuse Dual Diagnosis*. A glance at the bookshelf built into the hollow base of the window seat reveals similar numbingly academic titles. There is a heavy wooden desk stacked with a scramble of papers and files encroaching on a slim silver laptop at the center of it all, like the eye of the hurricane. Above the desk is a painting of a Zulu hut on fire, a deep phallic root extending into the ground and figures writhing around inside in torment.

"Heavy reading," I say as she shakes my hand. She has a grip like a pro golfer, loose, but in total control.

"Homework," she replies with an easy grin that furrows lines around her eyes. She's short, barely five foot in her heels and black trouser suit, but there is a sharp curiosity in her eyes that goes with her chin—the kind that jabs into other people's business. She has a calico pixie cut, russet streaked with gray. I get the impression she's the art buyer. It's the shoes. Teal-blue Mary Janes with playful detailing—purple and red flowers perched on the straps.

"I'm Veronique, obviously. Thank you so much for coming out."

As if I was the one doing her the favor.

"Thanks for accommodating me at such short notice."

"It's a catchy headline. Rehab safaris. Makes it sound so glamorous."

"It's all about the hook."

"Mandla Langa," she says noticing my interest in the burning hut. "His early stuff was all circumcision-related. It's about culture and tradition, rites of passage, the difficulties of being a man. And also being mutilated."

"Do your clients relate?"

"We call them patients. But, yes, I suppose some of them do. C'mon, I'll give you the tour." She's all brisk enthusiasm.

"I'd say about fifteen to twenty percent of our patients are foreign," Veronique says. Like a good journalist, I dutifully take notes. "A lot of them are from the UK. It's a last resort for the families—that old attitude of 'send the troublemakers to the colonies!' But we also get people coming in from Nigeria, Angola, Zimbabwe. Naisenya, the young woman you were talking to outside, is Kenyan for example. Mostly, it's a matter of money. Three months with us costs the same as a week in a UK treatment center like the Abbey."

She opens the door onto a spacious lounge with chairs arranged in a loose arc, facing a huge open fireplace—big enough to cook children in. Above the mantelpiece is a mounted Perspex light, featuring a naïve drawing of a cocky gentleman devil smoking a pipe, reclining in an armchair. On the opposite wall is a dreamy etching of a goat with its head bowed and a chain around its neck.

"Between the devil and the deep blue scapegoat?" I say.

"It's just art, Ms. December," she says, not meaning a word of it. "The most important part of what we do here is penetrating people's denial systems, removing the alibis that will trip them up."

"Sending their sins out into the wilderness to die."

"It's one of the theories of being animalled, of course," she says.

"I never liked that one. Give me the Toxic Reincarnation theory any day."

"I don't think I'm familiar with that."

"It's very now. Global warming, pollution, toxins, BPA from plastics leaching into the environment has disrupted the spiritual realm or whatever you want to call it, so, if you're Hindu, and you go through some terrible trauma, part of your spirit breaks away and returns as the animal you were going to be reincarnated as."

"What do *you* think about it?" I'm aware of her standing very still, all the better to psychoanalyze me.

"Does the therapy session come free with the tour?"

"Sorry, it's habituated. I'll stop." She holds up her hands in mock defeat.

"We were talking about art, I believe? The light is Conrad Botes and Brett Murray. The scapegoat is Louisa Betteridge."

"It's an upgrade from the rehab facility I went to. The only art we had was graffiti drawn on the toilet walls."

"Was that in prison? I've always wanted to do a prison program. We run an outreach project in Hillbrow, you know. We do good work. A lot of aposymbiots. You should visit."

"Maybe I will," I smile thinly to make it clear that this will happen when hell turns into a family-friendly summer resort. "Same deal?"

"Same tactics, different strategy. This isn't a broken leg, it's a long-term recovery. You don't want to do a story on that, do you? Make some noise? We've got some sponsors involved in our Hillbrow project, but it's difficult."

"Not really in my brief, sorry. I can pitch it for next time, maybe."

"I understand. Come, I'll show you the dorms."

We pass through the courtyard where a bunch of crazily beautiful boys and girls are lolling, smoking, and chatting. There is a high ratio of killer cheekbones per capita.

"You obviously get a lot of models," I say, walking up a flight of stairs to the dorm floor. Two beds to a room. They're bright and cheery and rich in personal detail.

"Also musicians. DJs. Journalists. Advertising people. There are certain lifestyles where high-risk behavior is endemic to the culture."

"Any names I'd recognize?"

"We take our privacy policy very seriously, Ms. December. I hope you're not fishing for some celebrity scandal. I didn't take you for a tabloid journalist." Unfortunately, that's one step *up* from what I actually am.

I decide not to ask her about Song or S'bu directly. Instead

I show her the contents of my folded-up tissue—the dried herbs I found in Song's bathroom.

"Actually, do you mind if I ask you what this is?"

She takes a pinch between her fingers and sniffs it. "I'm not the herb expert, but I'd guess African wormwood? It's very commonly used for cleansing, both by naturopaths and in traditional purification rituals. Some of our patients are into more alternative treatments."

"But you're not?"

"I like good old-fashioned medicine. Methadone is a very good thing. Although a lot of medication is based on herbal remedies. And you shouldn't discount the power of the placebo effect."

"Magic?"

"There haven't been enough studies to ease my mind about the efficacy."

I change tack, trying to circle back. "So what are the challenges?"

"With foreign patients? Language barriers, occasionally. The temptations of the exchange rate. It's very easy and very cheap to get drugs in Johannesburg. Not here, obviously. The problem comes afterwards, when they're in the third phase, out in the real world, staying at a halfway house."

"What about romance?" I fish.

"Sex addiction, you mean?"

"I was talking more about hookups."

"Totally inappropriate, of course. We try to discourage it. I say that because often it's a way of finding a substitute high, something else to latch onto, which ultimately doesn't help the patient."

"But it happens."

"It blooms like wildflowers. It's a very vulnerable time. Patients can form intense bonds that won't survive the fresh air of the real world. You're a recovering addict, so you would know. People can be very manipulative. They can end up enabling each other, falling back into old habits. And even if they don't, most of the relationships don't last in the world out there."

"Any chance I could speak to some of your clie—er, patients? Like Naisenya?"

"I'd be happy to set up some interviews for you. If you'd like to leave me with your card?" She holds out her hand.

I pretend to scruffle in my wallet. "Oh, hey. Fresh out."

17.

Masks of Existence: The Demystification of Shadow-self Absorption

ABSTRACT

This paper presents a case for the demystification of counseling approaches for Aposymbiot individuals who exhibit psychic trauma associated with fear of the phenomenon known psychologically as shadow-self absorption and commonly as the "Undertow."

While acknowledgement must be given to religious organizations and lay therapists and their work with Aposymbiot individuals, psychologists cannot ignore the continuing religious stigmatization of Aposymbiots within society and within the therapeutic community itself. Therapists who themselves, either tacitly or (in rare cases) overtly, subscribe to the idea of Aposymbiots as "animalled" or "zoos" and shadow-self absorption as "Hell's Undertow" or "The Black Judgment" perpetuate this stigmatization and very often fail to see the very real trauma that Aposymbiots

187

experience as a result of lifelong anticipation of shadow-self absorption.

This trauma, most often experienced as an irrefutable and ever-increasing sense of oblivion, commonly manifests as an intense obsession with self-annihilation, acted out through extreme hedonism and criminal behavior, or as a sexualized fetish with self-destruction, as in the well-documented bacchanalia of cults such as the Blood for Severance group, who engage in mass culling of their own animals to actively invoke the terror and rapture of shadow-self absorption.

While the sensationalism of animal sex and death has provoked the media into ever-increasing coverage of the exoticism of "zoos," society has largely ignored the true meaning of these acts: a desperate rallying cry from Aposymbiots who wish to take charge of their own existence rather than waiting to be led like the proverbial lamb, duck, or llama to the divine slaughter.

Clinicians have a responsibility to heed these calls and to change their approach to a more objective, empathetic, and scientific understanding of shadow-self absorption, one that will ultimately result in the delivery of more effective forms of treatment.

Current scientific thought tends toward an understanding of the "Undertow" as a quantum manifestation of non-existence, a psychic equivalent of dark matter that indeed serves as a counterpoint to, and bedrock for, the principle of existence. The process of shadow-self absorption is, in fact, such an integral part of life as we know it, that in *Dark Matter, Black*

Judgment (2005), physicist Nareem Jazaar states: "were intelligent life to be found elsewhere in the universe, it would be impossible to imagine that society without some form of the Undertow."

This type of understanding of the "Undertow," not as divine judgement but rather as a necessary part of the fabric of the physical universe, can only serve to relieve Aposymbiot individuals of the intense burden of guilt they often carry.

Van Meer & Reeves et al. (2002) in fact document robust differences in behavioral function between religious and secular Aposymbiot groups and their response to therapy. In the course of their two-year study, the religious group showed markedly increased levels of guilt, aggression, and suicidal ideation when compared to the secular and control groups.

Such studies form the basis for a shift in the clinical and ethical framework with which therapists, and ultimately society as a whole, approach Aposymbiot interaction.

18.

VUYO INSISTS ON meeting me at Kaldi's coffee shop in New-town, the funkified art, theater, design, and fashion capital of the inner city. They burned this neighborhood down in the early 1900s to prevent the spread of bubonic plague, and it occurs to me that they should consider doing it again, to purge the blight of well-meaning hipsters desperately trying to paint it rainbow. I should really try to be less cynical.

I squeeze between the tables packed with actors, dancers, trendy new media folk, BEE venture capitalists in suits with no ties, and capitalist wannabes (also in suits, but *with* ties) who have the ambition but not the office space, and come to use Kaldi's free Wi-Fi.

Vuyo is late. I check my emails on my phone and eavesdrop on the actorly bunch at the next table who are having a very heated and apparently hilarious debate about a proposed smackdown between David Mamet and Athol Fugard. Then again, they could be rehearsing lines from a play about the same.

There are another 312 responses to Eloria, including one from a French journalist who wants to do a story, is desperate to fly to DRC right away to meet. Vuyo would milk him for visa application fees, maybe even try to convince him to set up an emergency fund to help evacuate Eloria. I quietly delete it.

There is also another strangely anomalous message. Again, no return address. Maybe it is time to put up that firewall.

You said you would love me warts and all.

I forward the message to my personal address to add to the other one and nearly get bust by Vuyo, who has slipped into the chair opposite me. "Anything interesting?" he asks. He does not apologize for being late.

"Admin," I say.

He orders a black americano and waits for the waitress to leave before launching straight in.

"If someone has *the item* you're looking for, we don't know about it," Vuyo says. "But that item would be hard to miss. Hard to hide. You would have to be stupid."

"Bad things can happen even to famous people."

"Ah, but then someone would have to care. There is an insurance policy on that name, paid for by Moja Records. One point five."

"As in million?"

"And on the matching item. They come as a pair?"

"Twins tend to. Okay, what about the MXit account?"

"Sorry. Couldn't get in."

"What kind of slacker hackers are you using?"

"Hackers are Eastern Bloc scammers. The Company relies

on good old-fashioned African business as taught to us by our colonial masters."

"Bribery and corruption?"

"So much more efficient."

"And the phone?"

"Yes, my friend at Vodacom looked it up for me for a small fee. That phone number hasn't made or received a call since Sunday 20th 02h36."

"Do you have a record of what number was dialed?"

"That will cost you extra. Luckily, I anticipated that you would want this." He slides over a piece of paper folded in half. "One more thing," he says, before releasing the piece of paper. "You should see a friend of mine. At Mai Mai. Dumisani Ndebele. A *sangoma*. He might be able to help you in other ways."

"Am I paying extra for this as well?"

"Open the paper."

I unfold the note. There is an eleven-digit sharecall number. Underneath it is a handwritten scrawl that takes me a moment to decipher. It reads: "Hani Luxury Estates Format" and "Play along."

"What the——" I start to say, but Vuyo is already standing to greet the sweaty Japanese salaryman with a briefcase handcuffed to his wrist who has been directed to our table by the waitress.

"Ah, Mr. Tagawa," Vuyo says, turning the charm all the way up to eleven, "I hope you're not too jet-lagged. This is my investment partner, Lebo Hani, daughter of the great communist leader. But don't worry, she's a hundred percent capitalist. Don't mind the animal."

"You really are something." Gio's voice on the other end of the line is a combo of admiring and pissed off.

"Hello yourself."

"So, I just had this call."

"Uh-huh."

"Dr. Veronique Auerbach. About *Mach*'s journalist? Confirming that she's lined up some interviews for you. If you're actually doing a story, that is. She seemed skeptical. Suspicious even."

"Yeah, I'm in the middle of typing up my pitch. Sex, drugs, jet-set travel."

"I wouldn't have minded. Much. I mean, why would I expect anything less of you?" Gio says. The malice in his voice is justified. After all, I am the girl who stole his ATM card and eight grand out of his bank account, and blamed it on the cleaner.

"Only she didn't speak to me, she spoke to Montle, my editor. And I had to do a shitload of explaining. So, congratulations."

"I got the job?"

"Almost at the cost of mine. Helluva way to pitch an assignment, Zee. I need 1600 words in my inbox by April 23rd. Get some dirt, please. Something sexy."

"I'm all about the sexy dirt."

"And the reverse, if memory serves. So, what happens with the Sloth when you have sex?"

"You want a matching bite somewhere else?"

"Kinky," he says, but I can tell he's still simmering. "Maybe you can show me sometime. Laters, sweets. I gotta go."

"Yeah, me too," I say, turning the Capri in a lazy arc under the highway and into Anderson Street and the parking lot of Mai Mai.

The healer's market is less popular than Faraday, which is conveniently close to a major taxi rank. It looks like a cheap tourist attraction from the outside, with its mud-colored walls and the spread of herbs drying in the sunshine on the pavement outside the main entrance. Under a thatched deck, a man crouches on his haunches in front of a little urn on top of an open fire, wafting pungent smoke across the parking lot. A German tourist emerges from the toilets, forgetting to zip up his fly, and stops to talk to the guy carving up pieces of old tire to make sandals.

The sky has taken on that bright translucent quality that preempts a thunderstorm. The air pressure has changed. There are clouds rolling in on the horizon, cumulonimbuses that weigh down on the city. My mom used to insist we covered up the mirrors during storms to avoid drawing the lightning, scrambling round the house with towels and sheets at the first sign of a puffy cloud. It drove my dad crazy. "Superstitious rubbish," he always said, sticking his nose back in his cinematography books. "This is what's holding the continent back." He was always way too narrow about his definitions of what modern Africa meant.

We never were hit by lightning. But all my mom's precautions—slaughtering a goat for the ancestors in thanksgiving for the birth of Thando's kid, the ceremony when I got my matric results, the stupid sheets over the mirrors—none of it helped a damn against bullets.

As I get out of the car, a skinny boy, somewhere between twelve and nineteen, gets up from the shade of a scraggly eucalyptus tree at the edge of the parking lot and darts over, already hard-selling: "Lady, hey lady, look after your car, nice, lady. You want a car wash, lady?" He has buggy yellow eyes and an old knife scar in his hairline, like a side-parting. Sloth shrinks away from his breath.

"Not today, thanks."

"Cheap for you, sister! Special price!"

"Next time, my friend." He starts to slink back to his tree, where he's obviously sleeping rough. There is a tarpaulin precariously strung over the lower branches and a pile of rubble backing up against one of the highway support pillars. I can see the shadows of others huddled inside. "Wait, kid. Do you know where I can find Baba Ndebele?"

Yellow Eyes perks up immediately and prances towards the entrance. "This way, my sister. Come with me. I show you."

The square arch opens onto rows of red brick houses with ivy climbing the walls and a mix of equal parts flowers and weeds growing in planters. A black chicken scavenges between the bricks for crumbs. A woman in a white-and-red sarong with Zulu shields and beads crisscrossing her chest like bandoliers glares from a doorway, although I'm not sure whether it's at me or at the sickly boy.

There is a grisly *wunderkammer* in every window, hanging in every doorway. Tortoise shells, a wildebeest skull with a broken horn, shriveled twists of dead animal or plant matter, it's hard to say, and drifts of magic, like a static hum in the air, a harmony to the drone of traffic on the highway above. Sloth hides his head against the back of my neck.

"Here, my lady, in here," the boy says. I tip him with a five-rand coin and Yellow Eyes claps his hands together in a horribly servile gesture, waits to see me in, and then lopes down the alleyway, swiping at the black chicken with his foot as he goes past.

I step into a doorway of a tiny waiting-room-cum-apothecary. A woman sits sewing on a narrow bench. She gives me an incurious once-over and returns to her needlework without comment. The room is lined with shelves crammed with cloudy glass jars of unidentified substances. There are dried herbs hanging from the ceiling, twisting slightly in the breeze from a fan in the corner of the ceiling, cable-tied to the burglar bars of the window to keep it upright. The blades witter and creak like an asthma attack. There is a curtain drawn across an inner doorway.

"*Sawubona,* Mama, I've come to see Baba Ndebele," I say to the needlework woman. She puts her finger to her lips and looks at me out the sides of her eyes, then returns to sewing. She is embroidering beads onto an orange-and-white skirt. I sit down beside her and wait. A fly buzzes in an invisible rhomboid flight path, continually readjusting the pattern, an insect mathematician calculating geometries. Outside, a few doors down, a woman laughs brightly and then returns to a conversational murmur. The traffic takes on the rhythmic shush of a low tide, occasionally interrupted by the *brut-brut-brut* of a motorcycle or the roar of an exhaust with a hole in it. The fan judders abruptly, as if about to rattle itself right out of its jimmied mounting, then settles back into its asthma. And the woman sews, threading beads onto the skirt one at a time. I pull Sloth into my lap and lean my head against the cool wall. 281 alligator. 342 alligator. 719 alligator. 953 alligator.

I startle awake as a young woman emerges from behind the curtain. She is wearing a headband with a beaded fringe in front and a dried goat's gallbladder hanging behind. Red and white beads are wrapped across her chest and round her ankles and wrists. She is pretty, with dark blond hair that curls up at her shoulders, but her face is carefully blank. She kneels in the doorway, stands again, bows, and holds the curtain aside for me to enter. The sewing woman is gone. I nudge Sloth. He murmurs grumpily and tries to nuzzle into my lap to go back to sleep. "Come on, buddy," I say, poking him in his ribs. "We're up." My head feels hangover-muzzy, and as I stand up, the world reels away from me for a moment. It's either the incoming storm or the goddamn magic.

I swing Sloth onto my back and press a two-rand coin into the young woman's hand, because *thwasa* are not allowed to speak to you until you give them something silver. It could be tinfoil, but it's generally accepted that money is better for appeasing the ancestors, even when dealing with an initiate.

"Take off your shoes, please," she says and I slip out of my sandals and step into the consulting room. There is a sharp smell of *imphepho*—burning herbs.

"This is Baba Dumisani Ndebele, *sangoma*," the young woman says, indicating the huge man built like a pro rugby player kneeling on a reed mat in the center of the cement floor. He is wearing a white vest and a red apron, with a leopard skin tied over it and a matching leopard band across his forehead. His head is shaved and shiny with sweat. It is much hotter in here without the fan. I notice there's a D&G logo on his vest, so subtle as to be the real *makhoya*. Fong Kong goods tend to shout their fake logos as loud as they can. So much for the simple life of serving the spirits of the ancestors.

"*Thokoza khehla,*" I say in greeting to the spirits, more out of some residual deference to my mother than anything I might feel myself.

"*Thokoza,*" Dumisani replies and sneezes several times. "My *dlozi* has told me about you." He waggles his cell phone, a brand new iPhone, significantly. "He tells you do not want to be here."

"I didn't know the ancestors were SMSing now."

"No, he calls me. The spirits find it easier with technology. It's not so clogged as human minds." He taps his head for emphasis. "They still like rivers and oceans most of all, but data is like water—the spirits can move through it. That's why you get a prickly feeling around cell phone towers."

"And here I thought it was the radiation." I know I'm being disrespectful, but I can't resist. "So is there a spirit world

MTN? What are the tariffs like? I bet you get a lot of 'please call me's.'"

"*Hayibo, sisi*. So cynical and you with a *shavi*. What would your mother say?"

I flinch. Lucky guess.

"My *dlozi* says you will need a reading. The *amathambo* will help guide you."

The initiate says quietly, "Please put the money down on the mat. It's R500." I comply and the *thwasa* quietly withdraws from the room, letting the curtain fall closed behind her.

"Shame, *sisi*," Dumisani says. "It's because you carry your spirits with you. It's the state of the world, my sister. Seven billion people have a lot of ghosts. Sometimes they get lost. But spirits are heavy, *nè*? They weigh you down. You should cut your *shavi* loose."

"Very funny."

"No joke. There are ways it can be done. It's like soccer— you just need a substitute."

"Sloth has got me through okay so far, thanks. Can we do this?"

"I see you are a woman of action and forthrightness. Yes, we can *do* this. Please take these." He loads up my cupped palms with cowrie shells and stones, a chipped nautilus fossil, dominoes (one broken), a twist of white beads around a piece of wood, a bullet, an MTN pay-as-you-go SIM card—I guess it *is* the preferred network—and a tiny plastic figurine of an ugly purple monster with a shock of matted orange hair that might once have come in a Happy Meal.

"Now blow on your hands and throw them."

I just open my hands and let the contents fall. Dumisani looks irritated.

"You didn't do sports at school, hey?" He examines the constellation of objects, seriously. Sloth sneezes abruptly, once, twice, three times. The *sangoma* announces triumphantly, "You see, they are with us!"

I smile, but I'm thinking Sloth's propensity for discharging his nose is not so much a sign from the other side as a sign that the incense is getting up his snout. It must be obvious in my expression.

"You know, in my previous life I was an actuary," Dumisani says. "Audi S4. Four-bedroom house in Morningside, renovated. All the gadgets. Three different ladies I took care of, and they took care of me. Two children by different mothers. Private schools. Apartments. Cars. Then I got the call. In my heart, I mean, not on my phone. The *amadlozi* wouldn't leave me alone. *Hakking, hakking,* all the time. Like your neighbor's dog at three o'clock in the morning. These terrible dreams. The same one, over and over: my grandmother carrying a snake that climbed off her shoulders and walked up to me and entered my chest like a vagina. I got sick. So sick, my girlfriends thought it was AIDS. They left me, all of them. They were scared. I don't blame them. I lost forty kilos in two weeks. The skin was hanging off me like when you have bad liposuction. Trust me, one of my girlfriends had bad liposuction. It looks very ugly."

"What happened?" There is damp sweat pooling between

my shoulder blades and Sloth's belly fur. I want to shrug him off onto the floor, but I can tell by the way he's gripping my arms that he's not going anywhere.

"I stopped fighting it," Dumisani shrugs. "It's not so different, the statistical analysis, the number-crunching. It's just the same with the bones. It's knowing how to read them. Like here, you see." He turns over a white shell that has landed on one of the dominoes. It's the chipped tile, a blank and a three, with one dot dissected by the break.

"Now, this, this is bad luck. And here as well," he says, indicating the triangulation of the troll, the bullet, and the broken domino. "Very bad. There is a shadow on you."

"Trust me, I noticed." Sloth huffs, his breath hot against my ear. But really, I mean the Undertow. The inevitability of it is crushing. Sometimes I wake up in the night struggling to breathe, and my chest feels as crumpled as a car wreck. Maybe that's all your talent is for, a distraction to keep you preoccupied until the blackness comes rushing in.

"And here?" The *sangoma* nudges a fan-shaped shell with red striations with his finger. He seems impressed. "Whoo! Girl, either you have been messing with a very bad *umthakathi* or you're just a magnet for *imoya emibi*. I don't know if a chicken's going to do any good here. We might need a bull for *this*."

"I'm not really interested in sacrificing chickens or cows or witches or evil spirits or shadows. It's very simple. I'm looking for something. Vuyo said you could help me."

"Something? Or some*one*?" he asks slyly. "Because this

little stone over here," he rocks the bit of quartz backwards and forwards with his thumb, "says you're not being open with me."

"Some*one*," I agree, grudgingly.

"Two someones," he says, his finger darting between two practically identical smoothed bits of amber. "Is it twins? Twins are very powerful. In Zulu culture we used to kill one of the pair to kill the bad luck."

"Can I add humans to the no-sacrifice list?" But I'm impressed and a little bit shaken, and he knows it. I concede, "I'm sorry *baba,* I meant no disrespect to you or the *amadlozi.*"

He waves the apology away. "It doesn't matter to me what you mean or don't mean. Do you have anything belonging to these someones?"

"That's exactly my problem."

He holds up one finger with a quick little jerk. "One moment." He picks up his phone as if it's been ringing and pretends to answer it. "Yes, I know. Bloody cheeky. In her bag? *Ngiyabonga.*" He sandwiches the phone between his shoulder and his ear, as if he's still listening and taps his finger in the direction of my bag. "You have something in your bag that will help us."

"Is it perhaps my wallet?"

"*Hei.* If you don't want my help, *vaya.* Go."

"All right." I shake out the entrails of my bag, my own constellation of meaningful objects. Car keys. My notebook, stuffed with clippings on iJusi cut from music magazines and a Greyhound bus brochure on fares to Zimbabwe and

Botswana, both destinations en route to Kinshasa. Four cheap pens, only one of which is functional. My wallet, containing R1800, which is about R1300 more than it's seen in a long time. A lipstick (rose madder, matte, half-melted), Tic-Tac mints, S'bu's songbook, a crisp white business card (belonging to Maltese & Marabou), a pack of dented business cards held together by a hairband (belonging to me), a battered cigarette spilling crumbs of tobacco, crumpled sachets of artificial sweetener, spare change.

"Let's see," the *sangoma*'s shiny forehead accordions in furrows of concentration as, following whatever directions he's getting via his phone, he picks out the songbook and my notebook. "Good," he says. He shakes out the clippings and chucks the notebook aside. He shoves the phone in his pocket and then, holding the clippings and the songbook in one hand, he pulls out a Zippo lighter and flicks it open.

"What are you doing?" I grab for the songbook, but he yanks it away, holding it above his head as the corner of the pages starts to brown and curl in the licking flames.

"Helping you." The fire in his right hand has reached its height, flaring hot and bright and yellow, shedding burned pieces, like snowflakes, crisp around the edges. "You young people. No respect for your culture." A fragment drifts down: "Let's party, let's get together, *siyagruva,* baby, let's be free," a scorched society-page pic of Song and S'bu at the SAMA awards, posing in his'n'hers versions of a pinstriped suit with '80s-style braces and matching trilbies.

Dumisani yelps and flicks his fingers where the flame has

caught them. The scraps of paper fall to the reed mat among the strewn rubble and the contents of my bag, still burning. He whacks out the flames, then scrapes together the scraps and pieces, cupped in his hands.

His initiate enters, carrying a wooden pestle and mortar, already full of ground and reeking herbs, a tin cup, a syringe sealed in plastic and a two-liter plastic Coke bottle full of a viscous yellow liquid. She bows and retreats, and the *sangoma* funnels the burnt scraps through the V of his hands into the bowl of the mortar. He makes a big show of grinding them up. Then he passes me the syringe in its plastic pack.

"I will need some blood, please. Don't worry, it's perfectly sterile. Just a drop will do." But as I unwrap it and move to prick my finger, he motions for me to stop. "Not you. The animal."

Sloth retreats behind my back with a whimper.

"I can do it if you're scared," he offers, with a hint of impatience.

"No, it's all right. Come on, buddy, just a little prick."

Sloth extends his arm and turns his head away as I punch the needle into the thick skin of his forearm. It takes a second and then a bright bead of red wells up through his fur. The *sangoma* passes me a dried leaf, and I swipe up the blood and pass it back to him to be ground up in the mortar. Finally, he adds a thick glop of the milky yellow liquid, which is pus, mucus, or unpasteurized sour milk—I can't decide which is the worst possibility. I suppose it depends on the source. He pours it out into the tin mug.

"Muti?"

"Not for treatment. It's part of your diagnosis. Drink it."

I've drunk my share of dubious concoctions in my time, but I'm thinking more along the lines of nasty shooters. And there was the time I took a swig from a bottle of methylated spirits stolen from the art supplies storeroom when I was fifteen, but we won't get into that or the vomiting that followed. "If you think I'm drinking *that,* you're insane."

"You need to stop fighting," he says, and bashes the tin cup against my mouth so hard I cut my lip against my teeth. As I gasp in shock, some of the foulness washes down my throat. It is warm and slimy and bitter and sweet, like crushed maggots that have been feeding on rotten sewer rat. Like shit and death and decay. Sloth slides from my back, suddenly limp as a sack of drowned kittens. I drop forward onto all fours, heaving and gagging, but coughing up only long strings of spit. And then the convulsions start.

I am three years old, sitting in the park eating those small pink flowers that grow in the clover. They are unbearably sour and I shudder every time I mash one up between my teeth. And pluck another one to do it again. Thando falls off the slide. I am only peripherally aware of this, I am so intent on chewing up the sour little flowers. He runs up to show me his skinned knee with pride. Blood runs down his leg, sticky like honey.

There is a man with plastic gloves and a face mask picking out globs of brain and pieces of Thando's skull from the daisy bush.

The absence of my parents at the trial. When I try to call them from the prison pay phone, the electronic blips monitoring how many seconds I have left before my money runs out also count down the silence stretching between us.

Pacing outside the ambulance entrance to Charlotte Maxeke's ER, smoking ferociously, practically chewing up the cigarettes. So absorbed in the loop of please-don't-be-dead-please-don't-be-dead and still high, I don't notice the shadows starting to drop from trees and axles and other dark places and coagulating. Slime mold does the same thing in the right conditions: it masses together to form one giant community with a single-minded intent. Only slime mold isn't accompanied by a howling sucking smacking sound like the sky tearing at an airplane. Slime mold doesn't come for you, to drag you down into the dark.

I am laughing and swearing as Thando — always the fucking white knight — drags me down the stairs of Belham Luxury Apartments, which were never luxury and barely apartments. Some of the other junkies watch blearily from their doorways, but can't be arsed to intervene. The others can't be arsed to even look. Like my parents can't be arsed to get involved, not after all my prior offenses.

"Leave me the fuck alone!" I laugh and then scream and rail and kick and flail as my brother shoves me into the shiny new VW Polo that came with his shiny new promotion. "Why can't you just leave me——"

Songweza painting her nails purple in her anonymous bedroom. When she is finished, she spreads her legs and paints narrow stripes, like cuts, down the inside of her thigh.

The World Trade Center. Only the planes wheeling round the twin towers have dark feathers streaked with white, and long sharp beaks.

Afterwards, the daisy bush retains the impression of the impact of Thando's body. I am expecting a cartoon, a perfect Wile E. Coyote silhouette with arms thrown up in surprise. But it is just a crushed bush. Broken branches. Bruised and torn leaves. Stains on white petals as if from a rusty rain.

Where are your parents? the lady in the supermarket says, leaning on her knees to talk to me. She has kind eyes but her name badge reads Murderer! Murderer! Murderer! When my parents walk outside the ER entrance to find me, to tell me, gripping each other like gravity has fallen away and they are trying to find a new way to navigate the world, they see I already know. I am sitting on the pavement in the red-and-blue strobe of an ambulance light, shaking and making hiccupping gagging sounds of terror. Sloth is clutching my chest, his arms around my shoulders like a Judas hug. The Undertow deferred only for the moment. But not before I feel the dry heat of its breath.

The Tsotsis performing on stage in their Mzekezeke ski masks. They pull off the masks. They are all Songweza. Then they pull off their faces.

An email. Year, make, and model number. License and registration. Time and address. I don't feel guilty. Insurance will pay out for the car. I'll be settled with my dealer. Hijackings happen every day. I don't count on the white knight.

I am splashing through puddles in our garden, wearing my red-and-black spotty ladybug galoshes with smiley insect faces on the toes. There are pink flamingoes in the puddles, like a documentary I once saw on the Etosha Pans. Or was it Okavango? I dash forward in delight, windmilling my arms and shouting to get them to take fright / flight. Only the next puddle is not a puddle, and it swallows me whole. As I sink, I look up to the surface and I realize they were not flamingoes at all. And something is pulling me down.

19.

BIBLIOZOOLOGIKA: AN ENTYMOLOGY OF
ANIMALLED TERMS

M

Mashavi—a Southern African word (spec.
Shona) used to describe both the preternatural
talents conferred by an aposymbiot and the
aposymbiot animal itself.

The term first appeared in print in 1979 as "mashave" in an
unrelated text (*Myths and Legends of Southern Africa* by Penny
Miller, published by TV Bulpin, Cape Town) that nevertheless reflects today's common usage and meaning in contem-
porary Southern Africa.

"The *mashave* are spirits of foreigners, or of wanderers who
died far away from their families and clans and did not re-
ceive a proper burial. Owing to this, they were never 'called
home,' but continued to roam restlessly through the bush.
Homeless spirits like these are feared because they are always

on the watch for a living host in whom to reside; as the spirit of a wanderer cannot go back to the land of his ancestors, it seeks the body of one who is willing to harbor him.

"If the human is unwilling, an illness overtakes him or her which cannot be cured by European medicine, but must be treated by a diviner. If possession of a *mashave* is diagnosed, the patient must decide whether to accept or reject it. If he does not accept the *mashave,* the diviner will transfer it into the body of an animal (preferably a chicken or a black goat) by laying his hands on it. He then drives the animal into the wilderness in exactly the same way as the Israelite priests of old drove the 'scapegoat' into the desert after making it the repository of the sins of their people.

"Anyone unwise enough to take possession of these ac-cursed animals will himself become host to the *mashave* spirit.

"If a person accepts his *mashave,* the sickness leaves him immediately. A special ceremony is held during which he is initiated into a cult made up of groups whose members all possess similar *mashaves*. Some practice midwifery, others are skilled in divining or herbal lore. Some *mashave*-possessed in-dividuals are even believed to confer skills in such improbable things as football, horse racing, or attaining good examina-tion marks!"

20.

I OPEN MY eyes. I am sitting on the narrow bench in the waiting room. Sloth is curled in my lap. I am clenching an unlabeled cough-syrup bottle in my hand. The initiate is standing beside me, holding my bag.

"What's this?" I say, examining the glass jam jar in my hand. The viscous liquid slopping inside is a noxious sulfur color.

"*Muti*. For cleansing yourself of the bad energies."

"Like whatever you just poisoned me with?"

"It will help with the headache. Animal magic is very powerful. You may have some aftereffects. Use it as required."

"Thanks," I say, with every inch of sarcasm I can muster. I drop the jar in my bag with every intention of pouring it down the drain when I get home.

Thunder rumbles above, rattling the windowpane, the tin roof. The daylight has darkened. I stagger out the door, cradling Sloth against my chest. Everything feels flattened out. Or maybe it's just that I'm still feeling the effects of whatever the *sangoma* poisoned me with. Sloth groans and stirs, and I take off my headwrap and fashion it into a kind of sling to carry him.

There is a glitter of glass on the pavement beside my car. The side window is smashed. I realize that my cell phone was not among the objects I turfed out of my bag onto the reed mat, that I must have left it on the passenger seat after hanging up on Gio.

I have a headache that could rip off the worst hangover's head and piss down its neck. The cicadas are clicking. The traffic hums and buzzes. Fat drops of rain spatter like grease. I lurch over to the man cutting rubber, who is starting to pack up. Even the tourists are retreating from the storm, leaving the parking lot deserted. "Excuse me. Did you see who broke my window?"

He looks away.

"You were right here. You must have seen it."

He flicks an offcut of rubber at my feet. It's as eloquent a gesture of contempt as spitting. "Fuck off, apo."

I look around for my yellow-eyed car guard. There is no sign of him. The rain is getting harder. But there is a bright sweet smell in the air that leads me to the tarpaulin strung up under the tree. I duck my head under the tarp, but even as my eyes adjust to the darkness, I realize that the shelter extends much deeper, that whoever lives here has burrowed under the rubble to extend their den. I crouch down and shuffle forward into the haze of smoke, heavier than mandrax or *tik,* and with a sour note, or perhaps that's just the body odor. There's another smell in here too, one that's all too familiar—drains. I can make out three figures sitting on their haunches, passing a pipe between them.

"Hey *fokkof! Wat doen jy?*" a girl screeches, clutching the pipe to her jealously as I shuffle towards them. She is not so old, late teens, maybe early twenties, but the lifestyle has eaten into her appearance, and her face is pocked with scars and bruises. There is a sullen knot at her jaw and her hair is clumpy, with inflamed bald patches as if someone has been ripping it out by the handfuls.

"I just want my phone."

"*Jussis.* I told you, *mos,* I told you," says Yellow Eyes, looking wild and scared. An older boy moves forward, all aggro. If Yellow Eyes is a junkie rat, this guy is a seriously nasty piece of work. Behind him, someone *else* stirs in the darkness, making a rattling sound. I have badly misjudged this.

"There's no phone, lady. Now *fokkof,*" Yellow Eyes says.

"Even just my SIM card. It's worth money to me."

"How much?" the girl says.

"*Thula,* Busi!" hisses the older boy, and Busi cringes as if he's already hit her.

"R200 for the SIM card," I offer. "R300 if it comes with the phone."

"R400."

"Fine." I open my wallet, careful not to let them see how much more money I have in there, peel out four R100 notes and hold them up in front of them.

"What's to stop us just taking it, hey?" Busi says with a leer, creeping forward again.

"Me." My incarceration in Sun City taught me other things apart from how to wait. Like how to stare someone down.

My eyes have adjusted to the dim light and at the back I can make out a drop into a cave of sorts. The kids have excavated a storm drain, or maybe it was already damaged when they parked their tarp over it. They probably sleep down there, all tangled up together like a rat's nest. There is someone down there, shuffling backwards and forwards. The movement makes a dry skittery sound.

"You some kind of ninja?" Nasty Piece of Work says, smirking at the others.

"You want to find out? You want to know what my *shavi* is? What *muti* I just bought at the market?"

"R500," Busi says. This time Nasty does hit her, a cuff with the back of his hand. She whimpers, and glares at me as if it is all my fault. Maybe it is. Whatever is scuffling around in the back hesitates for a moment and then resumes its brittle nervous movements. The rain hurls itself against the tarpaulin.

"This is what I'm offering. Take it or leave it. It's good money." I wave the blue notes and Yellow Eyes snatches for them and misses. "Nuh-uh. Phone first. And tell whoever is skulking around back there to come out where I can see them."

Nasty looks amused. He pats his leg, as if calling a dog, and a Porcupine hauls itself out of the darkness, limping forward on three paws, its quills rattling. It nudges his knee with its stubby snout in wary affection. Thick ropes of drool hang from its jowls. Its eyes are dull. Its back foot is missing. The stump has healed badly, the tissue gray, the spiky hairs matted with dried blood and pus. It smells of damp and rot, like the broken concrete of the hole it crawled from.

"What the fuck did you do to this animal?"

"It's good money," Nasty wheedles, mocking me. "You want some? We can get a good price for that Sloth. Rare animal, hey? Start with a finger. Or a paw."

"Whole arm even," Busi says, emboldened, edging forward. "You won't miss it. You won't even notice." The Porcupine watches me with its beady little eyes, and despite myself, despite Sun City Rules, I start backing out, slowly. Fuck the phone. Odi can afford to buy me another one. But Nasty has managed to get round behind me, blocking the exit.

The rain buckets down, the sound like the roar of a stadium crowd. Outside, chunks of hail plink off the concrete. Nasty takes a screwdriver from his pocket, the end sharpened to a point. It's filthy — if you got stabbed with that thing, tetanus would be the least of your worries. I've seen bad stab wounds. A gangster in prison got herself a kidney puncture compliments of her girlfriend. It took her weeks to die from the infection.

"Don't go yet, cherry," Nasty says, raising his voice over the pelting rain.

"If you'd told me it was a party, I would have brought cupcakes," I say. I open my fingers and let the notes flutter to the ground, anticipating the girl dropping to her knees to pick them up. This buys me a second of distraction.

I grab Sloth's arm and slash his claws across Nasty's face, before he can raise the screwdriver. He screams and stumbles backwards, clutching his nose and eyes. I don't stick around to evaluate the damage. I turn and slam into Yellow Eyes with my full weight, knocking him over the girl, who is still on her knees, picking up the notes. Her head hits the ground with a painful thunk. I don't have time to feel guilty. Sun City Rules: take out the leader and get out any way you can. I barge past the Porcupine, sharp quills snagging on my jeans, and go in the exact opposite direction Nasty is expecting, dropping into the jagged hole and the darkness of the storm drain.

On my knees, I shuffle forward down the tunnel past the tangle of blankets that smell of smoke and sweat and urine, one hand against the rough concrete for guidance. My sneakers squelch in the rivulet of rotten mud. I can't see a fucking thing, but I can feel the water sloshing around me. "I hope you're looking where we're going," I mutter and Sloth, still shocked, manages a squeak in response. The tunnel should open up soon to a central flow. There will be maintenance entry points that'll take me straight up to the street. I just have to get there before they catch me.

I can hear the distorted echoes of angry voices behind me. Hopefully, they're still deciding if I went left or right. Hopefully, they'll split up. Easier to handle that way. I scuffle forward through the dark, now on my feet and hunched. Water is soaking through my shoes, and at first I think it's because the tunnel is widening, but it's the water level rising with the swell of rain. Another reason to speed up this getaway.

Sloth grunts in warning a second too late as the tunnel opens out onto a wide and slippery plateau and I go skidding over the edge of it, drop two meters, and land hard on my coccyx, on the edge of a step. The pain is like a railway spike driven up my spine. It knocks the breath out of me. I lie there stunned, while Sloth whimpers and moans for me to get up.

I'm lying on the edge of a massive staircase that slopes down, each step inclined thirty degrees. Looking up, I can see several tributaries convening on the steps, each of them spouting a dark churn of water. Beyond them, the vaulted ceiling stretches like a cathedral. I can only see this because of the bright circle, like a skylight, and the narrow metal ladder that leads up to the manhole, mockingly out of reach, one level up.

The voices are getting closer. Yellow Eyes pokes his head out from one of the tributary tunnels a meter or two above my head and shines down a torch. "Here! She's here!" he yells, his voice shrill with excitement. There's a muffled response, like someone talking underwater. "Help me! Help me climb down," Yellow Eyes shrieks. Sloth clicks in my ear, tugging at my shoulders to get up. I clamber painfully on all fours, pausing only to yank a porcupine quill out of my shin, and then scramble down the slope to the next step and the next.

The steps flatten out into a main artery a meter wide. I try walking along the narrow bank of the canal, but the cement is crumbling and slick with slime. I don't have time to teeter along the edge. I slide into the rush of water. It's hip-deep and horribly warm, like someone peed in it. There's a splash somewhere behind me, the sound twisted by the tunnel, so

I've no idea how close it is. I risk a glance back, but there's only darkness.

The water flows into an alcove, a place for the stormwater to back up before the artery turns the corner. The scenery has changed, the modern cement giving way to ancient brickwork here, a Victorian relic from the town's golden days. I pull myself out of the stream and take cover, pressing my back to the recessed wall and crouching down among the rubble, making myself as small as possible, but also ready to bolt. Sloth is curled against my chest, still in his sling. He's shivering violently. Scuttly things tickle my back. I resolve not to think about them. I'm *hoping* they're cockroaches.

"Here, chick-chick-chicken!" Nasty calls from somewhere down the tunnel. He sounds pissed. He's answered by a girl's nervous giggle. Which means either Yellow Eyes is keeping mum, or they know the tunnels better than I do and he's split off, lying in wait somewhere up ahead. I've got to get back to that ladder.

Splashing sounds resolve into Yellow Eyes with his torch, followed at a cautious distance by Nasty wading down the center of the canal, carrying his screwdriver above the water. There is a two-stroke gash across his face. I hope it gets infected. Wounds inflicted by animals sometimes fester in strange and horrible ways.

I shrink back against the wall, Sloth hunches his shoulders to make himself smaller, tucking his head under mine, and we both hold our breath. They pass right by, Yellow Eyes humming tunelessly. If they move far enough ahead, I can double back.

Somewhere in their wake, the girl squeals in surprise.

"Stop messing around!" Nasty shouts over his shoulder, not bothering to look back. Busi emerges a moment later, edging along the embankment, using my phone for light. She is shaking her foot like a kitten and holding up a soggy sneaker, its dangling laces black with grime.

"Tumiiiii," she whines, trying to wring out the shoe. "It's slippy."

"Then walk in the middle," Nasty snipes back from down the tunnel.

She bends down to pull her wet shoe onto her bare foot. Then she looks up, straight at us. I put my finger to my lips, pleading. She stares. One alligator. Two alligator. Three alligator. Four alligator. Five alligator. Six alligator. And then she yelps, "Here! Tumi! She's here, she's here, she's here!"

Shit. So much for victim solidarity. I shove her into the canal. She screams, a thin sound that cuts off abruptly as she goes under. She emerges a second later, thrashing wildly and spluttering, without her shoe *or* my phone.

"Stand up!" I yell at the idiot girl, who doesn't realize the water is only waist-deep, maybe chest-deep on her. Nasty Tumi is wading back towards me, grinning, Yellow Eyes splashing up after him.

"You might want to help your girlfriend." I stay where I am, back against the wall, searching out the rubble at my feet with one hand. "The water's rising."

"She can take care of herself," he says, but Yellow Eyes

stops to pull her up. She falls against him, sobbing, nearly pulling him under.

"What about you?" I ask Tumi. But it's just a play for time. I've found what I've been looking for. I close my hand over a broken brick, stand up, and hurl it with full force, not at his head, but his hand. Tumi howls and drops the screwdriver. It plinks into the water and disappears, the current sweeping it away with the other detritus. Busi shrieks in dismay.

Tumi scrambles out of the water and lunges for me. But it's Sloth's arm he grabs, tearing him out of the sling and swinging him out over the canal. Sloth drops into the water, too surprised to make a sound.

"Now what?" Tumi leers. He doesn't see Sloth resurface or start paddling for the bank, his long arms stroking elegantly through the water. But he's losing against the current, the angle of his trajectory towards the shore getting sharper as it tugs him away.

"Fuck you," I say and stab him in the side of his neck with the broken porcupine quill. I clutch onto my bag and plunge into the canal after Sloth without sticking around to see the results.

We wash up kilometers away, clinging to each other, battered from being hurled against the cement walls all the way down, with various additional minor wounds, including scratched arms and legs from a surprise collision with a broken branch wedged under the water.

It takes a long time to find the strength to stand up and carry on, and when I shrug Sloth onto my shoulders, he is so waterlogged, it feels like he's put on ten kilos. Sloth is ominously quiet. It's an indication of how much shit we're in because normally he's the first to complain, bleating rebukes in my ear.

The worst is that I don't know where we are. It's not like I'm the world authority on Joburg's storm drains, but I've been down here enough times looking for lost things to know the basic lie of the land. This is all unfamiliar. The tunnels are a scramble of pitch-black termite holes, some of them narrowing away to nothing, like whoever was digging them got bored and wandered off. The original gold diggings maybe, when Johannesburg was still just a bunch of hairy prospectors scrabbling in the dirt. Maybe we'll bring home a nugget the size of Sloth's head.

Sloth guides me through the dark, squeezing my shoulders like handlebars. If we could just find a lost thing, I could follow the connection back home, like a trail of breadcrumbs.

But hours later, we have not stumbled on anything, not a lost thing, not an exit, not even a passage that leads anywhere, just one dead end after another in the humid dark. Sloth squeaks once, a bleak little noise as I slump down against the wall. My feet are aching, my stomach is clenched, like hunger is a sweet it could suck on.

"Don't sweat it, buddy. We'll get out of here," I say. "No worries."

But he can tell I don't believe myself. It's so black down here, my eyes invent ghosts to make up for the sensory deprivation, ripples of black on black. It's as quiet as purgatory.

And then Sloth chirrups and looks up with a sharp jerk of his head. Swimming is not the only thing he does better than me. I strain to listen. My heart drops into my gut. "Is it them?"

There is a low rumbling sound, almost indiscernible, but it's building, like house music rising to a dance floor crescendo. I stand up in a hurry. "Water?" There are reports every year of kids who have drowned in the drains, caught out by flash floods that come out of practically nowhere while they're messing around in the tunnels smoking dope or looking for ninja turtles.

But Sloth clucks in irritation, shutting me up so he can listen. It's something else. He bats at my face with urgent pawings, the way he does when I've overslept. "All right, all right," I say, staggering to my feet and in the direction he guides me, towards the epicenter of the noise. It better not be a wall of water.

The sound reverberates through the tunnels, ramping up to a teeth-rattling earthquake. There is a glow up ahead, as if of civilization. Hope sparks in my gut. I stumble forward, round a corner, into blinding artificial light. I make out huge metal ribs lining the tunnel like the belly of a robot whale. And then a whip of glass and metal thunders past inches from my face.

The blur of one shocked pink face staring out the window, mouth open in a perfect O of surprise, is the only witness to the near-death of Zinzi December by Gautrain.

21.

BRIXTON IS NOT quite the new Melville, but since House of Nsako and now Counter Rev the area is definitely on the up, complete with irate residents complaining about noise levels and cars blocking their driveways. I walk up to the entrance, limping only slightly. It took hours to wash the smell of drains out of Sloth's fur, and I'm wearing a long-sleeved top under my '60s pinafore dress to hide the worst of the scratches. Otherwise, we're pretty good, considering the traumas of the day: having to talk my way past Gautrain security, finding a taxi in Sandton willing to take a filthy, wet, and stinking zoo girl downtown so I could rescue my car.

The sharecall phone number Vuyo gave me was for a taxi company, Quick-Quick. The operator was able to check the log for Sunday morning, 02h46. "Yes, we received a call," she said, gruffly. "Pickup was for 14 Highbury Road, Brixton. Some kind of club. Counter Revolutionary? Heading to Morningside. So you gonna pay for it?"

"Pay for what?"

"Customer never showed. Our driver waited for twenty minutes. Could have got two more fares in. That's lost income. That's—" But I'd already hung up on her.

The doors of Counter Rev are dramatically oversized, glossy black with huge silvered handles in the shape of a reversed C and R facing off against each other. Hip-hop booms from within, breezy lyrics over a richly malevolent melody. The bouncer is wearing dark sunglasses and a red-and-black jacket with a gold helmet insignia pinned to his lapel, accessorized with massively bunched shoulders and a hefty dose of aggro. But when I hesitate outside, he drops the attitude and lifts the velvet rope.

"Going in?"

"Waiting for someone," I say. "Thanks." Said someone is going to be another hour at least. I'm crazy early, but tonight isn't about seeing Gio.

"Warmer waiting inside," the bouncer says. "Just saying."

"Ah, but I'm not allowed to smoke inside." I tap out a cigarette from a box of lights purchased specially for the occasion. "Just like the song? I fought the law."

"Law won," he agrees and flicks a cheap plastic lighter under the tip of my cigarette. Smoking: still the number-one icebreaker known to humankind. His eyes flick down to the bruises on my wrist.

"The Sloth going to be a problem?

"You tell me."

"But there's no official policy?"

"Right of admission reserved."

"Who decides that?"

"I do."

"You're not a man of many words."

"Not what they pay me for."

"So who doesn't get past you?"

He ticks off the offenses on his fingers. His knuckles are lined with fine scars, and two of his fingers are splinted together. I'm guessing amateur boxing. No bouncer sees that much action in a nice part of town like this. "If they don't make the dress code. If they're already drunk. If they're known dealers. If I don't like their attitude."

"Do I make the dress code?"

"Yes."

"Do you like my attitude?" I drop the remains of the cigarette and crush the tip under the toe of my boot.

His demeanor changes abruptly. "Hey, you one of the new girls?" he says sharply.

"Maybe I'd like to be." I have not been expecting this tack.

"Because the staff entrance is round the back. Joey know you're here?"

"I'm not sure."

"You better go find out. And take your butt with you." It takes me a second to realize he means the cigarette.

"Thanks—I didn't get your name?" I say, picking up the *stompie* and putting it in my pocket.

"Ronaldo."

The staff entrance leads into the kitchen. A man unpacking pre-prepared maki rolls from the fridge directs me to just go on up the stairs. I make a mental note to pass on the sushi. I walk along a corridor with a row of staff lockers, past an open door leading into a bathroom where a cluster of exquisite and frighteningly young waitresses are touching up their makeup, and up the stairs to the door marked MANAGER. I knock and follow orders when a gruff "Come in!" is barked from within.

The door opens into an austere office overlooking the dance floor below, a view supplemented by a monitor linked to the CCTV that switches between cameras every twenty seconds or so, including the ones in the bathrooms above the washbasins. A giant of a woman is going through a spreadsheet, if the reflection in the window behind her is any indication. She looks up wearily and snatches off her glasses as if she's not used to wearing them. Or not used to being seen in them.

"*Ag* no. No-no-no," says Joey at the sight of me. She has ash-blond hair ironed straight as an army bed-fold and silver glitter eyeshadow that enhances the difference between her eyes, one blue, one hazel. She is wearing a tuxedo with a corset that somewhat restrains her generous frame, but not her boobs, which are doing their best to make an escape and take over the world. She must have made a fortune in her Former Life, which I'm guessing involved grinding up against a pole and many, many different laps. "I don't know who told you to come see me, my baby. But you are far too old. I'm sorry."

"Can't I even—waitress?" I hazard a guess.

"Sorry, my *engel*. That's a little too much exoticism even for our clientele. Dancers only. But maybe some place like the Foxhole would consider a mature girl like you."

"I really had my heart set on working *here*." I whine a little and try a petulant look. "Odi said I could."

"Oh, did he now? Well, tough breaks, *skattebol,* you're no little Carmen. You can tell Odi he can make calls on staffing when he shows his face around here, not before." Her attention snaps back to her computer screen as if it's magnetic. "Are you still here?" she says, not looking up. I take the hint and head for the bar.

Front of house, Counter Rev is twenties decadence meets electro glam. Great Gatsby by way of Lady Gaga, in shades of white and silver. A massive abstract chandelier cut from clear perspex hangs over the oval bar with its low, white neon counter, softly lit from underneath. Odi isn't fucking around. This is a far cry from the music venue grunge of Bass Station. The dance floor is hemmed in by a ripple of booths in cool cream-colored leather, the curve angled just right to allow each a modicum of privacy while still sustaining maximum potential for seeing and being seen. Opposite the seating above, the DJ booths are three grand archways with raised platforms all fenced off with white bamboo bars strung with ribbons.

"You the new girl?" the bartender says, jerking his head at one of the dancer's cages. He's pretty in a schmodelly kinda way, apart from a long nose and skin too pale to pull off all-white in a white neon glow.

"Just a regular patron. Can you get me a G&T? Hold the G."

"All right," he says, pouring out a tonic water.

"Actually, you know what, give me the full equation." I ignore Sloth's hiss in my ear. "I think I've earned it."

"Whatever you say," he says and pours me a double. Sloth reaches out and tries to swipe the glass off the counter.

"Frisky little guy," I reprimand, grabbing his paw midswing. "Sorry, he can't handle his booze."

"Yeah, I've heard of that," the bartender says. "You affect the animal?"

"It's a problem," I admit. "Do you have somewhere I could stash him? A coat check, maybe?"

The bartender shakes his head, amused, but the query wasn't for his benefit. There are no more attempts from the peanut gallery to prevent me having my drink. I'm feeling reckless. It feels good.

"I'm too early, aren't I?" I say, surveying the territory.

"Things only really get going round about eleven, twelve. Even on a weeknight."

"What's the crowd like?"

"Rich. Trendy. Beautiful. Lot of power people."

"Bet you get laid a lot. What's your name?"

He actually blushes. "I've got a girlfriend. And it's Michael."

"What do you do when you're not bartending, Michael?"

"I'm a student. Marine biology at the University of Johannesburg."

"Marine biology? Are you ever in the wrong city."

"No kidding."

"Can I make a contribution towards a transfer to a coastal facility?" I tuck R500 under my coaster.

"What's this for?"

"Just the name of the bouncer who was friendly with Song-weza Radebe."

"You from *Heat?*"

"Something like that."

"This going to come back to me?"

"Michael. Please. I don't even know your name."

He slips the coaster off the counter, the R500 vanishing seamlessly with it. "Ronaldo. Ro. But I don't think it went anywhere."

"Ro the jealous type?"

"Nah, man, he's a real sweet guy. He was always looking out for her. Didn't like her coming here so young. Bad influence, you know?"

"Oh, I know."

"He beat the crap out of some guy who tried to dope her drink a few months back. It happens sometimes. We found a girl passed out in the toilets last Friday. Had to break the cubicle door down. Joey was seriously pissed. Have you been in the toilets yet?"

"Not yet."

"You should go. Highlight of the venue. Those doors cost ten grand a pop."

"Lot of drugs going around?"

"Not according to official policy." He turns cool on me, suddenly very busy with grinding up ice for cocktails. I guess drug *skinder* isn't included in the fee. Most club "policies" are no more than lip service, or at best a system for keeping out unregulated dealers, the kind with dodgy product or who aren't willing to let the house have a taste of the profits. Most clubs have in-house service providers. They're not hard to find if you know where to look.

I sip my G&T and watch the place start to fill up. By "power people," the bartender meant older guys with younger girls in countless variations of suits and little black dresses. They occupy the booths and order top-shelf champagne and single malts. The younger, clubbier crowd are dressed more effortlessly casual in designer jeans and trainers, and tend to head straight for the bar. There's nothing interesting about these people.

I do spot the house dealer, or rather he spots me. Junkie pheromones reel him in like a pedophile homing in on a day care. He swings in to sit beside me, just a boy making a move on the lonely Sloth girl in the corner. He's a sweet-looking guy with sandy curls and a preppy shirt and chinos. The kind your dad would be pleased to have you bring home. "Heya, love," he says, "haven't seen you here before."

"First time."

"Having a good time?"

"Sure."

"Mike said you might be looking for something?" Michael is preoccupied on the other side of the curve, tending to a posse of chic girls in jewel tops and black business skirts who are starting to get a little loose and sloppy as after-work drinks turns into an all-nighter.

"Did he now?" Sloth hunches his shoulders and hisses at the guy.

"Hey, that's just what he said. If I'm bothering you, I'll go away."

"I'm sticking with this tonight, thanks."

His easy smile doesn't even falter. "Maybe later then, love." He winks, peels away into the throng and is next seen dancing with a girl in a satiny top and low-rider jeans that have ridden a little too low, revealing her bespangled underwear and a fair section of her arse.

"*There* you are." Gio collapses onto the barstool next to me. He still sounds pissy, although he's made some effort. He's wearing a very subtle, very expensive cologne. "Why don't you answer your phone? I've been trying to call you all night."

"My phone and I parted ways. Call it a tactical withdrawal." But he's not really listening.

"Was that guy bugging you? This place can be such a meat market."

"I need a favor."

"Whoa there, lady. I think you're already in the red on the Official Favors account."

"Have an argument with me. Outside."

"We're heading that way, let me tell you. Why would we be doing this?"

"We used to have great arguments, remember?"

"The neighbors three blocks over remember, Zee. As well as the Aftermath."

"Don't remember you complaining about makeup sex."

"I was too afraid," he grins. But he's getting off on this. We used to play games in bed, and our screaming arguments were always power plays.

"Come on. Outside. You may have to rough me up a little."

"That's a new one. You learn that kink in the big house?" He trails after me as I head towards the entrance. I just hope Ro won't completely destroy him.

Just before we reach the doors, I shove him hard in the chest, yell, "I *said,* just leave me the fuck alone," and storm out onto the street, exaggerating my limp.

He grabs my arm, bewildered. "Hey?"

"Get it through your head, Giovanni. It's over!" I may be overdoing it. The gin sings in my head. "There was never anything between us! And I'm sick of you following me!"

"Oh yeah?" Gio says, getting into it. "Well . . . what about the baby?"

"It wasn't yours," I spit, improvising.

"Bitch!" He raises his hand to pretend-slap me, but his arm gets stuck before it can begin its descent, clamped firmly in a fist the size of Gio's head.

"Your evening's festivities have come to a premature end, my friend," the man attached to the fist says. "Why don't you run along?" Ronaldo twists Gio's wrist down, forcing him to buckle to follow the trajectory of his arm.

"Ow. It's not what you think," Gio squeaks. "Ow."

"That's what I keep telling you, you stalker freak!" I say, my voice hitching. "It's over. Leave me alone!"

"You heard her. You have everything from inside?" Ronaldo keeps twisting until Gio is on his knees. Gio nods.

"Then have a lovely evening, sir," says Ronaldo, releasing his wrist. Gio scrambles to his feet. "Don't let me see you back here for a while."

"Jesus." Gio gives me a look so filthy it would make a sewer blush. "I hope you're fucking happy." He stalks away down the block, flexing his wrist and swearing under his breath.

"Thank you. You won't believe——"

"And you." He takes my arm firmly and speaks low: "I don't want to see you back here for a while either. I don't know what kind of game you're playing, but I'm not into it."

"Okay, I'm sorry..." I fumble, decide to come clean. "I was trying to get your attention. I know you helped Song Radebe and——"

"And look where it got me," he interrupts, taking off his shades, leaning close so I can get the full picture. Someone beat him ugly. His face is bruised, his right eye is a watering slit in a purple sack. There are cigarette burns on the inside of his wrist where he is gripping my arm. Perhaps the splinted fingers aren't boxing damage after all.

"I need to know where she is."

"I didn't tell them," he says, frog-marching me to the corner. "Why would I tell you?"

"Because I'm trying to help her."

"I don't know that. Maybe *you* don't know that."

"At least tell me who *they* are."

"I'm so sick of you fucking zoos."

"Wait, does that mean it was the Marabou? The Maltese?"

"It means, don't come back." He shoves me towards the corner so hard that my ankle twists and my heel snaps off. He turns and heads back towards the doors with the light and bass spilling from inside, leaving me standing under the streetlight with less shoe than I arrived with. Dignity, too.

Sloth opens his mouth to sigh in an I-told-you-so way. "Don't even think about it," I say, popping a breath mint to cover the gin.

22.

"WE CAN'T KEEP doing this," Benoît says, lifting my arm from the sweaty rumple of sheets. He turns over my hand and touches his mouth to my fingertips each in turn, the lightest of kisses.

"What, stating the obvious? What difference does one more time make to your wife? She'll have you for the rest of your life. Or until you get divorced over something incidental, like squeezing the toothpaste from the top of the tube. Or, you know, being total strangers to each other after five years."

"It makes a difference to me."

"Well, you'll have you for the rest of your life, too." I roll over to straddle him. "So, can you live with it?"

"Get off, wench."

"You don't mean that." I dip down to kiss him, leaning on his chest and the smooth dead scar tissue that doesn't feel anything.

"Don't I deserve some recovery time?" he says, pulling at my wrists as if he's going to wrestle me off. But he doesn't have any such intention.

"I'll show you what you deserve," I say, dipping lower.

I sit on the edge of the bed afterwards, my foot folded under me and fight with the cheap plastic lighter I stole from Ronaldo, which clicks like the luckiest game of Russian roulette ever. "Do you know where you're going?"

"Burundi. They're in a camp called Bwagiriza in the east, in Ruyigi. Safe from the fighting, they say. They're consolidating, moving all the people to one place. It's better."

"But still not exactly a holiday resort."

"They had to close the supertubes, it's true." He smiles, but it's as fake as the designer labels at Bruma Lake.

"Candyfloss machine broke down. The balloons have drifted away. The rebels took all the stuffed fluffy toys when they left. Have you spoken to her?"

"There's only one satellite phone."

"So you don't actually know it's them." I get a spark, but it doesn't last long enough for the cigarette to catch. Dammit. Flick-flick.

"The UN aid worker scanned a copy of her *carte d'identité*."

"Could be stolen. Assumed identity. They do genetic testing in the UK refugee centers now to make sure you're actually from wherever you say you are. Have you asked for a DNA match to your actual wife? Do they have her dental records?" Flick. Flick.

"This isn't easy for me either," he says.

"Oh piss off, Benoît," I say, flick-flick-flicking the lighter.

"I'm glad you've found someone else."

"That spying pigdog D'Nice can piss off too." Flick. Flick. Flick.

"It's good, Zinzi, it's what you need."

I toss the goddamn fucking useless piece of fucking shit lighter against the fucking wall. And instantly regret it. Now I'll have to go down the fucking stairs and buy another fucking lighter at the fucking *spaza,* which will probably be fucking closed at this time of the fucking night. I prowl over to the wall and pick up the lighter. The little plastic nib has broken off. It's well and truly fucked.

"Whatever is or isn't between me and Giovanni—you don't have a say in my life anymore, Benoît."

"I didn't know I ever did." He looks at me like *I'm* the bad guy. "Do you want to see photographs of them?"

"Why would I want to see photographs of the people you're leaving me for?"

"Because I'd like to show you."

"Oh for god's sake. Fine."

It takes him a couple of minutes to retrieve the photographs from his room upstairs. In the meantime, I manage to score a box of matches off a woman carrying a bucket of water up the stairs on her head.

Back in my room, Benoît takes the cigarette from my mouth and drags on it. I've never seen him smoke before. Then he sits down beside me on the bed with a bundle wrapped in plastic and bound with elastic bands in his lap. He starts slipping off the elastic bands and putting them neatly beside him. Some of them are practically rotted through. I'm curious in spite of the poison flower in my chest.

"When was the last time you looked at these?"

"Yesterday. Before that, I don't know. A year? Two years? I used to look at them every day."

He unfurls one Checkers packet. It's wrapped around another, which is wrapped around another, which is wrapped around a tight sheaf of papers bound in a piece of military green raincoat and tied with string.

It's a mix of photos and computer printouts of photographs, already faded, the paper worn soft with handling and the rigors of cross-continental travel. Benoît, a woman, and three children aged two to seven at a guess, posing formally, unsmiling in front of a low wall. Their features are indistinct. Washed out. They already look like ghosts.

The same woman, looking exhausted, wrapped in bright yellow sheets and holding a pinch-faced newborn, his eyes clenched against the light, a little girl poking her head into the bottom of the frame like she can't bear to be left out.

The same little girl holding the baby under his arms, carting him around.

The little boy sitting in a cardboard box, grinning to reveal one tooth.

The family posing formally again in front of a fountain in a city setting.

The same background, but this time Benoît is holding the little boy upside-down as if he's about to drop him into the fountain, while the rest of the family collapses in laughter.

But the one that yanks my heart into my stomach is the

picture of the woman hiding her face behind her apron with a coy smile, playing a game with the camera.

Or rather, the man behind it.

"Celvie," Benoît says. "Armand. Ginelle. Celestin. He's the smallest. Two and a half years old. He has so much energy. You need a leash to hold him."

I do the maths. "So six or seven now."

"Seven. His birthday is in April. Next week. Seven years old. Practically grown-up. I'll have to start saving for his university fees." The corner of his mouth twitches grimly, not even a Fong Kong smile. We're both considering the impossibilities of university fees, of universities in general, of where a university degree might get you. My BA. Benoît's third-year mechanical engineering.

He starts to put the photographs away, rebagging them in plastic, slipping the elastic bands back into place.

"What are you going to tell them?"

"That papa got lost for a while."

"And the Mongoose?"

"Ah," Benoît waves his hand. "He'll get used to them. They might pull his tail, but it will be okay. He's only mean to nasty Sloth girls," Benoît says, shoving me for emphasis.

"Oof. Well, I'm not going to miss you *at all*."

"I won't think about you for a second."

"I won't even remember you, I'll be so busy shagging other guys. I'll be, like, Benoît *who?*"

"You'll remember the Mongoose when the fleas hatch."

"I won't. I won't remember you. I won't miss you. I never

loved you. I never even liked you. And you smell funny. And your feet, your calloused nasty-ass feet? They're disgusting. I'll be glad to have them gone from my bed."

"You smell funny too," he says and kisses me on my cheekbone near my ruined ear. I tilt my head onto his shoulder. We sit quietly for a long time.

I'm swimming lengths at the gym pool at Old Ed's sports club. Back and forth, perfect tumble-turns — which I have never been able to do properly — at either end, back and forth.

I am the only person in the pool. The only person in the club, it feels like. I am churning up the water into choppy little waves. There is a whistle blowing out a rhythm I have to keep to, but I am falling behind. I can't keep up.

And far below me, so deep it's like this pool is suspended over a continental shelf, something is rising, swimming up towards me. Something with teeth.

23.

I WAKE WITH a start, my heart thudding. Benoît is fast asleep, lying behind me so we're curled together like a pair of quotation marks. His hard-on pokes into my back with innocent insistence, not privy to our decision to forgo the delights of each other. It wasn't the dream. There was a noise.

I sit up, listening carefully. There is the sound of running feet. A shout drifting up from the street. A door slams. More shouts. Gunshots. Unreasonably, I immediately think of Songweza. The way the sound is dulled, it seems like it's coming from the Twist Street side, and I glance out the window to check. The street is quiet, not even a plastic bag stirring in the trees.

The Mongoose's face appears at the end of the bed, nose snuffling as he stands up on his back paws to peer at me.

"Looks like it's just you and me." I slip out of bed, pulling on some clothes and a pair of slops. "The unholy alliance." Benoît doesn't stir.

The lights are on at 608. I rap lightly on the door and Mr. Khan, the little tailor whose wife has a talent for weaving antitheft charms into his work, opens the door a moment later. He used to have a small shop in Plein Street, but now he does what business he can out of Elysium Heights. His wife, Mrs. Khan, supplements her charm-making by advising residents on government grant applications. It helps that her Black Scorpion is easily hidden in her handbag when she goes down to social welfare, with applications and ID books in hand.

Mr. Khan beckons with little grabbing gestures for me to come in quickly before scurrying back to the window and the unfolding drama. I step over bolts of cloth and squeeze in round the sewing machine on the desk to the window, where Mrs. Khan, their twelve-year-old daughter, the sex worker from across the passage, and a man I can only assume is her patron for the hour have taken up viewing positions, all looking down over the street. We're not the only tenants enjoying a little 4 a.m. drama. On either side of us people are leaning out of the windows to look, smoking and chatting.

"It's these gangs," Mrs. Khan tuts, shifting her weight to balance the sleeping baby on her hip. "And that damn private security." The police are a joke with a punchline you've heard before. Armed response runs Zoo City and the downtown area the same way dogs piss on their territory. They're only interested in protecting their buildings. If a crime happens across the road, it's as if it doesn't happen at all. They lose interest as soon as it's out of their jurisdiction. Unfortunately, Elysium and Aurum fall out of the borders of privatized law. Our landlord is too *snoep* to pony up for protection.

There is another crackle of gunfire. A muzzle flash is reflected in the broken windows of the building on the corner. Then a man scrambles out from the cover of the trees lining the avenue, firing back over his shoulder. His trainers make a tennis-court squeal as he skids on the wet tarmac. A Bear lumbers out behind him and looks both ways, as if checking for oncoming traffic.

This is not the strangest thing I have seen in our street. There was the attempted rape that was interrupted—Mrs. Khan roused some of the larger men on our floor, and they beat the would-be rapist into a coma. There was the night D'Nice got stabbed, unfortunately not fatally. There was the murder in the stairwell a few weeks ago. But the weirdest was the night the owner of a local brothel paraded her girls and their menagerie naked down the street hoping to drum up new business.

"Dogfight turned bad," says one of the guys leaning out of the window of 610, with great authority.

"Not too late to place your bets," his goateed friend says. But their laughter is hollow.

"No, man," Mrs. Khan says, annoyed, "shows what you know. It's a gang war, definitely. The 207s were moving in on the Cameroonians two weeks ago now. This is revenge, you'll see."

Mr. Khan tries to shoo his daughter back to her bed. "Come on, my baby, you need to rest for school tomorrow." But the girl doesn't move. This is better than TV. And probably better than school too, as far as her life education is concerned.

On the street below, there is another shot. The Bear's shoulder collapses with a jerk. It roars in pain, rises to its full height, and then seems to think better of it. The man tugs at the Bear's arm, trying to get it to move. It roars again and then drops back on all fours. The man starts to run, gesturing urgently for the Bear to follow him. It starts after him. But it's too late.

More bullets, AK-47 rounds this time, rip through the animal, knocking it sideways. The man screams and starts running back towards the Bear, then hesitates. The Bear shambles another step and then collapses on its backside with a surprised whuff. It tries to get up, confused. The AK-47 stutters again. The Bear's forepaws slide out from under it. Its jaw strikes the curb with an audible crack. The people at the window wince. Very slowly, the Bear's head lolls to one side. The man turns and runs like hell is at his heels.

It will be.

We hold our collective breath. A *tsotsi* holding that favorite weapon of revolutionaries, criminals, and revolutionaries-turned-criminals walks cautiously out from beneath the scaffolding of the trees, the AK-47 at his hip ready to be swung up. There is a blur of wings hovering above his shoulder. A Sunbird. He walks up to the Bear and prods it with his foot. It doesn't move. He empties another clip into it anyway. The Bird darts forward to see, darts back again.

There are sirens in the distance. Private security, not police. You can tell by the pitch of the wail. The *tsotsi* looks up and sees half the building standing at their windows, watching. He gives us a cheerful wave and steps back into the trees, his Bird darting about his head.

We know what's coming. None of us say anything. The

Mongoose paces the window ledge, whiskers quivering. The sirens get louder. The Bear lies motionless on the pavement beside the metal frame of a licensed vendor's stall.

The air pressure dips, like before a storm. A keening sound wells up soft and low, as if it's always been there, just outside the range of human hearing. It swells to howling. And then the shadows start to drop from trees, like raindrops after a storm. The darkness pools and gathers and then seethes.

The Japanese believe it's hungry ghosts. The Scientologists claim it's the physical manifestation of suppressive engrams. Some eyewitness reports describe teeth grinding and ripping in the shadows. Video recordings have shown only impenetrable darkness. I prefer to think of it as a black hole, cold and impersonal as space. Maybe we become stars on the other side.

I turn away as it rushes down the road in the direction of the running man. Mr. Khan covers his daughter's eyes, even though it's her ears he should be protecting. The screaming only lasts a few awful seconds before it is abruptly cut off.

"Tsk," Mrs. Khan says, to break the silence that's weighing down on us, like someone has turned up the gravity. "This city."

But I've thought of something else. "Where are your parents?" I murmur, remembering the poison hallucination, the shop assistant with the name badge—*Murderer! Murderer! Murderer!*—bending over my five-year-old dream self.

"The parents? Someone will have to tell them," Mrs. Khan agrees. "Come you," she says to her daughter, hustling her away from the window, and all us rubberneckers too.

24.

BY MORNING, WHEN I wake up groggy and grumpy from lack of sleep, the municipal street-cleaning crew has already done the rounds. The blood has been hosed down. The Bear's corpse is gone. The only evidence that it was ever there is a black stain on the tarmac like a blast radius and the yellow police tape cordoning off the street.

If only the cleaning crew could do the same for my car. Benoît stares at it without saying anything. I wasn't the only thing that got knocked about yesterday—the Capri got trashed too. Comprehensively. The door panels have been kicked in, the headlights smashed, and a mostly illegible word, that might read "FUK" if you squinted at it right, has been carved into the paintwork on the bonnet in letters four inches high. The windscreen sags under fractal spiderwebs, caused by multiple blows from a metal object, like, oh, say the crowbar I found lying on the back seat. Which had also been used to gouge up the leather. The cherry on top was the smeared shit—human, judging from the smell—on the bonnet. I guess I should be grateful whoever made the deposit didn't do it on the upholstery.

"Hazards of the job," I tell Benoît. But it's easy to be off-

246

hand now. Yesterday, when the taxi I'd found to take me and my *eau de drain* downtown from Sandton pulled in to Mai Mai, the market was already closed up, evening shadows stretching across the parking lot, deserted apart from the ruins of the Capri. I insisted the taxi driver stick around while I got the car started. I didn't know if they were still there, hunched under the tarp watching, or loose in the city somewhere, but I gave them the finger anyway. I should have left the car there, but I'm stubborn like that. Also: not about to be overly intimidated by a cluster of junkie tunnel rats.

Benoît looks at the bruises and scratches on my arm as I drive. They look worse today. If I'd thought about it, I wouldn't have worn a sleeveless dress.

"You should have called the police," he says.

"The police don't care, Benoît."

"Then you should let me come with you."

"Don't you have your own day job?"

"I'm quitting anyway."

"And you have travel arrangements to make."

"You could just say 'no thank you,' *cherie*."

"You could do me one favor. It's dodgy, though."

He sighs. "I wouldn't expect any less from you."

"Hey, D'Nice is way worse than I am."

"But not nearly as cute."

"I'm telling your wife," I retort, but it's autopilot. Our easy banter is now laced with jagged edges.

"My *polygamie* offer is still open," he says, valiantly keeping up the façade.

"I might consider it, *if* you can get me the home address for one Ronaldo, bouncer at Counter Revolutionary, surname unknown. He works for Sentinel, same silly helmet on his badge." I flip a hand at the insignia on Elias's nametag.

"I'll see what I can do," he says, as I pull up outside the bottling plant where Benoît has been assigned to patrol today. Sentinel likes to shift security personnel around, so no one gets too comfortable, too familiar with the ins and outs, and sells the info on to someone like D'Nice. Who can be guaranteed to sell it to a gang of armed robbers.

"I don't have to do this," Benoît says, staying in the car. "They could live without a security guard for the day."

"What, and risk Elias's job?" I keep my hands on the steering wheel, the better to resist touching him.

"At least take my phone."

"I'll be fine. I'll stay away from storm drains and junkie tunnel rats with screwdrivers. Promise."

He looks pained. "I'll see you later, *cherie*," he says, and leans across to kiss me chastely on the cheek.

It's only pulling into Mayfields golf estate half an hour later that I realize he seized the opportunity to slide his phone into the change tray under the handbrake. Sneaky bastard.

Unfortunately, the smell of drains still lingers in my car and clings to me when I step into Mrs. Luthuli's. She's polite enough not to say anything, and she makes me strong tea, adding milk and sugar without asking. I drink it while she hunts upstairs.

After about ten minutes, she comes back downstairs with

a shoebox. She puts on her glasses and starts removing the photos one by one. "What is it you're looking for, exactly?"

"I'll be able to tell when I see it. May I?" I up-end the box onto the counter and sift through the photos. Most of them are cold dead things.

I latch onto one and turn it over. It's a photograph of a white wedding. A man and a woman—Song and S'bu's parents—squint into the sunlight at the bottom of a set of steps that could lead up to a community hall or a very plain church. His white suit has big lapels, she is holding a bouquet of pink roses and cosmos awkwardly. There is a faint wisp of attachment. Faded, fragile, hard to see in the light, but there. I've never worked with photographs before, unless the photograph was the lost thing in question. It never occurred to me to try to reach through the image. I get a flash of the World Trade Center again, which is frustratingly absurd.

"It's not fair," Mrs. Luthuli sighs. "They lost them so young."

"May I borrow this?"

"I don't know if I have the negatives . . ." She looks uncertain. But I am already out the door, following the tenuous wisp like Theseus and his ball of string. Let's just hope there's not a Minotaur on the other side.

It turns out that a Minotaur would be a dramatic improvement on what I actually find, which is nothing. Benoît's phone rings as I drive in aimless circles, trying to catch the ghosts of threads that keep fading, like bad radio signals. It's hopeless. Songweza could be anywhere in the city: sipping a mochaccino in a Parkhurst café or tied to a chair in a dingy garage in Krugersdorp. If I could get close enough, I might be able to pick up the thread, but where the hell do I start? I glance at Benoît's phone, which is pumping out the first twenty seconds of Gang of Instrumentals' "Oh Yeah" on repeat. The display indicates that the incoming call is from a private number. I let the call go to voice mail, but it rings again, insistently, distracting me so that I miss the dead-end sign and head down a cul-de-sac. The third time, it's easier to answer—even if it's his bloody wife calling from Burundi—than to have to listen to "Oh Yeah" one more time.

"Hola," I say, squashing the phone to my ear with a hunched shoulder, as I yank the car through a three-point turn. Oh, for power steering.

"I don't have an exact address for you," Benoît says, "but I can tell you he lives in Hillbrow."

"You have no idea how much that means to me right now," I say, steering the Capri back towards the highway.

"Even if I got it from D'Nice?" he says.

"I don't care where you got it, my love."

"Okay, good. He says you owe him R200 for the information."

That sours my mood, but only slightly, because as I get closer to the city, I feel like I'm tuning in to the right channel at last. The wisp of thread solidifies, still delicate, but now actually leading somewhere rather than tapering off into nothingness.

When I see it, it's like a smack in the face. Not the World

Trade Center. High Point. And the thread from the wedding photograph leads right to it. So close to home I could have tripped over it—if I'd bothered to look up, if I'd bothered to take the poison dream seriously.

I find parking two blocks away. The car guard does a double-take at the state of the Capri. *"Hayibo, sisi."*

"Just make sure it's still there when I come back," I say and walk down towards the twin towers of the apartment block.

If Hillbrow was once the glamorous crown of Johannesburg, High Point was the diamond smack in the center of the tiara, with swinging bachelor pads and luxury apartments for young ambitious professionals and urbane cosmopolitan families.

The entrance is situated inside a pristine open-air mall, an island of consumerist sanctity with clothing stores and a fast-food eatery, pavements you could eat off, and patrons not so desperate that they'd try. It's almost normal—practically suburban. I soon see why. The perimeters are tenaciously patrolled by boys built like bulldogs, with shaved heads and mace and bulletproof vests.

It's the broken windows model of law enforcement, the notion that smothering the sparks of civil entropy will help stomp out the embers that flare up into serious crime. No loitering, no littering, no soliciting—although it seems the sharply dressed dealers standing chatting on the corner have diplomatic immunity, as long as they stay out of reach, like the homeless sleeping in rotten sleeping bags across the road.

I head inside, up an escalator, and scout out the entrance to the apartment block. Four heavily trafficked security doors that open with a tag only. There is a caged security office beside the doors, and I try my luck.

"Hi, I'm a visitor. Flat 612," I say, making up a number.

"Name, please?" The bored security guard is a different breed from the youngsters outside.

"Zinzi December."

"*Cha, sisi*. There is no Zinzi December on this list."

"No, I'm sorry. *I'm* Zinzi December." I take a shot in the dark. "I'm here to see Ronaldo."

"Ronaldo who?"

"Ronaldo Flat 612."

"You don't have his surname."

"I've forgotten."

"You must phone him, then. Get him to come fetch you."

"I don't have airtime," I plead, pathetically.

The security guard shrugs, goes back to reading his tabloid. The headline reads MORE JOBS DOWN THE TOILET! The Bear murder didn't even make the front page.

"I'll go use the pay phone," I say.

I head back down, looking for a back entrance, a fire escape, anything. Instead, I spot one of the young bulldogs. I walk up to him, careful to seem innocuous and un-loitery. "Excuse me, can you help me?"

The kid turns to me attentively. He must be nineteen max, with blue eyes that burn with a puppy dog eagerness, the kind that might just as easily translate into a wagging tail or a nasty nip.

I weigh the odds of pulling the journalism card. Shelve it back in the pack of tricks. "I'm looking for a missing girl."

"Wrong block, ma'am. This building is clean. You should try across the road. Ask those guys," he says, indicating the sharps on the corner with a tight little nod of his head. "They know plenty of missing girls, believe you me."

"I'm sure they do. Mine is in this building. I absolutely know it and I need to get in."

"You with the police?"

"No. I'm a sort-of . . . a private investigator. I find lost things. People too. It's usually less investigating, more finding."

He brightens at the prospect of action. "Let me find out if it's okay." He speaks incomprehensibly into the radio hanging next to his mace spray. I look away politely, watching the sharps. I hope Song is in this building, and not the grim peeling low-rise across the road with its curtains drawn in the middle of the morning. Most traffickers don't even bother with shipping containers. They advertise instead. It's never prostitution. It's a secretarial or shop job that pays unreasonably well. People are desperate as well as naïve. Once they've got them, the girls are gang-raped to put them in their place, hooked on drugs, and then put to work.

"*Ja*, it's cool," says the boy, coming back to me. "But I'm coming with you and no making a scene to upset the tenants. This is a good block," he adds sternly.

"No problem." He escorts me back up the escalator and tags me through the security gates. The guard inside his cage doesn't even look up from his newspaper.

"Do you know someone called Ronaldo? Really big guy. A bouncer."

"Nope. Sorry. But we have maybe twelve hundred tenants living here. Sometimes more if they sneak guests in to stay, which is an eviction offense. Sorry, hey, but the lift is out, so we're going to have to walk up. It's the tenants. We have water supply issues. People turn on their taps, nothing comes out and they forget about them, so when the water comes back on, it floods. It's got into the elevator shaft. It's going to cost a million to fix."

"What do the people who live on the 26th floor do?"

"Walk. Even with groceries or prams. But it's okay, we've told them that until the lift is fixed, they can throw their rubbish out the window, and we get someone to clean it up. It's not nice, but you have to be fair to the tenants. So what floor is your girl on?"

"I don't know yet."

"Well, I hope you're fit," he says pushing the door open on a bleak cement stairwell. "I go up these stairs maybe eight or ten times a day. Disturbances with some guys drinking. Or a door gets stuck. We're like security and maintenance. We had something similar happen before, you know."

"Similar?"

"To your girl. There was a woman who was raped. We knew it was a tenant. So we just waited outside. Me and her, standing by the doors for two days until the guy came out. Then we had him arrested." He stands aside to let an old man carrying two bulging and battered Checkers packets pass. There are no numbers to mark the floors, but by my reckoning we've gone up seventeen or eighteen floors when Sloth grips onto my shoulders hard.

"I know, buddy." I can feel the thread tugging like an excited toddler.

Which is when the door above us bursts open and releases a flurry of girl into the stairwell. She collides with Security Boy, trying to barge past, but he catches her against his chest and holds her.

"Whoa, whoa, whoa," he says, restraining her. "You okay?"

"Let go of me, you cock!"

I was wrong. Songweza is not a Gothpunk princess, she's nu-'80s indie mod rocker. More colorful wardrobe, same amount of eyeliner. And she's a handful. Or an armful.

"Song Radebe?" The question is moot: she looks exactly like the photographs in the magazines. Slightly scruffier, maybe, with a mane of braids held back with a bright purple alice band and matching purple snakeskin cowboy boots. She sees me, or rather Sloth, and her eyes widen.

"Oh *crap*." She wriggles out of Security Boy's grasp and darts back up, taking the steps three at a time.

We emerge from the stairwell into a sun-drenched corridor and a standoff: Songweza is trapped between us and Marabou and Maltese. The door to room 1904 stands ajar behind them.

"Okay, people," Security Boy says, his hand hovering near his mace, ready to draw, "let's sort this out."

"Well, look who's here," sneers the Maltese.

"You're late to the party," the Marabou says. "And you haven't been answering your phone."

"What are you doing here?"

"Oh sweetie, don't you check your voice mail? Your services are no longer needed. We found her all on our own-somes."

"My phone was stolen."

"Very unprofessional," Maltese tuts.

Song looks from me to them and back again. Then she drops into a crouch, puts her hands over her ears, and screams loud enough to be heard in Cape Town. I don't know about her singing, but all that voice training has paid dividends. The screaming, one note perfectly sustained, sets off the Mutt, which starts yapping in a hysterical frenzy.

Security Boy clicks open the holster that holds his mace canister. "Okay, I mean it. What the hell is going on here?"

"Don't let them take me," Song says, sobbing. She throws herself at him, clutching onto his pants legs.

The door of 1910 down the way opens a crack and Security Boy shouts down the corridor, "Close that door. Mind your business!"

"As *you* should," the Marabou says.

"They're trying to kidnap me!" Song yelps, on her knees, hanging onto Security Boy's belt, looking up at him with huge kohl-lined eyes.

"She's been off her medication for a week," says the Maltese, slowly unbuttoning his blazer in a deliberate I-don't-have-a-weapon-in-here kind of way. "She's totally delusional."

"Wait. Wait a minute." Security Boy is flustered.

"I have a letter from her doctor." The Maltese reaches into the inside pocket of his jacket and removes a piece of paper. He carefully unfolds it, revealing the Haven's letterhead.

"Just wait! Let's start again. Who are you people?"

"This is a letter from the clinic that will elaborate on her condition. Severe paranoid delusions. She's been missing for days. We've come to fetch her home."

"Please. It's a trick. Don't listen," Song whimpers. The Maltese proffers the letter. But as Security Boy reaches for it, Song grabs at his mace, yanks it out the holster, and sprays him in the face with it. He recoils, choking, fists digging into his eye sockets.

Sloth starts wailing as we catch some of the misty residue. My eyes and nose start streaming with the burn, but it's not so bad that I can't lunge to grab Song's skinny arm and swing her back. The momentum swings her round so that she slams backwards into the window with a terrible crack. For a sickening second, I wait for it to splinter under the shock of her weight and catapult her nineteen stories down. But the glass holds.

"Ow! *Msunu!*" she swears.

"Calm down. No one's going to hurt you," I try to reassure her.

"Are you kidding me? You just did. Fuck you!" She tries to smash my instep with the heel of her boot, but I've already removed my foot from harm's way. Security Boy is half kneeling on the floor, one hand cupped over his eyes, gabbling into his radio to summon the cavalry. The Marabou and the Maltese watch, amused.

"A little help here?"

"Oh no. You need to earn your fee," Marabou says. Her Stork throws back its head and makes awful gulping motions, as if it's laughing.

Song is struggling and writhing like she's mid–grand mal seizure. When she throws her head back to smash my nose, I grab her hair, hold her head, and march her forward. And that's pretty much how we descend nineteen floors, with her squirming and swearing all the way. Security Boy stumbles behind, one hand against the wall guiding him down. I try to talk to her, softly so that the Marabou and the Maltese won't hear.

"Why'd you run away?"

"Fuck you."

"Was it something Odi did?"

"What *didn't* Odi fucking do?"

"I'm trying to help you, you little brat."

"By taking me back? Some help you are."

"What did you think you were doing here? Playing house with your bouncer boyfriend?"

"He's not my boyfriend, and it's not his place. Ro lives three floors down. It's mine. I paid for it." She adds for emphasis, "With my money. That I earned."

I try a different tack. "You had Mrs. Luthuli really worried."

That shuts her up, but only for a moment. "I'm sorry," she stage-whispers. "They're going to kill me, you know."

"I completely understand that. I'd quite like to kill you myself right now."

"Ask them what happened to Jabu."

"Who's Jabu?"

"Ask them. Ask them where he is now." She yells the name so it echoes down the stairwell. "Jaaaaabulaaaaani Nkutha!" She rolls her eyes at me. "Ask them!"

When we get downstairs, a police car is parked on the street outside, with a small cluster of High Point's security gathered around, watching disapprovingly. Their commander, an older man with features ravaged by sun damage and acne scarring, pours milk onto Security Boy's face to neutralize the mace.

The Marabou bundles Songweza into the Mercedes, which is parked across the road, and locks the doors. The Maltese walks over to talk to the cop and smooth things over with the official letter from the Haven That Explains Everything. As he hands it over, I get a glimpse of a wad of blue R100 notes folded inside.

"So who's Jabu?" I ask Marabou, playing innocent.

"Jabu? A horrible boy she met in rehab. He stole her money, broke her heart, and took off."

"Just disappeared?"

"Maybe he went back to his parents. How do I know? I didn't install a tracker."

"Is she normally——"

"Hormone imbalances. Manic depression. Whatever it is called. She is supposed to be on medication."

"And how exactly did you find her?"

"She made a call to a friend. The friend called us. Do not worry, you'll still be paid, as long as you are discreet." She gives me an appraising look. "I'd hate to see this feature in a blog." The Bird does that horrible swallowing-laughing thing with its head again. I have no idea what she is talking about.

"When can I get my money?"

"My, we are in a rush. We'll get it to you in the next few days. I assume cash is acceptable?"

"I'll come by tomorrow to collect it. And I'd like to see how Songweza is doing."

"Your concern is touching," she says indifferently. I glance up at her lost things. They're strangely sharp. Maybe it's just her, or proximity to her. The gloves and the book are still tethered to her among her lost things, but the firearm is no-ticeably absent.

"I see you found your gun," I say.

"What?" Her head swings my way. Her Bird clatters its beak at me.

"A Vektor?"

"Ah yes. One of my 'lost things'? I did find it, thank you."

"Is it licensed?" I glance over at the cops.

"If you understood what I had been through, you would know I would need something for self-defense."

"I've been thinking about that. Your tuna fish story."

"Yes?"

"You don't strike me as the tuna fish type. You're more of a shark. Were you really *inside* the container, Amira? Or were you on the outside, arranging passage? Another kind of procurement?"

"And *I* think you are a stupid girl with crazy ideas in her head." She jabs a long finger into my direction and stalks towards the car. I watch the Merc pull away, back towards the suburbs.

I'm out past the shark nets now.

25.

I'M MET BY wolf whistles and monkey whoops from D'Nice and his idiot friends, who are sprawled on the steps outside Elysium, already mostly drunk.

"Hey, Zee Zee On Top!" D'Nice catcalls. "You can ride me reverse cowgirl, baby!" He bucks his hips and pretends to swing a lasso above his head.

"You need to get a job, D'Nice. The beer is rotting your brain."

"Oh, I got one. You're looking at the new Elias. I start on Tuesday."

Upstairs, I find a printout tacked to my door that explains D'Nice's behavior, the Marabou's sarky remark. It's from *Mach* blog, a sneak peek of an upcoming feature (full story in the May issue!) called "Was It Good for Zoo?"

There are photos.

Some of them are five years old. Candid. He swore he'd deleted them.

Some are from a couple of nights ago. A kiss pinned against the wall of a grungy building. Dancing at the Biko Bar. Me looking wistful in the backseat of the car, streamers of city lights reflected in the glass. I don't remember Dave taking that one.

The naked pictures are not the worst of it. It's the words.

The copy is a mash-up of truth and invention. Gio writes about all the ways we have sex. Reverse cowgirl included. This, at least, is based on past experience, but he makes up the rest. How Sloth shivers and yowls when I come because we're connected like that. How he gets a little squeamish about it all. Calls it his pseudo-bestiality threesome. A gang-bang really, because the shadow of murder, of my sin, is like a fourth in the bed with us.

Mama always told him to avoid the bad girls, but hey, he writes, in a moment of tender confession, he loved me once.

"Cocksucking pigdog bastard mothercunt!" I kick the door for emphasis, leaving a vicious dent and cracking the paint-work. Mrs. Khan pokes her head out of 608, concerned. "Is everything all right, sweetheart?"

"Peachy," I snarl, and head upstairs to Benoît's apartment. He should be back by now. I just hope he hasn't seen it, but D'Nice is sure to have made extra photocopies to shove in his face.

Benoît is sitting in the middle of his floor sorting through a meager selection of clothes, in front of the sag-ging nicotine-yellow couch he and Emmanuel lugged all the way from Parktown when they spotted it dumped on the pavement.

The Rwandan kid sees me first. He's taping up a collection of tatty cardboard boxes salvaged from the superette. Every-thing Benoît has in the world. I could tape myself up in one of them and wait for his return.

"Benoît," Emmanuel says in a warning voice, a voice that tells me everything has changed.

Benoît looks up to see me standing in the doorway. He turns back to his job without comment, but he looks frayed, like a carpet that's been trodden down. The Mongoose gives me an evil look—our moment of bonding at the window last night forgotten.

"It's not true," I say, adding in exasperation. "Emmanuel, can you get lost, please?"

"Uh—" Emmanuel looks to Benoît for confirmation, but there's none forthcoming: he just keeps folding and rolling his t-shirts. Emmanuel has always been a little scared of me. He sets down the tape and ducks out the door past me. "Sorry," he says, like it's a funeral, and squeezes my arm.

As he finishes folding each one, Benoît places the sausage-roll shirts neatly inside one of those damn checked bags. I kneel down next to him.

"Please don't use that. I have a backpack I can lend you." He ignores me.

"Thanks for the phone. And the tip. I found her. I couldn't have done it without you. I'm getting the cash tomorrow. I can pay for fake papers, for your plane ticket."

"I don't want your money," he says, taking all the rolled-up shirts out again and starting to re-roll them.

"Oh for fuck's sake. Look, Giovanni and I had a thing years ago. He made up the rest. You can tell it's bullshit. That obscene stuff about Sloth coming at the same time—"

"Oh, that?" says Benoît. "I don't care about *that*, Zinzi."

"Where are you going?"

"Central Methodist Church. It's just for a couple of days until I leave."

"And fight over a piece of concrete floor to sleep on, an edge of staircase? Please. If you've got someone else moving in here already, you can stay at my place. I won't even try to have sex with you."

"I don't think that's a good idea."

"I can't believe you're letting this piece of shit's disgusting slander get between us. A couple of hours ago we're fine, and now this? Over ancient fucking history?" Sloth murmurs in my ear, soothing noises. He hates it when I shout.

"It's not him." Benoît hefts the bag onto the couch and stands up to face me. "It's *you,* Zinzi. I used your computer. I needed to email Michelle. The aid worker," he clarifies when I look blank.

"Oh." I sit down heavily on the couch next to his bag.

"I found your scam letters. I wasn't looking for them. But you had replies in your inbox. Many replies."

"So what? If you knew the circumstances —"

"Do you know *their* circumstances, these people you steal from?"

"I just write the formats, Benoît. You think this is easy for me? Living on money scrounged from finding a lost set of keys here, a passport there? I have debts to pay." I am aware of how childishly defensive I sound.

"We all have debts to pay!" Benoît raises his voice for the first time, gestures at the open doorway. "All of us here."

"Mine happen to be financial as well as moral."

"I didn't know you were this selfish."

"I'm an addict! It comes with the fucking territory. I'm sorry I'm not as perfect as your fucking wife. And I hope for your sake she's as fucking perfect as you remember. That she doesn't have an animal of her own. Five years is a long time, Benoît. How do you know she even wants you back?"

"I have a message from her."

"And I have a whole outbox full of messages promising untold riches. How do you know you're not just another *moegoe,* pinning everything on a dream that's patently impossible?"

"I don't. I just have to go and see how it is, see how to make it work."

"Fine. Whatever. Go live your life. Why do you care about these idiots giving away their money?"

He sits down next to me, the couch creaking mournfully. "It's because I knew a boy like Felipe once. The one who gets shot in the back in your Eloria letter?"

"I didn't know. How could I have known? It wasn't on purpose, Benoît. It wasn't to hurt you."

"Like your letters are not to hurt people? You don't care about anyone else, Zinzi."

"Of course I care, why the fuck do you think I took this missing persons job? And so far it's turning out more dodgy than all the scams I've ever been involved in. I did it so I could get out of this. Aren't you taking this a *little* personally?"

"I shot Felipe."

"What?"

"We used to sleep in a church, all the children and us older kids looking after them. I was nineteen. It was meant to be safe. They took us anyway. *Armée de résistance du Seigneur.* Lord's Resistance Army. Even before these troubles now, they used to make incursions across the border from Uganda. Or maybe it was a splinter group. They broke the windows. Used their rifle butts to smash in the heads of the little ones too small to walk. Anyone who resisted. In the forest, they did things to drive us mad. *Muti.* Drugs. Rape. Killing games. His name wasn't Felipe. But he was my friend. And I shot him because that was the choice they gave me."

"God."

He smiles wanly. "*Nzambe aza na zamba te.* God is not in the forest. Maybe He is too busy looking after sports teams or worrying about teenagers having sex before marriage. I think they take up a lot of His time."

"I didn't know."

"Your policy. No questions. It's all right, Zinzi, I wouldn't have told you anyway. I didn't tell my wife when we married. There are camps for child soldiers, where they try to teach you to be human again." His mouth twitches, more pity than smile.

"Was that when you got the Mongoose?"

"It was 1995. Before *mashavi.* But he was waiting for me. He waited eleven years for me. We were on our way to Celvie's father's funeral. We knew it was dangerous, but it was her father. We should have left the kids behind. The

FLDR attacked us. I fought back. Killed two of them. That's why they burned me."

"The FLDR?" I say, reeling. As if unraveling the acronyms could make sense of this.

"The *Forces démocratiques de libération du Rwanda*. I thought I'd left the fighting behind. It was like a different life for me, Zinzi, for many years. I met Celvie. We had children. I went to university. But the war in the Congo is like an animal. You can't get away from it." He runs his palm down the scars on his throat.

"What happens now?"

"Now I must hope that I can avoid the war. And this time, I will tell my wife. But you understand why I don't want your money."

In my chest, the poison flower bursts open, an explosion of burning seeds. I imagine Mr. and Mrs. Barber experienced something similar whenever they finally realized that the bearer bonds were forged.

It is the death of hope.

PART TWO.

26.

YELLOW LIGHT SLICING across my pillow like a knife would be the appropriate simile, but it feels more like a mole digging its way into my skull through my right eyeball. There is a boy in my bed, or at least I think it's a boy. It's hard to judge gender by the back of someone's head. But I have my suspicions, based on the sandy curls and the snippets of last night that my brain is starting to defrag.

A man built like a tank in a red-and-black tuxedo beside the velvet rope, because I couldn't face going to Mak's to get fucked up.

"Ro off tonight?"

"You want I can give him a message?"

"Can I give you my phone number?"

"Baby, you can definitely give me your phone number."

"Get out," I half-shove, half-drag the curly-headed thing out of my bed by the ankle and dump him on the floor.

"This is something special," Babyface Dealer says, chopping out another line, grainy like salt crystals on the dashboard of his car. Technically, he's not supposed to indulge with his customers. I can be very persuasive.

It burns going up, like speed cut with rat poison. He says that's just the magic. Sloth whimpers unhappily. Then the inside

271

of my head lights up like a Christmas mall display and my heart surges up in my chest and the world drops away in graceful slow-mo.

"What the hell?" Babyface Dealer yanks at the sheets around his legs.

A girl gyrates with an albino python in one of the elevated archways, pulling it between her legs and bucking her hips. It's the drugs or maybe her shavi, but lust seems like a tangible current moving through the crowd on the dance floor.

A used condom is still attached to his limp dick.

"House special," Babyface Dealer says in the bathroom as he chops out another line. "Specially imported."

"Odious maximus." I giggle and he shushes me, but I'm not sure if it's because he doesn't want to be bust or if I'm not supposed to mention Odi's name.

"It was wonderful. You were great. Now get the fuck out of my house."

There is a singer from Mali up on stage crooning into the microphone. Also specially imported. Or maybe procured.

"Not exactly a house," Babyface Dealer says, yanking on his pants, commando, over the shriveled condom. "Is it, love?"

I tip the marine biology student bartender my last R1000. "Buy yourself an oceanarium, honey."

"Don't get mugged and die on your way out," I snap. He slams the door behind him.

Despite the evidence, I consider going to the pharmacy for the morning-after pill. Maybe a shot of anti-retrovirals. Sloth is not speaking to me. He refuses to move from his perch in the cupboard and when I try to pull him out, he hits out at me, scratching my cheek. I had it coming.

I strip the bed, bundle up the sheets and throw them out the window. They get caught up in the branches of the trees below and hang there like dead things. Flaccid ghosts. Or my own personal white flag.

I think I've been here before. Rock fucking bottom.

27.

THIS WAS INEVITABLE. This grubby church basement with its grubby sign that reads NEW HOPE. The grubby men and women with grubby animals chanting the miserable litany of their grubby lives, mine included. It's supposed to be all relative. Degrees of awful that contextualize your own suffering. But what it really is, is painfully monotonous. There are only so many ways to screw up your life. We cover most of them in the first twenty minutes.

Even when the rich kids from the Haven join us halfway through, the only difference is in the details. But I feel saner for going. I also considered Phoenix, Fresh Beginnings, and even Narcononymous, but I'd already established the credentials of the New Hope program. Same principles as its plush sister facility, although there are less cheekbones per capita and I imagine the food isn't as good.

Lunch consists of day-old sandwiches sealed with stickers that proudly announce their providence as DONATED FROM THE KITSCH KITCHEN FINE FOODS DELI—CERTIFIED ORGANIC. Could have done with real cutlery instead of plastic, but hey, the patrons of this fine twelve-step establishment are a little rougher than those that frequent the Haven.

A cute black girl who came in with the rich kids slides in next to me and greets Sloth: "Hey, fuzzybutt, I thought I recognized you."

Sloth reaches out his arms to be picked up, and she takes him from me and gives him a cuddle.

"It's Naisenya, right?" I say, recognizing Overshare Girl from the Haven. "You can keep him, if you like. He's not exactly thrilled with me right now."

"Is that why you're here?"

"I could ask the same of you."

"Day trip. I'm the driver." She tilts her head at the rich kids, who are getting a nasty taste of what hitting real bottom involves. "We come visit every Sunday."

"Guess that makes me a passenger. The old revolving-door ride."

"No free will," she agrees and tucks into her only slightly stale pastrami sandwich. She offers Sloth a bite.

"He only eats leaves."

"Sorry, didn't bring any with me. I would have saved you some weeds if I'd known, cutiepie."

"Hey, did Songweza ever come here with you?"

"Oh yeah, Song was practically a regular. Wouldn't know it, huh? High-maintenance girl like her. I think she kinda gets off a little on slumming it."

"I get the same impression."

"This is where she met her poet."

"Would this be Jabu by any chance?"

"I see you're familiar with the tragic romance of Song and Jabu."

"Broke up with her via SMS?"

"Harsh, huh? Those two fell hard. Pop princess and wannabe-novelist breadline kid living with his charlady mom in Berea. He wrote poems for her when he managed to stay off the mandrax for long enough to catch the words. She promised to turn them into songs. And then, poof! He just never came back."

"Can't be that unusual. This isn't rehab proper. No one's exactly checking in."

"Sure, you get the drop-ins, drop-outs. But that was cold, even for a junkie. How do you know Song anyway?"

"Let's say I used to be in the music industry. Very briefly." I pack the Kitsch Kitchen wrappers and the plastic cutlery into the box, and stand up to go.

"See you again?" Naisenya asks, hopeful. I think she has a crush on Sloth.

"If you're here." I toss the box into the communal dustbin. "Working it, and all that."

It's strange to phone Songweza's number and actually get through, although it takes her twelve rings before she answers. I feel a stab of guilt for neglecting her.

"Lo?" Her voice floats up like she's answering from Atlantis—a dreamily drowning voice that is so far removed from the smart-arse diva persona, I'm convinced I've dialed wrong. Which is impossible. I put her on speed-dial two.

"Song?"

"Yes?"

"It's Zinzi. The woman with the Sloth."

"Oh. Oh yes. You weren't very nice to me." A hint of petulance spikes through the depths.

"Is everything okay? With you, I mean."

"I'm fine. Arno is cross that I came back. Yes, you, *doos*. But I had a talk with Odi, and he says as soon as this album drops and after the tour, we can talk about splitting up and going solo. He said it's like a good launch platform? For both of us."

"Well, that's good, right? Are you going to play indie music?"

"Odi said celebrities are little gods. You have to feed the people what they want so they can worship you properly."

"What about Jabu, Song?"

"Jabulani, Jabulani, he can kiss my *breyani*. I just made that up. Odi says he was cheating on me. Tried to hit on Carmen. Can you believe the nerve? He says he had a little word with him and that's why he took off. He says he didn't do it to hurt me. Odi, I mean. He has my best interests at fart." She giggles.

"Are you back on your medication?"

"I wasn't on these pills before."

"Do you know the name?"

"Misty-pisty-something-something."

"Do you have a pen?"

"What for?"

"I want you to take down my number. I want you to call me if you're worried about anything, or if you run into any trouble."

"So you can pull my hair out by the fucking roots again?"

"So I can try to help you."

"It's cool, your number came up on my phone."

"I'd like you to write it down."

"I'd like you to kiss my *breyani*," she screeches and lapses into manic giggles. "Shut the fuck up, Arno."

"Can I talk to your brother? Or Des?"

"Des is gone. Des was the bomb, but now he's gone. Here, talk to *doos* face."

"Arno?" There is the scramble of the phone being handed over.

"I told you. Didn't I tell you?" Arno whines.

"She's on some pretty heavy medication. Where is Des? Is Mrs. Luthuli there?"

"No, they went away for a coupla days. Back to the Valley of a Thousand Hills. For a funeral. Des's cousin hung himself," he says matter of factly. "He was twenty-two. It was probably AIDS."

"And S'bu?"

"He's writing songs in his room."

"Can you do me a favor, Arno? Can you give me the name of the medication Song is taking?"

"Uh, sure, hang on, I'll just have to go upstairs."

Song shouts in the background. "Hey! Hey, prick for balls! That's my phone."

"She's lost it completely," Arno whispers into the phone. "She's actually *worse* than before. And S'bu's just spacey. He's on meds too, now."

"Get a pen. Take down my new number. I want you to phone me if anything weird happens."

"Weird like how?"

"Like any kind of weird. Phone me first, okay? Not Odi. And then phone the cops."

"You're freaking me out here."

"I'm just worried about you guys with Mrs. Luthuli not being there. Tell you what, I'll call in every day to check up on you. And I'm going to speak to a social worker, okay?"

"Okay."

"You got the name of that medication for me?"

"Uh, hang on. Mi-da-zol-am. What *is* that?"

"Hang on, let me check." I do a quick search on my laptop. "Okay, it's cool, just a sleeping pill," I say. With one hell of a kick. "See if you can get her to lie down and actually sleep. And let me know if you run into any kind of weird. Anything at all."

"Does Song being a freak count?"

"Not unless she's being especially freaky."

The house has actually deteriorated since my last visit. It seems darker, dingier, and that smell of old people and vase-water has gotten worse. Carmen looks skinny and pale in a lime-green sixties-style handkerchief bikini. When she serves a tray of that disgusting tea, I notice that her fingernails are dirty, like she's been digging in the carrot patch all morning. Her Rabbit lies sprawled listlessly under her deck chair.

But the real shock is Huron. He is looking particularly odious in a faded *Oppikoppi '99* t-shirt that rides up to reveal his hairy belly. There is an old scar that hugs the curve of where his hip would be if his stomach wasn't in the way. Or rather a series of scars, slightly curved like surgical staples. Or teeth marks. His cheeks have sunken to flaccid jowls and, most telling of all, there is a drip on a wheelie-stand hooked up next to his ironwork chair. Above his head, the black tumor of sawn-off tentacles is thicker and squirmier than ever.

"I don't know why you felt you needed to see me," he says, antagonistic behind his oversized sunglasses.

"I actually wanted to see Songweza. Check that she's okay."

"After you cocked up the job, you mean. Check that you're still getting your full payout. So nice of you to care."

"Nice of you to pay me so well to do a job you were perfectly capable of doing on your own."

"What can I tell you? I hire good people. They got there first. Don't worry, you'll still get your fee."

"That's very generous. I take it it's more of a shut-your-face payoff than anything I really earned."

"Take it however you want," he says and slurps his tea noisily.

I lean forward across the table. "I'd ask if we could talk privately, but I think Carmen might want to hear this."

"Carmen's a big girl," he says.

"This is what I think. You've been sleeping with Song. And Carmen and anyone else within reach. Song ran away, maybe planning to blackmail you, maybe spill the story to the press, which would have been extra juicy considering you're also moving drugs through your club. It's a guess, but I figure the Marabou and the Maltese facilitate that. It's a kind of procurement, right? And you've got them doing a lot of international travel. Does that include drug smuggling? 'Cos I've sampled some of the wares coming through Counter Rev, and it was good shit, let me tell you. Wasn't that what got you into trouble with Bass Station?"

Huron opens his mouth to retaliate and I hold up a finger to silence him. "I'm not finished. Song's rehab boyfriend Jabu was probably helping her, maybe even instigated the whole thing, but you scared him off, so she turned to Ronaldo, the bouncer, in desperation. You had him beaten up already. I reckon the Maltese and the Marabou went back for round two and this time they got Song's whereabouts out of him. Might have even killed him. But hey, what's a missing Moroccan bouncer in the grand scheme of things? And I reckon you'll do the same to anyone else who gets in the way."

There is a long pause. Then Carmen says, "Excuse me," in a strangled voice. Her cheeks are bright pink. She picks up her Bunny and clip-clops into the house.

"You've gone and upset her," Huron says, not looking particularly bothered.

"It's upsetting stuff."

"This notion of yours," he says, pinching his thick bottom lip. "What should we call it—the Polanski-Sopranos Theory? It's original. Not bright. Not true. But original. Aren't you worried I'm going to put out a hit on you?"

"Believe me when I say I haven't got anything left to lose."

"So, what's next? You go to the police?"

"With what evidence? One half-baked Polanski-Sopranos Theory? No, I'm just letting you know that if anything happens to Songweza Radebe—anything *else* I should say—then I *will* go to the police. Inspector Lindiwe Tshabalala is an old friend. She'll listen to what I have to say." By "friend" I mean "one-time interrogator" of course, but I figure I can afford to be a little liberal with the truth.

"These are wild accusations. I might have to take this to my lawyer."

"Do what you have to."

"Do you have a physical address I can have the restraining order sent to?"

"Your people know where to find me. But so long as Songweza stays singing fit and healthy, I won't trouble you with the slightest, littlest thing, Mr. Huron."

"You assume I don't have my own insurance policy on you."

"Like the 1.5 million you've taken out on each twin?"

"You've been doing some research, little girl."

"I'd like my money now, please."

28.

I HAND OVER the cash to Vuyo in the lobby of the Michel-angelo. It's the most upmarket hotel I can think of that's still vaguely accessible. I've dressed accordingly in a sundress and dark sunglasses with a red faux snakeskin briefcase I pur-chased from the Sandton City luggage shop for the occasion, together with a brand-new phone. I can afford it. And for some moments in your life, it's worth making a scene. Espe-cially the kiss-off.

I sit beside Vuyo on one of the couches in the sumptuous flash of the lobby and flick open the briefcase on my lap, not caring who sees. I'm feeling reckless.

"All here plus the fee for the recent extras. Do you want to count it?"

"I trust you," says Vuyo, calmly flipping the briefcase shut. "We're rehearsing for a movie," he says smoothly to an over-weight man in a Cape Town t-shirt goggling at us.

"You shouldn't," I reply.

"Can I say that I am sad?"

"You could. It won't make a difference."

"I am sad. We worked well together."

"I worked. You ambushed."

"Ah. But I knew you would rise to the occasion. You are a hard-headed woman, Zinzi December. Sometimes you need a push." He still hasn't reached for the briefcase. "This isn't a sting, I hope. No cops about to swoop down?"

"I thought about it," I confess. "But I'm too busy trying to dig myself out of the plague pit that's my life right now."

He leans in close to me. "This money? I will give it back to you doubled. Another R500,000 a year from now. Come work with us. You're an asset to the Company."

"There's more chance of Sloth sprouting wings and starting his own airline. Not that I don't appreciate the offer. I'm trying to get clean."

"Zinzi. What are you going to do? Keep digging up trinkets for old people for spare change?"

"Something better. Or worse. Depends on how you feel about the media. I'm hoping for better."

"Well, if you ever need a dentist . . ."

"I have Ms. Pillay's email address."

He stands up to shake my hand and, just like that, I am cut free.

Or not quite.

There are 3,986 new emails in my inbox, unread. I set up an auto-reply to all of them.

This is a scam.
No one is going to give you millions of dollars for nothing.

Save your money.
Spend it on ice cream.
Go out to dinner.
Take your loved ones away for the weekend.
Pay off your credit cards.
Have an adventure.
Blow it on skydiving lessons or drink or hookers or gambling.
But please, don't send it to me or anyone else involved in this ugly little fiction.

And next time, don't be so fucking naive.

Vuyo is going to be pissed. But not pissed enough to have me killed. Not when he doesn't have an animal yet. And hey, there will be others. *Moegoes* are easier to come by than E. coli in a fast-food kitchen.

I add a final line, even though it's a petty revenge, far less than he deserves, even though it might implicate me, or at least my anonymous pseudonym, Kahlo999.

Questions? Please contact Giovanni Conte gio@machmagazine.co.za

It takes a long time to send 3,986 emails, watching the status bar count them off. There is a deep satisfaction in this. A satisfaction that is dented when one of the addresses bounces. It takes a techno-naif to fall for a 419, but they're usually not so unsophisticated that they can't even get their return address right.

This is the mail system at host smtpauth01.mweb.co.za.

I'm sorry to have to inform you that your message could not be delivered to one or more recipients. It's attached below.

For further assistance, please send mail to postmaster.

If you do so, please Include this problem report. You can delete your own text from the attached returned message.

The mail system <no-one>: Host or domain name not found. Name service error for name=inventedzoocity.com type=A: Host not found

Reporting-MTA: dns; smtpauth01.mweb.co.za X-Postfix-Queue-ID: D4AF5A024B

X-Postfix-Sender: rfc822; Kahlo999@gmail.com Arrival-Date: Sun, 27 March 2011 21:51:59 +0200 (SAST)

Final-Recipient: rfc822; <no-one>
Original-Recipient: rfc822;ghost24976@limboworld.za
Action: failed
Status: 5.4.4

Diagnostic-Code: X-Postfix; Host or domain name not found.
Name service error for name=<no-one> type=A: Host not found

From: Kahlo999
Date: Sun, 27 March 2011 21:51:59 +0200
To: <no-one>
Subject: RE:

This is a scam.

No one is going to give you millions of dollars for nothing. Save your money. Spend it on ice-cream. Go out to dinner. Take your loved ones away for the weekend. Pay off your credit cards. Have an adventure.

Blow it on skydiving lessons or drink or hookers or gambling.

But please, don't send it to me or anyone else involved in this ugly little fiction.

And next time, don't be so fucking naive.

Questions?   Please   contact   Giovanni   Conte
gio@machmagazine.co.za

========

From: <no-one>
Date: Sun, 27 March 2011 21:51:59 +0200
To: <no-one>
Subject: <no subject>

I danced until my feet broke off. Until my shoes turned red with blood. I always wanted to be a girl in a storybook.

It's too strange, too poetical to be spam. I open up the Word doc and add it to my collection.

It bothers me, like a pubic hair between your teeth. Or a ghost in the machine.

Hey, it's not like I have anything else to do with my life right now. I take my laptop downstairs and four blocks over to the Nice Times Internet Café to print them out. The guy at the shop wraps the hard copies in a brown paper bag for me, so it's only when I get home and spread them out over the floor that Sloth freaks the fuck out.

He's been resting on my back, half dozing, but when the pages are arranged on the linoleum, he starts hissing, tugging at my arms to pull me away.

"What's your problem? Is it this?" I pick up a page, and he hunches his shoulders and bats the page out of my hand. He scrambles off my back and backs into the far corner, behind the bed, bristling like the pages are possessed. Maybe Vuyo was right and this is bad *muti,* a hack spell from a rival syndicate. Maybe this is the cause of everything, the dark shadows over my life. I dig in my bag to see if I still

have that bottle of *muti* the *sangoma* gave me. How hard
can it be?

Sloth is not convinced this is a good idea. I'm kneeling
in the middle of my apartment, burning *imphepho* in an incense holder, a spindle of fragrant smoke rising in the air. I've
crumpled up the emails in a large empty pot. "Unless you
have a better suggestion?"

He opens his mouth.

"A better suggestion that doesn't involve going back to Mai
Mai," I add quickly.

His jaw snaps shut. And then he sneezes twice, abruptly.

"See? It's a sign."

Resigned, Sloth holds out his lanky arm and I take a pin-
prick of blood with a vintage brooch from my jewelry box
and wipe it off on the most recent email.

I pour a liberal dose of paraffin over the crumple of papers
in the pot, add a splash of the *sangoma*'s cleansing *muti* from
the cough-medicine bottle, and take a swig for good luck.
Then I light the email streaked with Sloth's blood and drop it
into the pot. Séance flambé!

What happens instead is that a two-foot-high flame shoots
up from the pot, singeing my eyebrows. I fling myself away
in surprise and my foot catches the pot. Flaming paraffin
splashes over the floor. Sloth screams in alarm and starts
crawling for his climbing post, moving amazingly speedily.
He clambers up his pole, reaches out, and hooks onto one
of the loops of rope hanging from the ceiling and swings towards the front door, which is probably the smart option. If I

had any sense, I'd be doing the same. Instead, I grab the first thing at hand, which just happens to be my yellow leather jacket, and start beating out the flames.

The fire resists valiantly, but I finally manage to whack the life out of the flames—and my jacket. The fire dies reluctantly, almost resentfully. Greasy, evil-smelling black smoke pours out of the pot and boils off the floor. Choking and gagging on the smell, I fumble to open the window. And then it hits me.

Dunes of powdery yellow sand. They swell and fall like ocean waves. Something you could drown in. Mounds erupt from the waves, spill termites onto the sand. They are swallowed up again. The waves roll on.

A king without his head. He holds it in his lap. The head rolls its eyes and grins with blood-stained teeth beneath its crown. Take me, take me, take me to your spider den. He is wearing a faded Oppikoppi t-shirt.

Birds circling in the sky, an aviary's worth, all different kinds, cranes, pigeons, hawks, vultures, sunbirds, sparrows.

A flash of an old movie. Soylent Green is people.

A barbed-wire fence. A bright yellow sign. Private property. Trespassers will be mutilated.

An artificial fingernail, half an inch long, ruby red with silver stars painted on it, lying in a gutter. A private galaxy in the dirt. There are faded letters stenciled on the curb. Kotch. Kozy. Kotze.

A supermarket trolley brimming with white plastic forks. It catches on fire. The forks twist and melt.

A snowfall of feathers. Some of the tips are clotted with red gobs of flesh. It turns into a rain of frogs.

Snap! Snap out of it. Snap out—

I open my eyes to find Sloth shaking me by my shoulders and whining.

"Okay, it's okay. I'm fine." I sit up gingerly, rubbing the back of my head, where I seemed to have smashed it against the floor, possibly repeatedly. My heels ache, as if I have been drumming them in a seizure. I'm lucky I didn't bite off my tongue.

Or break a nail.

29.

"DAVID LASLOW," THE voice on the phone drawls.

"Photographer Dave? This is Zinzi December. We met at the Biko?"

"I wondered if you'd call me." He sounds resigned. "You want to *kak* me out, I understand. It was a job. Gio was paying me. He didn't tell me what was involved."

"Forget it. That's not why I'm calling. I want to do a story, a real one. I want you to take the photographs."

"Whoo boy, did you pick the wrong week. I've got the Mbuli court case, the premier's portrait, the Springbok press conference, some new clinic opening—and that's not counting whatever comes up during the course of the day."

"*This* just came up. And besides, you owe me."

"I thought that wasn't why you were calling?"

"It isn't. But that doesn't mean you don't. Come on, I'll be your fixer on the zoo stories. Isn't that what you wanted? An all-access pass to Zoo City. You want drugs, sex, vice, dogfights? I can get you in. But you have to do this for me."

"You don't let up, do you?"

"No."

Dave is waiting by the One-Stop shop when I pull into the petrol station under Ponte. Once a glitzy apartment block famed for its round design, it's turned from housing project with gangsters, squatters, drugs and prostitution, garbage, and suicides piling up in the central well, back to reclaimed glitzy apartment block. I suspect it will go through its own revolving door soon enough.

"Get in." I pop the door lock for him. I still haven't got the window fixed. "My car is less likely to get us hijacked." He obliges with a dubious look.

"Where are we going?" he asks

"Did you pull the clips on the homeless guy killing I asked for?"

"Yep." He digs into his pocket and hauls out a slim bundle of photocopies. "Poor guy didn't get much in the way of column space. Here's *The Star*."

The Star 23 March 2011

Homeless Man Burned Alive

[Ellis Park] The badly burned body of Patrick Serfontein, 53, was found under a bridge in Troyeville on Tuesday, Gauteng Police said. Captain Louis du Plessis said the homeless man was apparently beaten before his attackers set him alight. The man was identified by his South African ID, found on the scene. The police have opened a murder investigation and appealed for witnesses to come forward. — Sapa.

"And here's my paper."

The copy features a grotesque photograph of a man's face, the skin black and bubbled, lips peeled back from the teeth, like he just got back from holiday in Pompeii.

The Daily Truth 24 March 2011

POLICE FILE
Crime Watch with Mandlakazi Mabuso

Homefried Homeless

I'm telling you straight. Some human scum burned a homeless *ou* to death on Tuesday. Patrick Serfontein lived under a Troyeville bridge in a cardboard box until he was beaten up and necklaced with a tire over his head by one or more *tsotsis* who are still unidentified and walking around free and easy because no one saw anything.

The poor homeless *ou*'s face was so badly burnt up that the cops had to identify him by what they hope is his ID book, which they found among some personal *goeters* in an old shopping trolley near the body. The SAPS refused to speculate on the motive behind the violent killing. Is this the first sign of another serial killer like Moses Sithole on the loose?

Other uglinesses that happened yesterday: The body of a missing nine-year-old in Ventersdorp has been discovered, drowned in a farm dam. At least his parents can make peace because his body *has* been found. The number of people who just *sommer* go missing in this city never to be seen again is just sad, *mense*.

The rest is ripped off. I raise an eyebrow. "That's some quality reporting."

Dave shrugs. "I just take the photographs."

"Nothing about his having an animal."

"Not every person living on the edge of society has to have an animal. What's this all about?"

"Patrick Serfontein is a hunch. Let's just say his death coincides with an email. Is there a Before photograph?"

"Just his ID. I got a photocopy of it for you from Mandla. She says if we find anything good, it goes under her byline. You can have an 'additional reporting by.' "

"I don't know if 'good' is the word I'd use," I say grimly.

"Where are we going?"

"To photograph a body that coincides with another email."

The ruby acrylic fingernail I recovered from Kotze Street lies on the dashboard. The thread that leads away from it is black and withered, but still traceable, if a vision dream of yellow sand dunes gives you a hint about where to start.

"You got a killer sending you emails? Do you know him personally? Some kind of gloating thing? They do that, right? Serial killers?"

"I don't know who the killer is. I think it's his victims sending me messages."

"But they're dead?"

"Exactly."

"Okay, whatever." Dave slumps back into his seat, fiddling with his camera.

I drive out south to where the last of the mine dumps are—sulfur-colored artificial hills, laid waste by the ravages of weather and reprocessing, shored up with scrubby grass and eucalyptus trees. Ugly valleys have been gouged out and trucked away by the ton to sift out the last scraps of gold the mining companies missed the first time round. Maybe it's appropriate that *eGoli*, place of gold, should be self-cannibalizing.

I pull off onto a dirt road lined with straggly trees and drive for exactly 3.8 kays. I measured the distance on my way back. As we get out of the car, a vicious little wind kicks up gritty yellow dust and stirs the trees to a disquieting susurrus. I haul the heavy blanket off the back seat and throw it over the barbed-wire fence. This time, I've come prepared, after shredding my jeans on my earlier foray. It was only after I got home that I noticed the gash in my pants, the dried blood on my leg.

"This is trespassing," Dave says as I lift Sloth over the fence.

"Don't worry. I was here earlier. It doesn't count as trespassing the second time round." I hold the ruby fingernail gently cupped in my hand. The thread is thicker now. We're close.

We scramble up the slope of the dump, the fine sand swallowing our feet to the ankle with every step. Away from the shelter of the trees, the wind is even more capricious. Eddies of dust whip and spiral around us, sandblasting exposed skin. I pull my hoodie up over Sloth, but it offers only scant protection. He ducks his head behind my neck and squeezes his eyes shut.

"Shit," Dave says. "I don't have the right lens protection for this."

"Here." I was hoping it wouldn't feel as bad the second time round. But the same mix of nausea and dread rises in the back of my throat. Dave raises his camera automatically and then lowers it again without taking a shot. "How did you find this?"

"It sort of found me."

The woman with the Sparrow is sprawled akimbo on the sand, looking blankly up at the sky. There is dust embedded in every hollow and fold of her body, in the scooped palm of her hand, banked up against her lower eyelids like unshed tears, encrusted in the bloody gashes over her arms and legs and stomach and head. Her nails are broken, as if she'd tried to defend herself. Acrylic. Ruby-red with sequins. They must have matched her shoes.

Dave opens his mouth and closes it again. There's nothing to say. He takes cover behind the lens. The wounds are approximately three inches long, gaping like red mouths. It's hard work to hack someone to death. Ask the Hutu. Whoever did this had a lot of enthusiasm for the job.

"Notice anything missing?" I say as he stops to switch to a new memory card.

"I—No. I don't know. *Is* there something missing? Wait.

There's not much blood. Which might mean she was killed somewhere else."

"And her animal isn't here."

"How do you know she had an animal?"

"She worked my street. It was a Sparrow."

"A Sparrow? That's tiny. You could miss that easily."

"Trust me. It's not here." I know this because I have searched this dune sideways and backwards for the corpse of a small brown bird with matchstick legs clenched up under its breast. But also because I can feel it. "It's lost."

When the cops finally rock up, only an hour and a half after I call them, they are pissy. It's the dust and the wind and the dead woman staring up into the sky as if she's cloud-watching. It's the paperwork. The evidence. It's the fact that I'm involved at all.

They send me up to the interrogation room for another two-hour session with the good Inspector Tshabalala. This time she cuts straight to the chase.

"How did you know where to find the body?"

"It's in my file. My *shavi*—"

"Your *shavi* is finding lost things."

"And I *found* her body."

"How?" she presses.

"I followed a connection."

"How did you know the victim?"

"I didn't. I'd seen her on the street. She is, was, *lekgosha*. A sex worker. But I don't think it was a client who did this."

"You don't *think?* Were you involved with the killing?"

"No."

"Where were you on the morning of Tuesday 22nd March?"

"Isn't that a different interrogation?"

"You tell me. Where were you?"

"As I said before, at the time Mrs. Luditsky was stabbed to death, I was at home in my flat. Apartment 611, Elysium Heights, Zoo City, Hillbrow. Postal code 2038. With my boyfriend Benoît Bocanga, who I believe has made a statement corroborating such."

"Benoît Bocanga. We've been reviewing his papers."

"Which are in order."

"But his refugee status application is due for renewal."

"If you want to blackmail someone, blackmail me. I'm sure you can dig up something."

"Indeed." She changes tack. "Ms. December. You—and your magical *shavi*—have been peripherally involved in two murders in the last week. How would you explain that?"

"Phenomenally bad luck, Inspector."

"Do you own any knives?"

"I have a kitchen. It's small and dirty, but it does come equipped with assorted cutlery."

"Can we search your domicile?"

"You'll need a warrant."

"That can be arranged."

"So can a lawyer, Inspector."

30.

IT TAKES COMMITTED former addicts to drag their sorry asses out of bed at ten in the morning. Or, judging by the faces, perhaps people who don't know how to sleep anymore. Pass the Midazolam.

I help distribute polystyrene cups of truly disgusting instant chicory-coffee mix to the patrons of today's early-bird meeting at New Hope, using the opportunity to show round the photocopy of the burned man's ID at the same time.

The problem is that all anyone wants to talk about is Slinger, and how he's not the real *makhoya* after all. They're passing round a copy of *The Daily Truth.*

"*Fo sho,* darkie's Hyena was a fake," a very tall, very nervy guy says with telltale ringworm patches in his hair. He is carrying a funky old baseball cap upside-down with a Hedgehog curled up in it.

"This whole time?" says a lanky redhead with drawn-on eyebrows. "And no one noticed? Don't you people have a way of telling if an animal is real or not?"

"'You people'? 'Real or not'?"

"*Ag* man, you know what I mean."

"It's not like being gay. We don't have some magic zoodar to detect other zoos."

"I think it's sad. That man was doing a lot for zoo relations."

"That man was doing a lot for his own publicity. Playing Mr. Big Tough Gangster Zoo Guy to stir up controversy."

"Can I see that?" I ask, indicating the newspaper. The guy with the Hedgehog thrusts it at me and launches back into lecture mode. "Man like that knows how to work the media and rile up parents. You check his album sales. Same with Britney Spears. And Eminem and that freaky vampire guy with the weird eyes? They're just going for a reaction."

There are two photographs side-by-side dominating the front page under the headline CIRCUS ACT. The first is of Slinger holding an Uzi, posing tough with the diamond-collared hyena and a veritable posse of pussy in gold micro-bikinis with assault rifles of their own. It's contrasted with a harried man in a dark green tracksuit with a jacket over his head, fleeing the paparazzi towards an SUV with the door open to reveal a woman twisted round to hide her face.

I flip through, past the page-three boobs and the story about the people who have been so hard hit by the recession that they're hunting house cats, until I find the report on the Sparrow's murder. Dave promised it would be front page, but Slinger's dirty has pushed it to a narrow block on page six, just another police file item.

The Daily Truth 29 March 2011

POLICE FILE
Crime Watch with Mandlakazi Mabuso

Hate Crime Hack Job

The body of an *oulike* young boy-*nooi* was found yesterday afternoon on one of the Crown Mine dumps in the deep dark south of the city. After a hot tip-off, our photographer was first to discover the hacked up body. The victim, said to be a ladyboy of the night, had apparently had magical and surgical alterations done before the madman killer did a little altering of his own, cutting he/she/it to bloody ribbons with a *panga*. Was it a hate crime—a dissatisfied customer complaint taken to the extreme? The Gauteng police say no comment.

I have some comments of my own, but they don't involve homophobic intersex hate crimes. I don't think that's the story behind this at all, but so far I haven't received any mysterious emails from the beyond to explain otherwise.

I stick around for the meeting, but no one recognizes Patrick Serfontein from the photocopy of his ID, including the facilitators. I wasn't really expecting them to. After all, Kitsch Kitchen's leftovers aren't quite the same thing as "eating things from planes," although it did give me the idea.

Along with the *muti* vision of a burning trolley laden with plastic forks.

I spend the morning on the phone to the airlines under the cover of doing a story for *Better Business Magazine* on "giving back." It turns out only two national air carriers donate leftover meals to the needy. As FlyRite's Corporate Social Responsibility person said, "We live in a litigious society. I can understand that other airlines might be afraid of the possibility of a food-poisoning claim. But we stand by the quality of our food. Even when it's a day old." She adds brightly, "If it's good enough for our passengers, it's good enough for those in need!"

Two phone calls later and I have a list of all the welfare facilities catered to by FlyRite and Blue Crane Air. Based on Patrick's age, I eliminate the Bright Beginnings halfway house for juvenile offenders and the Vuka! underprivileged schools feeding program, which leaves me with the St. James Church soup kitchen in Alexandra township and the Carol Walters Shelter situated just off Louis Botha, a stone's throw — give or take an Olympian athlete doing the throwing — from Troyeville. Call it a guess, but I go there first.

The shelter is a graciously decrepit Victorian house with cornices and *broekie* lace and blue paint peeling off the walls like sunburn. The interior is deserted and resolutely clean, but all the Handy Andy and Windolene in the world can't scrub away the air of desperation that hangs over the building like mustard gas. A man with a mop directs me towards the administrator's office.

Renier Snyman is somewhere in his early thirties, young enough to still believe in making a difference, old enough that he's beginning to feel the weight of trying. He's friendly, but wary when I introduce myself as a journalist on a murder story.

"I can't promise I can help you. We don't keep records of the people who come through here."

"Can you take a look at a photograph?" I unfold my photocopy and put it on the desk in front of him.

"Hmm. I have to say he doesn't look familiar. But that could be because this ID was issued in 1994. No one looks like their ID photo anyway, right, especially if they've been living rough for a few years. We could ask some of the long-termers. They're out at the moment. We cut them loose between ten and five, but a lot of them hang out nearby. Let's take a walk."

We head down to Joubert Park where the dealers are already out in force, as well as a few office workers taking an early lunch break in the sun. Renier heads straight for the public toilets where a group of obviously homeless people are huddled passing round a silver foil *papsak* of cheap wine. They glare at us suspiciously, and a gnarled woman grabs at the arm of the old man standing next to her and draws against him for protection.

"Wass'matter, Captain?" the old man calls out as we approach. The lines in his face are set so deep you could go crevassing in there. "Something got stolen? That *dief* back again?"

"Nothing like that, Hannes. This young lady would like to talk to you and Annamarie about a man who may have stayed with us."

I show them the photocopy and they hand it round with the same seriousness as the *papsak*.

"*Nee,* man. I don't knows this *okie,*" Hannes shakes his head.

"Are you sure? He might not look the same anymore." Definitely not after being burned to charcoal, but I won't show them that set of photographs. "His name was Patrick Serfontein."

"*Sê weer?*" asks the old lady clinging to his arm.

"Patrick Serfontein. He was fifty-three years old. From Kroonstad."

"No, lady," Hannes says again, shaking his head.

The old woman smacks his shoulder. "*Jong! Dis* Paddy! *Jy onthou!*" She grabs the photocopy with shaky hands, either Parkinson's or the drink. "*Ja, okie* with a beard, *nè. En dinges wat daar woon.*" She makes a scrabbling gesture at her chin as if scratching at lice. "You remember, Mr. Snyman. With the *Miervreter, mos.*"

"So he *did* have an animal?" I say.

"I do remember him." Snyman shakes his head. "That damn Aardvark used to get its tongue into everything, especially the sugar. It drove our cook crazy."

"And he used to feed it baby cockroaches, Mr. Snyman. You remember?" She holds her finger and thumb two inches apart to demonstrate.

"That's not a baby cockroach," a sullen man with a strong German accent corrects. He's leaning on a shopping trolley loaded with the remains of a single mattress.

"It *is* around here!" boasts the old lady, slapping her thigh, and even the sullen German and Snyman laugh.

"When did you last see him?" I ask.

"Must have been a few weeks ago," Snyman muses. "Maybe even a month. He came and went a lot, if I recall correctly."

"He was his own man," Hannes says, approvingly. "The shelter isn't for everybody, hey. Some people like their freedom. They can't be dealing with other people's rules all the time." He gives the old biddy on his arm a little warning nod.

"*Jy!* Don't make me laugh," she says.

Snyman says, "A lot of our residents come and go. They'll live on the street until it gets cold—our highest occupancy is in winter—or something happens. A fight, a beating, an accident. It's ugly out there."

"Is there anyone else you haven't seen in a while? Anyone with an animal?

They exchange looks and shake their heads.

"How would we know?" says the sullen German guy.

Exactly what the killer is counting on.

31.

MANDLAKAZI IS NOT just fat, she's enormous. Her belly rolls have belly rolls. She's chewing her way through a bag of vegetarian samoosas, one hand on the steering wheel, the other dipping into the bag and back to her mouth like an assembly line, as she drives us through to Cresta to meet the Witness. Sloth takes to her immediately, although per-haps that's just the butternut samoosas she keeps plying him with.

The Witness phoned this morning while I was checking out airline charity cases, claiming to have seen the whole thing. Dave phoned me to let me know, and I've insisted on coming along.

"Dave said you been hanging out with the juicy babies," Mandlakazi says through a mouthful of samoosa. It takes me a second to figure out that she's talking about iJusi.

"Yeah. I was doing an article on them."

"Past tense? Too bad, *koeks*. Dave tell you I was the gossip columnist past tense for the *Sunday Times?*"

"He mentioned it."

"He mention why I got fired? I got so big I filled up the social pages all by myself." She roars with laughter. "No, I'm kidding. I got sick of it. That stuff is cancer. All that celebrity bullshit, it'll eat you alive if you let it."

"And the crime beat won't?"

"Way I figure it, covering the celebrity beat is like dying from a nose job turned gangrenous. Or cancer of the arse. Just a stupid way to go. Give me a good headshot or a fatal stabbing. At least that's *worth* something. So what's your thinking on this unholy mess? Someone with an anti-animal vendetta and a *panga* to grind?"

"It's *muti* murders."

"If only! Screw Slinger and his fake puppy dog, we'd be riding the front page for a week. How do you figure?"

"Two murders in the space of the week. Both animalled. Both bodies found with no trace of their animal in sight."

"And you know these two murders are related because . . . ? I mean, on the one hand we got your homeless guy, necklaced. On the other, we've got a very nasty case of the stabs. Doesn't sound like the same MO to me, and baby, believe me, I got the hots for the serial killers."

"I got an email."

"From the killer?"

"From the victims. Ghosts in the machine. Their own special brand of lost things."

"Which is your bit, right? The lost things thing?"

"It's my bit," I confirm.

"But how do you know it's not just sick for kicks?" Mandlakazi wipes her fingers on her jeans.

"I met some junkie kids behind Mai Mai with a Porcupine. They'd cut off its paw to sell it for *muti*. They offered to do the same with Sloth. Someone's buying." But then, someone's always buying in this city. Sex. Drugs. Magic. With the right connections you can probably get a two-for-one deal.

"*Muti* from zoos?" Dave whistles appreciatively. "That's got to be expensive."

"Killing kids for *muti* is expensive," I correct him. It doesn't happen a lot, but every year there are a handful of cases that make the papers: prepubescents murdered and harvested for body parts. Lips, genitals, fingers, hands, feet. The more they scream, the more powerful the *muti,* although the morgues have a brisk backdoor business going too. A hand buried under your shopfront door will bring you more customers. Eating a prepubescent boy's penis will cure impotence.

"People miss kids. Zoos, especially homeless ones, streetwalkers, the ones nobody will miss, probably won't even notice they're gone. I don't know if that's expensive."

"Risky though," Dave says.

"Probably worth it," Mandlakazi says. "People pay a pretty penny for rhino horn or *perlemoen,* and that's before you add *mashavi* into the equation. Animals are already some heavy magic shit. Mix that up with *muti* and who knows what you can do? I sure don't. But it would be a great story, let me tell you."

We meet the Witness at an airy coffee shop on the lower level of the mall. She is sitting right at the back, curled up miserably in a booth. She's tiny, barely fifteen, with hunched shoulders that speak of a lifetime of making herself as unobtrusive as possible.

"You Roberta?" Mandlakazi asks, sticking out her hand to shake.

The girl gives a little nod so quick you'd miss it if you blinked. She doesn't extend her hand. She points at me and says, "Just her."

"Baby, I'm the reporter, you want to talk to me. I can send these other people away if you want to keep it private."

She shakes her head. "Just her."

"Zoos got to stick together, huh. Fine. We'll be at the table outside." She hands me her Dictaphone, disgruntled. "It's the red button on the right."

"Like riding a bicycle."

I emerge forty minutes later and take a seat at Mandla and Dave's table. "Okay, first up, she says no police. Not yet. Maybe you can talk her round. Second: she's badly scared. Too scared to go home. I need one of you to put her up for a couple of nights."

"Why can't you?" Mandlakazi says.

"Because I live in her neighborhood. Where the murder happened. To her friend, who happened to be a prostitute like her."

"She can stay at my place. For the night, at least. We can make a plan tomorrow. The paper can put her up in a hotel if this story is going to go somewhere. What did she say about

the murder?" Mandlakazi is practically choking on her eagerness.

"You should probably hear it for yourself. I made a note of
the timecode on the most useful quotes for you." I pass her
a napkin annotated with a ballpoint pen I borrowed from the
waiter.

"Well, look at you, intrepid girl reporter."

"Worth more than an 'additional reporting' credit?"

"Depends on what's on the tape."

I skip to 05:43 on the Dictaphone. They have to lean in to
hear Roberta's voice, barely a whisper, over the grind of the
espresso machine, the clank of cups.

> **ZINZI DECEMBER:** Okay, I just want to go back a
> minute. What exactly do you mean, "like a spook"?
> **ROBERTA VAN TONDER:** I'm telling you! Like there
> was no one there. One minute she's bending down
> to fix her shoe, that heel was giving her trouble all
> night, and then *Pah! Pah! Pah! Pah!*

In the coffee shop, she stabbed at the air, her face contorting unconsciously.

> **RVT:** [contd] There is blood opening up all over her. Her
> head, her arms, and she falls back against the wall,
> blood spraying everywhere. *Pssssh!* But *Pah! Pah! Pah!*
> More cuts. Blood! And she's on the ground, holding
> her head and screaming, but it's *Pah! Pah! Pah!*

ZD: How did her Sparrow react?

RVT: It's flying all over like it's crazy. *Shoooo shoooo.* Flying this way, that way.

ZD: Like it can see the spook?

RVT: Like it can see the spook.

ZD: Like it's attacking the spook?

RVT: I don't know. I don't know.

ZD: And you didn't see what happened after that?

RVT: No. I run. I run and run and run until I think my heart gon' explode.

ZD: I'm sorry, I just need to check that I understand. You couldn't see anything or anyone. No shadows. Nothing visible at all?

RVT: No, no, nothing. Well, maybe a gray. Like a shadow. Like a demon. An invisible demon!

"Oh this is gold, baby. This is gold," Mandlakazi says.

We spend the next few hours transcribing the tape and knocking it up into a rough.

32.

I GET HOME well after eleven, exhausted and pissed off at having to park two blocks away because of the roadworks outside Elysium. Maybe they're finally fixing the damn water. Roberta is safely housed at Mandlakazi's place. The news story is a solid little piece, even if I had to hype up the hysteria for the *Daily Truth*'s audience. From nowhere, anything is a step-up, even tabloid journalism. Maybe after this I'll write that rehab tourism story after all—for a decent publication, not *Mach*.

It's because I'm tired that I don't notice that the charms on my lock have been broken. I shrug Sloth off onto the climbing pole by the door and flick on the lights. Vuyo is sitting on the edge of my bed with a gun. He holds it loosely, his legs slung wide, so that it dangles between them like a penis. He looks resigned.

My phone chooses this precise moment to break into the jaunty *mbaqanga* jive of iJusi's "Fever." We both jump and the gun twitches in his lap.

"You want to get that?" Vuyo offers, but he doesn't mean it.

"Nah. I'll call them back later," I say, as casually as I can. It's a ringtone I've programmed for calls from certain numbers. Arno. Song. S'bu.

313

"Do you want some tea? I've had a really long day, I could use a cup," I blather, venting some of the nervous adrenaline that just kicked in harder than a Taekwondo champion, but also covering that I'm not getting out teacups, I'm looking for a weapon. "How do you take it? I like mine strong and black. That's not a come-on, by the way."

It takes all my nerve to keep my back turned to him. I can hear him jiggling his knee, the micro-sound of his jeans rustling. It's the only time I've seen him out of a suit, and that frightens me more than anything.

I yank open the cutlery drawer to be confronted with an anomaly worse than emails from dead people or a man with a gun sitting on my bed. It's a large carving knife with a viciously serrated edge and two broken teeth. It's tarnished with rust. It's not mine. And neither is the china figurine of a kitten with one paw playfully raised, also stained with rust. But it's not rust. It's not rust at all. Perversely, the thought that flashes through my brain is "I can haz murder weapon?" I laugh out loud, a sobbing hiccup.

"Is this yours?" I say, turning to Vuyo, holding up the knife by the tip like a dead cockroach.

"Don't make me shoot you," he says, sounding tired.

"You're going to shoot me over an email?"

"People have done worse for less. No girl, I'm going to shoot you because you made me look bad. Put the knife down." He points the gun at my head. I follow instructions.

"Are you sure you don't want tea?" I say numbly. My mother was a firm believer in tea. Also, my kettle is heavy, solidly built. Less expected than a knife. I take a risk, turn back towards the counter, reach for my old-fashioned metal kettle. But in that moment, he crosses the room, yanks me round, grabs me by the throat, and shoves me against the counter.

"No, I do not want fucking tea," he hisses, spraying spit into my face. He shoves the gun into my cheek. "I want my money."

I start to bring up the kettle, but he slams his knee up between my legs. Everything goes white. There is the clunk of metal dropped onto a linoleum floor.

He lets go of my throat and I sag down against the counter, trying to remember how to breathe. He watches impassively before tucking the gun into the back of his jeans, all the better to beat me.

"I don't—I gave—" I manage.

He backhands me. His knuckle splits my cheek open. "You made me look bad. Get up. I said, *get up!*" Vuyo drags me to my feet.

"I gave you the money!" There is blood in my mouth.

"Did you think I wouldn't fucking notice? Did you forget who you were dealing with?"

"Notice what? Wait—"

Still holding my arm, he punches me in the gut. I fold up around the point of impact, but he won't let me fall to my knees.

"Notice what? That it was counterfeit? Every single fucking blue note!"

"I didn't. It's a setup, Vuyo. They set me up."

"I am so sick of your mouth," Vuyo says, reaching into the back of his jeans. But he doesn't get to pull the gun, because Sloth drops onto him from the ceiling. Vuyo goes down under a ball of fur and fury. The gun goes skittering across the floor, skidding under the bed. I start to scramble for it, think better of it, and change direction.

Then Sloth screams. I stop dead, a frame-grab of a girl bending down to snatch up a kettle. I close my hand over the handle and turn, very slowly, to see that Vuyo has Sloth's arm wrenched backwards at a terrible angle, his knee between Sloth's shoulders, pressing him into the linoleum. There are deep gouges on Vuyo's face and neck. A chunk of flesh has been torn out of his cheek by sharp little herbivore teeth.

"You can break his arm, Vuyo, but I'll cave your fucking skull in before you can do anything else," I say.

Vuyo considers this. Sloth whimpers and squirms, trying to take the pressure off his arm. Our connection is one-way. I can't feel his pain, but it's bad enough to see it in his face.

"Stalemate," Vuyo says grimly. Blood drips off the end of his nose. The kettle is heavy. It would be so easy to bring it down. So complicated after.

"Or," I say through my teeth, "load saved game."

"What?"

"We reset to where we were before."

"Impossible."

"Who knows? That the money was counterfeit?"

"I do."

"Who else?"

"No one else. Yet." But he is starting to smile, a thin, appreciative smile.

"Two hundred thousand," I offer.

"Four fifty."

"That's insane."

"If you were anyone else, girl, you'd already be dead."

"But I'm an asset."

"You're an asset," he agrees, easing off Sloth's back. Sloth gives a little cry of relief and scrabbles towards me. I scoop him up with one arm, still holding the kettle half raised.

"Get out."

"My gun."

I laugh. "Add it to my fucking bill."

I'm an asset, all right. And as much a *moegoe* as any of the ones I've netted for him. If Vuyo had really wanted to punish me, all he had to do was shoot Sloth. Hell, chuck him out the window, save himself the bullet. He wouldn't have risked bringing the Undertow down on his head, getting animalled. Now he has me right back where he wanted, with triple the debt.

There is a commotion outside. Doors slamming. Footsteps. A kid scrambles past the door, yelling *"iPoyisa! iPoyisa!"*—the building's early warning system.

"You called the cops?" Vuyo says, incredulous. His eyes flick to the bed, to the gun under it. He wavers.

"Not me. Whoever left this knife in my drawer. Same people who gave me a suitcase full of fake hundreds."

"When you make enemies, you don't fuck around," Vuyo says, admiringly.

"You want to leave before they get here."

He tips his hand to his forehead. "I'll be in touch," he says, sliding into the chaos of people pouring out like cockroaches: hookers and dealers and *skollies* making a break for it.

I grab a dishtowel, wrap it round the knife and the china kitten and toss it in my handbag—Odi's insurance policy. But they killed Mrs. Luditsky before I even got involved, which means they're setting me up to take the fall for something else. What's worse than stabbing an old lady to death in her home?

I tie Sloth around my waist, like a pregnant belly, yanking one of Benoît's old t-shirts over my dress to disguise the lumpiness. The t-shirt smells of him, man sweat and Zambuk.

I barge out into the panic. There's a lot of noise, but the voice that yells "There! There she is!" has a note of self-righteous authority that could only belong to D'Nice. I don't look round. I keep moving forward and, at the last moment, sidestep into the burned-out doorway of apartment 615.

By the time the cops hit the kitchen with its ripped-out pipes and smashed sink, I've already dropped through the hole in the floor in the second bedroom, into 526. But instead of taking the main stairwell, I cross the walkway, climb through the window of Aurum Place's 507, clamber down the broken fire escape and drop the last half-story to the street. Queen of the shortcut. I casually drop the dishcloth with the knife and the china kitten into the storm drain as I pass by.

Police lights strobe the building. I count four cop cars round the front, which probably means at least another two round the back. The police don't mess around in Hillbrow. They're armed to the molars with shotguns and padded up the wazoo with bulletproof vests and riot helmets. Nice to see them taking a murder seriously, if only on the basis of a little old non-zoo lady getting brutally stabbed to death by a fratricidal Sloth girl. There's an e.tv news van already on the scene, parking in the riot vehicle.

I use it for cover, waddling round the back of it in the hippo-duck manner of the heavily pregnant. Unfortunately, the intrepid girl reporter spots me and the camera swings to catch me in its glass eye, before she spots something even better in the Human Interest vein—Mrs. Khan and her kids wailing and yelling as a burly cop escorts them out of the building, holding a fistful of confiscated fake passports. I slip away, past the roadworks and up the alley to my car.

The Capri maxes out at 140, which probably isn't a bad thing given that I'm dodging between lanes like Ayrton Senna on methamphetamines, listening to my voicemail on repeat, like torture. Because Arno's phone just rings and rings and rings.

"Hello? Hello!" Arno's voice hisses. "Are you there? Oh man. Zinzi, They're here. For real. Worse than zombies. They're like motherfuck-ing ghosts. Please answer. Please."

Arno is breathing quick and heavy like an obscene phone caller having an asthma attack. The breathing gets harder. Then there is the sound of a door crashing open. "Shitballs!" And then he screams. There is a muffled scraping sound accompanied by a dull drumming, as if of heels kicking the floor as he's being dragged away.

And then the phone cuts out.

The security checkpoint at the entrance to Mayfields is abandoned. There are sirens howling inside, black swells of smoke churning into an unnaturally pale orange sky. I duck under the boom to let myself in, and get yet another nasty surprise. There is a sign pasted up with a blurry web-cam photograph of me from the last time I was here. Someone has taken the time to highlight the important bits:

Housebreaker!

Crimewatch: All tenants!

Be on the lookout for this woman!

Zinzi December is a convicted murderer and considered very dangerous.

She drives an orange Ford Capri and has a Sloth.

If you see this woman, call security and the police immediately!

I tear down the notice and crumple it up, hit the button to raise the boom, and drive through, into a chaos of sirens, an ambulance parked halfway up one of the immaculate grassy verges, the road blocked by fire engines and cop cars. I pull over behind the ambulance and tug a baggy hoodie over my shoulders and over Sloth. The pregnancy shtick is too restrictive. "Keep your head down," I tell Sloth, my own personal hunchback, and start running.

H4-303 is a lost battle. The firefighters might as well be pissing on it. It's already been reduced to the black carapace of a building. Brilliant orange flames lash in the second-story window, S'bu's room. The heat is as dense as a wall, forcing the crowd of spectators to keep their distance on the clipped lawn. They're wearing various configurations of sleepwear.

"Media," I shout and barge my way through to the front where a body is laid out under fireproof sheets. A husky teen. There is an arm sticking out from under the sheet. The sleeve has pink robot monkeys. My heart lurches so hard I practically gag on it.

"Where are the other kids?" I yell at a shell-shocked security guard who is supposed to be keeping people back. He doesn't seem to hear me, mesmerized by the spectacle. A firefighter is dragging a blackened body out of the rubble, collapsed in his arms like a scarecrow. Scrawny. Girl-sized. Wearing purple cowboy boots. They are still smoldering.

"There's another one," someone shouts from inside the building.

"Get away from there!" one of the firefighters yells at me,

snapping the security guard out of his trance. But when I raise my hands in apology, I catch a glimpse of something else in the crowd. A shadow. The crowd is a tangle of lost things, but there is something moving through the threads. Like a ghost. Or an invisible demon.

"Come, lady, you can't be doing that," the security guard says, pulling me away. "What's the matter with you? Get back over there."

"Sorry," I mutter and let him shepherd me towards the crowd, which is shifting unconsciously away from the demon, parting like a magical sea to allow it through towards the parking lot.

I chase after it, pushing past people, grabbing at impressions as I go. Except that just like outside Mrs. Luditsky's on the morning of her murder, they're no longer just impressions. The images leap out at me in crisp high-resolution: a broken drum-stick scrawled with a band's name, a pair of girl's boyshorts with red lace detail, an orange plastic Casio watch, a keyring attached to a Bratz doll's head. And a tattered book with a golden tree on the cover.

"I know you're there, Amira!" I yell. But she keeps fading out, like a developing photograph in reverse, not so much like she's bending the light around her as bending people's minds, making herself unobtrusive, making your eyes slide away, your attention drift. Nothing to see here. Except that ruined book. I hold on to it as hard I can, but the crowd is resisting me.

"Oh come on!"

"What is *wrong* with you?"

Someone grabs my arm. It's the snooty waiter from the clubhouse. "I know you!"

I step forward into the waiter's hold, twisting his arm down and, at the same time, smack him in the throat with the open palm of my hand. He lets go with a strangled noise. Hey, what's an extra assault charge on my rap sheet tonight? They're probably going to lay the fire on me anyway. I turn and break for my car, people shouting after me.

I drive away, tires squealing. The Capri snaps the boom like a teenage heart.

33.

THE TENSION IN the car is as dense as a collapsing star. Benoît is quiet, looking out the window at the streetlights streaming past the car. I picked him up outside Central Methodist. He didn't argue, didn't ask questions, didn't try to convince me to go to the cops. He was the one who suggested using his uniform to get access, in case there was another "dangerous criminal" warning posted at the neighborhood security boom.

Reflected light catches on the brass-plated name badge, like an unspoken accusation. These are all the things he doesn't say in the silence: that I'm risking everything—his asylum status, his family's chance of a future here. The Mongoose says it instead, his beady little eyes glaring up at me from Benoît's lap. Those eyes say "useless backstabbing junkie slag."

I pull over a few blocks away, out of sight. It's unnaturally quiet. The birds will only start up in an hour or so. And in the meantime, dream city is dreaming.

"Give me ten minutes," Benoît says. I pass him the bag of Lagos fried chicken, and he gets out of the car and strolls down towards the security hut, chewing on a piece of chicken. It's more disguise than bribe. Who would suspect a man with chicken, particularly one in a Sentinel uniform and a name badge?

Headlights swoop over him and then past, not even slowing—it's not unusual for people to be walking at 3 a.m. It's like there are two different species inhabiting Johannesburg. Cars and pedestrians.

It's forty-two minutes before the official 4 a.m. shift change, but a man can be persuaded to go off duty early. It takes a little longer than anticipated. Not because the guard is diligent, but because he wants to shoot the breeze a little, share some greasy chicken before he heads on home. It takes all my willpower to stay in the car. Finally, he parts company with Benoît and starts walking up the road away from me, towards the main road. If he thinks there is a chance of a taxi at this time of the morning, he is a man who believes in miracles. We have twenty-eight minutes left until the actual shift change arrives and figures something is up.

The Mongoose scampers down the road towards the car. I open the door and he scrambles in, making urgent squeaking noises.

"Yes, I know, I saw him leave." I put the car in gear and drive down to the security hut to pick up Benoît, cursing under my breath when I see the cameras. Too late now.

The gate leading to Huron's house proves less of a problem. Benoît has been thoroughly trained in all the ways nasty burglars vanquish home-security measures, including, in this case, simply levering the gate right off the rails with a tire iron.

I stash the car a few blocks away, to throw off armed response when they click that all is not as it should be, and we slip up the side of the garden, sticking to the cover of the trees. The house is lit up for a party, all the lights blazing. Sloth squeezes my arms with his claws.

We follow the noise up towards the garage, passing the Daimler parked to one side. The double doors gape open. Light spills into the drive, illuminating James bent over the Mercedes, fussing around in the boot, which is lined with heavy plastic.

Benoît motions for me to stay back. He slides up behind James, and as he startles and begins to turn, Benoît slams the boot lid down on him. James yells. Benoît slams it down again, then once more, then swoops down to grab James's legs, heaves him into the boot, and slams it shut. The banging and shouting start up almost immediately. "Get the keys," Benoît says. I have not seen this side of him before.

I run for the front of the car and pull the keys out of the ignition. My hands are shaking as I jam the key into the lock on the boot and turn it. The noise from inside becomes more aggressive. I step back and nearly trip over an extension cord. It runs to a surgical saw, the kind you'd use for amputations, laid out beside the car, along with three different hacksaws, an axe, a pair of pliers, neatly laid out, ready for use. There is a chest freezer at the back of the garage, its lid propped open.

"Who is this Odi Huron?" Benoît says. The Mongoose is frozen, one paw raised, sniffing the air, whiskers trembling.

"I don't think I know." I feel sick. I think of Vuyo's gun lying under my bed.

"Won't he suffocate?" I glance back at the Mercedes.

"Do you care?" Benoît says, drawing his baton from its holster. "The house?"

"If they're still alive." I shake myself. "We should go round the side."

We slip round the side of the house through the shrubbery. The scent of yesterday-today-and-tomorrow is sickeningly sweet. My heart plays out a frenetic drum 'n' bass beat. My hands are numb and tingling. First thing to go in fight or flight: fine motor coordination. Way to go, evolution.

There are voices coming from the patio, but when we clear the shrubs, only Carmen is lying on a lounger in the dark with her sunglasses on, facing the pool. The fountain is on, water spluttering through the maiden's vase. A pallid underwater light shines up through the skin of leaves on the surface, highlighting every striation, casting dancing reflections over the tiles.

Carmen is talking to the radio and half-heartedly flopping one hand around as if conducting a haphazard choir.

"It's not like they even serve ice cream at the movies," she says, her face inscrutable behind the shades.

Her sunshine-yellow satin robe is drenched in blood like bad tie-dye. There is a shivering bundle wrapped in a towel under her lounger.

There is a flick knife and an empty martini glass on the table next to her.

"Kittens and mittens and teeth and teeth and teeth," she sing-songs.

She sees us, sits up on her elbows, and says brightly, "Oh. Are you here about the collection?" She takes off her sunglasses. If eyes are the windows to the soul, these are looking onto Chernobyl. "Because it's all about fur this season."

The glass doors leading into the house open and the Maltese emerges carrying two martini glasses, his little Dog at his heels. The Dog snarls and the Maltese pulls a face. "Ah," he says. "I'm afraid I didn't know you were here. Otherwise I would have made extra."

"What happened to the no-interference policy?" I ask. Benoît is tense beside me, muscles bunched for action. I put a hand on his arm.

"That's only for the victims," says the Maltese, as he sets down the glasses and sits down beside Carmen, stroking her leg. "It's like bottled water: best from a pure source."

"What is wrong with her?" Benoît says, barely restraining himself. He is holding the baton so tight that the strain is making his arm shake.

"She did it to herself, *mkwerekwere*. She's on a very potent dissociative drug."

"Midazolam?"

"Mixed with a bit of ketamine and the house special — to keep her awake. We've been playing. Show them, Carmen."

"Again?" she whines.

"Again, baby." He caresses the side of her belly through the robe. "I think you missed a spot over here."

She sighs sulkily, picks up the flick knife from the table and simply jabs it into her side. She pulls it out again and looks down at the bloodied tip of the knife with interest, but no indication of feeling. The blood starts to well up.

"Not so terrible, hey?" the Maltese says.

"Good evening Pasadena," she agrees.

"What about here?" he circles the skin above her kneecap.

"Enough," Benoît says.

"We're only getting started. Have you met Carmen's Bunny?" He reaches underneath the lounger and hauls up the trembling Rabbit by its ears. It closes its eyes in terror, nose twitching frantically. "We all thought Carmen was going to be the next Slinger, our animalled breakthrough artist. Better than erotic dancing. Although it turns out Slinger wasn't really Slinger himself, if you know what I mean. This is your fault, you know. Odi and Carmen were so happy together until you got her all riled up with your crazy accusations. As if he would have risked tainting little Song. It was bad enough that idiot Jabulani was fucking her."

"Where *are* Song and Sbu?" I say.

"Sailing away, sailing away, sailing away," Carmen sings.

He ignores the question. "Did you like the present I left you? It's a very distinctive knife, you know. Leaves very distinctive wounds."

"Were you going to implicate me in the fire at Mayfields too?"

"You should be ashamed." He grins. "Three teenagers died in that fire. After you stabbed them to death, you sick psycho."

"I only counted two," I keep my voice carefully level.

"Don't worry, they'll find the other one when they eventually get inside. Burned to a crisp. Unidentifiable."

"But they're not Song and S'bu, are they?"

"Don't they wish! Couple of unlucky street kids who match the general physical description. Collateral damage, can't be helped. We picked them up this afternoon. Made them feel special for a couple of hours. Let them play Xbox, fed them McDonald's, doused them in petrol. Same kind as in the half-empty container under your sink. Did you find that already? Or just the knife?"

"No one's going to believe this."

"Won't they? A psychotic junkie zoo bitch who killed her brother? Who was so celebrity-obsessed she pretended to be from a big shot music magazine so she could get close to the twins? Whose fingerprints were all over poor Mrs. Luditsky's apartment, who took her little china cat home with her as some kind of trophy? Are you kidding me? Better start working on your sound bites. The media are going to love you."

My head is spinning. I lean on the table, trying to fight back the wave of nausea.

"In fact, what are you even doing here?" Mark swirls his martini. Takes a sip. "Shouldn't you be on the run?"

"Where are they?" Benoît says.

"The real twins? Oh they're downstairs, sweetie, getting ready. They might have started already."

At the prompt "start," Carmen replaces her sunglasses and punches the knife into the flesh above her knee with cool reserve. It sticks there, trembling slightly as the muscle moves to accommodate her leaning back to take a sip of her martini.

Benoît can't stand it any more. He moves to pluck the knife out, but the Maltese is faster. He yanks it away and this time Carmen does flinch.

"You want to play too?" he says, tapping the flat of the blade against his cheek. "I have to tell you, this is my favorite game."

"Where downstairs? In the house?" I say, because there are more important things to worry about right now than Carmen, than being set up for quadruple homicide.

"I should really be getting down there. They need me."

"To cut someone up?"

"Oh sweetie, I'm just the magic battery to make the ritual even more potent. Or didn't you notice that your *shavi* is brighter whenever I'm around?"

"The invisible demon."

"Team effort," he agrees. "Amira's obfuscation is painfully obvious without me. Although we like to do the carving together. But we're wasting time. There are children to be sacrificed, getaways to make. Come on, *kwerekwere*," the Maltese says, brandishing the knife. "You look like you've seen a dog fight or two."

Mark lunges for Benoît at the same time as the snarling Mutt goes for the Mongoose. Yipping hysterically, the Dog rolls the Mongoose onto his back, biting at his belly, his face. Blood smears across its muzzle. The Mongoose writhes and kicks, teeth bared in pain, but he doesn't make a sound.

Another knife appears in Mark's left hand from a hidden sheath and, as Benoît smashes him across the ribcage with his baton, Mark manages to slice at his face, the blade glancing off his jaw and up his cheek.

"Carmen," I shake her. "Is there a gun in the house?"

But she shakes her head violently from side to side like she's having a seizure. "No-no-no-no-no-no."

I let go, and she pulls up her knees, clutching her Rabbit to her chest like a kid with a stuffed animal, and takes a sip from her drink, glaring at me as if I'm intending to take it away.

Sloth is making agitated little squeaks.

"I'm working on it!" I snap.

The Mongoose pulls up his back legs and kicks the Dog, contorting like a *koeksister* to scramble on top of it. They tumble over each other, but the Mongoose has the advantage. He's used to killing snakes and this is just a ratty little Dog. He has the Mutt pinned by the throat and squealing.

The humans are more evenly matched. Benoît and Mark are circling each other warily. Benoît jabs the baton into Mark's sternum with all his weight, keeping him out of reach. Mark staggers back, as if winded, but it's a ploy. As Benoît moves towards him, he ducks under the baton, stabs him in the side, and darts out of reach again. And then I smash one of the lacy ironwork chairs over the back of his skull.

It does less damage than I'd hoped. I was hoping for out cold, but instead he stumbles, drops one of his knives to clutch at the back of his head and turns on me, furious.

"You little cunt. I'll come back to you." But when he turns

back, it's straight into the baton that slams into the side of his head hard enough to knock him off his feet.

Carmen gives a little shriek of delight. "I can feel it coming in the air. Tonight," she says, matter-of-factly.

Mark starts to get up and Benoît hits him across the back of his knees. He collapses across the end of the lounger. I spring forward, push my knee into his back, and yell at Benoît. He breaks out cable ties, standard issue with Sentinel rather than handcuffs, and we work together to bind the Maltese's wrists and ankles and then cable-tie both to the heavy ironwork table. The Dog snarls and snaps at my fingers, but Benoît pins it down with the baton on its neck and I close a cable tie over its muzzle and chain it by the collar to one of the chairs.

"The water," Carmen sings, pointing at the pool. "Water, water. And not enough to drink."

A shadow swells up from the bottom of the pool, eclipsing the wan rays of the pool light. Something sickly white and huge with scales explodes from beneath the surface, snaps its jaws shut on Benoît, and slides back into the water before he can draw breath to yell. Like a fucking dinosaur. I'm still blinking from the icy shock of water that burst up with it— and Benoît is gone, like he never was, the choppy waves the only sign that something happened.

"Pop goes the weasel!" Carmen says, clapping her hands in delight.

34.

I DON'T THINK about it. I jump in after him. The water is cold enough to knock the breath out of me. I hear the Mongoose scream and splash in after me. But Mongooses can't dive. I fight my way through a dense skin of slimy rotting leaves, Sloth clutching my neck in terror. I hope he knows how to hold his breath. I dive into the pallid gloom lit up by the underwater light. There's a hole at the bottom of the deep end, a tunnel wide enough to steer a truck through. I swim into it, following the curve down into pitch darkness, like swimming into the heart of the Undertow. The pressure in my ear gear-shifts from a dull ache to a screaming drill bit in my head, but then the tunnel curves up again, like the U-bend of a sink, into water that's brutally cold and black. I can hear distorted music through the water and a slapping sound. Lungs burning, I kick up to the surface toward the pale streamers of light burning through the water, and emerge into the cool air of an underwater cavern strung with lamps that still leave swathes of darkness.

There is music pumping. An innocuously sweet pop ballad. One of iJusi's.

Baby it's a drive-by, drive-by . . .

The slapping is the sound of the blast as the monster breaches, twists in the air, and flops back into the water, Benoît hanging limply in its jaws. Not a dinosaur. An albino crocodile, six meters long. It's rolling to drown its prey.

I start to swim for the thing, but Sloth tugs at my arms, to hold me back. He's right. There's nothing I can do until it stops its death roll. I tread water in the darkness and try to slow my heart and take in what's going on, try not to focus on the monster's thrashing.

The cavern is maybe twenty meters across. Natural rock with manmade features: the speakers pumping out iJusi, the bare neon bulb mounted on a set of stairs so steep it's basically a ladder, rising from a cement outcropping that juts into the water like a pier. The smell of damp and rot is overwhelming. Old vase water.

Drive-by love

Huron, bare-chested, his belly hanging over his shorts, with a gun holster strapped under his arm, is standing on the landing with the twins who are naked, handcuffed together and swaying slightly. Their faces are empty. The Marabou is spreading a plastic sheet over an old-fashioned wooden butcher's block.

There is a cage at her feet big enough to hold a medium-sized dog. There's something else—not a dog—inside the cage. A hunch of mammal with brown fur. A flutter of feathers.

It's not even love at first sight, it's love at a glance

Huron shouts over the water at the Crocodile, "That better not be Carmen!" He laughs, but adds to the Marabou, "Go see what's going on."

"I'm sure Mark has everything under control," she says.

"Then where the hell is he? And who is *that?*" he says, pointing to the water. For an awful moment, I think he's pointing at me, but he's indicating Benoît in the monster's mouth.

"Whoever it is, he's not a problem anymore," the Marabou shrugs.

"Hurry up, you overgrown fucking gecko!" Huron shouts. "We need to get this show on the road."

Saw you in the back of a taxi, passing me by

Sloth makes little panicky gasps in my ear. "It's okay, buddy, they can't see us." I hope. Sloth gives a little sob.

Tried to raise my hand, tried to catch your eye

I retreat into the darkness, to the wall, find a low rock to cling to. Sloth clambers onto it, shivering.

"We should start on the animals," the Marabou says. "There might be other intruders."

"Don't we need booster boy?"

"The twins will be enough. The doubling effect——"

"Yeah, yeah, yeah, you're the expert here, baby. I'll do whatever you say," Huron says. "Let's get this party started."

"Indeed," she says and opens the cage to pull out a rabbit-eared creature with a long piggy snout. Patrick Serfontein's Aardvark. Still alive. She picks up a machete from the butcher's block.

But you looked straight past, didn't see me

The Crocodile slows its thrashing. It rises from the water and shakes its head violently as if testing the resistance of the body in its mouth. Benoît's right arm flops grotesquely from his body. He's not moving. The Crocodile smacks its jaw against the water and then sinks under, dragging Benoît with it.

Baby it's a drive-by, drive-by, drive-by love

I take a deep breath and dive down, reaching for my own lost thing. The tea-colored blackness swallows me whole. The faint distortion of the lyrics, mixed with a terrible high-pitched squealing, accompanies me down.

Drive-by, drive-by

I clamp down on the panic, the claustrophobia, and the vertigo of blindness, following that slender thread.

There is a rush of current. And something massive sweeps towards me in the darkness. I can't see but I can sense its mouth gaping and I fight back the terror, the urge to thrash for the surface. Its hoary tail sideswipes me as it brushes past, hard enough to crack a rib.

I have to be close. I have to be. I swim another couple of meters or maybe a mile, and bang my wrist against a rock. I grab it and feel the shape of it with my hands, like a blind woman reading a face. The rock face curves under. I follow it down and grasp a revoltingly soft hand. The flesh gives way under my grip. I can't help it. I scream into the water, expelling valuable air.

Get a fucking hold of yourself. I reach out for the hand again. It's pliable and doughy like wet bread, but I can feel a hard edge. Bone? No. It's a splint. Two of the fingers are bandaged together. Ronaldo. His face looms into view, bloated, unrecognizable. But this time I'm ready for it.

I drag myself past him, deeper, grasping for Benoît, terrified of what else might be down here in the black. I run my hand along a fracture in the rock, over a body jammed into it. I grope my way up, trying to find a way to identify it, to pull it loose. Tiny bubbles escape from a fold in the shirt, like little fish nibbling at my fingers. I touch plastic. Benoît's burns.

His arm is caught in the crack and I'm running out of air. Dark spots pop in front of my eyes. I brace my feet against the rock and ease his shoulder loose. It rotates obscenely under the skin, his arm flopping loosely from the socket. I pull again, hard, and he comes away. Only Ro comes with him. I kick out in blind panic as the bulk of the rotting bouncer drifts into me. My foot sinks into his stomach. A stream of thick bubbles erupts from between his lips, and his head flops back and up, his arms dragging, like a man called to the Ascension, the trapped gases sending him bobbing up to the surface.

I kick up after him, but I have the disadvantage of a cracked rib and 95 kg of my one-time lover in tow. The black spots have turned to bright sunflares. My lungs have moved beyond burning to the sear of napalm. And I break into the air and the music, gasping and choking. And it's not even nearly over.

Baby you can drive me crazy, drive me anywhere you please

Huron's voice carries across the water. "Kids, this is my friend, Mr. Crocodile. Say hello, Mr. Crocodile. He'd like to be your friend too. Your special friend. Because quite frankly, I'm sick to death of the thing."

But baby don't break my heart, baby don't tease

I drag Benoît to the rocks. Sloth tries to help, yanking at his shirt with his teeth. I heave him up, but his legs are still dangling in the water, the current wafting at his pants. I scramble out, crouch down beside him, shivering. I hadn't realized how cold the water was.

Benoît's not breathing. I tilt his head back, squeezing his

nose shut with one hand, and press my mouth against his. Two deep exhalations. Then I push two fingers against the artery in his neck.

Sloth whines, seeing the blood seeping through his shirt. "Shut up, buddy."

Please. Please. I count out the faintest of pulses. One alligator. Two alligator. Thirty beats in a minute. That can't be good. And he's still not breathing. And he's bleeding to death.

One thing at a time, Zinzi. I have no idea what I'm doing here. If he has a pulse, do I do chest compressions anyway? Fuck.

We'll keep on moving, keep on cruising,
Journey through the night

I tip his jaw back again, press my mouth down, inflate his chest with my breath. "Fuck you, breathe. Fuck you, breathe." Like we're some kind of obscene machine, a conjoined human bellows. "Fuck you, Benoît, breathe."

It's okay baby, just stick with me
Everything will be all right, be all right

"I don't want to," Songweza says in a little-girl voice from across the cavern.

I don't look up. Can't afford to.

"We all do things we don't want to sometimes," Huron says. "It's like a game."

"Like *Blood Skies?*" S'bu asks, his voice vague and distant, an echo of a human being.

"I don't know what that is," Huron snaps.

"It's a video game."

"Yes, exactly like a video game," his voice turned wheedling.

"Cooperative or non-cooperative?"

"Definitely non."

Baby it's a drive-by, drive-by, drive-by love

I place the heel of my palm against Benoît's sternum, fingers interlaced. Fuck it, chest compressions can't hurt, right? Only when I push down there is a horrible grinding sound in Benoît's chest, like his ribs are cracked. That makes two of us. "Good luck explaining *that* to your wife," I hiss at him. "Come on, you cheating shit." Sloth puts a paw over my hands.

"Okay, you're right. No compressions." I take a deep breath. Try to calm down.

Baby it's a drive-by, drive-by, drive-by love

"Here's a knife for you, Song. And one for you. Don't worry, they have spells on them. You ready? First to kill the other wins."

"Yaaa!" Song giggles.

We'll keep on moving, keep on cruising, journey through the

Benoît's body heaves against me, his teeth smashing into my mouth as he convulses. I pull away as he starts to choke, coughing up a thin stream of water and vomit. I turn him onto his side. He doesn't open his eyes. Sloth looks at me expectantly, but I don't know if this is it, if this is enough. It's not like the fucking movies. Benoît splutters and dribbles, then takes a deep wet gurgling breath. And then another one, slightly less wet. He doesn't open his eyes. But it's enough. He's breathing.

You stick with me, babe
Everything will be all right, be all right

His arm hangs grotesquely from his side, but if it's broken, it hasn't torn through the skin. Maybe just dislocated. The tooth punctures that run in a massive arc down the right side of his body from his collarbone to his groin are something else. I just hope the fucker didn't puncture an organ. I tie his shirt round his side the best I can to stanch the blood, haul Sloth over to the wound that's bleeding the most, over his appendix, liver, spleen? Christ, why didn't I pay attention in biology?

"Push down with all your weight, buddy. Don't let up on the pressure. I'll be back as soon as I can." He might yet bleed to death. Might still drown from the water in his lungs. Might have already sustained brain damage. We need to get to a hospital. We need machines and doctors. I try to blank the fear as I strike out for the landing.

Be all right, be all right, be all right

The track fades into silence. And then starts right up again.

Song's giggles turns to a shriek of indignation. Unfortunately, now I can see what's happening as well as hear it. The cage is standing open. There is a mound of limp fur and intestines and downy brown feathers lying on the butcher's block. The plastic sheeting is slick with blood. The Aardvark's head dangles off the edge, its eyes glassy as a stuffed toy. The Marabou is holding a Toad down on the block. It croaks in loud desperate gulps, its mottled throat inflated like a blister. She raises the machete and chops off its head. Blood sprays up in a bright gush.

"By these deaths, bind them," she says, wiping the spray of blood off her face with the back of her hand.

The Crocodile is lying on the other side of the platform, its mouth gaping open. Song and S'bu are circling each other, no longer handcuffed together, working around the giant reptile, while Huron and the Marabou watch from the bottom of the stairs. Or rather he's circling her. She's standing there, pressing her hand to the deep gash in her arm. "Ow, what the hell, S'busiso?"

"Die, Cthul'mite!" Sbu shouts, slashing frantically at her,

video game–style. He slices her hands, her arms, as she tries to cover herself. She drops her knife. "Seriously, *doos*. Cut it out. You're hurting me."

It's not even love at first sight, it's love at a glance.

"S'bu," I scream from the water, shoving past Ronaldo's bobbing bloated corpse. "It's the drugs. Stop it! Put down the knife!"

The Crocodile turns its head as if about to slide off the slipway into the water. "No, stay," Huron instructs. "It's nearly over." He snaps at the Marabou, "Taken care of, huh?" He pulls the gun out from under his armpit, and aims it at the water. "Never mind, I'll do it my-fucking-self." He points the gun. I dive.

But I can't let you go, I have to take this chance.

Underwater, the gunshots sound like staccato snaps.

Three of them in quick succession. I imagine I can feel them burrowing through the water, leaving silvery trails. Something tears at my ankle. I twist away in panic and blunder into Ronaldo. I pull the rotting body over me as a shield, as a fourth gunshot echoes through the cavern. The trajectory is slowed by the water, by the corpse. Slowed, but not stopped. It rips through the mushy flesh and into my chest, wedging into my collarbone.

I scream into the water, swallowing half the lake. But I

stay under. Counting down. Holding my breath. 74 alligator. 92 alligator. 118 alligator. Until I can't anymore. But when I surface, it's under the cover of Ronaldo's armpit. I kick for shore, pushing my Trojan corpse ahead of me, staying low.

But you looked straight past, didn't see me

"Hurry this up," Huron says, gesturing impatiently at the Marabou. She looks at him coolly and then moves forward. The Stork spreads its wings and beats the air behind her. She grabs S'bu's wrist, swats Songweza's arm out of the way, and, still holding S'bu's wrist, drives the knife into Song's chest.

Now I'm wondering if the thought of you will let me be

The knife rasps against bone as the Marabou jerks it free. S'bu gives a little shriek of surprise, but he gets the idea. She doesn't even have to force him to make the next thrust. Or the next. Or the next after that. Song's screaming is a jagged counterpoint to the gleeful chorus.

Baby, it's a drive-by, drive-by, drive-by love

Songweza drops into a curl on the cement, trying to shield her body. The Marabou urges S'bu down over her. He keeps the knife moving like a darting piranha as Song screams and howls and is finally silent.

"Enough," Huron says.

S'bu looks around, dazed. The Marabou plucks the knife from his hand and passes it to Huron. S'bu smiles at her, uncertainly, and then notices his sister. He kneels down to shake her shoulder. "Come on, quit messing around," he teases. "Re-spawn, you big baby." But the air pressure has changed, and I understand that Song is dead. The Undertow is coming.

A thin howling sound starts up, like wind through narrow spaces. Instinctively, I retreat, paddling backwards in the water.

"Eat," Huron says to the Crocodile, nudging Songweza's body with his foot. "Fucking eat!"

The Crocodile slithers forward and reluctantly rips a piece out of Songweza's leg. It swallows with obscene jerks of its head, its white gullet undulating with the weight of flesh. S'bu moans in horror.

I look away. Shadows are peeling off the walls, congealing in the water. The howling reaches a new pitch, underscored by a dull *click-clack,* as if of teeth. Huron looks uneasy. All zoos do with the Undertow coming. Even the Marabou has retreated against the white-painted rock closest to the stairs. Huron uses the knife to slice open his left palm and then drags it through the bloodied tangle of animals on the butcher's block. The howling gets louder.

Marabou prompts him, like a priest at a wedding ceremony. Huron repeats the words after her, dully. His hands are shaking. "I offer this boy in my place. Let him not be animalled. Let him take mine. Bound by flesh, bound by blood." He lunges forward and slices across the Crocodile's snout with the knife, as it tears at Songweza again. It yanks its head away in fury and hisses at him with open jaws.

"Now you," Odi screams at S'bu. "Say: I take this animal."

"I don't underst—"

"Say it! Fucking say it!"

"Please." S'bu starts to cry.

"Do you hear that sound? Do you know what that is?" Odi yells. "That's the fucking Undertow, my boy. Now say it, or it's going to swallow you up and drag you down to hell."

"I take this . . ." S'bu stutters.

"Animal!"

"Animal. I take this animal." He looks to Odi for approval. Odi looks to the Marabou.

"Did it work?" Odi screams. "Did it fucking work?"

The Marabou shakes her head. She doesn't know.

"It better have fucking worked!"

S'bu is rocking backwards and forwards, staring at his sister, his arms hugged around his body. His chest heaves with sobs.

The darkness seethes and boils, like a slick of oil. It separates to flow around S'bu. He waves his hand at it feebly, trying to ward it off. The Undertow rises like a wave, tendrils reaching towards him, as if tasting his skin. I shudder at the memory.

"Song?" S'bu says, his voice trembling.

The Crocodile suddenly bursts forward, its belly rasping over the concrete, snapping its jaws at the Undertow, sweeping its tail through the thick black. The darkness turns to steam instantly, as if it was only ever mirage. S'bu screams as the reptile lunges for him. But it's only moving to lean its massive head against his leg in something like affection. Horrified, he tries to shove it away. The same way I did with Sloth, until I realized he was the only thing between me and the rising dark. Of course, Sloth didn't have my sibling's blood on his teeth.

"This isn't how the game goes," S'bu sobs, bewildered, standing stiff and frozen with the Crocodile nuzzling his leg.

"He's yours now, kid. Congratulations," says Huron. "I'd say enjoy feeding the fucker, but you won't live that long."

"I—" S'bu starts, but Amira steps forward, holding a retro gun. She puts the muzzle of the Vektor to the side of his head and pulls the trigger. S'bu falls onto his knees and tips slowly forward onto the remains of his face. I look away.

Drive-by, drive-by

Without the howl of the Undertow the music is audible again.

"Well, that went well. Turn that racket off, will you?" Huron says. Amira clicks a switch and the music dies, leaving a heavy silence, broken only by the waves lapping at the pier and the muffled thump of the Crocodile nudging at S'bu with its head, as if to make him get up.

"Well enough," Amira replies, sheathing the gun in a concealed holster under the straps criss-crossing her chest.

"Good luck getting that fucking thing out of here."

"Don't trouble yourself. We have a plan. Alive would have been better of course, but you take what you can get." She eyes the Crocodile evaluatingly.

"Shhhh." Odi laughs. "He'll hear you."

I wait until they're both up the ladder and then count out another few minutes, 289 alligator. 294 alligator, until I'm sure they're not coming back. I creep out of the water as quietly as I can so as not to disturb the Crocodile, which is still head-butting S'bu. I've seen animals live for months after their humans have died. But they're never quite the same.

I can't raise my arm, courtesy of the bullet in my collarbone. Every step sends shards of glass stabbing through my chest and causes sunbursts in my head. But I have to get upstairs, have to get to a phone. There's no way I can drag Benoît out of here on my own.

I skirt round the side of the butcher's block, trying to avoid looking at the mess of animals, but the Crocodile sees me. It swings its bulk between me and the stairs in a rapid jerk, faster than should be allowed for something that big. Its mouth gapes, a clear sign of aggression. I hold up one hand, all I can manage, in surrender.

"They're planning to kill you. Chop you up for *muti*. They've got all the tools waiting." It studies me impassively with slit gold eyes. I persevere. "Monster like you? You're probably worth a fortune. I can help you. I can *try* to help you. But I have to get out."

It jerks its head at me. I flinch, but it's not attacking, it's motioning towards the stairs. For me to go. I step past it gingerly, still half expecting it to lunge, for those bonecrushing jaws to snap around my body, but it doesn't, and I haul myself agonizingly up the ladder, one-handed, pain screaming through my chest.

The stairs lead out into the back of a music studio. A fake back wall behind the mixing desk, reinforced with foam soundproofing that nevertheless can't mute the smell. The glass doors are standing open onto the garden. Dawn streaks the sky with pale yellows and pinks.

I edge down the hill towards the pool, hugging the line of shrubs for cover. Amira and Mark are on the patio, Mark rubbing the red lines on his wrists from the cable ties. Amira is stroking the Bunny's head. It trembles violently in her arms. Underneath the upturned metal table, the Mongoose paces and snarls, throwing itself against the ironwork curlicues in fury. Amira's phone bleeps and she glances down at it. "Transfer's through," she says to Mark.

Huron emerges from the house, freshly showered, wearing a satiny bathrobe. In the distance, sirens howl. He stops to look at Carmen, slumped limply on the deck chair in a pool of blood.

"You did make a mess of little Carmencita," he says, with only the faintest smack of regret.

"She was no good to you," Mark scowls. "And now we can use her as bait." He tips the recliner up onto its wheels, to demonstrate, and carts Carmen towards the pool.

"I'll skip. There's been too much activity around here already." The sirens are getting louder. Sentinel finally catching a wake-up. I crouch in the shrubbery, wondering how to get the Mongoose out.

"We won't be long," Amira says as Mark tips the recliner, sending Carmen sliding into the water. She bobs up, floating limply, her back like a pale mushroom growing from the surface of the water, her blond bob drifting in a halo around her head. "It should come right up—"

The Crocodile is already there, disguised under the leaves. It noses at her body. Odi leans over to look, despite himself. It's a simple matter for the Crocodile to just reach up and fold its jaws on him. It's almost gentle. But then it clamps down. Its teeth rip into his stomach. Huron screams like a slaughter-house pig in a PETA video.

The sirens are getting louder. Lights flash between the trees at the bottom of the driveway. Huron fumbles for his gun. "Help me, you fucks!" he yells at Amira and Mark. But they don't move an inch.

Swearing, Odi manages to reach between the Crocodile's jaws to yank his gun out of the holster. He presses the muzzle to the Crocodile's eye and fires. It bursts in a gelatinous spray and the Crocodile jerks its head back in shock. Odi screams as teeth tear through his gut. A gray coil of greasy entrails is dragged from the wound. The Crocodile thrashes, slamming its tormentor against the side of the pool. Odi struggles, swapping the gun to his left hand. He reaches deep into the creature's mouth. There is a muffled bang.

The Crocodile goes slack. Its jaw unlocks. Huron starts

pulling himself free, but the monster's weight is dragging them both back into the water.

"Help me, Jesus, fuck, help me! Amira!" Huron extends a meaty hand.

"What do you think, sweetie? Should we help him?" Mark muses.

"I think our business is done," Amira says. "Goodbye, Odi."

"Please," he begs. The Crocodile slips further back into the pool, its shoulders disappearing into the water. "At least don't let me drown. At least give me that."

"It's been good working with you," says Marabou, stepping forward. She extends her boot, braces it against Huron's chest, and shoves. The tangle of man and Crocodile slides over the edge of the tiles and sinks into the water.

A muffled shout comes from the bottom of the driveway. "Armed response!"

"A pity to lose the Crocodile, but what can you do?" Marabou says, watching as Odi chokes and splutters and goes under. She starts to fray around the edges like the light is unraveling around her.

"Oh sweetie, there'll be other procurements," the Maltese says. Then he takes her hand and they simply vanish. A smudge of movement against the torchlight as footsteps thud up the driveway towards us.

Armed response finds me sitting slumped by the pool and the Mongoose bristling at my side, staring at the ripples on the dark water.

35.

The Daily Truth 30 March 2011

POLICE FILE
Crime Watch with Mandlakazi Mabuso

The day the music died

They said the music industry had teeth—but who knew they meant literally! Legendary music producer Odysseus "Odious" Huron got himself chowed last night by his secret animal, a *moerse* white Crocodile after slaughtering twin teen pop sensation iJusi in a gruesome *muti* murder! Turns out the man behind some of the finest talent in this country was also a big-time *tsotsi*, running drugs, killing homeless zoos for *muti*, feeding others to his Crocodile, and cultivating talent only so he could slice them open! Some 20 bodies so far have been recovered from a secret underground lake, including a woman's skeleton that police refuse to comment on, but let's just say my sources on the inside say

353

the investigation into Lily Nobomvu's fatal car crash is being re-opened! *Yoh!* Turn to our special eyewitness report on page 10 for all the *verskriklike* details!

Police have seized all assets, but I hear there's a *moerse* sum of money missing from his account. Just goes to show you never know who's a zoo. Rapper Slinger isn't. Odious Huron is. Who else is hiding an animal under their bed?

Meanwhile, a pretty-boy journo has a lot to answer for. Seems one of lad-mag *Mach*'s senior people has been running email scams from his office address! Tut-tut, *skat*. Don't you know when it comes to porn and fraud, you don't use your work email?

36.

IT'S 4:30 A.M. AND the queue to the Beit Bridge border is already more than a thousand cars long, and that's on the South African side. Never mind the torrent of refugees trying to cross over from Zimbabwe. Barbed-wire fences barricade the dusty scrub on the riverbank from anyone stupid or desperate enough to try to swim across from Zimbabwe. After all, there are crocodiles in that river.

The high drone of cicadas rises with the heat as we inch forward one car at a time through the carbon-monoxide fug. There is a bus two cars ahead of me loaded down on its axles with bags and chickens and a cram of people. The tangle of lost things on that bus swarms like a cloud of spaghetti.

And even here, there's that Zoo City hustle going on. Maybe it's not peculiar to Hillbrow. Maybe it's South Africa. You do what it takes, you take the opportunities. Vendors walk up and down the line of cars selling warm cold-drinks and chips, single *skyfs* or packs of Remington Gold. Two girls in short skirts and dusty high heels lean in the window of a 4x4 flirtatiously. It's a 24-hour border post. People have 24-hour needs.

Sloth is hidden in a rattan bag full of clothes with a hole

slashed in the side for him to breathe. The bag is stacked on the roof amid a jumble of other bags, loaded with the kinds of things returning Zimbabweans bring home for their families. Clothes and canned food, blankets, appliances, toilet paper, sanitary pads. I will dump these on the other side. They're only a cover while I'm still in South African territory. Still in Inspector Tshabalala's jurisdiction. Never mind Vuyo's.

The Capri has had a paint job. It's now black. The window has been fixed. It has new plates to go with my new Zimbabwean passport in the name of Tatenda Murapata, twenty-nine, full-time nanny going home for a holiday. D'Nice sourced the papers for me, to make up for pointing the cops in the direction of my apartment. But only after I threatened to frame him for Mrs. Luditsky's murder. He doesn't need to know I already handed over the knife after I retrieved it from the drain along with the china kitten. He even got me a good exchange rate on my counterfeit notes. Just because they're fake doesn't mean they don't have value, particularly when dealing with border officials who don't look too closely.

Benoît is still in hospital. Critical condition, the doctors say. They speak in medical terms, but what I understand is broken ribs, a bruised heart, a punctured lung, nerve damage to his dislocated arm. He will need months of physiotherapy. He may never recover the full use of it. But the worst is the bite. It's the magic. Animal wounds take longer to heal, come with stranger side effects. He sways between fevered moments of wakefulness and unconsciousness that's borderline coma, but with more erratic brain activity, like he's still fighting monsters in there. The Mongoose paces the corridors, looking thin and miserable.

There was nothing I could do there.

Eight days to Kigali if I keep to the tar, and don't hit any potholes or roadblocks I can't bribe my way out of.

Day one: Johannesburg to Harare
Day two: Harare to Lusaka
Day three: Lusaka to Mbeya
Day four: Mbeya to Dar es Saalam
Day five: Dar es to Nairobi
Day six: Nairobi to Jinja
Day seven: Cross into southern Uganda
Day eight: Mbasa to Kigali

The place names sound like new worlds. I have only ever traveled to Europe. On a skiing holiday with my parents when I was eleven, when Thando broke his leg, not on the slopes but slipping on an icy pavement. On a working holiday to London when I was eighteen, which lasted a month before I decided to hell with living in a shitty apartment and working a bar and returned to the creature comforts of my parents' Craighall house with the pool and the gardener and the char lady who made my bed. Before I met Gio, before I killed my brother, before Sloth.

I have an *amaShangaan* bag full of fake cash. I have a bundle of photographs. I have printouts of emails from a UN aid worker. I have Benoît's family's names and ID numbers and application papers for asylum in South Africa.

What I do not have is permission to leave the country in the wake of a multiple homicide/serial killer investigation.

Celvie. Armand. Ginelle. Celestin. It's going to be awkward. It's going to be the best thing I've done with my miserable life.

And after that? Maybe I'll get lost for a while.

ACKNOWLEDGMENTS

Making the fantastic seem credible is hard work. I was lucky to have co-conspirators.

Special thanks to Johnson Sithole of JBS Security, who was my fixer in Hillbrow and Berea (special thanks for not bringing your gun), and to photographer Marc Shoul for recommending him.

Thanks to Lindiwe Nkutha for taking me to Mai Mai and Faraday healers' markets and for getting bounced from the Rand Club with me when we weren't appropriately dressed. I'm grateful to the management of High Point and their passionate young security team, who gave me a complete tour of the building and really did catch a rapist.

Nechama Brodie's fine pop-culture history of the city, *The Jo'burg Book,* became my bible, and Nechama sent me additional personal recommendations and annotated maps, and provided general fact-checking. Thanks also to my great friends Georgi Guedes and Ter Hollman for playing host.

My music industry insiders/informers were Esther Moloi, Jason Curtis, Gabi le Roux, Shamiel Adams, and music journalist Evan Milton, who insisted on being allowed to interview Odi Huron, albeit for a fictional magazine. Thanks to you all, and to travel writer Justin Fox for helping me plot Zinzi's travel arrangements.

Thanks also to Charlie Human and Sam Wilson, who were roped in to write additional materials for this book, the psychological paper on the Undertow and the prison interviews respectively. Both pieces added a depth to my story and provided perspectives I wouldn't have thought of on my own.

Dr. Meg Jones and Cape Medical Response paramedic Chris de Meyer were invaluable in providing expert medical opinions on fictional conditions and injuries.

I'm very grateful to Jamala Safari, who shared his journey from the DRC to South Africa (hopefully soon to be a novel), and unraveled acronyms and the tangle of conflicts over resources that has resulted in an estimated 5.4 million deaths in the Congo since 1998. James Bocanga, another DRC émigré who runs his own security firm in my neighborhood, patiently explained slang and daily life, and provided translations for me.

Bishop Paul Verryn invited me to visit the Central Methodist Church, where, at the time, over three thousand refugees were living in terrible, dehumanizing conditions — that were nevertheless better than sleeping on the street. It was a shocking and humbling experience that has stayed with me, even though I couldn't find a way to fictionalize it. The church offered shelter during the xenophobic attacks of 2008, and continues to offer support and assistance even as many try to ignore the dire situation of refugees in South

Africa. There's been ongoing controversy about it, especially recently, but the people I met there were courageous and empathetic, and doing the best they could in the worst possible circumstances.

Tim Butcher's *Blood River: A Journey to Africa's Broken Heart* provided a great perspective on the DRC, while Jane Bussman's book *The Worst Date Ever: War Crimes, Hollywood Heart-Throbs and Other Abominations* was a brilliant, awful, and very funny resource on the LRA, specifically their actions in Uganda.

Other books that proved invaluable include Bongani Madondo's *Hot Type;* Kgebetli Moele's sad, funny, gorgeous Hillbrow novel *Room 207;* Melinda Ferguson's harrowing autobiographical account of addiction, *Smacked;* Kevin Bloom's devastating *Ways of Staying;* and especially Penny Miller's riveting and sadly out-of-print *Myths and Legends of Southern Africa*—which haunted my childhood with its wonderful stories and distinctly disturbing illustrations.

Matt Weems's fantastic website *warlordsofafghanistan.com* was such an intriguing and wonderful reference, I was tempted to abandon this book and write about that instead.

Friends on Twitter leapt to help me with research questions on anything from storm drains to good places to dump a body (only a *little* creepy, guys). Thanks especially to @6000 and @ghostfinder for medicinal advice, @mattduplessis, @brodiegal, @gussilber and @louisgreenberg for general Joburg advice. And to everyone else who tweeted back about different species of gun or how easy it would be to lever a gate off its hinges.

Various 419 scammers were very helpful in sending reference material direct to my inbox (you're welcome to contact me to claim a percentage of my royalties, although there may be a small administrative cost involved), but I owe greater thanks to the good people of *419eater.com* and *ScamWarners.com*, the South African 419 Unit of the SAPS, and the victims I interviewed for *Marie Claire* and *Cosmopolitan* stories for their insight into scams and scamming syndicates.

Thanks to my meticulous and highly critical readers: Sarah Lotz, Sam Wilson, Zukiswa Wanner, Lindiwe Nkutha, Verashni Pillay, Nechama Brodie, Charlie Human, Louis Greenberg, and Matthew Brown—you all helped make this book what it is.

Genius illustrators John Picacio and Joey Hifi created the two most beautiful covers in the world for the international and South African editions of the book respectively. They're both incredible in different ways, and both artists took time out of their insane schedules to do the work. I'm grateful.

Marc "Marco" Gascoigne and Lee Harris at Angry Robot, and Pete van der Woude and Maggie Davey at Jacana have been exceptional and brilliant people to work with, as has been my editor, Helen Moffett.

Finally, thanks to my family and friends—especially to Keitu—for making everything worth it.

INNER CITY

An essay by Lauren Beukes

"HEY, WATCH OUT," João says, yanking me back under the safety of the overhang as a black garbage bag drops onto the rubbish piling up on the landing, like the yellow silt of the mine dumps that used to rise up around the city. He's nineteen years old with a sharp face and a blunt nose and pit bull puppy eagerness. He pokes his head out from the safety of High Point's undercover parking lot—an action hero checking for snipers—and then beckons me over, to safety.

It's 2008. I'm researching my book *Zoo City*. The idea of the great South African novel is all about the journey into the interior, the wide expanses of the Karoo scrublands that expose the interior of the soul. I wanted the journey of my story to be vested in more corporeal things. Forget the soul, I wanted the sparking nerves, the guts, the pounding heart of the cityscape.

João explains that the building's lift is out. The water goes off periodically, people try their taps, cursing and cranking them wide open. They forget to close them and when the water comes on again, it floods the sinks and bathtubs, spilling down the walls. The last time it happened, it drowned the lift's electrics. It will cost a million rand to fix. And in the meantime, building management has told residents it's OK, as a temporary measure, to throw their garbage down onto the landing rather than lug it down twenty-four flights of stairs.

We carefully skirt the garbage drop zone to the edge of the landing that looks down onto the street, me and João and his young burly blond partner, Mike, and my fixer, Johnson, a Zimbabwean recommended by a photographer friend to escort me through the wilds of inner-city Johannesburg. Tour guide, translator, bodyguard. We have agreed he should leave his gun at home. "It just makes more trouble," Johnson says, and we are not here looking for that.

Hillbrow is the place of breathless TV specials: documentaries following paramedics on New Year's Eve, dodging refrigerators thrown from tenement-block windows in some kind of high bacchanalian consumer backlash; Louis Theroux cringing coquettishly in the rear guard of private security officers in bulletproof vests storming up the stairs of abandoned buildings that have been hijacked by squatter slumlords.

As a teenager, my friends and I used to drive through here, on our way to the alternative club, the Doors, where you had to check your goth wannabe-weapons at the door. We never told our parents where we were going. Singing along to Tori Amos or Sisters of Mercy, jumping red lights on the lonely streets, always with that jagged catch in our throats of danger that made us feel restless, electric, alive. Because if there's one thing everyone knows about Johannesburg, it's that it's capital-D Dangerous.

I read everything I could on Hillbrow: Bongani Madondo and Charl Blignaut's essays on the '90s scene, Ivan Vladislavic's restless meditations, Kgebetli Moele's spiky provocation of a novel, *Room 207,* but it was a blog about the death of Johannesburg that got under my skin. I won't name it, but it's one of those smug, hand-wringing then-and-nows contrasting photographs of how vibrant the inner city used to be and the *wrack* and *ruin* and *decay* it has fallen into.

The thin subtext of the captions and comments is that it's because of "the blacks." Always the blacks. As if apartheid's (white) secret police, the Civil Cooperation Bureau, didn't meet at the Quirinale Hotel on Kotze Street in Hillbrow to orchestrate atrocities, assassinations, and political unrest in their efforts to derail democracy. As if a hundred years before that Cecil John Rhodes and the (white) mining magnate Randlords didn't scheme in the library of the gentlemen's club downtown to bring the colonial Empire snaking into the interior on railway tracks.

But for all its shrill hysteria, the photographs on the blog don't lie about the decay. Businesses have fled the city center to soulless business parks surrounded by soulless townhouse complexes in Midrand, a purpose-built suburb halfway between Johannesburg and Pretoria.

The premises they left behind *have* become dilapidated, boarded over, and in extreme cases bricked up to prevent them being gutted for copper piping or taken over by squatters. A few kilometers away, Forest Town, the suburb where I grew up, where President Zuma lives now, has jacaranda trees that bloom in purple archways over the streets. Whereas the Hillbrow "blossom" is the plastic bag, tangled and shredded in the branches.

There are a thousand pocket worlds in Johannesburg, rubbing up against each other. The student and art scenes in Brixton and Braamfontein, the black hipster hangout of Newtown around the Market Theatre and Café Sophiatown, the suits and shiny cars in Bank City by the Diamond Building. Hillbrow has always been a separate animal.

The twin towers of High Point used to be the most desirable blocks in the most cosmopolitan neighborhood with restaurants and bars and clubs. When my dad was considering divorce in the '70s, he planned to buy an apartment here as the perfect swinging bachelor pad.

That was before Hillbrow turned bohemian: sex and drugs and rocking disco soul thanks to the likes of Brenda Fassie, the Madonna of the townships, who hung out here, got high here, made love here, in the middle of the hip multi-racial scene of artists and musicians and gays and lesbians in the '80s and '90s.

Now it's the place people bring their hopes, packed up in *amashangaan,* the ubiquitous cheap plastic rattan suitcases used by refugees and immigrants from small towns in the rural areas, looking for work, looking to break in. Low income, high aspirations.

Mike, swaggering for my benefit, goes to the edge of the

ledge and calls down to a man on the street who is tossing away his cigarette, "Hey pick that up, you can't throw your *stompie* here!" Each building is a private fiefdom and the security guards are the protectors of the realm with batons and mace. What happens across the road is none of their concern. They manage the building, keep crime out, deal with troublesome tenants.

"We caught a rapist in the building. It took three days, but we knew he lived here, so I stood outside the gate with the woman who was, you know . . ." João takes a swig from his Coke to hide his discomfort. It is exactly the same red as his canister of pepper spray. "Until the guy finally came out and she pointed at him and we grabbed him and took him down to the cops."

"But there was this other time, I felt *kak,* hey, because I had to evict this old black guy who hadn't paid his rent. And I had to hit him with the baton to get him to move because he wouldn't go. And it made me feel *swak,* like he must think of old times, like apartheid, this young white *oke* beating him, but it's my job, what am I supposed to do?"

Johnson nods in understanding. When he's not playing fixer for journalists, he runs his own security firm for other buildings in Hillbrow. He has the same problems with tenants, but even more so, he says, with their guests. "As a security guard, you learn to understand the characteristics of people. You can get to know people in the building and their behavior. But visitors are a problem. You cannot understand the visitors."

There are old attitudes that endure. The ghosts of the city. But people find ways to live with ghosts and that's why we're here, because despite the horror stories, the flying refrigerators and the drug dealers on the corner in their sharp shoes and cell phones, and the low-rise across the way that João says they raided last week with the cops to bust a sex-trafficking operation, Hillbrow is somewhere people live.

The city *has* changed. Cities do. It's in their nature. Like language. *Tsotsi-taal* (gangster-speak) is the word on the street here, a patois of English, Afrikaans, and Zulu that has stolen the best slang from other tongues and remixed them.

And maybe that's the best way to think of Hillbrow and the inner city. As a remix.

Unlike the manicured pavements of the leafy suburbs or the glossy consumertopias of Sandton and Rivonia, the city streets are flush with people. Hawkers sell cheap plastic flip-flops alongside sandals hand-made from Nguni leather, in front of cell phone shops and Internet cafes and fashion boutiques and a church built in a reclaimed mall. Flyers pasted to a brick wall advertise the services of the Prophet Nkhomo, the St. Paul's Preschool, safe abortions, youth worship services. The big brands are moving back in—KFC and Jet clothing—to compete with the cheap clothing stores and the place on the corner that does Lagos-style chicken. It's '70s Harlem: hectic, alive, on the rise.

As Moele describes it in *Room 207,* the city of gold is actually the city of dreams. Because dreams, like ghosts, are unpredictable. They can be good or bad. You have to live with them.

It's driven home when we venture downtown to the Central Methodist Church. I have been intending to set a major scene in *Zoo City* here and have arranged with Bishop Paul Verryn to attend the Sunday night service.

We're here a few months after a nationwide outbreak of horrifying xenophobic violence, where black South Africans turned on black Africans. A group of Somalians were thrown off the roof of a building, like refrigerators. They burned a Zimbabwean man alive in the streets.

There is a 40 percent unemployment rate. Someone has to carry the blame and the middle class are safe in their suburbs with their high walls and their private security and their jacaranda trees. The "blacks" again. Blacker than black. Us versus them. The colonials knew this, exploited this, indoctrinated this. They taught us there is always someone blacker than you.

People have fled to the church to take shelter from the violence, the same way activists hid out here during the struggle against apartheid. But now there are new struggles. There will always be a struggle. It's the legacy we're left with, from all those whites with their schemes.

The friends who drop me and Johnson off outside the church are reluctant to let us go. There is a mob clustered around the fence and the Portaloos around the church. The anger in the air is a living thing.

It is the first time I feel a spike of fear. Nothing like in

Hillbrow, which was daytime, admittedly. Not even when the boy brushed past me and hissed, "Put your cell phone away, they'll rob you." And not like driving to The Doors a decade ago. The acupuncture prick of dread. This is a pitchfork twisting my guts like spaghetti. "Don't worry," Johnson says, "They're my people. Zimbabweans." And although there are also Malawians, Zambians, Congolese, he's right. Far and away, the greatest numbers are those fleeing Mugabe.

We make our way inside the church, to the upper pews. There is a constant murmur, people talking through the preamble of announcements and hymn-singing. Kids tumble over the stairs. There are chains of coughing, babies crying, a choir of cell phone ringtones. A man is coughing bloody sputum into a tissue, his whole body wracked with the effort of it. He has no shoes. His bare feet are like knots of wood. His toenails are cracked and yellow.

We find a place to sit next to a nurse, Melanie, dressed immaculately in a white linen suit, just in time for Bishop Verryn to deliver the sermon. He seems exasperated. "It is not satisfactory for you to live like this. I am not saying I don't want you here, but I worry about the humanity of people in this place." He seems worn down.

It has taken this to make me realize that dehumanizing is not only something that other people do to you. It can be self-inflicted too. Switch off the light behind your eyes. Focus on the lowest rungs of Maslow. Get through the day, however you can.

From the pulpit, Verryn rails against the city council that

keeps trying to move them: "Treat us like human beings. Don't move us like furniture, because we are not furniture." Outside, a young man tells me, "They use us like a ball. They kick us everywhere." He also says they go looking for trouble, seeking out Zulu guys and beating them up. Reprisals for the way they have been treated. He is thinking of going home. Even with no jobs, the messed-up politics, it is better than here. But he can't afford the trip. He is stuck.

Melanie, the nurse, explains that she came here via Harare, via London, via Cape Town. She offers to show me where she sleeps and confides, "I don't have friends. Only to share my jokes with, but not to share my secrets." She doesn't tell me how she manages to keep her white linen suit so spotless.

It is a fever dream, following her down the stairwell to the basement, pushing and shoving through a crush of warm bodies in the dark, stepping over people who are bedding down for the night, on a scrap of cardboard for a mattress if they are lucky. On bare concrete if they are not.

We break free into the basement where the women and children sleep, the sum of their belongings arranged around them in *amashangaan* and battered suitcases. We are standing shoulder to shoulder, packed like tin cans. I cannot see how there will be room to lie down. Several women are bathing babies in buckets. "From Musina. The border," Melanie says. "The guards demand sex sometimes for getting you across."

I reel away from the horrors of a refugee camp condensed into a church building, into the crisp Joburg night air, where young men cluster restlessly on the pavement, and into a warm car that will whisk us back to the suburbs. I feel shaken and raw.

"How was it?" my friends ask, and Johnson, who has been dead quiet, *tjoep-stil,* this whole time, bursts out in furious contempt, "It was pathetic." He shakes his head in disgust. *"Pathetic."*

I'm speechless. He told me earlier about how he came to South Africa as a refugee fourteen years ago. How his wife is a refugee. How these are his people. And now he is denouncing them.

It's a coping mechanism, I realize. He is distancing himself from the possibility that he could ever find himself living through a similar experience. He is saying that somehow he would be different in the same circumstances. We all want to be the exception. We all want to believe it couldn't be us.

But then we were only visitors there. Who can't be understood. Or understand. We can only imagine.

This essay originally appeared in *Granta* online, June 2013.

ABOUT THE AUTHOR

LAUREN BEUKES writes novels, comics, and screenplays. She's the author of the critically-acclaimed *Broken Monsters,* the international bestseller *The Shining Girls,* and the *New York Times* bestselling graphic novel *Fairest: The Hidden Kingdom.* She has worked as a journalist and as show runner on one of South Africa's biggest animated TV shows and directed an award-winning documentary. She lives in Cape Town, South Africa.

MULHOLLAND BOOKS

You won't be able to put down these Mulholland Books.

CLOSE YOUR EYES *by Michael Robotham*

THE EXILED *by Christopher Charles*

UNDERGROUND AIRLINES *by Ben H. Winters*

SEAL TEAM SIX: HUNT THE DRAGON *by Don Mann and Ralph Pezzullo*

THE SECOND GIRL *by David Swinson*

WE WERE KINGS *by Thomas O'Malley, Douglas Graham Purdy*

REVOLVER *by Duane Swierczynski*

SERPENTS IN THE COLD *by Thomas O'Malley, Douglas Graham Purdy*

WHEN WE WERE ANIMALS *by Joshua Gaylord*

THE INSECT FARM *by Stuart Prebble*

CROOKED *by Austin Grossman*

ZOO CITY *by Lauren Beukes*

MOXYLAND *by Lauren Beukes*

Visit mulhollandbooks.com for
your daily suspense fix.

MULHOLLAND BOOKS

You won't be able to put down these Mulholland Books.

Visit mulhollandbooks.com for
your daily suspense fix.

ABOUT THE AUTHOR

LAUREN BEUKES writes novels, comics, and screenplays. She's the author of the critically-acclaimed *Broken Monsters,* the international bestseller *The Shining Girls,* and the *New York Times* bestselling graphic novel *Fairest: The Hidden Kingdom.* She has worked as a journalist and as show runner on one of South Africa's biggest animated TV shows and directed an award-winning documentary. She lives in Cape Town, South Africa.